IAN L...

THE CARMODY CASEBOOKS

CORGI BOOKS

CORGI BOOKS

UK | USA | Canada | Ireland | Australia
India | New Zealand | South Africa

Corgi Books is part of the Penguin Random House group of companies
whose addresses can be found at global.penguinrandomhouse.com.

www.penguin.co.uk
www.puffin.co.uk
www.ladybird.co.uk

Part I of this edition first appeared as *The Disappearance of Tom Pile*, published 2015
This edition, including *The Miraculous Return of Annick Garel*, first published 2017

002

Text copyright © Ian Beck, 2017
Cover artwork photography: boy, girl, war scene and
plane silhouettes copyright © Shutterstock, 2017

The moral right of the author has been asserted

Set in Goudy Old Style 11.5/17pt by Jouve (UK), Milton Keynes
Printed in Great Britain by Clays

A CIP catalogue record for this book is available from the British Library

ISBN: 978-0-552-56819-7

All correspondence to:
Corgi Books
Penguin Random House Children's
80 Strand, London WC2R 0RL

Contents

For Michael and Iris Holloway

IAN BECK has worked as a freelance illustrator for many years (including such notable artwork as the record cover for Elton John's *Goodbye Yellow Brick Road* album). Ian turned to writing and illustrating children's books when his own children were born.

Part 1

THE DISAPPEARANCE OF TOM PILE

PROLOGUE

'Tell us your story,' the voices said. 'We want to hear your story – all of it . . .'

That was when I started speaking out loud to the night stars all around me, and to the music, the voices in my head. They said, 'That's it. Go on . . . go on . . . tell us, tell us all . . .'

My mother died when I was seven. I remember so clearly the simple coffin box in our little cottage parlour. It lay there closed and screwed down, resting on trestles, and even then I knew that she was inside it. My father sat beside it with his head bowed, his mug of tea resting on the lid. The parlour was almost dark, with just a single lit tallow candle on the mantel, and still he sat there quietly all night.

She was buried in February – on St Valentine's Day, to be exact. The dark earth was tamped down hard and wet. The grave was dressed with greenery and one or two hothouse blooms from the Rectory. Mr Woolard had cut the grave and Mr Woolard's son had made the coffin. There was no stone or marker as yet, only the few pale flowers under the sleet and the ivy.

I stood at the grave while the Woolards lowered the coffin down on wide hessian straps. My father was standing at the graveside in his black Sunday best, one hand on my shoulder. He was the first to throw in some of the wet earth and flowers from the heap by the open grave. I looked around at the expectant faces: the Reverend Stone, Miss Gladwyn, my uncle and aunt, and then my father, who was hatless in the cold. His beard and side whiskers were grey, and his teeth were clamped together, making his cheeks look hollow. His hair was whipped by the wind that blew across Gallows Hill, where we would see the lights together for the first time, years from that night . . .

The Dorchester Weekly Courier & Advertiser

Friday 25th July 1890

Reports of shooting stars, falling meteors and unusual lights in the sky have been made from various towns and villages in the west of the county during the last week. The director of the County Historical and Archaeological Museum at Dorchester, Hector Brewer Esq., announced that he would be happy to receive and examine any pieces of fallen meteorite material that may be found at or near the area of the sightings. Falling stars were observed near the villages of Swyre, Puncknowle, Burton Bradstock, and on Gallows Hill at Litton Cheney. The sightings were reported over three nights, and alarm was caused when some residents reported sightings of what were described by some as 'angels' on Gallows Hill itself and in the surrounding landscape. However, no evidence of any such manifestation has been forthcoming.

Several of the witnesses have been interviewed by a representative of the London Scientific, Philosophical and Spiritual Society, a Dr Frobisher, who has been able to draw no firm conclusion from his findings.

He stated that, 'In such cases there can sometimes be in effect a kind of mass delusion or hysteria which can lead perfectly sane, level-headed and practical country people to conclude that they have seen supernatural apparitions such as ghosts, will-o-the-wisps and even serious religious manifestations such as sacred saints and angels and the like. In my own mind I am satisfied that what the witnesses observed was no more than a series of optical illusions brought on by the effects of the apparently unusually bright lights arising from the local meteor activity. In rural areas such events have throughout history been interpreted as signs and omens, and ideally we should not allow ourselves to be too troubled by them in our more scientific and rational age.'

Cover Note

I don't want to waste too much of your valuable time by telling you all about myself. I am not very important. You don't need to know much about me personally. I will simply say that I did something very secret during the Second World War. All that was, of course, some twenty-four years ago now, although the results of our work are still very much with us.

What I did was rightly categorized as secret, for I was dealing with the mysterious and the unexplained – it would perhaps be better described as the inexplicable. I was always viewed with suspicion. Some thought I was wasting valuable war resources by looking, as I did almost daily, into reports of odd and unexpected things: sightings and events that were, in the majority of cases, the ravings of the deluded, the drunk and the insane. I was there to thoroughly investigate the five per cent or so of those reports which were not so easily explained away; those strange and deeply troubling events that happen all the time, whether there is a war on or not.

The idea of investigating such things made some

of the high-up folk in the War Office very nervous indeed. Some of them found it almost laughable, and said so endlessly in circulated memos. In the end, of course, we were proved right, but our stories have remained secret and classified. The secrecy embargo has finally been lifted; I would suggest this is because the astonishing events of last July have finally made it unnecessary, hence this volume – the first, I hope, of a good few.

I am all too aware, however, that the licence to publish could be revoked at any point, so my concluding dateline below could, in fact, be out of date by the time these words reach the public.

I had actually been conducting these investigations since I graduated from university many years before the war. But when the conflict began, and the threat to our democratic freedom and our very way of life became ever more real, I gained the strong support of the highest authority, in the form of Winston Churchill himself. He was only too aware that in the 1930s the Germans had founded a secret department: the Office of the *Unerklärliche & Übernatürliche*, which roughly translated as the 'Unexplained and the Supernatural'. It was a subject the Nazis and Hitler took very seriously indeed, and Churchill knew that; he was of course unwilling to take the risk that the

Axis powers might stumble on an advantage of any kind, however bizarre and remote, that might be denied to us, the Allies.

I was thus allowed to recruit my own small unit, with a very similar aim to our German counterparts. We were known as Department 116 – which was simply the number on our annexe door. We comprised a handful of technicians and research scientists, and one very bright young man from the East End of London. As a child he had shown a kind of genius for recognizing the mathematical patterns behind the seemingly random and disordered. He also had a strong – indeed, an almost uncanny – sense of intuition, which proved very helpful in certain circumstances. His name was Jack Carmody, and he was to become my man in the field, my special investigator; my 'go to' man, if you like. We were given offices close to Churchill in his Citadel and the Admiralty buildings, and more or less left to get on with it.

This, the first of our cases to be published, will be told partly in Jack Carmody's words, because he kept a detailed journal of our adventures, and partly in my own, because I did too – although of course it was not encouraged by the authorities. Now, in retrospect, I am glad that we did keep such detailed journals. With the help of these, and the other evidence, the whole story of Tom Pile can be told.

I have added in certain previously classified documents: direct transcripts of wire recordings, various intercepted messages and more, which all add their own layers of truth to the narrative. Some of the documents date back to long before the war; before the twentieth century, in fact. Each entry adds another little piece to the strange jigsaw puzzle of past, present and future which makes up Tom Pile's story. These events were so mysterious, and revealed something so huge and potentially dangerous, that they had an effect which went way beyond what might have been expected at the time.

So the roots of this story were laid down long before the war – and not just in these islands, but on the mainland of Europe too, as you will discover. I have tried not to interfere with the original testimonies, some of which I intend to present here in facsimile form. It will be up to the reader to read them carefully in order to see the big picture, which I hope will be revealed as each piece finally falls into place.

M. D. Holloway
(Captain, retired)
Glynde, Sussex

CHAPTER ONE

'Down to darkest Dorset today, then,' Captain Holloway said to me with a friendly wink. I was about to set off and was, you can bet, excited enough about what I might finally find there. Still, a tiny part of me wished I wasn't going away and leaving poor old London. There were too many things I had to leave behind – and who knew for how long? And it was not just that. I would miss the terror and drama of the Blitz. I was worried that, what with the bombs falling, and the destruction of dear old London, which seemed certain in those early days, I might never see the place the same way again. I couldn't let that stop me, though. Fear was a curse, and I wasn't about to give in to it. I could trust my aunt Dolly to look after herself, and she would look out for my own place too. Anyway, there I was, all ready to go. I was kitted out in my very stiff and uncomfortable new uniform, and I felt not only self-conscious, but a bit of a twerp too, to be honest.

'That's right, sir,' I said, looking down the length of my new and very itchy khaki strides (that, by the way, is slang for trousers in these parts).

'You might remember to return a salute to an officer, by the way, Carmody. You may be a pretend soldier and I might be one too, but we must at least play the part for our lords and masters.'

'Yes, sir, sorry, sir,' I said, and brought my hand up beside my forehead in what I hoped was a correct salute, as fast and as smartly as I could without laughing.

'Better,' he said, and he smiled his smile, and I could see that he wasn't taking it all that seriously after all. The bluster and noise was for the sake of the others who might be listening in the outer office of the Citadel annexe.

'Now, you've got the camera, plenty of special film and everything else?'

'All packed, sir.'

'Then good luck. Remember, anything you can get of these lights – the more the better. Of course, you know what else to look out for?'

'Yes, sir,' I said, grinning again. 'An actual live

person, if I can manage it.' Another smart raising of the hand.

'That's right, Jack. The real thing, and remember to get into the saluting habit and stay in it. You're supposed to know how to salute. You're meant to have gone through all that in basic training.'

'Right, sir.'

Viktor Prejm, a tame Polish airman who is said to be 'walking out' with our general office assistant and copy typist, Miss Greville, was perched, as casually as ever, on the edge of her desk while she tried to work. She was giggling when I reached the office.

'What's funny, then, Ruth?' I said.

'Nothing funny about you, Jack,' she said. 'Mr Prejm here just said he wanted to whisk me away to a romantic hideaway like one of these.' She gestured to the frosted glass panel to one side of her work area, over which she had taped dozens of picture postcards. There were sunny seaside and cottage scenes and the like, making it her own personal blackout area, shielding her from the worst of the bustle in the big office. 'Fat chance, I told him,' she added. 'I was laughing at his ruddy cheek, that was all.'

'I was only asking Ruth to file a translation document for me.'

'Dear Viktor,' Ruth said. 'Look, it's already done. I do know how to file – and I don't mean my nails. I used to be an archivist, don't forget. I know my way around all kinds of files.' She smiled.

Viktor raised his hands in mock surrender and shrugged, as if to say, *English girls*, and then gave me an ironically appraising look as I turned to struggle up the stairs and out of our inner sanctum, all crouched over (we have a low ceiling) and weighed down with the army kit bag over my shoulder and an overstuffed army-issue suitcase in each hand.

'Take care now, young man,' he said, helping me up the steps and along the corridor. 'Where are you off to? Somewhere more exotic than I was proposing to take your Miss Greville, I trust?'

'Can't really tell you that, now, can I, Viktor?'

'No, of course not, er, Corporal,' he said, his eyes widening a little as he took in my smart uniform. 'Well, now, look at you. Whatever else you do, just mind out for the girls, looking like that, eh? What would your girlfriend say if she were to find out?' And then he laughed.

I laughed too, but the joke was on me. Unlike Viktor, I didn't have a girlfriend.

It wasn't until I had struggled off the dingy train at Dorchester South and had been standing for a while in the poorly lit, bone-damp, cold station forecourt, waiting for the army truck from Burton Bradstock to come and collect me, that it properly hit home.

I was in the army, and I was in 'darkest Dorset' all right, just as Captain Holloway had said.

Standing there shivering on that late afternoon made me feel homesick for life in the good old smoke. I had no idea how long I was likely to be stuck down here on what might be just another wild-goose chase. We'd had plenty of those to contend with in our time.

There was one tiny saving grace, though, at that moment. The station was near a brewery, and that telltale warm, malty smell drifted over occasionally on the wind. It was almost as good as standing near Truman's in Brick Lane.

CHAPTER TWO

I have to admit something. There's no getting away from it. I'm a London boy through and through. There were times during those first few quiet days down in the country when the thought of a nice warm picture house – like the Sphere on Tottenham Court Road, or the Rialto on Coventry Street – showing a good old horror picture or a Marx Brothers comedy, and sharing it with a crowd of jumpy, laughing Londoners, was like a vision of heaven itself. After all, the deep dark countryside wasn't meant for everyone, but in the end that wasn't the point. I should at least have brought my travelling telescope with me for those rare clear nights. My army-issue binoculars had to stand in for my stargazing (and by that I don't, of course, mean looking at Miss Greta Garbo), but they just weren't as good.

It's hard to say exactly when everything started for me; hard to date when my path in life was suddenly clear. It was long before I first met up with Captain Holloway, in any case.

I was born in August, so I was always the youngest in my class at the local school. School didn't last long. Not that being the youngest held me back at all, as it is meant to – far from it, in fact. I was always a bit of a whizz. I could read almost anything before I ever went to school. I surprised the teachers with my abilities right away, especially for my age, and with my background. I was part of the dirt-poor but very respectable London working class, and I still am in a way. I'm not saying I was especially proud of it, but I certainly 'wasn't ashamed neither', as my aunt Dolly would have said, and did say, over and over, to anyone who would listen.

She brought me up on her own, Dolly did. She was my father's sister. Salt of the earth, and a bit more besides. She was fierce in her determination to look after me. I was, after all, her brother's only son. She was fierce too in her ambition to get me properly educated. Dolly had enough drive, pride and loyalty for about ten people. She was a force to be reckoned with.

I never knew my parents. To me, growing up in the streets of Hackney, Aunt Dolly had to be both mother and father. She saw my promise early. She moved

heaven and earth and worked the system sideways, backwards and upside down for me. She applied for scholarships. When my abilities really started to show, I was tested and probed and questioned so often it felt normal to me. I suppose it must have been some of the strange things I did when I was very young that alerted her. First there was the thunder, and then there was the lady in grey.

She never tired of talking about the incident with the thunder. Aunt Dolly didn't like thunder. I noticed it once in a storm. There was one of those particularly loud claps of thunder overhead, the kind that almost shake the room, and she went all to pieces. I suppose I was about four years old, and her fear must have made a big impression on me. A year or so later, I was sitting in the back garden with her on a warm afternoon when I suddenly went and stood right in front of her and pressed my hands very tightly over her ears.

'Whatever are you playing at, Jack?' she said.

A moment or two later there was a huge and terrifying clap of thunder overhead. I saved her from hearing it: I just knew it was coming. Even at that age I could read the seemingly random patterns in the sky and the atmosphere. Aunt Dolly couldn't get over it. She told the neighbours, she told Lew the barber, she told everybody. They mostly looked at her like she was a bit touched. It just served to further convince her that her late brother's son, her only nephew, her Jack, was 'special'. It was quite something to live up to. Every time I got my hair cut – and in those days it was pretty often – Lew would tell all the customers, 'This little boy 'ere knows when the thunder's going to bang off before it happens. How about that, then? 'E ought to go on the halls.' I blushed with embarrassment as I looked at myself in Lew's mirror while he laughed and rinsed out his comb in a cup of white liquid.

I would have liked to go on the 'halls', as he put it, but not in variety. I wanted to be up on the silver screen. I wanted to be a Hollywood actor, like Ramon Navarro or Douglas Fairbanks. I suppose what I have done since has involved acting at various times; playing a part to deceive.

My childhood bedroom was at the back of the house overlooking the garden patch. Dolly slept in the middle room. She had the big front bedroom with the two windows all kitted out as a study for me. I would sit up there working even on bright summer's evenings. The other kids would all be out playing street cricket or generally roughhousing about while I sat there and read my books and solved things. I didn't mind. I didn't feel deprived. Sometimes I roughed it up with the best of them. I wasn't weak or scared; I had my share of fun and games. I played knock-down ginger and the like, and generally annoyed the neighbours from time to time like all the local kids.

'It's only natural, after all. Boys will be boys, you know,' Dolly would say, arms folded across her wide shelf of a bosom, head nodding in apparent sympathy with whoever had banged on the door to complain.

Every year I enjoyed our little backyard blaze

on Bonfire Night. Aunt Dolly let me set off bangers and jumping jacks and sky rockets out of our Brock's selection box, just like everybody else. However, I didn't much care for the stuffed homemade Guy Fawkes that kids used to wheel around in old prams, collecting 'pennies for the Guy' long before November the fifth. When I was very little, my overactive imagination gave those poorly stuffed straw men life. I felt them watching me from behind their papier-mâché masks, which I saw hung in rows on string in the local paper shop. I knew they weren't real, but once they were put on the dummies, I believed in them.

I wasn't like everybody else. I don't say that to show off. It is the simple truth.

I saw things.

I saw the bones behind the mask.

I saw the structure under the surface.

I also saw the patterns in large groups of numbers. I could pick out the connections and links between seemingly random events. I could see the core shapes in apparently formless things – like cloudscapes, for instance, or crashing waves and rushing water torrents. I could decode almost everything, or at least it seemed that way. I saw these patterns and connections fast, and I saw them clearly and simply; I didn't have to think or try or struggle. I solved things.

And I suppose you might say I even had visions of a kind; the sort of thing people referred to as 'being psychic' or having 'second sight'. I couldn't predict the Derby winner or anything like that, but I had something else. It was a kind of sixth sense, if you like, for odd and unexplained things. If predicting the thunder wasn't enough, there was the other incident; the one Aunt Dolly *didn't* tell everybody about. The woman in grey.

My aunt Dolly supplemented her income by doing bits and pieces of fine needlework, dressmaking and knitting for people. She was very skilled at it, and often made things for the locals who were that bit better off, too busy or too idle to make their own. Sometimes she took me to their houses to show me off. One of her 'ladies', Mrs Burtenshaw, lived a bus ride away, up in Hampstead. She had a large house with railings around it and a big gate. I had to be on my best behaviour. After we were given tea, with tiny triangle-cut sandwiches and fruit cake ('Only one slice now, Jack, and don't ask for another!'), I needed to go to the lavatory. I put my hand up and asked as if I were still at school.

'Please may I use the lavatory?' I said, and I saw Aunt Dolly beam at my polite approach.

'Of course,' Mrs Burtenshaw said. 'Just go out of here and turn left, keep on down the passageway, and there is a door on your left, and that is the cloakroom. Inside there is another door, and that leads to the lavatory.'

The hallway had a shiny marble floor with black-and-white squares like a chessboard. I could easily imagine big scaled-up pawns lined up along one side protecting the knights and bishops. I dawdled along, counting the squares to see if there was an even number between the front parlour and the cloakroom. Then I smelled something very sweet. I looked up, and saw a woman in the hallway looking at me. She was dressed in a long grey dress and a straw hat with a wide brim. Over her arm was one of those trug gardening baskets, full of cut roses.

'I was just going to put these in water,' she said, opening the cloakroom door and letting me pass by. It was the roses that smelled so sweet. 'There ought to be a suitable vase in here somewhere. You carry on, young man, don't mind me.' She looked down at me and smiled, then turned her back and began rummaging on a shelf. I went through the door to the lavatory.

After I had finished I went back out into the cloakroom. The roses had been arranged in a china vase. The lady's straw hat was hanging from a peg behind the door. I was careful to wash my hands because I knew Aunt Dolly would make very sure that I had.

When I got back to the parlour, Aunt Dolly said straight away, 'I hope you washed your hands, Jack.'

I held them out for inspection, back and front.

'Good boy,' she said.

'You found it all right, then?' Mrs Burtenshaw asked.

'Yes, thank you,' I said. 'The nice lady showed me.'

'Nice lady?' she repeated, a frown creasing her brow.

'What nice lady?'

'The one I just met; the one with the roses,' I said.

There was a silence after I spoke, and I knew I'd done or said something wrong; I had somehow upset this woman.

'Roses?' she said, quietly and intensely. 'How was she holding them?'

'In one of those flat-bottomed trug baskets. She was looking for a vase to put them in.'

The colour drained out of the woman's face. She looked like a sheet of paper. 'You saw her?'

'Yes, Mrs Burtenshaw.'

'She spoke to you? You spoke to her?'

'Yes. She said something like, "Don't mind me, you carry on."'

'Are you all right?' Aunt Dolly said.

The woman was staring at me in shock, her hand to her throat. 'No, I'm not,' she said. 'He says he's seen her.'

'Who's he seen?'

'My sister. What was she wearing?'

'A long grey dress and a hat.'

'It really was her . . . My God. Did you put him up to this, Miss Carmody? Have I ever spoken about her to you?'

'Of course I didn't, Mrs B., and I swear you have

never mentioned your sister to me, not once. Have you fallen out with her or something? Is she not meant to be here?'

'My sister used to wear a straw hat and an old grey day dress. She wore them for gardening. Tell me again what she said to you.' She seemed even more intense now, and she leaned forward and held my wrist hard, as if to stop me getting away, or daring me to be wrong.

'She said, "I was just going to put these in water," and then, "There ought to be a suitable vase in here somewhere," and after that, "You carry on, don't mind me."'

'There was no message for me? Nothing at all except talk of the flowers?'

'No,' I said.

'Has he done something wrong?' Aunt Dolly said, putting her hand on my shoulder.

'Not as far as I know. He is the first to see her. I hoped I might; I felt something once in that hallway, not long after she died, but I never saw her.'

'Died?' Aunt Dolly whispered.

'I never saw her,' Mrs Burtenshaw continued, almost to herself. 'And we had such a strong connection too. Surely she would have shown herself to me . . .' She shook her head then and let go of my arm.

'I can show you the flowers,' I said – even then,

young as I was, aware that none of this was normal. It was almost as if there were a charge of electricity in the air, as if a thunderclap were imminent.

'Flowers?'

'The roses she had. They are in the cloakroom, in a vase.'

Mrs Burtenshaw took my hand in hers and held it slightly too hard. 'You are not teasing me, are you?'

'No, Mrs Burtenshaw,' I said.

'He wouldn't do that, Mrs B. Jack's a good boy, bright as a button. Gets up to larks like any other boy, but he's not cruel.'

'Show me the flowers.' Mrs Burtenshaw led me back out into the tiled corridor. We all three stood just inside the door frame looking down the empty space. The polished floor, the rugs, the wood-panelled walls. I sniffed the air, and there was still the sweet rose smell.

'I smell the roses,' Mrs Burtenshaw said, and her voice, I remember, was quavery and suddenly nervous. She led the way down the passage. Aunt Dolly had her hand on my shoulder. The silence in the hall was deafening. It was quiet and calm, but it seemed to me that everything around us was screaming, there was so much tension, such a strange force of veiled energy in that house. I didn't experience that kind of pent-up and hidden force again until one night many years later, on a hilltop in West Dorset.

Mrs Burtenshaw closed her eyes and quickly opened the cloakroom door. The roses were there, neatly arranged in a white vase on an old sideboard below a row of shelves. White and sweet-smelling, they were, at least a dozen of them. We stood huddled together in the doorway, just looking at them.

'Perhaps you put them there and forgot,' Aunt Dolly said, doing her best to be helpful.

'Oh, no,' said Mrs Burtenshaw quietly. 'That bush has long gone over. Madame Hardy, a damask rose – the old kind. They only flower once or twice a season.' She leaned forward, picked one of the roses out of the bunch and brought it up to her face. 'It ought to be a comfort,' she murmured, 'but I can't help feeling cheated.'

She turned to Aunt Dolly. 'I think you arranged this to trick me. I don't know why, but you hid those flowers somehow, and then the boy put them in there and made up that story. I think you had better leave.'

Aunt Dolly frowned. 'I'm sorry, Mrs B., but you're quite wrong. I told you before that this boy is special. You remember, I said he could tell when it was going to thunder, and he covered my ears to protect me from it? Well, now he's gone and properly seen a ghost, by the sound of it.'

'I shall pay you for your work and that will be that. Just be thankful I haven't called the police.'

'How ridiculous!' Aunt Dolly protested. 'Call the police! He's not a liar and nor am I. We are respectable, honest folk.'

'That may be. I would still like you to leave, thank you.'

On the way home we stopped off at a café. Aunt Dolly bought me an ice cream. 'I could do with a brandy after that. Always said you were special, Jack. You weren't scared, were you?'

'No,' I told her honestly. 'She seemed a nice lady. I didn't know she was a ghost before.'

It was one thing to see the patterns in things, to see through them. That was all connected to links and fast thinking. I suppose I was a bit like one of those adding machines most of the time. Seeing that lady in grey, though, was very different. Part of me sensed something about that hallway before I saw her. I knew there was something up: some part of my inner antennae told me. It was as if I had opened another undiscovered part of myself that afternoon. I realized, almost with a shock, that there were unexplained things, deep mysteries just at the edge of my understanding. I had somehow lifted a curtain on a new world.

Aunt Dolly drank her tea, but I could tell she was troubled. What had just happened had scared her, and she wasn't someone who scared easily. It hadn't scared me, though – quite the opposite. I was excited by what else might be behind the curtain. Aunt Dolly never mentioned what I saw in that house in Hampstead. She didn't tell Lew the barber or anyone else – it worried her too much. I think she thought that I had somehow conjured up the lady in grey.

As I got older, I developed a keen interest in astronomy, and in the worlds beyond our own – which is how I came to be taken up by Captain Holloway.

When they discovered what I could do, I was soon whisked away from my local infant school. I was tutored at home instead, and that's when all the testing started. Aunt Dolly would regularly take me in to appointments in the West End. We went to impressive but fusty offices in places like Russell Square, where I was set difficult theorems and mathematical problems. We would visit various institutes where my intelligence was tested. It was all very friendly, but it involved us both getting dressed up and me having my hair strictly parted and smarmed down with horrible brilliantine, which Dolly bought at Lew's.

I had to be polite, and hang my gabardine raincoat up on the hook, and sit at a desk in a plain brown varnished room all on my own. Then I would have to answer the questions.

'Just do your best, Jack,' Dolly said. 'You can't be expected to do more than that.'

I was asked by a friendly examiner after one of the tests if I 'had an ambition at all'.

'I would like to look at the craters on the moon through a proper big telescope, sir,' I said. I was just fourteen at the time.

A week later we got a letter.

Dear Miss Dorothy Carmody and Master Jack Carmody,

Allow me to introduce myself. My name is Michael Holloway and I have been told by an examiner friend of mine, Mr Anthony Paine from the College of Preceptors in Russell Square, that following a very successful recent mathematical examination Jack expressed an ambition to observe the moon through a proper telescope. I have a private observatory in my garden near Lewes on the Sussex Downs. I would be delighted to welcome you both here for just such an observation. I would suggest a date in mid March when the moon will be at the half phase, which allows for better viewing of the craters, etc.: March 19th would seem to be the best date. We must pray for a clear sky. If you are agreeable, a car will be sent to collect you from your home and will also take you back again. There will of course be no charge for this. I look forward to hearing from you both and very much look forward to welcoming you here.

Yours faithfully,

M. D. Holloway

(Captain – ret'd)

We were collected by a uniformed driver. He was behind the wheel of a Humber 12. I had never ridden in such a car before, and nor had Aunt Dolly.

'My word,' she said, 'this is a very nice car. I hope her at number fourteen saw us getting in, Jack, toffee-nosed old cow – pardon my French.'

We were driven to Mr Holloway's house high on the South Downs. Luckily it was a rare clear night. The sky was cloudy over south London as we drove out. The ground was still white after the late snowfall. Even though the car had a heater, Aunt Dolly sat with a heavy picnic blanket over her lap all the way down. The weather had been overcast and cold for most of the year. That night, though, away from the city, the moon was clear. I could see it as the car climbed the hill up to the house, which was hidden in a copse of trees.

Mr Holloway was a tall man. He came out to meet us with his pipe clenched between his teeth; he waved, a broad smile on his face. His hair was thin at the front and swept back over his ears. He had a high forehead and looked like the kind of professor you might see in a film. He stooped forward a little to shake my hand. 'Welcome, Jack,' he said. 'And you, dear lady, must be Jack's aunt Dolly. Well done, both of you, for getting here.'

'We ain't done much,' Dolly said. 'Your driver fetched us here; we just sat.'

'I meant partly in regard to Jack's education. It's you we all have to thank for encouraging his great talents, I gather?'

'I do my best. You have to, don't you? Always knew he was a clever boy.'

'More than clever.'

I liked Mr Holloway right away. He was friendly and engaging; a bit like some of the examiners I had met, but more jokey. I felt comfortable with him. Later, when I came to know him better, I realized that whenever he said something, it was with a special kind of authority, a certainty; it seemed that he knew everything about whatever the particular subject was. It was as if somehow he carried with him, all hidden away, the contents of a huge electric brain, which, like the nine-tenths of an iceberg, was floating under the water. In his case the waters of the everyday.

'Anyway,' he said, 'the moon is our business this evening. Come on – we've no time to waste.'

Aunt Dolly sat it out in the kitchen, chatting to the driver over a pot of tea.

Mr Holloway had a big wooden shed on a circular set of rails in the garden behind the house. The roof had a sort of dome, which could open in half, allowing for a view of the night sky.

There was a big refractor telescope set up.

'You see, Jack, I use this place as a summer house in daytime and good weather. I can move it around along the rails to follow the sun. At night it becomes my home observatory like it is now.'

Mr Holloway pointed to a chair set up under the eyepiece of the telescope. 'Park yourself there, Jack,' he said.

I sat down in the chair.

'Now, on the side there you will see the small sighting scope – got it? Good. Now line up the visible edge of the light and shadowed area on the moon with the cross hairs. When you move that small scope into place, it moves the big scope as well – that's it. Now look through the eyepiece of the big scope.'

There it was. My first view of an alien world. I could

see details of the craters on the defined edge between the light and the dark area. They were thrown into sharply detailed relief. I probably said something stupid like, 'Cor,' or 'Blimey.' Something uncouth anyway.

'Never fails to impress, does it?' Mr Holloway said. 'Think how far away it is. It's about 238,900 miles from Earth on average. At its closest approach, which is called the lunar perigee . . . I bet you know that word too.'

'Yes,' I agreed.

'The moon is 221,460 miles from us here on Earth. At its farthest approach—'

'That's the apogee,' I said.

'That's the one, well done – *then* the moon is 252,700 miles away.'

'It's moving,' I said.

'Of course, and it looks fast through there, doesn't it?'

I spent a happy hour examining the edge areas. I checked the details of crater names against the moon map – the Plato crater, and the Mare Imbrium.

'I am certain that one day we will settle a colony on the moon,' Mr Holloway said.

'I want to go and live there,' I told him.

'Maybe you will, Jack. It's not entirely impossible, you know.'

He settled himself on an old sofa which was pushed up against the back wall under the moon map. He lit his pipe. 'So you have two more years of study – although looking through some of your results, I can't imagine what they are finding to teach you any more.'

'You've seen my exam results?' I said.

'I see everything, I'm afraid. I'm a very nosy person, and because of my job I'm allowed to do and see all sorts of things that most people can't. What would you like to do after your studies are over, Jack?' he said.

I turned from the eyepiece. 'I don't know – find a job, I suppose.'

'What kind of job would you like to have?'

This was where I always came unstuck. The jobs I wanted to do either didn't exist, or were impossible for someone like me. First off I had always wanted to be an actor in the pictures. Aunt Dolly took me twice a week to the Dalston Odeon. I loved films. Secondly, but most of all, I wanted to be a detective who could solve mysteries through making all the odd connections that only I could see. A kind of clairvoyant secret sleuth operating on the edges of instinct and science. How could I, a fourteen-year-old boy with brilliantined and badly cut hair, explain that to anyone older, anyone in charge? How could such a job exist? It was mad.

'It's hard to explain to anyone,' I said, my confidence

rising just a little as I looked over at Mr Holloway, who seemed to be willing me on. I felt I could confide in him and it would be all right. 'I think, sir, that most of all I would like to be a kind of detective,' I said awkwardly, both expecting and fearing that I would be laughed at.

'That's very interesting,' he said, not laughing at all. 'What kind of detecting? Do you mean criminal stuff – fingerprints and all that?'

'No, not really that. Like I said, it's hard to explain. It's more to do with the mysteries of science; more to do with unexplained things – finding out about them and investigating.'

'What you mean is: are there little green men on Mars, and what really happened to the *Mary Celeste*, and is there a spirit world – and all the time pretending that you are not doing it and keeping it all secret; that sort of caper?'

'Something like that, yes,' I said.

'Well, then, it looks like you have come to the right place.' Mr Holloway cheerfully banged the arm of the sofa so that a cloud of dust rose up in the lamplight. He reached out his hand. 'Shake that, young man,' he said. 'I think you and I are going to work well together in the not-too-distant future, because, you see, the job I just described to you – that is exactly what I do.'

CHAPTER THREE

As far as I could see, as I sat there hugging my knees
under the dripping wet tarp in the back of the lorry,
looking out at all that gloom on the way over to my
billet, Dorset was just a lot of bare wet trees and cold-
looking hills. There were some buildings, I grant
you – farms, barns, cottages, and I don't know what,
all clinging to the round hillsides for dear life. It
was all very Thomas Hardy and bleak and doomed-
looking in the November dusk; and romantic, I'm sure.
There wasn't much in the way of actual pavement,
though. There weren't too many shops, either, and
no picture houses – at least where I ended up. Just
a lot of cows and sheep, and noisy cockerels, and all
of them started making their big racket well before
dawn.

Oh, and another thing: it was bloody freezing cold too.

The village where I was billeted, Litton Cheney, was in the Bride Valley in West Dorset. Not much of a centre to it, not many houses; a tiny place really. You could walk the length of it and hardly notice you had come out the other side. There were two ways into the village proper. It was as if one half was attempting to make its way up Gallows Hill, and the rest was content to stay in the flat valley. One road snaked its way down gradually from the main top road that eventually led to Honiton via Bridport. The other way in was from the same main road but was much steeper. There was a fine view of the valley and the sea from the top. This route ran directly into the village all the way down Gallows Hill. Litton Cheney had a church, and there was a pub, the White Horse, off to the south – where I had my rooms. There was one general grocer's and tobacconist's shop.

The church was north of the main route through the village. You could reach it in two ways. One was along a narrow track called Church Path. There were half a dozen labourers' cottages on one side looking out over the valley, with the Rectory at the far end behind its iron gates. Then there was another path that led up from the lower edge of the village past the steep border of the Rectory garden, where there was a spring which bubbled out and ran back down the side of the path. A corrugated-iron 'tin tabernacle' club house with a pitched roof, which looked like a cricket pavilion, was set at the very top of this path, and this was my main office. I shared it with the officer of the local centre for Air Raid Precautions – or ARP, for short – Mr Feaver.

Almost every day there was some new fear or alarm in the village. As soon as I started on my regular patrol, villagers either came running up to me with some story or other, or went and reported to Mr Feaver in the tin hut. They were all full to bursting with panicky rumours and stories.

For instance, a Mrs Hinde-Smith claimed that the German invasion had started already: her maid had spotted some Hitler youth spies near the village. Turned out to be just some Boy Scouts out camping in what was called Rocks Field, looking after a few evacuees.

There were constant rumours of Nazi landings too. One morning Mr Fry, a particular nuisance, and a bugbear of mine, swore he had seen dozens of parachutes dropping down onto Gallows Hill in clear daylight. When the ARP warden went up there to investigate, the parachutes turned out to be nothing more than an innocent flock of sheep.

With more than one aerodrome based around Dorchester, just a few miles from us, the whole village, and even those further west, had witnessed the recent Battle of Britain. This had lasted from July until October. I think this had set the mood of panic up nicely, because the villagers went on about it all the time.

When I was first stationed there, I just about saw the tail end of it all. At least, I saw a skirmish – a bit of action in the sky. I noticed some Spitfires and Hurricanes just after takeoff from the hills above Dorchester, and soon after that I heard the air-raid sirens. None of it seemed to be real at first. The planes were all so high, they were just little silvery dots; they looked like toys. Though toys would never have left the distinctive white vapour trails that everyone in London had got used to seeing. There was the distinctive droning sound of the engines too. Then I heard distant ack-ack guns. I saw the shells explode with those soft-looking puffs of dark or light smoke. They drifted in a fixed velocity pattern which I could read clearly against the background colour of the sky. The vapour trails crisscrossed each other, and I heard the machine-gun fire, both from our planes and from the Germans'. Once shot down, the planes fell quickly, spinning and turning, the vapour trails echoing the seemingly chaotic patterns of the falling craft – which of course were not chaotic to my eye. I noted a number of parachutes. More than one surely meant that the crew had baled out of a German bomber. The distant siren sounded the all clear. I was lucky that day: one of our fighters flew low over the village and went into a victory roll as he barrelled out over the top of Gallows Hill, which was exciting to watch. I heard no more about any arrests or the survival of the parachutists. Life at Litton Cheney was mostly aggravation, routine and tedium.

As my cover was to be the local support service to the ARP office, I heard all the rumours of invasion and tales of hidden spies – and worse.

There was a group of London evacuees who played in and around the village. They upset some of the villagers one Sunday morning by jumping out of the bushes at them, holding wooden rifles and shouting out in what they thought was German. All of this was reported to our office with a straight face.

The fear and panic was everywhere, and it was mostly irrational. If one of the locals saw a piece of broken glass or mirror, or even a bit of shiny tin, by the roadside, it was seen as a possible signalling device put there to alert enemy aircraft. If someone hung out their washing on a Tuesday, when on the Monday morning the weather had been good for drying, some of the villagers found it deeply suspicious, and would report the possible signal to us very seriously.

All sorts of strange advice and rumours circulated about what to do if anyone actually found a possible invader or spy. In the White Horse pub one evening, I heard the theory that you should go up to a suspicious person and ask, 'Excuse me, sir, but how tall are you, if you don't mind my asking?' If the suspect answered in metres, then they were plainly the invading enemy.

The other option offered up in the bar was that you should suddenly stamp on a suspect person's foot and see what language they swore back at you in.

Mrs Gladwyn's unmarried sister Ada told me once that she carried a brown paper bag full of pepper in her handbag at all times to 'throw into the invader's eyes should they get near enough'.

I will admit it was hard to picture poor little Miss Ada throwing her bag of pepper over a hulking great storm trooper.

The night things kicked off properly, it was not only freezing cold, it was raining too. Well, actually, no . . . sorry . . . start again – let's be more accurate here. It wasn't *exactly* rain. You see, back in London, rain was rain, and fog was fog. We had plenty of both, but we kept them apart. We wouldn't allow them to muddle themselves up and get mistaken one for the other. It was not the same, though, down in the country. For a start, it was so close to the sea; within hearing distance on a windy night. The rain down there was sometimes really more of a heavy sea mist – a 'precipitation', I suppose it would be termed officially (I might be a cockney lad, but I am, as you can tell, well educated). It was more of a 'soak you right through' sort of a fog. You could smell the salt water and the acrid engine oil and that rank whiff of seaweed; they were all mixed up in it as it rolled in off the sea – that is, if you could bring yourself to breathe it in at all.

That night I was on my 'reassuring presence' rounds, walking my preferred circuit of the village not far from my billet. There were no stars to be seen, nothing much to look up at, just low cloud and the general cold wetness. I stopped in the most sheltered corner I could find on my regular beat.

I had a decision to make.

I stamped my army boots (have you ever tried on a pair of army boots? They don't bend at all), just to try and get the blood flowing again. Anything to warm up my poor cold feet.

I had been doing my level best to look and behave like a regular soldier; of course, I wasn't one at all, just acting the part. I saw myself as a plucky young soldier in a propaganda film. The others weren't meant to know about me, which is why I had to work extra hard on my act.

I pushed myself further in under the high overhanging bushes to get out of the wet stuff, and tried my hand once more at rolling a blessed cigarette.

It seemed to me that the British army ran on Naafi tea and hand-rolled cigarettes. Nearly all the other soldiers in the barracks over at Burton Bradstock 'rolled their own', and whenever I went over there, I felt like the odd one out for being unable to do it properly. I never even had any cheap Woodbines to offer round like everyone else.

I was under Captain Holloway's strict orders to do my best to fit in. I had to try and be like all the other regular soldiers. So I practised rolling rotten filthy fags. I did it again, and for the last time, on that fateful evening.

I held up the thin paper tube, already stuffed with Gold Flake tobacco, and sealed it, as I had seen the other soldiers do, by running my tongue along one edge. I turned so I was facing out of the wet as much as I could, and tried to light it – and then that was it.

I'd had enough.

I made my decision.

I threw the horrible soggy thing away among the

tree roots. Who was I trying to kid? Smoking wasn't for me, Jack Carmody.

'That's it. Enough is enough. It's finished, Jack,' I said out loud in my very best Leslie Howard voice to the wet leaves pressing in all round me. Even though no one but the leaves was listening, it somehow had to be said, and out loud too. I was giving up smoking, and the idea of smoking, and anything to do with smoking, for ever and ever amen. And that was before I'd even got properly started on it.

Everybody in the regular army smoked like chimneys. Captain Holloway had his pipe. But I didn't like it, and I couldn't get the hang of it anyway, even though I knew it would make me look older and more like a proper soldier if I could. Part of me enjoyed that aspect – the pretending. As I said before, it was like being an actor in a big film. I played my part. The only problem was, it went on all day. I wasn't like the rest of the soldiers: I was undercover, and when I was with them, I think they sensed something about me; something a bit off kilter. Anyway, since I was posted to the village, away from the main barracks, the smoking didn't seem so important. There was no one around here to impress or notice in any case.

'No more fags ever, ever, ever,' I said out loud to the dripping leaves. 'Decision made. Good boy,' I added.

To someone who'd spent as much time as I had skiving off to old horror films in the picture houses of the West End, the whole village looked like a properly haunted place. The odd bit of light that got through the wet fog only made it look worse. All that was needed to make the setting perfect was the jagged silhouette of a ruined castle looming up on Gallows Hill above the village; now, that would have really completed the picture.

The heavy fog (the locals called it a 'sea fret') had been rolling in all afternoon from the nearby Chesil Beach – a weird-looking place where they carried out practice bombing runs . . . but that's a whole story in itself.

The fret masked the full moon. I have studied the moon; I know the moon. I could look up at the moon and identify all the so-called seas, and the craters too; the larger ones are all named. The Sea of Tranquillity didn't seem to fit any more, though, what with the bombing raids and the Blitz. A bomber's moon, it was called now. There were so many new words and phrases with the coming of the war. Just like the rumours – and not just of the approaching German invasion. There were rumours of secret bombing raids too. Mr Feaver told me last week that a stick of bombs had been dropped from a German plane near Bridport. 'Just to soften us up for when they land,' he said.

I suggested to him that it was most likely on its way to attack the naval docks down at Plymouth, further west, and 'Jerry just let some go for the hell of it.'

'I heard that the only casualties, Jack, were an outhouse roof that lost all its slates, and two rabbits – and luckily one of those was still edible and some clever beggar put the poor thing straight into a pie and baked it,' he told me.

All this might have been true; then again, it might not. There were so many stories and rumours flying about then, most of them best taken with a pinch of salt (rabbit pie . . . pinch of salt . . . ha ruddy ha) – like the one about German paratroopers dressed as nuns. There were rumours, and there were counter-rumours, and there were straight-out lies.

I had been billeted in the White Horse 'Hotel' (so called). I had two rooms upstairs, which were cushy enough compared to an army barracks. I was forced to spend some time down in the bar, obviously, and the locals wasted no time in bending my ear with all their tales about this and that. One or two of the older ones remembered the stories about the 'lights in the sky' from way back in the 1890s, which of course interested me, though I couldn't really let on how much.

'The newspaper sent a man down here from London

back then in the old days, when it was happening before. He sniffed around and interviewed all the local folk who had seen them and all. Now some say the lights they have seen, 'tis the Germans and their planes and parachutes and all that. Well, answer me this: what about back then in 1890? Where were *those* lights from? It weren't no Germans then, was it? They never did find out.'

'Was no one there at all; was the beer talking,' seemed to be the popular view about the reported lights seen above the village in the distant past.

Of course, I knew a lot more than that, but I couldn't tell them. I was on special, 'need to know only' secret duties for Captain Holloway, but as far as anyone else was concerned, I had been sent down to help out with the local ARP.

I'd been teased all the time back in the outer office before I went off to Litton. 'Too scared and skinny to load mines and too young to play with the big boys, eh, Corp? You might as well enjoy cream teas with the farmers' daughters down in that village of yours.'

I only wished some of that had been true, but things were not like that in the deathly quiet village of Litton Cheney, I can tell you. Nothing much happened that wasn't ancient history or panicky ill-informed rumour; at least, not until that evening.

Communiqué 1

Translated from the <u>GERMAN</u> original
(Cl./Capt Holloway office 116 title for future use)
December 1939

Greetings from the other side. I am now in place, 'old chap', and
am of course fully trusted. In fact, it is all better than we
could have hoped for. There are some limits, and we shall soon
no doubt be suffering from some of what you might call priva-
tions, 'old bean'. The English, though, have already been lulled
into calling it the 'Phoney War', as if nothing else were going to
happen to inconvenience them but another pile of sandbags
heaped up outside the office and the 'terrible bore' of carrying
a gas mask with them at all times. I shall report again when and
if. Until then I am lying as low as I did before; as low as it is
possible to lie. I am not to be disturbed; indeed, I am lying so
low, I might as well already be forgotten and forlorn in my own
grave, such is my silence and my deep overhead cover. I do
remember one thing, though, from my earliest days – an old
soldier saying: 'Cover from view is not necessarily cover from
fire.' I always keep it in mind.

CHAPTER FOUR

I knew that there would be no sign of my friend Mr Feaver, the fussy ARP warden, before it was fully dark and the start of his official rounds. 'Finishing up his cooked tea, no doubt, in his nice cosy cottage,' I said to the wet bushes next to me, and they shivered a sort of reply at me, and we all waited together while my watch ticked.

I wondered what he would be eating. I could imagine his plate only too well. Whatever was on it would be swimming in flour-thickened gravy, which would cover most of the blue and white pattern. There would be a couple of nice big boiled spuds and some carrots sliced in rounds, topped by a meat pie – pigeon or rabbit, I guessed – and maybe some boiled cabbage on the side. Sort of thing my aunt Dolly would have set in front of me before the war, except her pie would have been steak and kidney. Things weren't in such short supply in the country.

There was something about that evening, something odd in the air, and not just the sea mist and the smell of diesel oil. I felt little ripples of apprehension, shivers and goose flesh across my neck. It was what I would describe as my 'thunder' feeling, and it meant something was up. I walked the length of Church Path. Most of the old labourers' cottages were closed off and in darkness. Some evacuees and land girls were expected to be using them soon. Now they looked forlorn and doubly neglected in the dark. I finally saw our ARP headquarters through the fog. By the time I reached the corrugated-iron hut, it was properly dark. That real-country, no-light-at-all dark. The rooks (I was actually getting to know the names of birds and trees) were squawking and calling out as they settled for the night in the tall beech trees (see?) that skirted Gallows Hill and the edge of the big Rectory garden.

Mr Feaver would surely be in there by now, fussing about and getting all his fire buckets and stirrup pumps lined up nice and ready, just in case, along with our three chairs, a table, a telephone and a tea urn sitting together in the dingy tin tabernacle.

'Such a ruddy depressing racket those birds make,' I said as I went in, rubbing my hands. 'Give me the shivers, they do.' In fact, the whole winter countryside either gave me the shivers or bored me rigid; it was all pretty depressing and bleak. Warden Feaver nodded at me, his finger to his lips. He was standing bolt upright listening to someone on the telephone, looking as official as he could manage. He wore his navy blue siren suit tightly buttoned up. I am sure he thought it made him look like Winston Churchill himself. In one respect he was right: they were about the same size around the waist.

His tartan muffler was tied under his chin and then stretched up over the top of his carefully but oddly hand-lettered ARP tin helmet, which was perched squarely on top of his head. Even inside his own village hall, he was taking no chances. However, to be fair to the old chap, he had already brewed up some very welcome tea in the big brown teapot.

He nodded his head again and pointed at two enamel mugs steaming nicely on the trestle table next to the lamp and the regulation issue field telephone (official use only). 'Nice and fresh brewed, mind,' he said quietly, his hand over the mouthpiece.

'Won't say no, Mr Feaver,' I mouthed. 'It's brass monkeys out there tonight, and it's that damp cold too – seems to get right through to your bones,' I added in a whisper. I held my hands out to the paraffin stove.

'We've had a report,' the warden said as he put the receiver back, picking up his clipboard. 'That was local area command on the telephone, and our old friend Mr Fry was up at my cottage earlier too. Said he saw something as well – I've noted it all down here for you – "Odd-looking lights in the sky up over the top road," and then he says he saw a strange low-flying aircraft when he was out on Gallows Hill, walking his dog. He reckons he's seen these things more than once. Says he's reporting it direct to someone he knows in higher authority, if we can't be bothered to do anything about it. Says we ought to "go and have a look for ourselves instead of drinking tea in here all night" – damn cheek. Oh, here y'are, then – I did sweeten it, Corporal.' And he pushed one of the mugs across the table at me. 'Two lumps.'

'Two lumps.' I nodded my appreciation and gratefully swallowed some of the hot sweet tea. I kept my cold hands wrapped around the mug.

'Damn cheek is right,' I said. 'When was this all supposed to have happened?'

'Not half an hour ago. Mr Fry said he *heard* something too – sounded like low-flying aeroplane engines; the kind, he said, that land Nazi parachutists.'

'How would he know that?' I wondered. 'I ask you – it'll be another flock of sheep, no doubt.'

The mysterious lights were in fact the very things I had been sent down to investigate; those and the possible sighting of an actual person of interest, of course. I couldn't share any of that with Mr Feaver, though. It was all I could do to mask my rising sense of excitement. 'Strange I didn't hear anything while I was out on my patrol. Tell you what,' I said, as casually as I could, 'we'll satisfy Mr Fry for once: we'll go up Gallows Hill in a minute and have a little poke about. That'll shut him up for a bit – but only when I've finished this cup of tea.'

I hoped I had remembered to put film in the camera. My real job, my secret job, after all, was to faithfully record and report such things to the captain, not clump around the village listening to rumours about people signalling to the enemy by leaving bits of shiny tin or broken mirrors by the road, or hanging their bloomers out on a Tuesday morning instead of wash-day Monday.

CHAPTER FIVE

The sea fret had grown even thicker by the time we left the hall. The top of Gallows Hill had almost vanished into a vague dark cloud. Warden Feaver went ahead, holding up his home-modified version of a blackout lantern. We would have looked like a couple of those protesting villagers in *Bride of Frankenstein*, if I'd only been holding a pitchfork instead of a rifle. The lantern gave out such a faint beam of light across the chalky ground that it made the surroundings look more like a horror film setting than ever.

Mr Feaver had a first-aid box ('just in case, Corp'), attached to an old Sam Browne belt left over from his Great War service. I had my rifle and the camera strap across my back and round my neck. I had put my heavy army greatcoat back on before we left the hut. For once I was glad of my stout boots as we clumped our way up the chalk road surface.

'Shouldn't want to climb this just after it's snowed,' I said. Gallows Hill had a gradient of one in four.

'Snow don't come very often down here,' Warden Feaver told me, 'but when it do, the whole village might be cut off. You can't get any sort of lorry up or down this road. Snow has been known to lie as high as the tops of these hedges so that you can walk over them. No deliveries get through – nothing.'

We carried on up until, looking back down the hill, we could just make out the very faint shimmer of the golden cockerel on top of the church weather vane, down among the bare trees of the churchyard. We stopped to catch our breath and listened. At first all I could hear was the faint roar of the sea four miles to the south. There was another sound, though, in the background; it could have been a low-flying aircraft, but it was hard to gauge which direction it was coming from.

'That might be it,' the warden said. 'The aircraft Mr Fry said he heard. What should we do now?'

'Wait,' I said. 'We don't even know if it's anything at all yet. Let's just give it a moment, shall we?'

We waited, and as we listened, the sound, whatever it was made by, came and went, as if it too were being momentarily blurred and then magnified by the swirls of wind and sea fog.

Then a bright shaft of light appeared some way higher up the hill and touched the white roadway. There were others too, but further away, near the crest of the hill.

I got the captain's camera ready at once. Luckily I had already loaded it with special-issue extra light-sensitive film. 'It might just pick up something,' I said, and I clicked and wound through a couple of times, and then the light moved off. My own 'thunder meter', as before, was properly clicking into place. I was getting the shivers around my neck, the goose pimples too, and one further thing: whenever I reached this state of heightened awareness, ever since the lady in grey, I smelled the sweetness of those roses. I could smell them then, out on that bleak wintry hill. My inner needle was spinning around the dial. Something really was up.

'Can't see why you'd want to *photograph* them; shoot at them maybe. What on earth could they be anyway?' Mr Feaver said.

The lights showed again, a little higher up the hill: one was a shaft of pure white like a sudden searchlight turned on the road out of the clouds above. There was sound now too – a faint rippling thud like a giant footstep.

'Sounds like they could be laying mines or even dropping incendiaries,' I said, clicking off two or three more hopeful shots. I knew that this was certainly not the case, but I couldn't risk letting Warden Feaver know what was really happening. I ran further up the

hill. 'Could even be parachutists, I suppose,' I called back to him, for he was struggling to keep up.

'Can you see them, then?' he shouted breathlessly.

'I can see something,' I said. 'Though God knows what.'

We were nearly halfway up the hill when the lights came again, only now they were directly over our heads, and dazzlingly bright for just a second or two.

'The aircraft noise is stronger too,' I said, 'although it doesn't have the distinctive rumble of a Heinkel or a Junkers.'

The line of lights moved on, like lightning, further back down the hill. They touched the ground on the way, one after the other.

'Damn,' I said. 'Back down there, Mr Feaver – look.'

Above the church, somewhere among the tangle of shrubs and trees, the lights appeared again in a blinding flash. I photographed what I could manage in a rush, and then raced past old Feaver back down the hill again. 'Wait for me,' he called out, and ran after me, his dim lantern light waving about in the fog.

CHAPTER SIX

I stopped in my tracks, hesitating near the steps that led up to the churchyard. The sweet smell had come again out of nowhere: somewhere nearby there was something strange. I knew the signs by now . . .

The lantern on the iron arch over the gates was switched off, but bright light suddenly flooded out of the open door of Mr Fry's house. He was standing on his porch in a grubby old dressing gown, with a broom raised above his head.

'Now you've heard them and seen them,' he said, 'perhaps you will believe me. Invading Germans, you see, just as I told that fool Feaver earlier. Now perhaps you'll believe what I saw and heard – and not for the first time.'

'Please close your door at once, sir, and respect the

blackout,' I said. 'And please keep it closed. We are dealing with this now.'

'Why would I take orders from you? You look like a ten-year-old. Answer me that,' Mr Fry said.

I was used to this sort of thing.

'It has nothing to do with my age, sir, which I assure you is not ten. It is a question of the law. We are at war and the blackout must be respected, and you surely know that.'

He glared at me, then turned on his slippered heels and slammed the door shut. His dog started barking loudly from behind it.

The warden arrived, out of breath, still holding his helmet onto his head. He put the lantern down on the ground and stayed bent low for a moment with his hands on his knees, getting his breath back.

'You all right, Mr Feaver?' I said.

'I'll be right as ninepence in a mo', young Jack,' he said, straightening up and holding the lantern high above his head. 'Just not used to running at my time of life. I'm guessing, from all the noise, that Mr Fry's been on at you?'

'Yes, he has,' I said. 'I put him straight.'

'What should we do now, then?' Mr Feaver asked.

'I think we should go up into the north churchyard.'

'You sure, Corp?' he asked. 'Looks empty to me –

nothing there but sleepers, if you catch my drift.'

'I agree, Mr Feaver, but I have a strong feeling that someone or something is hiding there.'

I had a real horror of treading on the grass humps and mounds of earth above the dead. I've never liked cemeteries much – who does? – especially in the dark, and especially after some of the things I've seen. It was like the game we used to play back in the smoke when I was a really little kid: avoiding the cracks between the paving stones – except now I knew that it was all real. It couldn't be helped. To go any further we had to clamber over the ancient green mounds of the village dead. It had to be done; the sweet smell was calling to me and I had to act on it.

The place looked abandoned and haunted on that wet November night. The older monuments and high gravestones loomed up out of the pitch darkness, dull-white and grey. The rusty iron gate was half pulled open, and it was covered in drops of water which caught the low light from Mr Feaver's lantern. Ragged swirls of sea fog floated all around it. We went up the steps side by side: Mr Feaver held the lantern out in front of us, and I pointed my rifle forward with the bayonet, my 'pig sticker', fixed in army regulation fashion.

We crossed the wet grass over the sleeping mounds and went up the second short set of steps into the

higher, north part of the cemetery. The next instant, I heard the same throb of aircraft noise, somewhere in the fog right above our heads, and then there was another blinding flash of light, which dazzled me as it hit the ground, accompanied by those thumps – which felt loud and deep enough to wake the sleepers under our feet.

The sea fret had somehow gathered here in this corner too, and had grown even thicker. When my eyes had recovered from the light, the darkness seemed extra dark again and the lantern was having little effect.

There was no aircraft sound anywhere now, just an uneasy silence.

It was then that something large and white rushed out of the darkness at us.

I already had the camera raised in case, and I clicked just the once before I had to sidestep. A terrified-looking albino stag with large antlers leaped straight at us out of the fog. I could read the fear in its glaring eye as it rushed past, and then careered off through the tangle of bushes. I watched it clear the steps in a single bound, and then it dashed off to the side in a swerving panic. It was soon galloping up the chalk road of Gallows Hill.

'Good God!' Mr Feaver shouted. He had fallen back in shock, and was leaning against one of the taller gravestones. 'What the bloody hell! Where did that come from? I've never seen the like – nearly gave me a ruddy heart attack, it did.'

'I thought they lived wild in the forest, not here,'

I said, only just regaining my own balance.

'They do,' he replied. 'They do, Jack. I've never seen anything like that here, ever – not a white hart, not here in the village like that.'

We waited, recovering from our shock in the uneasy quiet. 'Not even those awful rooks are squawking now, and they're never quiet,' I said. I breathed in deep draughts of Dorset air, cold and damp, but overlaid with that sweet rose smell. I looked around carefully. I was sure that the deer was not the only living thing in the churchyard.

'Wait a moment,' I said. I set off further in among the tombs, aware of something just out of reach.

'Shouldn't we get back inside, Corp?' Mr Feaver called out to me. 'There's nothing left for us here.'

I was soon in total darkness: the light from the warden's lantern was so weak it had no effect at all if you stepped just a few paces away from it. The churchyard was almost completely silent now; I could only detect one sound – of something or someone breathing heavily among the shadowy gravestones.

'Who goes there?' I called out suddenly, as loudly as I could, into the quiet air.

'Is that . . . is that you, reverend sir?' a voice called back to me fearfully from among the graves. 'I didn't hurt it – I couldn't do it, not with that knife – it didn't seem right. I was trying to save it, honest. I promise I was.'

'No,' I called back, my heart pounding, 'it is not the reverend anybody. It is Corporal Carmody of the Ninth Essex Regiment. I am patrolling here with Air Raid Precautions Officer Feaver. I should warn you now that we are armed. Who might you be, friend or foe? Step forward slowly now and show yourself.'

A shadow emerged and took a nervous step forward.

'Mr Feaver, your lantern up here please,' I called out.

The warden was soon next to me, puffing and wheezing. 'What is it, Corp?'

I took the lantern and held it out at arm's length. Standing in front of us was a boy of about thirteen or fourteen, not so very much younger than myself.

'Well, look at that,' Mr Feaver said.

'Do you think we have found a parachutist?' I asked, doing my best to play along and so keep Mr Feaver in the dark. I knew that this boy was no German paratrooper.

'I thought you m-might be the r-reverend,' the boy suddenly said haltingly, ignoring what we had just said. His teeth chattered – I presumed from the cold. He stood stock-still and shivered. He was wearing a rough-looking dark waistcoat and breeches and a dirty white shirt. He was shaking all over and wide-eyed, apparently with fear.

'Was that animal anything to do with you, then?' I said.

'I didn't hurt it, honest, sir. It was old Gawen's idea – he wanted it and promised me a share, but I changed my mind, and now I don't know where he is.'

'Right,' I said, pulling myself together and sounding as convincingly official as I could manage. 'Warden Feaver, sir, if you wouldn't mind just looking behind all these stones here for anything that may have been hidden – a discarded pack, weapons, parachute, anything at all.'

'Right you are,' he said and moved away, taking the lantern light with him.

The darkened shape of the boy stood staring ahead and not always straight at me. His face was deathly pale. He looked dirty too, and the whites of his eyes were just visible in the gloom as he flicked his gaze right and left, then back to me. He was clearly terrified of something.

'First thing now,' I said. 'Please put your hands up high above your head where I can see them.'

The boy obeyed at once, lifting his arms straight up into the air.

'Where are you from?' I asked.

'From round here, course,' the boy said in what I recognized as the local accent.

'You sound as if you might be, but then accents can be learned and faked, and you Germans are clever devils, aren't you,' I said, keeping up the pretence that I thought the boy might be just that.

My feelings about this boy being there had been correct. Once again there was a stirring, a quickening of something around my sixth sense, my thunder meter. Something was wrong with all this. The boy didn't fit; my readings were, as they say, 'off the scale'. Here was the very thing – the 'person of interest'. I had to dampen my excitement down in front of Mr Feaver, but there was something distinctly odd and at the same time familiar about everything that had happened.

Warden Feaver returned from his search behind the graves. 'Nothing there,' he said, and moved closer to the boy. 'I don't know this lad by sight at all.' He shook his head. 'Certainly not local to us.'

'You're not from this village, then?' I asked.

'I am, though. I live very close by – just down the path there.' The boy lowered his arm and pointed. 'I live at the cottage down there, the first one past the steps on Church Path.'

'No one lives there – it's boarded up, and has been ever since the last tenants left. It's up for requisition for possible evacuees,' the warden said.

'But I live there with my father,' the boy insisted.

'I think you'd best come with us,' I said. 'Slowly now – come forward. You look frozen, and the least we can do is get you into the warm.'

The boy was shivering violently, as if he had just been pulled out of freezing water and saved from drowning. He came into the dim circle of lantern light, and I saw that he had a tangle of dirty-looking dark hair.

'*Woher kommen Sie, junger Mann?*' ('Where are you from, young man?') I asked suddenly, as if trying to trick him and catch him out with my best LCC-board school-certificate German.

The boy just looked back at me; his face was a complete blank. Not a flicker of recognition at the German.

'All right, come on, then.' I waved my rifle, the bayonet pointing up the slope back towards the tin tabernacle.

The boy walked hesitantly between me and Warden Feaver. Mr Fry appeared again, scuttling out of his now darkened doorway. In one hand he was holding a threatening garden shovel instead of the broom, while in the other he held his muzzled dog, which growled and strained against the lead.

'So you actually caught the little Nazi swine,' he said. 'The first of many, I'm sure. Why not let me at him?'

'Step back, please, sir,' I said.

'Not much to look at, is he? Some soldier *he* is – not

much to worry about if they are all like that. Looks more like a damned gypsy.'

'Back inside please, sir. We have this under control now.'

The boy broke away and blundered ahead for a few feet in a sort of panic.

'He's escaping now,' Mr Fry said. 'Fat lot of use you are. Shoot him, man.'

'No, sir. He has not escaped, sir, if you look properly. There will be no shooting.'

Warden Feaver had hold of the boy by the scruff of his shirt.

Mr Fry went reluctantly back into his cottage, grumbling to himself.

Communiqué 2

Translated from the <u>GERMAN</u> original
(C2./Capt Holloway Office 116)
Undated – filed early 1940

I have met someone. They think I am 'quite the thing'. In turn
they could in fact be quite the useful thing too. I need someone
like this – a natural cover. Couples can do things and go places
here in London with more ease; the individual cannot wake up
without suspicion. The idea of a romance is a pleasant
distraction in itself.

   They work for one of the War Office Ministries – nothing too
sensitive. I was told there were bombing raids on the cities
outside London, although the newspapers here are censored. They
fear a coastline invasion. I have joy to determine that the
submarines can now operate out of Brest.

CHAPTER SEVEN

Mr Feaver pushed the boy gently over the threshold of the hall. He stood blinking in the sudden brighter light and I gestured for him to sit down at the warden's table. I moved the black Anglepoise lamp up and round a bit so that I could get a good look at him. The boy watched me, shivering in silence. It was a fearful silence rather than a sullen or defiant one.

'You look like you could use a cup of tea,' I said, as casually as I could manage.

The boy nodded a yes while he continued to stare straight ahead at the upturned electric light bulb. He reached his finger out suddenly, and before I could stop him he touched the bright glass. The bulb seemed to react. It brightened momentarily, and the boy pulled his finger back as if he had been stung.

'Careful now, lad, you'll burn yourself,' I said. 'You

should know better than that – or are you playing the simple card now, I wonder?' It was an interesting moment. It seemed that a surge of something had passed through the light filament when he touched it; as if he himself were charged with energy in some way.

I moved the base of the lamp back to keep it away from him, and then picked up the camera.

'Look at me,' I said. The boy stayed still and I took a photograph of him and then wound the film on and took another.

'What you doing?' he asked.

'Taking a photograph,' I replied.

The boy said nothing; he just stared back into the camera lens.

Warden Feaver slid a mug of tea across the table, along with a tin bowl with three or four sugar cubes rattling around in it.

'Sugar?'

The boy said nothing, so I stirred two of the cubes into the tea for him.

'Steady on now – our sugar is in short supply,' the warden said.

'I think he needs it more than us, Mr Feaver,' I said.

'Lucky to get it at all, if you ask me, Corp.' He shook his head.

The boy picked up the mug and held it up as if for

an inspection. He looked at it in wonder, as if he had never seen anything quite like it before. He put it to his lips and carefully drank some of the tea with his eyes tightly closed. He kept the mug up close to his mouth, as if he were savouring the heat and steam from it as much as the tea itself.

'Time to ask you some questions, I'm afraid,' I said. 'You must understand our position here,' I added. 'We have had several reports of low-flying aircraft, and then you and some unlikely wild animal suddenly turn up in the local graveyard together straight afterwards.'

'I live here,' the boy said quietly. 'This is my home and we were going hungry. I didn't want to hurt it.'

'So where did that deer come from? You know, you shouldn't be out at this time of night. You were obviously up to no good. There's a war on, and a strict blackout and all that.'

'Obvious to me, Corp,' Mr Feaver said.

'Go on,' I told him.

'He's most likely one of those badly behaved London evacuees and he's been sneaking out with this mate of his, Gawen, from wherever they're billeted – over at Burton, most likely, or I hear there are some at Puncknowle. They've been doing a bit of venison poaching and we caught this one. The others ran off.'

'Is Mr Feaver right? Are you from London – is that

it? Grabbing some free venison off the ration?'

'No, I live here, in this village. I was born here and my poor mother is buried up in the churchyard, may God rest her soul.'

'I see. Well, we can check up on all that later. What is—'

I was interrupted by the field telephone ringing suddenly and shrilly into the quiet. The boy jumped forward off his chair as if in terror of the phone. He lunged forward to touch it and knocked the receiver off its cradle. I watched as it fell awkwardly to the floor.

It was as if, for just a split second, an invisible hand had steadied the receiver as it fell.

It visibly slowed in the air.

The warden didn't notice anything because it was on the far side of the table from him, but I did, and my interest in the boy was suddenly doubled. A tinny voice came floating up out of the fallen receiver. The boy, startled, backed away from the table.

'What's that?' he said.

'Now, you shouldn't have done that, should you? That belongs to the WD, that's Government property, that is,' Warden Feaver said, bending down and scrabbling awkwardly under the table for the telephone receiver.

'WD?' the boy asked, looking at me with a blank

expression on his face. 'WD?' he said again.

The warden picked up the receiver and spoke quietly into it. 'Yes, sir, as a matter of fact we *are* aware of it. Yes, we saw it ourselves. Yes, sir, I'm sure someone will be looking into it.' He put the receiver back.

'Someone has reported seeing that white stag,' he said. 'Been running wild up on the main road over to Honiton.'

I said to the boy, 'WD means War Department. We have that telephone in here because it is the year 1940 and we are at war and we are keeping a lookout for enemy aircraft. Now, come on, calm yourself and sit back down.'

He looked at me with a frown on his face, as if he was working something out. He closed his eyes and mumbled something which I didn't catch.

I took a pen from the table and a sheaf of Captain Holloway's incident report sheets.

'Have the Boers won, then?' the boy asked. 'Is that what you mean?'

'The Boers?' I said. 'No, that all ended in – ooh, what was it? – 1902. We are at war with Germany now, of course.'

'We are at war with Kaiser Bill as well now?'

'Kaiser Bill? Where have you been living? It's 1940,' I said, carrying on with the standard question and response for the benefit of Mr Feaver.

'No,' he said under his breath, his head shaking from side to side. 'No, no, no – can't be.'

'We're at war with Herr Hitler, of course. You know, the one who looks like Charlie Chaplin but is not at all funny.' I touched my index finger to my upper lip in an attempt to look like a caricature of Hitler and his moustache.

The boy continued to shake his head slowly. He certainly wasn't faking his ignorance.

'First things first,' I said, opening the pen. 'Let's start as we mean to go on. Your name?'

'My name is Tom – Tom Pile,' the boy answered, staring ahead past my shoulder into the darker part of the hall.

'And how old are you, Tom?'

'I'm fourteen – in any case, that's what I was told last birthday.'

'Why were you out in the churchyard this evening?'

'I started from there with old Gawen this evening, but I don't know how I got back there. I can't seem to remember anything much about tonight.'

'Were you sent here from Germany?' I said for Mr Feaver's benefit. I knew full well that Tom might well have come from a lot further away than Germany.

'No, course not. Like I said, I'm from here. I'm

from this village. I've lived here all my life . . . all my life . . .' His voice trailed off and his eyes lowered, and he suddenly looked very sad and young and dirty and bewildered.

'All your life, you say . . . But,' I pointed out, 'the warden here doesn't know you at all, and he knows everyone in this village and hereabouts.'

'Well, I don't know him,' the boy said, shaking his head wildly. 'I don't know anything or anyone any more.'

CHAPTER EIGHT

It was late when I finally led Tom off to my billet in the White Horse. I took full responsibility for him. Warden Feaver made me sign a letter to that effect, which he folded into his report ledger.

'Just in case, Corp, you understand.'

I understood all right. It was called 'covering your back'. Everyone official seemed to do it – must have orders in triplicate, must keep flimsies, must have letters and files all backed up with carbons, responsibility shifted far away down the line. That was how everything worked now with the war.

We didn't go in through the public bar. I didn't want to draw too much attention to the boy. If word got out that we had found a possible German invader in the local churchyard, then I might have a lynch mob of Dorset peasants on my hands, all carrying flaming torches and pitchforks, and we would soon be back in the churchyard burying him. I was sure that this boy was no German. I could see it clearly enough. He was not part of some pre-invasion force. If he was – if this was the best they could come up with – then it was surely all over for Hitler, and no mistake.

Luckily the upstairs rooms had their own side entrance. I took him up and sat him down by the table and told him to stay there. Then I locked him in from the outside and went to find the landlord.

The bar was full of the usual locals – though it was not a place frequented by Warden Feaver. He was church warden as well, and would have considered himself a cut above the public bar at the White Horse. The news about the boy wouldn't have come through yet, but it would only be a matter of time.

'Evening, Corporal,' said the landlord, Mr Cox.

'Evening. A half of bitter, please, squire – and is there anything to eat?'

'Could get the wife to make you up some sandwiches. Nothing hot left tonight, I'm afraid.'

'Sandwiches will do well enough. Two, if you could. I have an extra mouth staying tonight.'

'Oh, I don't know if I can allow—'

'Yes you can,' I interrupted, tapping the side of my

nose. 'It's an army matter. Very strictly hush-hush,' I added.

'Understood,' he said, and handed me a dimpled glass.

Mrs Cox came through from the kitchen and said, 'I can do cold lamb and mustard piccalilli – that do?'

'Very nicely,' I said.

One of the older villagers, Mr Gladwyn, who was always to be found sitting by the big fireplace in the public bar, called me over.

'Any chance of a bitter, Corporal? Only I've got something to tell you, just between you and me, mind.'

I was used to this. No doubt he had seen one of his neighbours signalling to the Germans by putting a mirror in the hedgerow or heard someone in the village speaking German. After all, I was down there to dig around and find things out, so I shelled out for a pint of the finest and took it over to the fire. He drank a good quarter of it off and then spoke to me quietly.

'Post office van driver from Bridport was just in 'ere earlier, Corporal. Said he saw some low aeroplanes. Well, he said there were bright lights up in the sky. Says he saw them, and then, after that, on his way 'ere, he saw a white stag running free and wild up on the Honiton road. Nearly forced him off the road, it did. Gave him a shock. He said it looked like a ghost creature out in the fret like that. Never 'eard the like. Rum things happening round 'ere all over again.'

'All over again?' I said.

'Aye, it's not the first time for seeing the lights hereabouts and more. Ask any of the older folk: they might remember it – lights in the sky and all, 'bout forty years ago.'

'I'm sorry,' I said, playing dumb. 'I'm obviously missing something here. What exactly do you mean?'

'Look it up, lad – must be records of it all somewhere that will tell yer. I don't know much about it, only heard the stories. My old father – God rest his soul – told me he had seen them, but then I never did. The post office man was all shaken up by it too – 'ad to 'ave a brandy and water, not like himself at all – 'e's a cider man normally. I say it means invasion for sure. Bad omens, I reckons they are. We'd best brace ourselves for it – looks like Ada might need her bag of pepper after all.'

Back in my room I found the boy slumped down on one of the single iron beds which had been pushed up under the window. He had fallen asleep. His position and his pale colour reminded me of that old painting, *The Death of Chatterton*; the boy looked dead too. I went over and felt for his pulse. He wasn't dead, but he was dead to the world. I covered him with a blanket and let him be.

The landlady brought the sandwiches up. I opened the door just enough to allow her to get the plate through. They would see the boy soon enough at breakfast time; I didn't want to fuel their curiosity just yet.

I ate one of the lamb sandwiches. It was good, as far as it went, but I already had strong yearnings for a fried fish-and-chip supper, all sprinkled over with salt and malt vinegar. After seeing a film in Leicester Square. That wouldn't happen any more – not for now anyway. I saved the boy one of the sandwiches in case, and finished up my report for Captain Holloway. I had set up a film-developing tank in the cupboard, and I loaded the film from the camera onto the holder in the pitch dark, closed it off and set the crucial timer. When the negatives were dry, they would go up to London in the pouch, to be printed up along with my notes for Captain Holloway. We would see then if I'd managed to get anything of the lights.

CHAPTER NINE

The boy slept right through, past breakfast time. I wondered what dreams were spooling through his mind, if any, while I enjoyed a good rasher or two of bacon and a fresh egg on a fried slice down in the public bar. One saving grace of the Dorset countryside: there was not so much evidence of shortages and rationing at that time.

'Your, er . . . companion not up yet, then, Corporal?' Mrs Cox asked.

'No, Mrs Cox, he's not.'

'Not one of your soldiers, then?'

'Not really, no. We found him hiding in the churchyard. We think he might have been out poaching. He seems lost.'

She looked startled at this. "'E's more of a prisoner, then, is he?"

'In a way, I suppose he is, for the moment, yes,' I said. 'Nothing to be frightened of, missus. He's very low risk. He's only a boy – no more than fourteen or so. He looks worn out and harmless enough. Might even be a bit simple-minded. He says he lives in the village, but the house he claims to live in is apparently all boarded up – has been for some time.'

'You sure 'e's not a German spy, then? He could be fooling you?'

'No,' I said, 'I'm not sure of anything at all, and that's why I'm taking him over to the barracks later for proper questioning. He seems confused to me. I would like to give him some breakfast, though, later on, if I may.'

I took a cup of strong tea up with me. The boy was sitting on the edge of the bed looking out of the window at the road below.

'The road is black,' he said to me in a puzzled tone, almost as if he was asking himself a question, as if he had only just noticed it.

'Yes, it is. The grass is green too, when you can see it,' I added, trying to make light banter with him.

'Road wasn't that colour yesterday.'

'No? What colour was it, then?'

'The usual colour, of course,' he said defensively. 'Someone's painted it all over black since yesterday.'

I put the tea down for him. 'Cup of tea for you there,' I said. 'Tell me some more about what happened last night before we found you.'

'Can't remember much of anything.'

'All right,' I said, as breezily as I could. 'We'll be off soon. We're going into Dorchester to see if we can find out a little bit more about you.'

'I live here, though. My father will be wondering where I am. I ought to go and see him.'

'Tell you what: you drink that tea, and there's a sandwich I saved for you, if you want it, and we'll go and see if we can find him.'

I used the bar telephone to warn Dorchester barracks that we would be coming over later, and also to ask for a delivery driver to go to the station with an urgent package by rail for Captain Holloway in London.

I also checked if there was enough hot water for the boy to have a bath. He certainly needed it.

'I suppose so, Corporal,' Mrs Cox said grudgingly. 'Here's the key. Keep an eye on things, mind.'

I ran some hot water and encouraged the boy to get in. He smelled like an old tramp – as if he hadn't washed in weeks.

'We might find you some better clothes too, or at least get these cleaned.'

His clothes stank as badly as he did. I had my suitcase of civvies in the room, and as I wasn't much taller than him I thought I could kit him out until his stuff could be washed and possibly even de-loused.

I locked him into the little bathroom on the landing. I sorted his clothes out and took the chance to feel inside his pockets. A penny and a farthing, dating from 1882 and 1883 respectively, a rough linen handkerchief and a bone-handled folding fruit knife in one. Not much to carry about – wouldn't get very fat on that. A penny farthing wouldn't buy you much nowadays, I thought.

What I found in the other pocket was something else altogether, and it set my pulse racing. It was a thin square, apparently made of metal. It weighed next to nothing, almost as if it were cut from a bolt of fine silk, and yet it was hard and felt very dense. The intense colours shimmered, even in the dull light of my bedroom. The effect was similar to the rainbow patterns you see in a puddle under a car when the oil or petrol has leaked out. The whole metal surface looked like that, and as I stared down at it, the colours actually seemed to shift and glow, move a little and then settle. I had never *seen* the like before, and yet I looked at it with a shock of recognition. I then realized that I had read a *description* of it. It was in a secret file document, one of the many copied and smuggled in from Germany before the war. The evidence had been found and examined by the German security office – their own secretive Department X, which is a close equivalent to what we are doing. Captain Holloway showed me that particular file, and I remember we went through it carefully because it contained a description of the only piece of hard evidence.

I had a spare WD evidence envelope, and I prepped it ready but I couldn't let it go. The little square of metal (if that is what it was) sat there like a spell. Studying it for any length of time was like looking into the burning coals of a fire. I remembered feeling that same lost sensation on winter nights while Dolly toasted a slice of bread in the flames on a long-handled toasting fork. I saw a sudden expansion. It was as if the tiny crags and fissures among the flames and the red-hot embers of coal had grown, filled my field of vision and become a real and huge landscape. It was hypnotic, and so was this strange sliver of rainbow. I could feel my concentration slipping, and the little pulsing square of colours seemed to be getting bigger as I looked at it. I quickly turned away and broke the spell, but I had to force myself to do it. I quickly opened the despatch bag and put the shimmering metal square very carefully into the WD envelope. I included my notes from the night before and the negatives, adding a note to explain that the boy had actually had the square of metal in his pocket when found. I added the words *Günzburg Clinic File,* and a big exclamation mark, knowing – hoping – that Captain Holloway would pick up on it at once and realize and understand.

I hurried back along the corridor to the bathroom. I didn't want to say anything about the small scrap of metal to the boy. I unlocked the door. He was sitting on the edge of the bath, wrapped in a towel. He seemed almost cheerful.

'I bet you feel a lot better now,' I said.

'I would do,' he said, 'except for this.' He showed me his upper arm, where there was a neat scar and evidence of what looked like a bullet wound.

'How did you manage that?' I asked.

'Wasn't there before,' he said. 'I've never seen it in my life. I never been wounded there.' He pulled and stretched out his pale, almost blue-white skin.

'Maybe it happened when you were very young,' I suggested. 'You have just forgotten.'

'No,' he said.

'Well, it's very well healed and neatly done.'

He shook his head. 'Don't understand,' he said, and

then added, 'Never had a bath in one of these before,' patting the enamel rim of the bath tub. 'We use one o' them metal tubs. Dad keeps it in the outhouse at the back.'

His bath water looked like dirty river water. I pulled the plug out and allowed it to flow away.

'They got a bath just like this up at the Rectory. The Reverend Stone has one in there.'

'That's nice for him,' I said. 'I've laid out some clothes of mine. They should fit you all right – they're good, and clean too. My Aunt Dolly in London looks after me very nicely. I'll get your clothes washed meanwhile – they certainly need it.'

The boy dressed himself in a pair of my old grey flannel trousers, a striped work shirt with no collar, and a sleeveless Fair Isle patterned pullover that Aunt Dolly had knitted for me a while ago. I watched him test the scar on his arm again before he rolled down the shirt sleeve; the wound plainly bothered him. He had to pull the belt buckle up to its tightest notch to keep his trousers up, but all in all it wasn't too bad a fit.

Mrs Cox tapped on the door. 'A messenger's here for your London parcel, Corporal,' she said. 'Oh, and there's a policeman wants to see you too.'

'All right, Mrs Cox. Thanks.'

I went downstairs with the WD package and gave it

to the messenger. The boy followed me down hesitantly and hovered somewhere behind me. The copper stood to attention, all official, upright and ready in the dingy snug bar, with his notebook out, waiting.

'Good morning, Corporal,' he said with a formal nod. 'Now, Warden Feaver over by the church tells me that you personally took charge of a possible vagrant or suspected poacher – perhaps even a German agent – last night. Is that correct?'

'As far as it goes, in a way, yes.'

'Is that him, then?' He indicated to somewhere behind me with his pencil. "Cos I need to ask him a few questions.'

'There's no need, Constable. I will be taking him to Dorchester with me in just a mo for that very purpose. This is an army matter now and I have taken full responsibility.'

'Is that so?'

'Why, yes, I am afraid it is,' I said.

I tugged at the copper's sleeve and pulled him away, out of hearing of the boy, further down into the gloom at the end of the bar. I grew up in the East End of the smoke, after all, and I knew how to talk to coppers.

'Between you and me,' I said, in a hushed, confidential tone, 'I think this boy is in need of all sorts of help.' And I winked, as if to say he was sixpence short of a shilling, which at that moment was, after all, still a possibility. 'Before I get him over to army HQ at Dorchester, I thought I would take him up to Church Path. He claims he lives there. It shouldn't take a moment to sort out. Perhaps you would like to come with me, sir?' I said, gushing with extra respect.

'Do you know, I think I should do just that,' he said, closing his notebook.

'Thing is,' I said, 'the boy needs a bit of breakfast first – he looks half starved. He refused a cold lamb sandwich earlier – can't say I blame him for that, but I think he needs something hot on a morning like this, don't you? I should think you could do with a cuppa too,' I added, sensing his weakness.

We sat in a corner of the snug. The boy ate eggs and bacon; actually, he more like wolfed them down. The copper watched him, plainly suspicious.

'You a Romany, then, lad?' he said. 'Look like a traveller – are you?'

'No,' the boy said between mouthfuls, shaking his head vigorously. 'Ask the Reverend Stone, if you don't believe me,' he added, pushing away his empty plate.

I had met the local vicar during my first week in the village and he wasn't called Stone. I said nothing.

'I haven't made the acquaintance of the local reverend yet,' the copper said, 'but then, I've only been down at the Burton station for a couple of weeks. I seen your regiment down there, though, Corp.'

'I can't say anything about that, Constable, obviously.'

'No, of course not,' he said, looking over at the silent boy, who watched us seemingly with no understanding at all, holding onto his mug of tea with both hands.

'Come on, then,' I said.

The boy put on my old civvy overcoat and scarf, and we set off to walk through the village back to the church.

The boy looked around as if puzzled by almost everything we passed.

'Whole road has been painted black,' he said as we turned onto the main village street. I felt like saying that it wasn't paint, just the natural colour of the tarmac, but held back.

The grocer's shop was open, and there were some vegetables in boxes outside the door. The shopkeeper came out in an apron and added some potatoes to one of the boxes from a sack. The boy stopped and watched him as he filled the box.

'What is it?' I asked.

'New grocer,' the boy said.

I stepped up to the man, a ruddy-faced figure wearing a cloth cap and a muffler. I had been in his shop more than once.

'Mornin', Corporal,' he said. 'Some Gold Flake for you at all?'

'No thank you, never again,' I said. 'Given it up for good. How long have you run the shop here, if you don't mind my asking?'

'Let's see – we first came over from Honiton in early thirty-four, I think – so six years, give or take.'

'Do you know this young man?' I asked, indicating the boy.

'Can't say I do,' the grocer said. 'What's he supposed to have done?' he added, noticing the copper standing a few feet further off.

'Doesn't matter,' I said.

I turned to the boy. 'He's not the new grocer. He's been here in the village for six years, he says.'

'I've never seen him until today,' the boy said. 'He wasn't here yesterday.'

'He was, though, because I bought some tobacco from him yesterday afternoon.'

The boy looked back at me, mystified. He just stood hunched and huddled up in my old coat. I could see that he was feeling out of his depth, out of his life, out of his mind, out of something. If he was acting, then this was first-rate stuff and he should have been in the pictures.

We soon arrived at the small farm cottages that lined the path up to the church. We went up to the one closest to the church itself. A fence, once painted white, now patchy with lichen and the wood mostly rotten, ran along the narrow front garden. It was deep enough for a couple of overgrown, tangled hedges and not much else. The same fencing also ran along the front of the twin cottage next door. Both places were boarded over. The doors were sealed off with crossed planks. The upstairs windows had curtains in them but they were filthy and torn. The downstairs ones were boarded up like the door. The boy looked at the house, and his face set at once in a strange rictus of both agonized shock and disbelief. He walked up to the door and banged on it and rattled the handle.

'Dad!' he called out. 'Dad, what's going on?'

I watched him carefully for any sign of acting or overacting, but there was none. He seemed genuine. It gave me goose pimples just to watch him.

Then he pulled at the planking that was nailed across the door as hard as he could. 'No,' he said. 'No.'

'You claim this is where you live, then?' the copper said in his official voice.

'Yes, I do. I *do* live here, I've *always* lived here. I've lived here since I was a baby,' the boy said, his voice cracking.

There was no doubt in my mind that he was telling the truth as he saw it. The agony of disbelief on his face was too real. It was the kind of weird grief that would be impossible to fake. It came from the heart; from inside; from his soul. He had it, he felt it, and to him it was real.

'I think it's clear,' the copper went on, 'that no one lives here and no one has lived here for quite some time, by the look of things.'

'I'm afraid he's right,' I said quietly, putting my hand on the boy's narrow shoulder. 'Just look at it.'

'I have gone quite mad, then,' the boy said, equally quietly, 'and will surely be up in the Herrison Asylum before long.'

He turned his back to us and looked down from the front of the cottages back over the sloping landscape as it fell away to the sea. Above, there were ragged scraps of darker grey clouds chasing after each other on a westerly wind. I followed the boy's gaze, and saw the pattern in the clouds as they rolled together. I could clearly picture the opposing air currents and wind pressures that had made them form these particular shapes at this particular moment, in terms of equations and the subtle application of various elements.

My thoughts were interrupted by the boy saying, 'This is all the same as it should be, all of this,' and he raised his hand as if to trace the areas that remained familiar to him. 'Nothing else is,' he added, his voice flat. He continued to look out at the unchanged landscape and the not so distant sea.

'Last night,' I said, 'when I first called out to you, and this morning, you mentioned the Reverend Stone.'

'Yes, my dad does jobs for him around the big garden. The reverend knows me well enough. He lives up at the Rectory, just through those gates there.'

'Let's go and see him, then, shall we?' I said, turning away from the sky and the shabby, dismal-looking cottage.

CHAPTER TEN

From Captain Holloway's journal

My morning started badly. I left the house without my gas mask and its accompanying and very annoying square bulky case. I hadn't got very far when I realized. An office girl wearing a bright yellow scarf walked past me. I noticed her gas-mask case swinging from her shoulder. She wore it casually, almost jauntily, like a fashionable handbag. I automatically reached for the empty space where my own usually hung. I knew that they were a nonsense, a kind of placebo to reassure a frightened population. As far as intelligence was aware, there would be no gas bombs. However, I had no wish to draw attention to myself or risk a fine or a court appearance. I like to stay nicely anonymous; in the shadows, as it were. I groaned to myself and ran back up to Adur Terrace. My landlady was already out on the step polishing her brass door furniture.

'You've forgotten it again, haven't you, sir?' she said, shaking her head.

'Yes, of course I have,' I said.

I wore a captain's uniform. I was, of course, a captain in the first show, but had no real regiment now. Mine was a token posting – a camouflage, if you like – enough to stop anyone wondering what I was up to. As far as my landlady and neighbours were concerned, mine was a dull but vitally necessary job in army and navy administration. My very close friends knew little better. I lived 'out' – that is, away from any form of barracks. It was just a short suburban railway ride to our office, which was housed in a deep and secure underground annexe somewhere near the Admiralty building.

I was forty-seven years old, and as yet unmarried, and not likely to be. I was wedded to the work, I was wedded to the idea. I was in many ways the keeper of the biggest secret. Pursuing the truth of that secret was what I actually did for the war effort. It was a far cry from administration – that at least I can tell you.

I waited with the other commuters on the platform at Putney station. There were a scattering of uniforms among the business suits; I even caught a glimpse of the girl with the bright yellow scarf again. She added a welcome touch of colour on a cold November morning. Everyone had their gas-mask box with them. Some stood awkwardly reading the morning paper, trying not to let it get in the way. Others tapped on the outer case, drumming their fingers while they waited impatiently for the train. I doubted I would get a seat – I rarely did: by the time the Waterloo train reached Putney on the Kingston loop line, it was pretty full.

I looked out of the train window. The glass, like most other windows all over London, was partly obscured, crisscrossed with anti-shatter tape. As we rocked slowly past Battersea and the river, I could make out through the drifting steam and flying smuts the barrage balloons floating on their tethers high above the chimneys of the big power station. They shone silver in the cold sunlight.

I finally got a seat after Queenstown Road and found that, by chance (in my experience, few things are down to mere chance; there is usually the hand of a designer there somewhere), I was sitting opposite someone I recognized. It was Viktor, the Polish beau of Miss Greville, who worked in the outer front office. He had apparently been among the first wave of refugees who saw just what was looming from Herr Hitler and his crew, and fled to Britain long before the actual war. He was often called into the outer office to act as a linguist on translation questions. There was inevitably a lot of chatter and traffic now from occupied Eastern Europe. He had some unpronounceable-looking surname . . . Prejm. Viktor Prejm.

He nodded politely and said, 'Good morning, Captain,' with a faint apologetic smile.

'Morning,' I said. 'It is Viktor, isn't it?'

'Indeed, Captain, it is,' he said, and made a slight bow of acknowledgement, then quickly turned away, indicating his book.

I had my own reading matter in my attaché case, but it was not something I could take out and read on a public train. All my documents were marked either TOP SECRET or MOST SECRET. I only read them in my rooms on Adur Terrace or in my chilly brick-lined tunnel of an office.

The set of offices that made up Department 116 were to be found in a very low basement not far from the so-called Citadel near Admiralty Arch. They were not marked at reception, and any visitor was always there by appointment and certainly always expected. The rooms were safe enough from any air raids, but they were cold and damp in the winter, being far below river level, and stiflingly hot in the summer, when you couldn't even crack open a window. Part of me envied my young protégé, Jack Carmody, and his outing down to Dorset: at least he was in the open air, and would have a chance to look at the stars now and then. In fact, I hoped there might be a pouch report from Carmody waiting for me when I got in; one was certainly due.

In the event I had to wait around for the delivery until late lunch time. Finally a motorcycle courier was announced in the outer office. Miss Greville had already signed for the pouch by the time I reached the office. I took it back to my desk and opened it.

CHAPTER ELEVEN

All three of us walked up the curving drive from the gates. As we rounded a bend in the drive, the Rectory came into view. It was an old house surrounded by a wild and overgrown garden. There were tall beech trees to our left, and the gloomy rooks were at their business as usual, cawing and cackling in the cold air.

A gardener with his back to us was raking up leaves from the front lawn. They were being heaped up on one side – I supposed for a bonfire.

The boy broke away from us at that point and ran forward up the drive.

The copper moved to stop him but I held his arm.

'No,' I said. 'Let him go.' I wanted to see how this would play out.

Tom called out, 'Dad, are you all right there? What happened to the . . . ?'

The gardener straightened up and turned round at the commotion, and the boy stopped dead in his tracks.

'What is it, lad?' the man said, shielding his eyes and looking over at him.

The boy had his back to us, and I saw his shoulders slump, and then he just fell forward as if in a faint, down on the grass beside the driveway.

At once there was chaos and confusion. The gardener shouted out for help, and both the copper and I ran forward. A man in army uniform came out of the house. I noticed that he was an officer, and luckily enough I remembered for once that I was in uniform too, and saluted him as smartly as I could before kneeling down and cradling Tom's head.

'What on earth is going on here, Corporal?' the officer asked.

'Sorry, sir,' I said. 'I had no idea the house was an official billet.'

'Oh no, this isn't a billet. I am just here on a private visit to my parents.'

'Would your father by any chance be the Reverend Stone, then, sir?'

'No, I am afraid he would not, Corporal,' the officer said.

The boy struggled to sit up, and looked at the gardener standing over him, and then at the officer, and then at the copper, and then finally at me.

'It can't be true,' he said. 'None of it – it's not possible.'

'I imagine this might be the young poacher, then,' the officer said. 'The one who was arrested last night. Mr Feaver was telling me about him earlier. I'm Captain Boulter, by the way . . . And you are . . . ?'

'Corporal Carmody, sir. Ninth Essex. This was the boy we found after the deer escaped, yes. I'm not entirely sure he is a poacher, though, sir.'

'Sounded pretty straightforward to me. Seems like he was caught red-handed with the animal.'

'In one way it does, sir, but the boy seems genuinely distressed and very confused.'

'Of course he does. He was caught, wasn't he? No doubt just playing for sympathy.'

'Maybe, sir, but I was bringing him up here to the house to find his father or the Reverend Stone. He says they can vouch for him.'

'The Reverend Stone,' the gardener said. 'I remember him all right – tall, skinny, pinch-faced man with not much hair on top. He was the vicar here, and over at Puncknowle as well. Mind you, this was a very long time ago – forty or so years. When he finally retired, I was still in the choir, but only just. He must have died a while back. He was one of the last vicars to have the living here at the Rectory.'

'My mother is buried just up there,' Tom said quietly.

'Show me,' I said.

He got up without brushing the leaves and mud off my old trousers. There was a set of steps that led from the east side of the lawn up into the churchyard. We followed him. He held on tight to the rickety rustic hand rail as he climbed the steps, and then, once he got in amongst the tombstones, he slowed down. He went a few paces further down the path, and stopped before a simple headstone as if he couldn't bear to go any further.

'My dad's brother – my uncle – is a mason at Bridport,' he said. 'He cut the stone for her. It's all wrong – it shouldn't look like that.'

We gathered around it. There was a mass of lichen and moss across the surface. I knelt down and brushed it away so that finally the deeply cut letters were legible.

From my kneeling position I read the inscriptions quietly; there were four of them.

I stood up and turned to face Tom. I spoke gently. 'It says here that Thomas Pile went missing or died in 1900.'

He had already stepped backwards onto the path. He shook his head from side to side and stood there trembling, with a bewildered expression on his face.

OLIVE ALICE PILE NÉE
WOODBURN 1864-1894
GREATLY LOVED AND TAKEN
BY THE LORD
BEFORE HER TIME

THOMAS EDWARD PILE
HER ONLY SON
1887
A LAMB LOST IN THE AUTUMN
OF 1900 AND NEVER FOUND

THOMAS EDWARD PILE SNR.
HUSBAND TO OLIVE AND FATHER
OF THE ABOVE 1855-1917

ALL GATHERED AT LAST
BY THE GOOD SHEPHERD.

I couldn't help but feel for him: if he was mad, it was
tragic; if it was all true, it was equally sad for him,
however exciting it might be for me.

'No,' he said suddenly. 'No – someone's playing a
terrible trick on me. It's not true, none of it – the house,

the stone. It can't possibly be true! Look, I'm standing here in front of you. This is all a terrible dream, and in a minute I'll wake up in my bed.'

Tom wasn't acting any kind of part; this was real and raw.

'You'd better bring the boy into the house,' Captain Boulter said. 'He looks all in. He'll collapse in a minute.'

'His name is Tom, sir,' I said. 'I think we should use it, don't you?'

It was warm inside the house, and Tom sat awkwardly perched on the edge of a sofa, looking around the large L-shaped front room. It was a cheerful place, with a good log fire burning.

'It's all wrong here too. It's all been changed since the last time,' Tom said. 'There's different colours on the walls, and there wasn't never a fire laid in here in this room. No, it was always cold in here. The reverend only kept the back kitchen warm, not this room here. This was all covered in books on shelves, all the way round from top to bottom.'

'When do you think you were in this room here before, then?' Captain Boulter asked.

'Just a week or two ago. I came up and was told to wait in here for my father to finish up his work in the garden. It was raining hard, you see, and it was proper cold in here then.'

'What if I was to tell you that my parents have lived in this house since 1933, when my father retired from his office in London, and that Mr Legge here has been the only person working in the garden for them since then and that he works for nobody else?'

'Then I would say you were surely mistaken, begging your pardon,' Tom said, now almost defiant, looking around at us.

'I was taking Tom in to the Dorchester barracks, sir, as I said, to question him properly. Nothing he says seems to make much sense,' I said.

'I'll take you in my car, if you like. It'll save time,' the captain said, rubbing his hands. 'I'll admit I'm intrigued – I can't deny it. I'd like to help you interview him, then I can get a recording done. I'm very keen to try out one of our new machines. Would you mind at all?'

'No,' I said. How else could I have replied?

'I think you can safely leave this boy with the army now, Constable. We'll get him to Dorchester, I can vouch for it.'

'If you're sure then, sir,' the copper said.

'I'm very sure.'

CHAPTER TWELVE

Captain Boulter drove us into Dorchester. I was a bit worried by what he said about helping with the interview and recording it. That was my job; well, at least, it was Captain Holloway's job, and I needed to get that done, not this Captain Boulter. How was I supposed to pull rank on a ruddy captain?

Tom sat next to me in the back of the car. He pressed himself hard against the seat and stared straight ahead. Every now and then he looked out of the side window at the scrolling grey winter countryside. He looked as if he were in a trance, almost completely mystified by everything he saw and felt. He had surely never travelled in a car before. Every time we picked up speed and there was that slight lurch forward, he grabbed hold of my arm.

'It's all right, Tom,' I said. 'We are in a car – perfectly safe. It's just fast.'

He shook his head and looked down at the floor. Captain Boulter said, 'I don't know why you are humouring him like this. Surely he's seen a car before?'

'I honestly don't think he has, sir,' I said.

'Where has he been then? On a ruddy desert island all his life?'

'In a manner of speaking, I think he has, sir.'

Tom seemed especially puzzled by the tops of the surrounding hills. I noticed that there were now tall poles on some of the higher fields – I presumed to prevent enemy gliders and planes from landing.

'What is it?' I asked finally. 'You look like you're seeing ghosts.'

With his face pressed close against the window he said quietly, 'I am the ghost. It's all changed, all of it, everything I see.'

He stared out of the window as we approached Dorchester. He looked at everything as if he had never seen anything like it.

Finally Captain Boulter parked at what had been the old castle prison and was now Garrison HQ.

A sentry at the gate saluted him sharply.

'Can you find an interview room for us?' Captain Boulter said. 'And can you bring one of the new wire recorders and a mike down from the ops room?'

The sergeant showed us into a room on the ground floor and then left us. It was near the back of the building, and I guessed it might have been a cell or the warder's office originally. The bricks were painted in that same sickly, pale-green, almost shiny distemper that the army always favours. There was a glossy darker green line halfway up the wall under the one window, which was partly covered with a green holland blind and which looked out on a far brick wall and not much else. There was a basic table, a few canvas and metal hall chairs, a black Anglepoise desk lamp, and a notice board with a big map of Dorset pinned to it, but no telephone.

'This do you, sir?' the sergeant said when he came back with a recorder and microphone.

'Perfect,' Captain Boulter said.

After the sergeant had left, the captain set up the machine on the table. He plugged in the mike and switched on.

'Now then, testing . . . testing,' he said. 'One, two, one, two, testing.'

He played the recording back, and Tom looked startled. I ignored it. I was still working out how I could put a fly in the captain's ointment without arousing too much suspicion.

Boulter offered me a cigarette from a smart silver case.

'No thanks, sir, I don't,' I said.

'You sure?' he said, nodding. 'I find it calms the nerves.'

He lit up a cigarette and said to Tom, 'Why don't you take your coat off, lad?'

The boy didn't reply, but just sat where he had been put. He had hunched himself down as far into my overcoat as it was possible to go without disappearing. He looked on the verge of collapse. It was as if he were trying to crawl inside himself and vanish.

'I don't quite get your role in all this business, Corporal,' Captain Boulter said, blowing out a long stream of smoke. 'If this boy has gone in for a bit of petty larceny and poaching, why didn't you just leave him with the police? Why bother?'

I saw my chance. I decided to go public, just slightly. 'I'm not at liberty to explain my position fully, sir,' I said, with just a note of defiance, eyeballing him directly.

'Ah, I think I see,' he said, looking down at his watch. 'Cloaks and daggers, eh? I thought you were billeted in the village to help Mr Feaver with his ARP duties, but there's more?'

'Officially I am just that,' I answered, keeping up the

defiance. 'But yes, there is more.' If the worst happened, I would at least get a chance to let Captain Holloway know, and rank and strings and all else would surely be pulled then.

He sighed and nodded, and looked at me through his smoke as if he heard that sort of evasive answer all the time. First of all I explained what had happened. I was careful not to say too much about the lights in the sky and the photographs, and all the while Tom just sat there staring at the dull green wall.

'Old Feaver told me much the same story,' Boulter said when I had finished. 'Only he said you were taking some photographs out in the dark. Is that right?'

'That is right, yes.'

'I see. Some new kind of film, then, I imagine. One thing you can say for war time, it certainly increases the pace of invention. This recorder is a big improvement over the old ones, but there we are. I imagine that is all I'm going to be told about it, isn't it? This is all a bit of a hush-hush effort.'

I didn't reply. I just looked back at him.

'I didn't hear any aircraft at all last night, but then the Rectory walls are thick and I was dog-tired. I went to bed early and slept like a baby.'

The sergeant bustled in with some mugs of army tea and a bowl of sugar laid out on an old tin tray.

'Very thoughtful indeed. Thank you, Sergeant,' Captain Boulter said, stirring his tea.

'Now, as far as I'm concerned personally, I think this boy's just a poacher and a bit of a nuisance,' he went on. 'I'm guessing that he is most likely an evacuee from the city. And certainly a good and well-practised liar. I suppose you think he's some kind of fifth columnist or something, or has a secret agenda. My advice normally would be to take him down to the police station here in Dorchester, get him charged with poaching, and then leave him there. We aren't in normal times, though, are we, Corporal?'

'No, sir.'

'So, assuming that whatever your other duties are, they include secret photographs and all, I think we should let this boy talk and see what he has to tell us.' He drank off his tea and stubbed out his ciggie.

'I'll let you ask the questions. I'll just work the recorder. Good luck, Corporal,' he said and switched on.

At first I encouraged Tom to drink his tea, but he just stared at it.

'Come on, it's all calm now. Perhaps you can tell me where you are really from,' I said.

'From Litton Cheney,' he said after a silence. 'Like I keep saying, I was only out last night to get us some meat. I was helping old Gawen and he tried to get me to shoot at . . .' He faltered and looked up, and then closed his eyes. 'I remember one thing: there was a bright light in the woods like I seen twice before, ages ago. Then I don't remember anything else.'

'Try talking it all through from the beginning, Tom. Tell us all about yourself. By doing that you might be able to remember more. Who is old Gawen, for a start?'

'Gawen were testing me. He were getting me to shoot it – it was to see if I had the guts. See if I could do it. My dad and me, we needed the meat, see.'

'Where is this Gawen person now?'

Tom looked down at his feet and mumbled his answer. 'Don't know.'

Captain Boulter asked, 'Which woods were you in, then, exactly?'

'We was up somewhere near the village of Powerstock,' Tom said.

The captain went over to the map. He found Litton Cheney and marked it with a pin, then followed the line of Gallows Hill with his finger up to the old Honiton road. The village of Powerstock was up beyond that, north of the main road by a long way; among other things, I noticed that there were some new airfields marked there. 'It's a long walk,' he said.

'How did you get that stag all the way down to Litton from there with just two of you?' I said.

'I don't know how we got back to Litton at all. I just seemed to wake up, to come to there.'

'Did this Gawen have a light with him of some kind? Was that what you saw in the woods and what I saw in the churchyard?'

'Only had my dad's rifle and a knife and some sacks, that was it.'

'Start again, then. Tell me about your life, Tom,' I said. 'Take your time, don't rush. Tell us everything about yourself and all the people around you.' I sat back in my chair.

Tom leaned forward, his arms on the table top, and started talking quietly into the microphone. His testimony sounded almost as if he had said it all once before, to a room full of strangers perhaps. His voice was hushed, controlled and monotonous, almost as if he were in some kind of trance. He hardly drew breath . . .

My mother died when I was seven. I remember so clearly the simple coffin box in our little cottage parlour. It lay there closed and screwed down, resting on trestles, and even then I knew that she was inside it. My father sat beside it with his head bowed, his mug of tea resting on the lid. The parlour was almost dark, with just a single lit tallow candle on the mantel, and still he sat there quietly all night.

She was buried in February – on St Valentine's Day, to be exact. The dark earth was tamped down hard and wet. The grave was dressed with greenery and one or two hothouse blooms from the Rectory. Mr Woolard had cut the grave and Mr Woolard's son had made the coffin. There was no stone or marker as yet, only the few pale flowers under the sleet and the ivy.

I stood at the grave while the Woolards lowered the coffin down on wide hessian straps. My father was standing at the graveside in his black Sunday best, one hand on my shoulder. He was the first to throw in some of the wet earth and flowers from the heap by the open grave. I looked around at the expectant faces: the Reverend Stone, Miss Gladwyn, my uncle and aunt, and then my father, who was hatless in the cold. His beard and side whiskers were grey, and his teeth were clamped together, making his cheeks look hollow. His hair was whipped by the wind that blew across Gallows Hill, where we would see the lights together for the first time, years from that night . . .

The church and churchyard of St Mary's stands a third of the way up the hill above the valley. The beech trees march up the hill beside the churchyard. They are always full of rooks cawing in the wet air.

My uncle had arrived by trap from Bridport, where he

worked as a stonemason. He stood on the other side of me, his hand resting on my other shoulder. He was older and taller than my father, and he stood with a bowed head. His wife, Anne, was beside him, a handkerchief held to her eyes and her head lowered and turned from the biting wind, which I remember sounded like the sea on the pebbles on Chesil Beach as it ripped through the beeches.

My father spent much time there at that grave, and would talk to my mother when he used his scythe on the grass which, if left, grew long among the headstones. The same long grass where later I lay sometimes near my mother's stone on a hot summer afternoon, hiding. My mother was a 'gentlewoman', so said my father, whom God had 'taken to his bosom too early', she being young herself at the time. His name was Thomas and, yes, I was named for him, and he was commonly called Tom, just as I am. He was old; I should say at least thirty-five years at the time of our loss. All the hair had gone from the top of his head, on which, of custom, he wore – no, he wears, he wears . . . he is not dead – he surely lives. All of this is a bad dream. It is me, rather: I am the one who is most likely to be dead, shot down in the woods by old Gawen. So my father wears an old battered hat made of soft felt. He used to wear high boots, and a pair of well-polished leather gaiters, or leggings. He also used to maintain the woods and copses, and he even grew fruit and vegetables for the reverend. That was in the good time when he worked hard every day, excepting, of course, Sunday. Once he even sang in the choir, and was, I think, well enough liked by all. Miss Gladwyn, a woman of the village, gave us the balsam for my chest in winter and was always polite and kind with me.

When I was younger, on certain nights of good weather my father would take me on the long walk to the Chesil Beach, to night fish, or perhaps up Gallows Hill and on over to Bridport. The beach was a wild place, long and flat with the deep water right close to the shore. Father said that some of the Popish sailors from the armada of Spain were washed ashore there hundreds of years ago, and how even some in our own village, those who were darker of skin and hair, owed them their origin, and how some were like as to a Spaniard or Turk.

That was when we saw the lights in the sky. That was before my father took to drinking in the White Horse most every night and 'pissed away his wages', as old Gawen said.

Father once said that 'God and the angels would perhaps take me as well', as he eased my misery of cold nights when I couldn't breathe too well, and needs must hold my head over a pudding basin and breathe in the fumes from Miss Gladwyn's dark liquid balsam which steamed there. My father would hold a cloth about my face and pray for me. He was a bear of a man, with much of the outdoors about him. He would say that I was a good boy, and that I was all he had left, and that I was so like my mother. The angels came for her, and then they came for me . . .

Our own house was – no, not was, is – old, but it is still there; it endures. It is a cottage, not a house – don't run away with that idea – and it is made of stone, and is Church property. It stands halfway up a steep hill, the Gallows Hill, and looks down over the Bride Valley. It lies between the towns of Dorchester and Bridport, of which Bridport is the nearer place, and where there were boats, and ropewalks where rope is made.

When we had done our chores, and on days when my father didn't need me, I walked over to the village schoolhouse. A mile or so directly across the fields, though I followed the route around the village, which is formed by the natural lie of the water that flows out from the Rectory garden, where there is a spring. The water was always cold, even on the hottest summer day, and in the good weather of early summer we would come back from the schoolhouse wading in the stream against the flow. Now and then a dark spotted trout would dart between our legs.

With no mother, I needs must help my father at home, and often made his evening meal. Miss Gladwyn showed me how I must wash and prepare the vegetables, and I was soon in the habit of it. In the good days we had cheese in a steady supply from the rector, who allowed his field to be used for the grazing of sheep and cattle, in return for fresh milk, butter and cream, and meat. Miss Feaver would on occasion deliver us a good pie, and there were our chickens, which I fed and cleaned, and collected the eggs, Mr Fox permitting. That was in the good time before Father took to drinking in the daytime, and fell out with the reverend, and we went hungry, always hungry.

My father saw them . . . saw strange things when he saw the lights. Twice he was with me; once, though, he was on his own. He was fearful of what he had seen. He supposed the drink had made him mad, although he didn't tell me about it at the time. No, he waited until we were both filthy and starving and it was the bad times, and he was drunk on cheap cider and was threatening to hit me, and sitting in the cold and dark with no fire in the grate, with no meat, nothing to eat – that was when he told me about it. He told me that he had seen Heaven itself, and angels, and my late mother's face up in the sky. She was looking down on us. Others had seen the lights too, and he said that he had seen my poor mother as a ghost. He said a man came all the way down from London. A doctor, he was. He came down to interview those that had said they had seen the lights. All those in our village were interviewed, including my father, and they were also investigated for insanity. No one heard any more about it after the doctor had gone away. When I saw the lights, I didn't tell anyone else I had seen them . . . not until now.

The first time was one summer night when I was walking along the top road with my father. I was about ten years old and we were going towards Bridport. It was the full dark, and a sky full of stars, when the white light came. The light fell slowly, like a distress rocket as you might see off the beach from a ship in trouble, but this was bigger. It fell close to us, down into the dark copse of trees beside the road. We heard a single loud thump on the ground somewhere in among the trees. This was near Walditch, just south of the main Bridport road. We left the thoroughfare and went to see what had fallen. He thought it might be a piece of shooting star or meteor or similar, and so might fetch money from the museum at Dorchester, if it could be retrieved whole or in large part. Once we were beyond the road we tried to find an area that would show damage from a falling weight, or perhaps burns, as the rock – if that is what it was – must have some weight and the light must also have some heat. I was worried about my father, and was afeared we might face danger from the lights. Despite the darkness, it did not take us long to find damage. There were scattered branches along the ground in the centre of the copse, and then a light shone down on us, and where it touched the ground it made a deep booming sound such as might be made by the striking of a bass drum in a silver band. I looked up into the light. It was brighter than day in that one place just above the trees. I found myself unable to move, but just stared upwards, and at that moment I fancied I saw a figure somehow from within the sphere of light. Then it went dark. We looked around the area but could find no trace of any burned rock. We quickly rejoined the road, but said nothing one to the other; nothing of what we had seen or thought we had seen. I especially did not wish to upset or trouble my father.

On the second occasion we were returning to our cottage. My father had been in the White Horse public house and I had gone to fetch him home. He was not intoxicated, having, as he said, 'drunk little but had mostly stayed there at the inn to be by the fire and to be in good company'. As he neared the area of the church, we saw a bright light, and then another up on Gallows Hill. Strong beams of light striking the ground as if in a lightning storm. There was no sound this time, but the lights were not falling. They stayed in one place, high above the chalk roadway. We passed our own dwelling and made our way up the hill towards the lights. My father was frightened then, and he admitted it to me, and he wished he had his hunting rifle about him as we approached the place of the lights. There were two distinct ovals of light above the roadway. One was beside the other; we stood below them, alone on the road. We looked about us, but there was no one else to be seen. The flock was higher up the hill, but we could see no sign of a light in the shepherd's bothy, not even a wisp of smoke from the chimney. We were the only living things on that steep *road. Then my father said, 'Look,' and he pointed to the light. 'An angel, boy, and it has the face of your poor dead mother, and she's smiling on us.' I couldn't see it.*

My father was never the same after that night. That was when he started drinking all the time, and not working so much, and we went hungry for days at a time and we stayed hungry. Being hungry was my doom and my downfall . . .

Tom was suddenly quiet after that, and after a moment or two he slowly moved further forward across the table and rested his head on his arms. He went into a kind of sleep.

'Poor boy's a deluded faker, I'm afraid, just rambling on like that. I shouldn't wonder if he isn't some sort of Romany. Perhaps he's taken opium or laudanum or something,' Captain Boulter said.

'You may be right, Captain,' I said. 'It was all very odd. Might I have that recording, though, please?'

'Hmm, I suppose it will be all right. If I don't give it to you, you'll just request it through official channels, if I'm any judge. Well, all right, but let me just check that it worked first.' He rewound the spool. 'You haven't fallen for any of that desperate nonsense, have you?'

He played a fragment back. It had worked.

'All the evidence needs evaluating,' I said. 'I wouldn't want to jump to any conclusions. Is there a secure telephone I can use?'

'Yes, of course. The sergeant will show you. After that I expect you will be off with your prisoner. Take my advice, Corporal. March him down to the police station and hand him over. He will, I am sure, turn out to be a waste of your valuable hush-hush time.' He clapped me on the shoulder and handed me the recording.

'Thanks, sir,' I said.

CHAPTER THIRTEEN

From Captain Holloway's Journal

The whole thing was laid out in front of me, and for the first time I felt a kind of shiver of certainty. We had a real breakthrough, and there were pieces of physical evidence too. This could turn out to be the definitive test case. I read young Carmody's report through quickly, and then read it again while I waited for the negative roll of his photographs to be printed up. Reading between the lines, I sensed Jack's excitement at what had happened.

I was called to the dark room about twenty minutes later. The red light was on inside and there was the pervasive smell of Hypo.

Our technical whizz, Staff Sergeant Martin, had pinned a series of images up on the softboard cork wall that ran down one side of the darkroom. As soon as I was in and the door was secure, he switched from the red to the white light and produced a linen tester glass.

'I think we've got something – look,' he said.

The photographs were in a numbered sequence. At

one end of the wall were images of the lights. I could see the crest of a steep hill, and at the top a shaft of light beaming down from a cloud and lighting part of the roadway and a STOP sign.

'This fast film still gets enough detail, then,' I said. There were more of the lights in the sky – blurred oval-shaped discs, just above the low cloud layer. Then came the fourth picture, taken down the slope of the hill. Something solid could be seen through the ragged edge of cloud and fog. It was metallic-looking, a sweeping curve – perhaps part of a wing formation, but with no markings visible, German or otherwise. And then the shafts of light were shining in a churchyard, and the shapes of the tombstones were clearly visible, and the true intensity of the beams of light seemed clear as well, incandescent and very strong. It would be hard to determine exactly what kind of aircraft would produce such a beam, and also why. Then came the startling picture of a white stag caught by the camera, a gleam of terror in its eye. And then pictures of the boy, at first out among the tombstones, a pale and overexposed face with eyes wide. Then one of the same boy sitting at a table, his expression inscrutable, but at the very least bewildered.

'Jack did well,' I said. 'Is there anything we can do to make that section there bigger, clearer?' I indicated the wing edge in the fourth picture.

'I can try,' Sergeant Martin said. 'I'll keep enlarging, but in the end all we'll get is the grain of the film itself.'

'Agreed, but I would like you to try, if you would, please.'

I let myself out, secured the darkroom door behind me, and went back to my desk. Among Jack's notes and reports there was a single WD envelope that I had yet to open. I tipped its contents out onto my desk.

Something astonishing sat there on my official WD blotter. I had seen a similar thing described just once before – in a smuggled and translated document from a restricted German scientific journal of 1936. It was one of the key pieces of evidence that I longed to see with my own eyes, and here it was in front of me on my own desk, safely gathered in, deep in the bowels of the Admiralty. A little shining trinket, roughly three inches square – slightly smaller than a postcard. A souvenir, perhaps, but a souvenir of where exactly? It certainly wasn't Skegness.

I sat down and moved it a little with the tip of my pen until it was under the direct beam of my desk lamp. It sat there, pulsing and glowing. I looked carefully at it; watched the colours cross its surface. I fumbled for my lower desk drawer and pulled out a magnifying glass of the sort that would not have shamed Sherlock Holmes in his heyday. It was limited in its magnification, but it was enough.

I studied the surface, and after a minute or so became almost hypnotized by the shifting patterns and colours. I found myself drifting a little. I pulled my eye away from it and put the lens down. Maybe that was the point: perhaps it was some kind of beguiling device; a hypnotic. The thing seemed alive. I sat up straight and shook my head. I picked up the surprisingly light, dense square and tucked it back into the envelope that Jack had put it in. He must have realized the significance of what he had found; we had been through all the various reports from our German counterparts together a year or so ago.

I went at once down to our file system, which was awkwardly placed high under the curved vault of our inner office ceiling. I pulled out the relevant file, took it back to my desk, and sat and read through it all over again. I put in a call to Jack Carmody. There was no time to lose.

Translated from the GERMAN original
From BERLIN Registry File
Department 116

MOST SECRET
From: The desk of the Chairman of Regional Special
Intelligence Investigations Authority
BERLIN September 1936
CLASSIFIED AND CONFIDENTIAL

Following on from a series of interviews (transcripts
supplied, see APPENDIX B — not for release) carried out at
the isolation clinic of Günzburg Sanatorium soon after the
discovery, arrest and protective custody of suspect A:
Fräulein V—

In summation I found the girl claiming to be V— (Warrant
No. 17847) of a reasonable educational standard and of some
school learning, although she was suspicious and evasive
and apparently ignorant of any recent history. She claimed
to know nothing of the Führer, for instance, which would
seem at the very least a foolish position to pretend to, and
a very dangerous game to play in the circumstances.

The girl showed some intelligence and a very thorough
and unlikely knowledge of the period of history that she
claimed to be living in. She also claimed that I was an evil
spirit; some sort of chimera conjured by angels to torment
her. She communes with angels, apparently. She is also oddly
consistent and convincing in her false world-building. She
says that she was apparently well enough thought of by
the town of —, which she claims to come from, and named
several residents who might vouch for her and prove her
claim. Even on a cursory investigation it was easily
discovered that all the persons she named were long dead.
However, from census records it was clear that each and
every one of those persons she mentioned had indeed lived
in — at the time she said they did.

There are two possible explanations:

1. At first the girl was believed to have developed some sort of obsession with a very old missing persons case from —, which happened sixty or more years ago. It was thought that she had somehow identified herself with the girl who was originally reported missing (according to the local police ledger, believed murdered) and was playing the part of the same missing person in that case – see original warrant. Incidentally, I strongly recommend sending someone to conduct a thorough search and literally dig around in the place and facts of that original case, all documentation from local records, burials, etc. However, judging from the ignorance, naivety and youth of the girl in question, the ability to come up with such an invention and identification, let alone all the simple fact-checking and collating involved seems highly unlikely.

2. In my opinion it is more likely that this girl is the third one so far to be found — and indeed as yet only surviving example — of the so-called disappeared. It would, of course, be more convenient for all to put her firmly in the former group. However, for me all evidence points to this second explanation. Her persistence of belief and her self-identification show her as one of the missing/returned, and the fact that she seems to be honestly telling the truth as she sees it demonstrates that my position may be upheld.

ADDENDUM

Fräulein V— later demonstrated the ability to move objects independently by mind, demonstrating under laboratory supervision the trait known as telekinesis. The Soviets have been secretly trying to develop this for some time. Her power manifests itself mostly through stress. One such demonstration proved fatally dangerous, and details were sent at once to BERLIN. (See attached Note C.)

However, there is of course still a strong possibility here not only of power, but also of a disturbed and unsound mind, and I would recommend that the continued complete protective custody order be kept enforced, along with supervised detention in a secure asylum and the administration of drug therapy, followed by a series of further interviews and investigations in order to discover her true identity and, indeed, the truth.

She had a bag with her on arrest, and among the contents was the item described in the attached APPENDIX D document.

NOTE C
April 1937

After much coaxing and not a small number of threats, the
girl was taken to a secure space, the abandoned aerodrome at
(B). A plane was loaded with explosives and flown in a circuit.
She was tasked with the job of bringing it down from the air
and onto a specific target, a complex of old buildings. The
pilot knew nothing of the test and was in any case
expendable. She was set to work, and after twenty minutes she
had worked herself up into an odd state. She first of all
destroyed the buildings on the ground. They were FLATTENED,
just as if a hurricane had passed over. Then she brought the
aeroplane down directly onto the ruins in a huge fireball.
She then proceeded to destroy two of the doctors who were
supervising and recording. The results of this may be seen in
the sealed can of film logged in the evidence file depository.
This film is to be viewed on a strict need-to-know basis only
and is not for general distribution within the department.

It was necessary to restrain her after the test. The girl
known as V— shortly afterwards <u>died</u> in protective custody in
April 1937.

Müller, H.
Here signed ....

APPENDIX D
CONFIDENTIAL

Among the items found on the detained girl V— was something
which was at first thought to be some broken item, a shard of
cheap jewellery. Closer examination and analysis of this item,
however, have revealed it to be something else altogether,
and so far it is of unknown origin. A more detailed analysis
is contained in a further APPENDIX E (not released).

CHAPTER FOURTEEN

We locked the sleeping Tom in the interview room, and I was taken to another office. By using combinations of numbers and certain key code words, I was immediately put through to Captain Holloway's office. The army could be efficient when they needed to be.

'Carmody, where the hell are you? I've been trying to get you since the courier turned up with your envelopes.'

'I'm at army HQ in Dorchester. Been recording an interview with the boy in question.'

'Get on down to the station and take the next London train, and bring him with you. And go now, this very minute.'

'So do you think that this is what we have been looking for? That this might be it, sir? And by the way, this recording is something you need to hear.'

'I am quietly optimistic,' he said. 'Actually, I'm a lot more than that, but that's enough said on an open line. Now come on – jump to it and get weaving.'

It was hard not to show too much excitement or even to think straight after that. It looked like we had finally found our evidence. Early days, though, and I didn't want to get too excited. I went back down to the interview room, and the sergeant unlocked the door.

The boy was gone. The window was fully open and the blind pull was tapping against the windowsill.

At first I panicked, I will admit. I ran out into the corridor and charged up and down a couple of times like a headless chicken. The kind sergeant saw me and calmed me down.

'He looked harmless enough, that lad. What's the panic?'

'He's a security risk, and much more,' I blustered.

'I'd better fetch the captain then,' he said.

'No,' I said. 'Don't bother him. This is my responsibility.'

'He can't have got very far,' the sergeant said. 'Not if he got out of that window. It doesn't really lead anywhere – just to a closed-off yard and a high wall. I doubt he will have got over that.'

We went out through a side door into what used

to be the exercise yard for the Napoleonic prisoners who were once held there. The boy was tucked as far into the corner of the square as he could get. He was hunched down into my overcoat as if he were inside a tent.

I sat down next to him, pressed my head back against the flint wall and said, 'Look lively. I'm taking you up to London. There is a man there who wants to meet you. He's a good man too – kind, and not any sort of policeman.'

'Why would you want to do that?' the boy said, his head bowed, his mouth pressed into the collar of the coat.

'You're not in any trouble, Tom. You're of interest to us,' I said. 'Both you and your situation – your story.'

'I've got no situation. I'm a ghost, I am. I'm nothing but a will-o'-the-wisp.'

'You are as real as me. You are awake and I am awake.' I turned to him and shook him by the shoulders. 'Feel that? You are alive, and we are both sitting here in this old prison yard in the year 1940. The world is spinning away on its axis and getting further and further into trouble.'

'I don't know what you're talking about,' he said, looking at me with real fear in his eyes, like a trapped animal.

'We can do this calmly. I'm here to look after you, Tom. I can understand what you are going through. First we are going to stand up. Then we are going to leave here and walk down to the railway station. Then we are going to get on a train and travel to London to meet this kindly man who wants to talk to you. That is all,' I said, as slowly and matter-of-factly as I could.

He looked doubtful, but eased himself up, keeping his back against the wall. The sergeant stood a few feet off, plainly puzzled by the odd transaction and my tone.

I turned to him. 'It's all right, Sarge,' I said, tapping the side of my nose with my index finger, implying that I was dealing with a loony. 'We'll be off in a minute. He's coming back to London with me.'

'You have the authority, do you, Corp?' he said, his eyebrows raised.

I pulled my warrant card out of my field jacket pocket. 'Special operations,' I said.

'Fair enough,' he said. 'I can organize a car for you, if you want.'

'No thanks,' I said. 'We'll walk.'

Communiqué 3

Translated from the <u>GERMAN</u> original
(C3./Capt Holloway Office 116)
Undated - filed late 1940

I have noticed a rise in activity. Something has happened at the office. An AGENT (A) was sent off. I later found it was to the WEST country. He sent something back which caused, in the colloquial words of hereabouts, 'A FLAP', which is slang for great <u>excitement</u>.

'A' was called back.

I am on alert for anything which is let drop. It is a tight ship now, however, and I cannot force anything or I will risk complete exposure. I shall keep a close eye and prepare for the capture and flight option if necessary.

CHAPTER FIFTEEN

There was no time to go back to the White Horse and collect my stuff. We just left the barracks and set off on foot for the railway station. I wanted to get moving before Captain Boulter decided to interfere again. The high street was busy with army and civilian traffic, and even here, down in the country, there were sandbags around the shops and anti-shatter tape on the windows.

Dorchester was a garrison town, and as we walked through the centre, there was evidence of soldiers everywhere. I knew that the Parachute Regiment was based just outside the town at Piddlehinton Camp. I was told there had been extensive work in Dorchester preparing for the expected invasion. I could see signs of it everywhere in the town. There were concrete blocks set up near the roads and on the surrounding hills.

The locals called them 'dragons' teeth'. Squaddies had been hard at work digging anti-tank ditches, and there were pillboxes set up on main junctions; we were told that the bridges had been prepared with explosive charges for when the invasion started. There were rolls of barbed wire across the side roads, especially near the railway station. I half expected to see a German armoured car followed by a marching division of the Wehrmacht turn into the road outside Dorchester station.

Tom Pile trudged along beside me. His hands were pushed deep into the coat pockets. He made no eye contact with anyone, just shuffled along, occasionally looking up at a building or sentry post or installation.

'I never been on a train before,' he said as we waited on the station platform. There were other soldiers there too, a dozen or so of them at the far end of the platform. After a few minutes the London train up from Weymouth chuffed round the curve and into view. The engine must have been green originally, but it was so covered in mud and dirt that it looked almost khaki, as if it were in some way an official army engine. Wartime meant dirt and neglect, along with everything else. Resources were stretched, jobs were skimped; no one there to polish up the engines. Standards were slipping, or had already slipped. The shirker's phrase was:

'Don't you know there's a war on?'

I got us a good compartment to ourselves by flashing my special travel warrant card at the ticket inspector and saying that Tom was my security prisoner. We sat facing one another on the window side. It soon darkened as we travelled through the afternoon. I had to pull the blinds down and secure them when the lights finally came on. The bulbs were very dim in any case. I might as well have left the blinds up as far as any enemy aircraft were concerned. It was so dim in the carriage it would have made little difference.

'It'll be dark by the time we reach London,' I said.

'This is the way to Hell, isn't it?' Tom Pile said. 'I know it is. It explains everything to me. We are being taken there now. I know it. That tombstone said I was dead, along with my mum and dad, and I suppose you are dead too, and now I am being taken there with you and them, and all those dead soldiers on that platform. We are going all the way to Hell. The angels showed us the way last night. Old Gawen must have shot me instead . . . and I – I heard the bang and then . . .'

His eyes widened even as he said the word 'angels'. Then he fell silent, and pushed himself back in the seat as if he were struggling to dig himself into the springs and fabric.

I thought of the secret report I had read – the one

smuggled out of Germany; the one in our files which described the 'self-belief' of the found girl. Here was Tom displaying that self-same conviction and complete self-belief. He believed everything that had happened to him. He was not pretending and nor was he mad. He was the real thing.

'It was them – the angels, the bright light, it was them. I saw them. I don't want to go.'

'Who did you see, Tom?'

'The angels – they came for me, and here we are now, all on our way.'

I leaned forward in my seat and took his hand. He looked back at me, puzzled.

'Tell me what they looked like, then,' I said.

He pulled his hand free, stood up quickly and stretched both his arms up towards the ceiling. The four lights in the carriage just below the string lattice of the luggage rack brightened and burned with a sudden fierce intensity. They gave off a kind of tungsten white heat, like the flash gun of a Speed Graphic press camera, just for a second or so, and then they all blacked out altogether. The carriage was plunged into total darkness.

'That's what I see. That's what they looked like,' he said.

The compartment door slid open and the ticket

inspector blundered in.

'Did your lights just flare up before they blacked out?' he said.

'Yes,' I said. 'What was it, then?'

'How many in here now? Just the two of you?'

The lights flickered back on, but if possible they were even dimmer than before.

'Yes,' I said. 'Myself escorting my prisoner,' I added quickly.

'I was worried about sabotage, you see. Lot of military on this train.'

'Should you even be talking that way?' I said. 'Careless talk, and all that.'

'You're quite right. Could I see your warrant once more, then?'

He took the paper from me but hardly looked at it. Instead he seemed more interested in Tom Pile.

'What's this one supposed to have done?'

'I can't discuss that, obviously,' I said.

'Couldn't he get to a barber's shop, then?' the inspector asked.

It was true that Tom Pile had longer hair than most, like a painting of a gypsy horse dealer.

'He's been living rough,' I said. 'It'll be cut soon enough when we get to London.'

The soldiers left the train at Southampton. I went

out into the corridor and watched them disembark on the steamy darkened platform. I beckoned for Tom to come and join me, and pointed them out as they shuffled into line.

'They are not dead, you see, Tom,' I said, 'and nor are you and nor am I. We are alive, and in an hour or so we will be in old London town, which to me is a kind of Heaven. To a country boy like you, I suppose it might seem like Hell, but let's wait and see, shall we?'

We settled back in the dimly lit carriage, and Tom nodded off for a while with his head tucked down against the stale velvet moquette of the seat rest. A framed photograph of Durdle Door rattled loose in its frame above his head. I dozed for a bit myself, but not for long.

CHAPTER SIXTEEN

I was jerked from sleep and woken up by a loud clanking noise, the squeal of metal brakes on metal, and a reverse thrust as the train shuddered to a sudden halt and then seemed to slide back on itself. I also heard the newly familiar wail of an air-raid siren somewhere in the distance over the chuffing of the engine. I knelt on the floor of the carriage, shuffled over to the side window and lifted just a corner of the blind. I could see the beams of gun emplacement searchlights piercing the dark. I could hear the drone of aircraft too, passing somewhere overhead. I guessed we were near London and there was a raid on. I shook Tom awake and let him look out at the scene. There was a sudden thump, and the ground shook, making the train shift back, and I heard more clanking. Another thump followed the first. Then the familiar deep crump of a distant explosion, a mile or more ahead of us.

'What is it? What's happening?' Tom said, gripping me by the arm.

'It's an air raid somewhere over West London. I told you before, we are at war now. Those are German aircraft. They are most likely bombing a factory, or it might be Isleworth Dock, west of London proper. I don't know, but I expect we are stopped here until the all clear. Might even be here all night.'

Tom stayed crouched, peering out through the crack in the blind, watching everything.

'I suppose that really does look like a vision of Hell to you, doesn't it?' I said. 'Are there flames now?'

'I can see a big fire over there,' he said. 'I don't understand.'

'Incendiaries,' I said. 'Those are bombs that cause fires. They start the raid by dropping a run of the incendiary bombs which mark the target with fire, and then they follow that up with the high-explosive run.'

'Where are they coming from, though?' he asked.

'From the sky, of course. From a formation of aircraft – bombers. That's why the lights are shining up: to try and isolate them so that the ack-ack guns can pinpoint them and shoot them down.'

Then, as if on cue, the guns started up with regular deep bangs.

'Keep looking – you will see the tracer fire up in the sky in a moment.'

'I do see something up there,' he said.

At that point there was a loud shout and a whistle blast outside our window.

'Put that damn blind down in there! Are you mad? There's a raid on. Do you want to alert the enemy, for God's sake? Respect the blackout!'

'ARP,' I said. 'Just like Mr Feaver back in Litton. You'd better get back over here, Tom.' I tucked the blind strap back into place. After that we sat in the dull amber lamplight, facing one another across the carriage, listening to the nasal drone of the aircraft engines overhead, the thump of the falling bombs, and the pounding of the anti-aircraft fire. Tom looked wide-eyed but calm, considering what he had just seen.

'Welcome to London,' I said.

CHAPTER SEVENTEEN

By the time our train limped into Waterloo with a final loud sigh and release of steam, it was early morning. Outside the busy station there were signs of the recent air raids everywhere. 'We can walk from here,' I said. 'It's not far to the office.'

A pall of smoke and a smell of burning and ruptured gas mains and worse hung over the city as we walked across the river on the west side of Waterloo Bridge. The pavement was crowded with Londoners on their way to work. There was that 'business as usual' spirit about; a kind of drab, resigned cheerfulness in the face of misery, as if to say, 'Well, at least we survived another night.' People picked their way through bits of shattered glass and rubble, nodding politely and making way for one another. It was hard for the British not to be polite. I had to pull Tom away from the edge of the bridge and the view of the river. He seemed to want to stand and gawp at the dirty water traffic under the drifting fog and smoke.

'*Old London can take it* is what they kept telling us on the newsreels. I'm not so sure,' I said.

'Are we really in London now, then?' he asked.

'Course. Where did you think we were?'

'My dad went up to London once with his brother, my uncle, the one who is the stonemason,' Tom said. 'They had to deliver a memorial stone somewhere – came up in a horse and wagon. Took them a long time.' He fell silent, and I saw a horse and cart making its way across Waterloo Bridge on the other side, behind a tram.

'You still see horses and carts around town even now,' I said. 'Usually brewers' drays and the like – especially with the petrol rationing,' I added.

It was painfully obvious that none of my attempts to distract Tom with cheery chatter or interesting facts were getting through to him. The boy still walked along beside me obediently enough, but he was all hunched up, still lost in my civvy overcoat like a sleepwalker or someone in a daydream.

After crossing the bridge we turned left onto the Strand. A policeman was directing the busy traffic from the middle of the junction with the bridge. There were sandbags piled outside the bigger shops, and barbed wire was laid in rolls across dangerous sections of road and pavement where there was obvious damage.

'This is the result of the sort of thing we could see and hear from the train last night. Blitzkrieg, the Germans call it. Total war – that's what we are experiencing here: total war. The whole city could be reduced to a pile of rubble, like all that lot over there, if this goes on for much longer.'

'How long has it been going on, then?' the boy said. Perhaps he was waking up after all.

'Just started last year. We had a few months when everyone thought the worst was going to happen, and it didn't, and then all of a sudden it really did. Some would say I've been lucky – I've been and missed most of it down in Dorset. Part of me thinks that I ought to have been here, lending a hand to poor old London. But then, I've been doing my bit looking out for the secret enemy, and also I found you.'

'You think I am the enemy, then?'

'That's a good question, and that's what we are about to find out. If it's any help, I don't think you are an enemy at all. I have a sixth sense about things. I have hunches and intimations, and I've got a good one about you, Tom.'

There were gaping holes in one of the buildings tucked behind the Strand. It had taken a direct hit. I could see exactly how it had fallen too. How it had collapsed in on itself, leaving the back wall that faced the river intact while the front was a neatly stacked pyramid of shattered bricks and broken and charred timbers. There was sure to be a mathematical equation explaining the pattern in the seeming chaos and the way all the bricks had ended up in relation to one another, and the force of the high explosive used, and the angle at which the bomb had hit – but I couldn't even begin to tackle thoughts of that. I wasn't in the mood.

'Are we safe?' Tom said, looking around at all the shattered glass on the pavement and the gully of rubble and pools of water from the fire-fighting.

'They usually come at night,' I said. 'There have been some daylight raids, but not many. It's much easier to shoot them down in daylight.'

'What are those?' he said, pointing up to a line of silver barrage balloons floating over Charing Cross station.

'Barrage balloons,' I said. 'They confuse and damage the low-flying dive bombers. Well, that's the idea. Trouble is, Tom, there haven't been any low-flying dive bombers like there were on the beaches at Dunkirk or over Guernica in Spain a few years ago. The Germans use their high-altitude bombers to pound poor old London – Heinkels and so on, not Stukas.' I might as well have been speaking Serbo-Croat as far as Tom's reaction was concerned. I guessed he just couldn't take it all in.

We passed a barber's shop that was open for business, even though the shop window was all taped over. I persuaded Tom in and told him to sit in the barber's chair.

'He's had a bit of a shock,' I said to the barber. 'He was shipwrecked. Just got picked up off the coast. He can't talk at the moment.'

Tom was given a good, almost military haircut. It looked like he hadn't had one in months.

'That's better,' I said to him after I had paid the barber. 'You'll blend in more easily. We won't get so many looks now.'

We walked under Admiralty Arch and then turned off to the steps down to the Citadel annexe.

An MP stood guard at a sentry post outside the door among a tower of sandbags.

'Corporal Carmody and suspect to see Captain Holloway. We are expected,' I said, and remembered to salute smartly.

'Wait here please.'

There was a constant stream of people in and out of the bunker below us. Our offices were deep down at the end of a long low corridor. We were not first priority, but we had our place; according to the good captain, this was because we had Churchill's interest and blessing.

Miss Greville escorted us once we were past the guard. Viktor passed us in the corridor. He doffed his trilby at me and winked – I presumed at Miss Greville. We went down the staircase to the outer office, and the captain was already there, beaming out one of his smiles.

'Well done, Jack,' he said. 'Mind you, you look like Hell. A tiring journey and a rough night, I imagine.'

'Very much so, sir,' I said, saluting again.

'Come through into the inner sanctum, both of you. It's been a long time coming, but I have been looking forward to meeting you, young man,' he said, extending his hand to Tom and smiling from ear to ear, just as he had when I met him for the first time.

'We have a lot to talk about, but first I think a cup of strong, sweet army tea.'

CHAPTER EIGHTEEN

'I imagine that all of this, every last bit of it, is a puzzle to you, if my hunch is correct,' the captain said.

He sat down behind his desk with his back to the wall – a wall which was painted that same drab institutional green as the army office in Dorchester. I sat to one side of the desk, and Tom, the boy from forty years away, sat facing Captain Holloway. A set of my photographs was pinned to a framed cork board stretching behind the captain's head so that the boy could not fail to see them. There were the lights on Gallows Hill, and the boy's own face staring back, starkly lit by the Anglepoise lamp. There was the stag, much enlarged, the terror evident in its eyes.

'Quite a gallery, isn't it?' the captain said in his

best friendly uncle voice. 'Take us through it, would you, Jack?'

'Yes, sir,' I said, and got to my feet. I picked up a pointer from the desk and went through the images one by one.

'These are the bright lights I saw on the hill near the top. They moved very quickly: here they are directly over us, and here below us, down the hill near the churchyard. This is just at the northern part of the churchyard, and here is the stag that rushed out at us.'

'I didn't hurt it,' Tom said, staring at the photograph. 'I couldn't. It wasn't right.'

'No, you saved it, I think, Tom,' the captain said.

'Can't say I did – I saw it shot. Saw it fall down, shot. I was meant to go and finish it off. I couldn't do it, though, and I threw old Gawen's knife away, far as I could. Then the light came, and next thing I knew, the poor creature was on its feet again, racing past me.'

'You say it was shot?'

'Yes, it was Gawen shot it.'

'Where did the bullet strike – did you see?'

'Creature turned its chest to us, and the bullet struck it there, over the heart.'

'I see.' The captain stood up and tucked his chair under the desk. He took the pointer from me. 'If I may, Jack,' he said. He went close to the enlarged picture of the stag, and tapped the pointer on its chest.

'If you look carefully, you can see there is a scar that has been left by a line of tiny neat stitches. So, you see, the stag was indeed shot, and then there was time for someone to stitch its wound and help the healing process. Who was that? Did you do it?'

'No,' Tom said. 'No.'

'Who did, then? This Gawen character, perhaps, took pity on the animal.'

'No, sir. He wanted it dead. He wanted the meat, the venison. Must have been them, the angels, that healed it.'

'When did all this happen?'

'The day before yesterday – but then things have changed since then. It's all gone mad. I can't explain it.'

'Have you ever been to Germany, Tom?'

'No, never. Never been to London before, let alone Germany.'

'Something happened to a girl once in Germany very like what I think has happened to you down in Dorset. It has happened more than once or twice. I think it has happened many times. I doubt you have ever heard of the Office of the *Unerklärliche & Übernatürliche*, which roughly translates as "The Unexplained and the Supernatural". In fact, I would be very shocked if you had, because very few people, even those inside the

German Reich itself, know about it.'

'No. What does any of that mean, then?'

'No matter, for the moment. What do you make of this?' The captain picked up the little piece of metal I had found in Tom's trouser pocket. He held it out so that it shone and glowed in the lamplight.

The reaction was instant.

Tom stood up and said, 'The angels gave it to me. I must have it back.' His voice was blank, almost impersonal.

'They gave it to you?' Captain Holloway handed the little fragment over, and Tom took it quickly and put it in his trouser pocket.

'Yes, they gave it to me.'

'Who exactly are they, Tom?'

'Hard to say,' he replied. 'I can't describe them. I don't really see them, but I hear their voices when I have that with me. I haven't heard their voices, their music, for a while now, and I need to. They love me – they love me like . . . like a parent.'

'This is really the heart of the matter,' Captain Holloway said. 'The nature of these creatures and what they want with you or feel for you, Tom.'

'Don't follow you.'

'Your manner has changed since you took possession of whatever that little thing is.'

I had noticed the change too. Tom seemed confident now. He was standing upright, not slumped or slouched, burrowing into my old coat as if trying to hide himself.

'It's true, Tom,' I said. 'You have. It's as if you've had a sudden burst of energy; of confidence in yourself. Do you remember the lamp in the ARP office in Litton Cheney? Do you remember what happened when you touched it?'

'Like this, you mean?' he said, and he stretched out his finger to the lamp on Captain Holloway's desk. There was a sudden intensity to the light from the bulb, and from the ceiling lights as well. Instead of their usual underpowered yellowish glow, they went through white to a kind of dazzling tungsten silver blue; I had to turn my head away, it was so bright.

'Yes,' I said. 'I mean just like that.'

'Remarkable,' Captain Holloway murmured. 'Quite remarkable.'

Miss Greville burst through the door. 'What on earth—? Is everything all right in here?' she said, plainly out of breath. 'We thought there was an explosion or a fire . . .'

'Nothing to worry about, my dear,' the captain said. 'Just a little power surge in the system.'

She looked over at Tom and frowned, as if uncertain,

and then back at the captain. 'Well,' she said, 'if you're sure, sir?'

'I am perfectly sure. Really, Ruth. Thank you.'

She left then, but I could see she was puzzled – worried, even, by what she thought she had seen. After all, it wasn't every day that lightning appeared to flash in our dingy basement offices.

'That was a truly remarkable demonstration. I imagine you might be able to do much more if you put your mind to it.'

'I'm not . . . certain,' Tom said in his broad Dorset accent. 'But if the voices tell me how, then I might.'

'Sit down, Tom. Relax,' the captain said, and I sensed he was nervous now, as if the boy had suddenly become unpredictable; a ticking bomb or some other unknown deadly weapon that might suddenly go off without warning.

Tom sat back in the chair, but he was alert now, sitting up straight like an eager pupil.

'I'd like to tell you what we know, Tom. Are you comfortable? You look tense.'

Tom just sat quietly, expectant.

'Now, Jack Carmody here and I have worked together for a number of years. We investigate things, Tom. We dig and see what is what. We investigate odd things that no one else takes very seriously, like ghosts and séances, like apparitions and spirits, automatic writing – all of that and more. I suppose we are, for want of a better phrase, detectives of the supernatural or the paranormal. Does that make any sense to you, Tom?'

'No.'

'I think your experience comes very much into our remit. You have had a very strange experience, Tom, haven't you?'

'I can't make much sense of it.'

'You must be in a very disorientated state at the moment. Your confusion is understandable. Here is what I think has happened. You have met with some kind of non-human creatures of considerable power, and this meeting has happened more than once in your time. Now, I suspect through their agency, you have been brought to our time. There is a big missing piece of this jigsaw puzzle. How many years have elapsed? As far as you are concerned, you went out poaching a night or two ago, and then Jack here found you in the churchyard – found or disturbed you maybe – because of course, there was this animal with you which ran off before you could shoot it.'

'I saved it. I don't remember getting back there,' Tom said.

'I know you don't, Tom, and at some point I want to help you to remember. The thing is, forty years have passed between your time and our time, and you are still just about – what . . . fourteen, Tom?'

'I don't understand,' he said. 'I feel like I am dreaming all the time, or like I have died and come to life again, or I'm just in Hell. That's what I think.'

'My opinion is that your memory has been closed to you by these – for want of a better word – angels; these non-terrestrial beings. I want to find a way to open it all up to you and to us. I think that there is a deep dark secret locked away there. You see, I've been digging around a bit, Tom, in the newspaper archive. That's a place where very old newspapers are kept in big bound volumes. I found many things of interest, but mainly this . . . Here, read it – no, better, I'll read it out to you. It's from your local newspaper . . .'

Captain Holloway read the piece aloud. Tom looked shocked. He asked to see the paper, and Captain Holloway handed it to him. He looked down at it. 'I used to read little bits of the *Illustrated London News* out loud to my father of an evening. He used to bring it back from the Rectory sometimes when they had finished with it. Never thought I would be in a newspaper.'

He looked up. He suddenly seemed defeated again,

The Dorchester Weekly Courier & Advertiser

Sunday 16th December 1900

The hunt for the missing youth, one Thomas Pile, a labourer's son, aged 14 years approx, of Litton Cheney in the Bride Valley, continues. The boy has been missing without trace for a month. A gamekeeper recently handed in a discharged rifle to the police. It was found in the forest near the village of Powerstock, along with some discarded poacher's sacks.

The rifle was licensed to the boy's father, a garden labourer, who claimed to have no knowledge of where his son was or how his own rifle came to be where it was found. He said he had last seen his son into bed, and that in the morning when he went to wake him he was gone, and the bed cold. Police have searched and dug extensively in the area near where the rifle was found, so far with no result. Foul play cannot be ruled out.

slumped and even paler, if that was possible. 'My father really is dead now, then, along with my mother?'

'Yes, Tom,' the captain said quietly. 'I'm afraid so. This must be very hard for you. You see, Tom, you went missing forty or so years ago, and then suddenly you have turned up again. If you really *are* you, and we think you are, you are not the first. It has happened before. In Germany, for instance, this girl disappeared, and then, many years later, a confused girl was found wandering in a forest not far from the remote village where the original girl disappeared. She claimed to be that same missing girl from all those years before. *Impossible*, you will cry out in common sense. I might have agreed with you at one time. You are no Rip Van Winkle, Tom. You haven't been asleep in a hollow for forty years, but you have been somewhere else, and I don't think it was here.

'I think you are just one of many people who, over the years, have been abducted by – for want of a better word – some sort of aircraft, but one not of this earth. There, I've said it. The beings you call angels are, I believe, extra-terrestrial alien creatures from another world or universe who would appear to you – and, indeed, to most people – to be just that: angels. It is perfectly possible that these "angels" have been visiting this planet, our earth, among others, over many centuries. This would account for the old descriptions, and the fear and wonder that accompany such sightings. A few years before your disappearance the local paper reported sightings of lights in the sky. The very same lights which Jack here managed to photograph so recently.'

'I saw the lights before when I was little – same lights. Later on I saw them again: falling, they were, into the woods near Bridport.'

'That's right. Several locals saw the lights in about 1890. There are two reports – one in the paper, and one written by an investigator from London, who went down to interview the witnesses. It was seen then as a mass delusion, a kind of hysteria. At some point we need to get to your closed-off memories and unlock whatever it is that is inside you. Don't worry – I'm not suggesting we do anything now.'

'No need, Captain,' I told him. 'Like I said before, we have just such a recording: I made it in the garrison at Dorchester.'

'Good,' he said. 'I shall of course listen to it at once, but you need to rest, Tom. Jack will take you to a safe house for today and tonight. Back here bright and early tomorrow, and we will talk again. Take it easy, Jack. No doubt there will be more air raids tonight, so be careful. No risks, remember.'

CHAPTER NINETEEN

'First of all,' I said, once we were back outside, 'a good breakfast, and then the Underground home.'

We went to a Lyon's Corner House café north of the Strand.

Tom hardly spoke. I'm not sure how much he had taken in of Captain Holloway's theories.

He was soon wolfing down a plate of sausage, bacon, grilled tomato and fried bread, washed down with a cup of strong tea, and all for 10d. I had poached eggs on toast for 8d. SAVE FOR VICTORY, BUY WAR BONDS was printed across the bottom of the menu – as was the following, which made me laugh: *Notice is hereby given that margarine of the finest quality will be served with all goods except bread and butter.*

'Tom,' I said, 'when we were in the hall at Litton Cheney, you knocked the telephone off the table onto the floor. Do you remember that?'

'No,' he replied, 'not really.'

'Well, I do, because I noticed that you stopped it hitting the ground too quickly. You controlled it in the air – well, that's what it looked like. Do you remember that?'

'Not sure,' he said.

'Do you think you could do it again?'

He looked across the table at me, and for the first time, he smiled just a little. The metal milk jug rose off the tray and travelled the few inches over the table to land gently next to my china mug of tea.

'I see. Clever stuff, Tom.'

I looked at the table next to us. A woman in a hat with a raised netting veil was looking at Tom, open-mouthed. I wiped my mouth with a napkin and said, 'All a trick – 'e's a conjurer, you know.'

She nodded, but her mouth stayed open.

After that we walked along the Strand the other way, through the Aldwych and up to Holborn. Tom was still looking around as if he were in a dream. To be fair to him, after the quiet of Dorset it was rough, chaotic and smelly. Before we descended into the Underground, we went to Lincoln's Inn Fields. We just sat together quietly and watched some office girls out playing netball in the cold. What with the girls and the busy crowds on the pavement, I doubted whether Tom had ever seen so many people in his life.

'What do you make of it all?' I said.

'I can't make sense of anything,' he replied. 'All the carriages with no horses, and the train we were on . . . All so fast – and everything has changed, everything is so different, I don't really know what's going on. I feel like I am suddenly going to wake up and have to collect the eggs from our little henhouse. I'd like that to happen, to tell the truth.'

'I don't think that will happen, Tom,' I said. 'I think you are here with us in our time now, and you are here for good.'

I was worried what his reaction to travelling in the Underground might be. If he found the busy streets disturbing, what would he make of that?

Holborn is a frighteningly deep station, with especially steep escalators, or so it seemed to me, suddenly looking at it through Tom's eyes. The place stank of cheap fags and the body odour of people more or less living down on the platforms during the air raids. I doubted whether the smell would bother him as much as the dark and the chaos.

I had to encourage him to get on the moving staircase, because of course he had never seen anything like it before. He stood one or two steps below, looking up at me like a worried pet. He gripped the moving handrail with both hands while people hurried past us on their way down to the trains.

Even though I called out, 'Watch out for the last treads,' he panicked at the sight of them folding down into the dark space under the grille, and he tripped over his own feet at the bottom and sprawled across the floor. People tut-tutted and skirted round him as if he were a drunk.

'Come on,' I said, helping him up. 'I did try to warn you.'

'I thought I was going to be pulled down under there,' he said.

'I know,' I said. 'I should have warned you sooner. It's my fault. Children always think that the first time.'

'Yes, but I'm not a child, am I?' He was red-faced with embarrassment, brushing down the front of his trousers.

'In a way, though, Tom, you are. All this is as new to you as it would be to a seven-year-old on his first trip.'

'I suppose,' he agreed.

The platform was crowded with busy, hurrying people, though there were others who were already making space for themselves on the platform for later in the evening, hanging clothes from the pipework and generally settling in. The telltale rush of warm stale air came flooding out of the tunnel.

'Here comes a train,' I said. 'Hold on.'

It rattled towards us in a rush, pushing more foetid air ahead of it. I heard it as I imagined it might sound through Tom's ears now, and it really was unbearably loud. I saw him flinch beside me. He turned his head away and brought his arms up as if to shield his body.

'It's all right,' I shouted over the racket of the squealing brakes. The doors slid open with a whoosh, and a crowd of people left the train, pushing and barging carelessly past us. Then I had to push and shove to get us on, and of course there were no seats. I put Tom's arm up and got him to hold onto one of the straps above the seats.

'You're a straphanger like the others now, Tom,' I said. 'Like one of the daily commuters. A proper Londoner.' I tried my best to make light of things as the train lurched forward. I could see that he wasn't paying any attention to what I said. There was just that unmistakable look of panic in his eyes.

The carriage was very crowded. There were a lot of tired and worried Londoners, all squashed in tight, together with their awkward hard-edged gas-mask holders, with me and Tom. I was used to it, but he wasn't. At the next stop, Chancery Lane, more people got on, closing in on us even further. We were heading east on the Central Line, and at the Bank interchange, things got really bad. A whole crowd surged onto the train.

'Move right down inside the cars please. Make room now,' a voice called out from the platform. We were soon backed up hard into the corner near the doors on the other side of the carriage. I could see an almost mathematical pattern in the flow of figures pushing forward. There was surely a formula, an equation describing the way in which people tried to edge themselves into the remaining spaces by turning and squirming, as if the fit were almost preordained. I did my best to shield Tom from the worst of the pressure, but I could sense that the panic was rising in him.

''S all right, Tom,' I said, now having to turn my head awkwardly to be able to see him at all. 'Only one more stop.'

The pressure was unlikely to be relieved until we reached Liverpool Street. Everyone would get out there. But among those who had just joined the train at Bank were firemen, nurses and ARP auxiliaries, fresh from the horrors of the bombings, by the look of them. We were now under the worst of the blitzed areas at the centre of the city, and near the docks too. I could smell the smoke on them; their faces were soot-streaked, and they all looked drained and exhausted.

The train set off again, and the lights in the carriage flickered on and off for a minute. For a whole stretch the carriage was in total darkness. Then we just ground to a halt in the tunnel.

There were coughs and throat-clearings, and even some nervous laughter. Someone shouted out, 'Be a pal and turn 'em back on, would you, Adolf,' which was followed by more nervous laughter and another cry of 'Put that ruddy light out,' which was the kind of thing the ARP wardens would shout out to hapless folk who left their curtains open. More laughter gave way to groans and mutterings of displeasure.

'This is all we need,' someone near to us said.

This was a common occurrence – a train stuck at a signal in a tunnel. The lights stayed off. I was getting my approaching-thunder feeling.

'We'll be off again in a minute, Tom,' I said, as reassuringly as I could. It was not enough. If I felt the hot and oppressive sense of suffocation and burial, then what was Tom feeling? Someone struck a match to light their cigarette, and I saw that Tom had his eyes tight closed.

'Put that light out,' someone said in a mock posh voice. 'Don't you know there's a war on, old chap, what, what?'

More nervous, edgy laughter from the rest of the

passengers, all squashed up tight together in the carriage, breathing each other's body odour and anxiety. Death, after all, could come roaring down out of the sky at almost any moment.

Tom wasn't laughing. He still had his eyes shut. Indeed, he looked as if he was in terrible pain. I could do nothing. We were too tightly squashed in to even try to move, and in any case the train was between stations and in a tunnel and in the dark.

'Your mate all right, is he, son?' someone close to me said out of the muddle of shapes surrounding us.

'He's not used to all this,' I said, as cheerily as I could manage. I felt Tom's other arm moving out and up beside me. A harsh, low hum started up, and then an electrical buzzing and crackling sound, which rose through the carriage, along with Tom's arm. I was worried about what he might do, or be able to do, or be doing. According to her file, the German girl had been able to bring down an aircraft out of the sky.

The lights in the carriage suddenly sparked back into life.

''Bout time,' someone quipped. 'Thanks, Winston.'

The lights came on again all right, only now they were suddenly much brighter, and then they were brighter still; unnaturally so. The bulbs glowed tungsten blue-white bright, and the carriage was lit up as if by a lightning bolt, and everyone was picked out in alarming frozen detail. The train lurched forward suddenly too, and then, one by one, all the way down the carriage, the light bulbs blew out, one after the other. They shattered explosively, showering bits of super-heated glass down among the crowded passengers.

There was immediate chaos and panic. It was clear that everyone thought we had been hit during a daylight bombing raid or a previously unexploded bomb. The train moved on, building up speed as it rattled and swayed along the tracks in the now pitch dark, while the passengers also crashed back and forth and into one another as their terrified voices called out above the train noise.

'What the hell?'

'Help!'

'For God's sake!'

'Oh, help, please help me. I'm bleeding. There's glass in my hair . . .' and so on.

Trapped in the corner, I could do nothing to help them, and besides, I had a good idea of the cause of all the chaos.

'Let go now, Tom,' I said close to his ear. I held onto his arm and tried to calm him as best I could. 'Enough – let go. It'll be all right.' I could feel the tension in him; the stiffness in his bearing and all through his body, as if his nerves were strung out like wires.

The train seemed to gather speed. The rocking motion got worse. Some people stumbled into one another and even fell to the floor.

'Calm down now, Tom. That's enough,' I repeated.

He finally slumped back against the door and I felt the tension leave him like the air out of a punctured tyre. The train returned to its normal speed too. We finally pulled to a sudden jolting halt at Liverpool Street station, and that was when pandemonium broke out. In the light filtering in from the platform I could see that several of the passengers were covered in cuts from all the flying glass. The doors slid open and everyone fought to get off the train. Those who had been injured, the walking wounded, were helped off our carriage, and from all the others as well. Tom looked paler and more exhausted than ever, as if he had been drained of all his energy.

There were policemen on duty at points along the platform, and the train driver was reporting to one close to where we stood.

'It happened after Bank,' he said. 'I thought we must have hit a mine or an incendiary. The whole train seemed to get away from me at one point.'

'No explosions – nothing like that reported to us,' the copper told him.

People were milling all around us. Some were being treated by nurses for minor cuts and abrasions. The train doors were stuck open and the carriages gaped all the way down the platform.

The policeman turned to me. I suppose I must have stood out among the mostly civilian crowd in my uniform coat.

'See anything unusual, Corp?' he said.

'Only the same as everybody else here, mate. Not sure what happened really. One minute we were barrelling along as usual. Then we stopped, and the next minute the lights went out; then they came on again, really bright; then they shattered all over everybody – bulbs, glass, shades, the lot.'

'No explosions? No fire? No external intrusion? Nothing like that?'

'Not as far as I could see. Seemed, if anything, like an electrical fault to me – a surge in the system.' I shrugged. 'Sorry I couldn't be more use.' I turned and started to walk off, only to find that Tom was no longer beside me. I couldn't see him anywhere in the muddle on the platform – but I did see Viktor Prejm, some way back along the platform, looking over at me.

'Tom,' I shouted out. 'Tom Pile, where are you? You all right?'

There was no sign of him on the platform. I looked

back to where Viktor had been standing, but there was no sign of him either. At that moment I was more worried about what Tom might do, but an alarm went off somewhere in my system at seeing Viktor there. Surely that was more than a coincidence?

A NO EXIT sign led down a long twisting tiled corridor, and I just caught sight of a figure I thought must be Tom, running away ahead of me. I dodged through groups of injured people.

'Tom,' I called out. 'Tom, it's me, Jack. Stop!'

Halfway down the tunnel-like corridor, he stopped and turned to face me, and then raised his arms. The lights around him flared bright, then shattered, one after the other, and I was plunged into darkness.

CHAPTER TWENTY

I made my way along the dark corridor, back out to the ticket hall, where passengers were being treated. A ticket inspector blocked my way out.

'Can't any of you read?' he said. 'This is an entrance, not an exit. You're the second one to try this trick.'

'Where did he go?' I said.

'Who?'

'The first bloke – the one who came through here just now.'

'Oh, him. He pushed past me like you just tried, and then he ran off through there, and he didn't show no ticket neither.' He pointed to the street exit.

'He was my prisoner,' I said.

'Well, if that's the case, you should have taken better charge of him, then,' the inspector said.

I pushed past him myself, and set off running across the forecourt.

'Oi,' he called out. 'Where's your ticket, mate?'

'Don't need one,' I shouted back without even turning. I ran outside and joined the stream of people walking up the incline below the station spire and clock tower. Finally, out of breath, I reached the street. Tom had apparently vanished: there was no sign of him. I had lost him, and I had lost Viktor too.

I found a telephone box and gave the correct coded combination and got through to Captain Holloway in his office.

'I've lost Tom,' I said. 'He got away from me.'

'How?' The captain's voice was suddenly brisk and no nonsense. 'What happened?'

I told him. I also mentioned seeing Viktor on the platform. 'I think he must have been following us.'

'Seems that way. Hmm . . . Wait exactly where you are in that telephone box – I'll be with you soon.'

Communiqué 4

Intercepted radio message
Translated from the <u>GERMAN</u> original
(C4./Capt Holloway Office 116)
November 1940

The required parcel has been safely taken.
I will arrange collection and delivery at
the earliest.

CHAPTER TWENTY-ONE

We spent a fruitless hour and what must have been a whole tank of precious petrol driving around those streets that were still passable, looking for Tom Pile and Viktor. We must have gone into a dozen Lyon's Corner Houses and ABC Cafés; nothing much else was open.

We had a contact address for Viktor so we drove out towards Newington Green. Viktor lived in a tall run-down boarding house in Mildmay Park, overlooking the North London railway lines. A few cars were parked along the road close to the house. No one used their private cars much any more, what with the petrol rationing. I noticed a gap in the line of cars like a missing tooth, just outside the house.

'That's where Viktor kept his car, I'll put money on it,' Captain Holloway said, pointing to the gap.

The landlady was eager to help after we showed our special warrant cards. She took us up to Viktor's room, and then stood at the doorway jangling her ring of keys.

'Is he in trouble? I do hope not. He has such lovely manners – a proper gent. Nice-looking too. I shouldn't like to think he had done anything *wrong*.'

'I'm sure we all feel the same,' Captain Holloway said with a smile. 'When did you see him last?'

'He was off earlier today, and all of a rush. He packed a suitcase, but left most of his things behind, far as I can see – even his overcoat and the rest.'

I searched Viktor's wardrobe. It was full of good suits, and racks of shoes, all neatly lined up. There were good cotton shirts neatly folded in drawers, and a selection of silk ties hung from the brass rail attached to the inside of the door.

There were two suitcases in the wardrobe.

'Look at these,' I said.

'Better open them, Jack,' Captain Holloway said. 'Carefully, mind.'

'It isn't going to be a woman's body, is it, all cut to pieces, in that case?' the landlady said, putting her hand up to her chest and fluttering her fingers.

'No, nothing like that – at least, I don't think so.'

'Only you hear of these things, don't you – what with all the terrible bombings and the blackout? It seems a person can easily get away with murder these days.'

I flicked the locks on first one, then the other, and lifted the lids.

'No dismembered ladies,' I said.

'Oh . . . thank God,' the landlady said with just a hint of disappointment in her voice.

Both cases were stuffed full with what looked like sheets cut or torn from old newspapers, and even some hardbound clerk's ledger books.

'What shall I do with this lot?' I said.

'We'll take them with us. I'll go through it all at some point. He must have had all this stuff here for a reason.' Captain Holloway turned to the landlady. 'I doubt he left you a forwarding address, did he?' he said.

'No. He'd already paid for another two months in advance, in cash, like he always does; he said he would be in touch with me later. What's he done, then?'

'We don't know yet. Could be anything. We just get sent to check on these things,' Captain Holloway said with a smile and a shrug.

'Murder?' she said.

'I'm sure you will be safe enough here, but if he should come back, please telephone me at this number' – he handed her a card – 'at once.'

'I will. I can't believe anything bad of him, a nicely

mannered man like that, though – not murder, surely?'

'Most likely they just want to talk to him because he's involved in some petrol coupon swindle, something of that sort. I don't really know why we were brought in on this at all. Bit of a sledgehammer to crack a nut, if you ask me,' the captain said reassuringly. 'He has a motor car, though, doesn't he?'

'Yes – it's gone now. It was always right outside. A black Austin Six, it was. He must have gone off in it.' She gestured to a photograph on the bedside table: it showed Ruth Greville and Viktor standing in bright sunlight in front of the same car.

'I took that picture for him with one of his girls,' she said.

'I doubt he used it much, did he, what with the petrol rationing. Oh, and just look at that – now we have the registration number.'

Once we were outside, a train rattled past from Canonbury station, sending plumes of white steam across the road.

'Travel by car or by train, I wonder?' Captain Holloway said as the steam billowed and cleared. 'What would you do, Jack?'

'Tom is in a very odd, fragile state,' I said. 'He hardly knows what he is doing. He's like a mine. He could go off at the slightest thing.'

'I wouldn't risk taking him on public transport. Not after what happened on the Underground. And as it turns out, it seems that our tame Nazi friend Viktor was there, so he surely knows that.'

'I find it hard to believe that Viktor is a Nazi,' I said. 'I wonder if he realizes that Tom's power is growing . . . I swear, from one light bulb to a whole trainful in just a day!'

'I suspect Tom has no real idea of what he could unleash if he wanted to,' Captain Holloway said. 'Trouble is, the Germans already know very well what someone like him might be capable of if handled properly. They had one of their own, after all, until they lost her. She pulled an aeroplane down right out of the sky, if we are to believe their reports. They pushed her too far, and it killed her, I suspect. That worries me.'

'Worries me too.'

'Car it is, then,' he said, ushering me back into our unmarked staff car. 'But where would they go?'

'Either get him over to Germany somehow, or to some place here in England where he could do some serious damage to the Allies; to our war effort?' I said.

'An even more worrying thought,' the captain murmured. 'Take him, hide him away, win his confidence, train him up. The poor boy is a bit of a lost soul, after all, and our Viktor is a charmer, if nothing else. Then let him loose on one of our valuable targets – makes horrible sense to me. If you were looking after him and you knew he could inflict serious damage on your enemy, that's just what you would do. They don't care about him; to them he is a human weapon, no more. All they have to do is wind him up and watch him go. He'll only be kept alive as long as he's useful to them.'

'Poor boy has no idea,' I said.

'I'm not sure he has no idea at all. From what you said, he's finding out what he is capable of, and that could possibly play into our hands.'

CHAPTER TWENTY-TWO

Back in the office, while we waited for any news of sightings of the car, radio intercepts or short-wave chatter, I looked through all the file material on the German girl, poor little Fräulein V—.

I wondered what she made of her angels experience. It hadn't taken the Nazis long to realize that her 'power' or 'gift', if that was what it was, could be used as a weapon. She had, it seemed, died in some mysterious way after unleashing some of her power – or whatever she, like Tom Pile, was blessed or cursed with. Perhaps they had simply disposed of her as being no longer required, which was hard to believe; or perhaps just using her powers to the extreme had killed her . . .

It meant that Tom Pile was in danger in more than one way. It made me even more determined to find the poor boy before it was too late. Where would Viktor take him?

An impression of laughter came to my mind: it was a woman's laugh, and I remembered something that Ruth Greville had said:

'Mr Prejm here just said he wanted to whisk me away to a romantic hideaway like one of these.' She gestured to the frosted glass panel to one side of her work area, over which she had taped dozens of picture postcards. There were sunny seaside and cottage scenes and the like.

I went out into the office, where she was normally plugged into her earphones. She wasn't there. Her desk was piled up with all the usual paper traffic, but there was no sign of her. I went through to the outer area. 'Anyone seen Ruth – Miss Greville lately?' I said.

'She left shortly after you did this morning,' one of the photographic technicians said. 'Heard her speaking to someone on the phone first. Assumed she was off to meet her Viktor.'

'Oh, right,' I said, and went back to her desk.

It was neatly arranged. Her typewriter had the cover pulled over it as if she wasn't expecting to come back that day. Her coloured marking pencils were all lined up on a sheet of corrugated cardboard – 'Keeps them from rolling around on the desk,' she once told me.

I noticed a break in the pattern. One pencil was out of place, a black one. It was under the mounted desk sharpener, next to a mound of fresh shavings, and I noticed a broken lead. Her spiral-topped shorthand notebook was open and slewed across the desk on top of a confidential file which had not yet been returned to the registry. I picked up the notebook. The indented marks of what she had last written were visible. I lifted the page and held it at an angle under the desk lamp, then rubbed the black pencil lightly across the ghost letters.

She had written: *Gallows Hill Litton Cheney.*

Captain Holloway had a map of Great Britain pinned up on the wall; it showed, among many other things, all the secret locations of new airfields and military installations.

I went over and studied the Dorset section. There weren't many bases to choose from. There was an airfield at Warmwell, and there was a bombing target run base near Chesil Beach. Captain Holloway was in his office, with the contents of the suitcases taken from

Viktor's room spread out across the two desks and on a trestle table as well.

'Bad news,' I told him. 'Ruth went off to meet Viktor. He called her out earlier – she wrote *Gallows Hill Litton Cheney* on her notepad afterwards.'

'Looks like he's taken her there too. Now, why would he do that? Bit risky.'

'Maybe he's using her as cover. A couple looks less suspicious travelling with a boy than a single man would.'

'Tricked her into a romantic weekend, you mean,' Captain Holloway said. 'How would he explain it to her, poor girl?'

'He'll tell her it's official, hush-hush . . . Department wants a test run of Tom's powers,' I suggested. 'There's even a glider base somewhere up on Gallows Hill, above Litton Cheney, of all places – near where I found Tom.'

'Makes some sort of sense now,' the captain said. 'Odd thing is, there was a label in the lid of one of the suitcases – sort of thing you put your possessions in when you are sent away to school. Just had *R. Greville* written on it in blue ink, so Viktor must have got it from our Ruth to keep all this stuff in. Poor girl, she's in for a shock, I'm afraid, after all this.' He indicated the papers scattered across the table. 'Someone's been on to all this for a while now, Jack,' he said. 'Look, just sit here for a moment and read this. Just as I was saying, the German Office of the Unexplained and Supernatural have obviously been covertly trawling for cases of what they call "the disappeared" like this for years. Gathering and collating the evidence, just like Herr Viktor – or whatever his name is really. He's been doing a lot too, judging from all his loot here. It looks to me like he has been quietly stealing ledgers, police records and the like from reference libraries, and ripping pages from the newspaper archives, among other things. Read the section I have marked there, and you will see that young Tom Pile has been telling us a blinding truth in his halting way, just as we thought he was. It makes those pictures you took all the more remarkable – as you will see when you read the evidence in this ledger which our friend Viktor has so usefully marked and flagged.'

I sat down. The ledger was open on the desk; the entry was halfway through it, the place kept with a bookmark, which was itself part of a book dust jacket. It was neatly torn down the middle and had been cut from a library copy of H. G. Wells's novel *The War of the Worlds*. Viktor had a sense of humour all right.

This was what I read:

Transcribed from the third evidence ledger 1900 - 1902

*Originally taken at Dorchester Police Station & subsequently
at Herrison Asylum for the Insane
Spoken by the accused-witness under oath over a two-day period.
Faithfully recorded by Mr Alfred Stevens Esq.,
Clerk/Recorder to the Court.*

*Disclaimer
I, Gawen Dilke, unemployed farm labourer of the County of Dorset,
do swear by this as a true account of the events of the night of
November 15th in the year of our Lord 1900, God Save the Queen.*

I here add my mark in confirmation.

X

I have known the boy Thomas Pile for some time – not
since his birth, mind, but not long after. I know his father,
the sometime gardener at the Rectory, who is also called
Thomas. I have supped ale – well, more usually cider – with
him at the White Horse on many an evening. Seemed to me
lately like he was drinking away his pittance, was guzzling
all his hard-earned money up in the cider after his poor wife
passed and he saw the lights. The boy and him was going
hungry. I made the boy an offer. I'm not getting any younger
– thought I might need a young body to help me cut and
carry, help me tote the sacks of a night on occasion; share
the spoils too. I meant no harm to him. Folk in that village

have a grudge agin me a mile wide, and would say anything to watch me swing on the end of the rope out in the yard there. I know 'em all well enough to know they hate me, sinner that I am, may God forgive me, but they hate me no more than I hate myself.

I arranged to meet the boy in the cursed village of Litton Cheney, and well after dark. Church clock struck the half-hour after ten just before I found him. He was waiting below Church Path playing silly beggars on the cart tracks at the bottom end of Gallows Hill. Poked him in the back with this same finger.

(Prisoner held up his right index finger.)

'Move along, then. Come on,' I said. 'Quick as you like.'

Made him jump like as if the Devil hisself had touched him. Well, maybe he had, poor child, wretch that I am. Made him slip his foot in a puddle along the cart track.

'Been here long enough. I thought you weren't coming,' he dared say back to me, quick as you like and sharp as a tack.

'I said I would come, didn't I,' I said, 'you ungrateful whelp, and here I am. I ain't no clock watcher, no time keeper to you, and you can scram off back where you came from, quick as you like, if you want to. It'd be no skin off my nose, young Tom Pile.'

That shut him up.

We set off up the steep path beside the precious reverend's garden. We went past the cottages, which were all dark. We walked together uphill onto the white chalk road that is Gallows Hill.

''Tis a long walk, 'bout as far as Powerstock over the top road – that's where he last saw it,' I said.

'He?' the boy asked, still sullen.

'Aye, 'twas Ruben the shepherd who saw it, large as life, and he says it's a fine big beast too.'

He had promised to help me for a share. I didn't doubt that meat was rare on their table, and a good haunch of venison would keep for weeks, hung up in a cold scullery.

'Here, you can carry these sacks. 'Tis a steep walk too.' And God forgive me if I didn't lump those heavy sacks, those very ones (Prisoner indicated sacks among the evidence pile on table), across the boy's shoulders. Sacks that was stiff and crusted and smelled, even in that cold air, of blood and stale meat.

'We shall 'ave to lug the best of him back between us. You prepared for that, boy?' I said.

'Course I am,' he said.

'No one knows you are out, do they?'

'No,' he said.

'Good,' I said. 'Behave yourself tonight – do as you're told when I tell you, and I might, just might, take you with me again. I en't getting any younger and I could maybe make something useful out of a wet-behind-the-ears pup like you.'

We crossed the top road, and then, after a while, we walked downhill again, this time on the single track – the one that winds through the woods. We was surrounded by trees, and it was all darkness, and we was near that ruined chapel – the place they all say is haunted, where everyone died from the plague hundreds of years before. A properly haunted place, even on a good day in bright sunshine. I never felt anything strange there before, but I would allow it now, believe me.

The boy slowed his pace, seemed afeared and stumbled along behind me.

'What is it?' I said, turning. 'Walk steady, now. Keep up and keep quiet. We could be on him anytime from now.'

We walked together side by side after that: a boy of fourteen, a garden hand's son, you would say, and he was of previous good character too. And me with him, old Gawen, sinner, drinker, poacher. I wonder what you would say of me? 'Previously known very bad character', no doubt.

We neither looked at the other as we walked through those dark trees.

There were all the usual rustling noises from either side – twigs snapping. 'An old brocky badger sniffing about, most like,' I said. 'Or it might be a dog fox. Could be anything. He'll be more scar'it of us than we should be of 'im, so don't worry yourself.'

'I'm not worried,' the boy said, all defiant, furious that he should even be thought to be worried, as if he had been out in the surrounding woods on his own every ruddy night.

'This is where Ruben says he saw the white hart,' I said, 'so go carefully now. Nice prize that. Good bit of gravy he'll make to stick your bread in, eh?'

The boy said nothing.

Suddenly there it was in front of us. It stood all on its own. The white hart. It was ghostly white in among those dark trees. It was sniffing the air and listening and its ears were forward. I gripped the boy's arm and stopped him in his tracks. Then, quiet as a church mouse, I took the rifle from across the boy's chest.

'Go on,' I whispered, placing the gun in his hands and – oh, may God forgive me – I said, 'Here's your chance . . . prove yourself.'

The boy quietly shouldered his father's rifle, and he sighted right enough and careful down the barrel.

The stag stood still.

'Go on,' I whispered. 'Time is a-wasting – gently now.'

The boy lowered the rifle. 'No,' he mumbled to himself.

I waited a moment – couldn't believe he would be so stupid – then I snatched the rifle from him. 'Coward . . . useless puppy,' I whispered, and I steadied the gun against a tree.

I waited, lining up for the kill shot. The animal shifted slightly and presented a good view of its chest. Even the boy held his breath. The animal breathed out as I watched it. I marvelled at its strength and its whiteness, and then the boy suddenly went mad and shouted out loud at the stag.

'Go on!' he cried.

And I fired my kill shot just as he shouted.

I was sure I had hit it. The creature's legs buckled under it and it slumped down to the ground.

'You little fool,' I whispered, and I sincerely pray that the Lord may save me for saying this; for doing what I did. 'What were you thinking of? You put me off my aim, and now it's mortal wounded and suffering. You'll have to go and finish it off now.'

The stag was lying down, still alive. I could see its breath. I pushed my sharp hunting knife, handle first, into the boy's hand.

'Quick blow to the heart now and I'll let you off. Then we can cut it up and take it back.'

'I won't do it,' the boy said.

'Then you'll get none of it,' I said, 'and 'tis the last time you come out with me to line your larder, young Pile.'

The boy stepped away from me and let those there very sacks fall from his shoulder.

'Give me the knife,' I said. 'I'll do it, you useless—'

'No,' he shouted out, loud enough to wake the dead,

and then he threw the knife away, somewhere among the trees.

'You ungrateful little idiot,' I called out in my anger, and then he suddenly sprinted off like a roebuck, away into the darkness, as far from me as he could get. He ran towards the stag.

And then it happened . . .

(The prisoner collapsed at this point. The interview resumed the following morning.)

It was a blinding light and it came suddenly from deep in the trees near the ruins of the chapel; from the graves of the dead. I had heard about the lights. People in the village had seen them off and on a few years before, and now here they were again, right in front of me.

I can see him now. The boy just stood there for a moment, haloed by the light. It was like looking into the noon sun on a bright July day. I squinted my eyes tight shut and shielded my face with my hands.

'What the—?' I cried out suddenly, mostly fearing to have been caught in the act.

Then a second light moved across the ground in bright shafts from above. I looked up. I could see a strange shape moving back and forth somewhere high above the trees.

The boy moved further off towards the light. I thought, 'Tis the keepers, and that means prison for sure. Forgive the thought, but then I raised up the rifle again, and forgive me again if I didn't say out loud to the trees, 'May as well be 'ung for a sheep as a lamb. I'll leave no witness anyway,' and I sighted the rifle right over to where the boy was standing.

I watched him walk steady through the trees for another few yards beyond the stag towards the light.

I had no idea what kind of machine could be giving such a fierce light on a cold winter's night. I couldn't let myself think that the lights were those lights. My hand worked the trigger, and without thinking I found I had let off a shot directly at the boy. The bang was deafening. There was a roaring noise, followed by a kind of wailing scream, and the light went out at once, and darkness fell suddenly.

Then I had the unbidden thought. It was as if it had been suddenly planted there in my head. I were being punished. The light was from above, and it was God punishing me for poaching the squire's livestock. I were being punished for even thinking of shooting that white deer and then killing the boy.

I trembled then. I knew what those lights were – I couldn't fool myself any longer – and I felt such fear deep in my bones. Here was an apprehension of angels, of God in Heaven's own judgement on a miserable sinner like me . . . just as the others had seen them all those years ago. I fell then, right down onto my knees on the cold ground, and

I clasped my hands, these very hands, like this together in prayer.

'Forgive me,' I said out loud, my voice sobbing out into the cold over and over – and it was then that I saw it: the angel. It was like nothing I had ever imagined an angel to be; perhaps it was even . . . God himself?

I tried to call out for forgiveness, but my tongue felt as thick as an ox tongue and it stuck suddenly, and my mouth was dry and no sound would come. It was as if all my breath had been suddenly sucked from me. I remember crying, though. I remember my tears falling like a newborn. My tears flowed as I tried to look at the light; at the angel, which was made of light.

A cold wind blew then between me and where the angel of the Lord stood. I fell forward onto the cold mud and leaves. I pressed my face hard into the dirt. I thought of a rabbit and I pushed myself down. I tried to burrow into the earth itself for safety. I heard more noises now, and was sure they were the agonized cries of the damned as they waited to welcome me down in Hades. 'Spare me, Lord. Spare me, spare me,' I cried out into the freezing dirt.

I stayed with my face pressed hard down into the filth and the darkness. There was a kind of whispered wailing noise, which was high-pitched and went right through me; it hurt my ears and made me feel sick to my stomach. I lifted my head up and looked along the ground. The light had brightened again, more so than ever, and the heaps of fallen leaves and the now upright body of the stag were all suddenly lifted, as one, into the air by the power of the Lord, up over the mud, just a yard or so from the ground.

I floated up too, and I was held there among the leaves which all spun around me, and I was sure now that it was God himself made real. I clasped these hands tighter together in prayer as the noise got worse. It was like a police whistle blowing right in your ear. The ground rumbled and shifted below, and my eyes seemed to give out at that point. I sensed the lights rise up above the trees. I fell back to earth with a bump. There was nothing after that but silence and complete darkness. After a minute or two, with my face pressed to the ground in fear, I dared look up. Where the boy Pile had stood there was nothing at all. I looked at the mound of bloodied sacks on the ground. I stood up, expecting to be struck down at any moment, either by armed keepers or by the angel of the Lord come to smite me.

Young Pile was gone, and the white hart was gone too. I staggered off then in fear, into the darkness towards Powerstock. I never saw Tom Pile again.

(Testimony ends.)

CHAPTER TWENTY-THREE

It was all there: the white hart, old Gawen – everything just as Tom had said and I had seen. The poor boy and the stag had leaped through time by forty years or so; no wonder he was so disoriented.

I looked again at the line of photographs I had taken down in Dorset. I was haunted by both Tom's face and the expression of the stag, the glint of terror in its eye. What had the poor dumb animal made of the angels who had so suddenly and mysteriously abducted it and so perfectly tended its gunshot wound?

'Right,' Captain Holloway said. 'We have no choice. We are driving down to Dorset and we have to go this minute. It'll take a while. We'll stay at your billet, and we will hopefully track down Viktor before he gets up to anything.'

'In my experience down there,' I said, 'they will be reported to the ARP authorities if they so much as hang a pair of underpants out on the washing line on the wrong day, or open a shiny tin of marrowfat peas in the open air.'

We left London in a fog. It was early evening, and as yet there were no air raids. Our progress was slow. There was less inessential traffic on the roads, but the dimmed and semi-obscured headlights of our staff car combined with the fog to make the going slow and potentially dangerous. Our conversation on the way down through the western suburbs and out was about the nature of the 'angels'.

'I wonder which part of the solar system or beyond they are from,' the captain said.

'Nowhere that can be seen even through your telescope,' I replied. 'Further – much further.'

'Yes,' he agreed. 'How do such beings, if that is what they are, even choose their subjects – victims, if you will? A girl in rural Germany, a boy out in the woods in Dorset and a shot stag, and who knows what else? Why them? It's all very rum; no one else will believe it.'

'The Germans believe it,' I said, 'and that is surely the point?'

'Indeed it is, Jack. Indeed it is. If we were at peace,

just think of the possibilities: we could share and pool our intelligence, but . . .' There was no need to say more.

We made such slow progress that by the time we reached the White Horse at Litton Cheney, it was closed and in darkness. There were, of course, right on cue, trailing wisps of a sea fret swirling round the building in proper Dorset fashion – wouldn't have been right if there hadn't been. I banged on the door at the side, and one of the upper windows opened and a cross voice called down in a loud and worried whisper, 'Who's there, and what the hell do you want at this time of night, may I ask?'

'Sorry, Mr Cox,' I called back. 'It's Jack, Corporal Jack Carmody, here with my superior officer, Captain Holloway. We just drove down from London. Took us longer than we thought.'

'Hold on, then.'

I pointed out Gallows Hill to Captain Holloway while we waited to be let in. 'That's the place,' I said.

'Looks bleak enough on a November night for anything,' he muttered.

CHAPTER TWENTY-FOUR

By morning Captain Holloway had already commandeered the telephone at the White Horse and was busy arranging for the intercept and triangulation of any odd shortwave traffic via the coastguard listening stations, and for searches of unoccupied buildings – or at least those known to be empty in and around the Chesil Beach area. Later that morning I took him up to meet Mr Feaver at the ARP hut.

'What happened to the poacher lad?' the warden asked us over a cup of ARP tea.

'Well, that's the thing,' Captain Holloway said. 'He was a bit more important than a poacher, and that's why Jack's come back here with me. We need everyone to be on the lookout for him. Any sighting of him, any rumour – anything at all, however trivial, however unimportant seeming it may be – call me at the White Horse.' He handed him a card with the number.

'What's he done, then?' Mr Feaver said.

'It's not so much what he's done; it's what he might do that worries us – can't say any more than that.'

'Oh, I see.' The warden nodded knowingly at me.

'I was never here just to assist the ARP,' I told him. 'Sorry about that – and leaving you with no warning or message. Couldn't be helped.'

"S all right, Jack – no harm done, though Mr Fry was up here earlier with the local paper. Seems some others have noticed those lights we saw up on Gallows Hill the other night. They been seen again – look there.'

I picked up the newspaper from the trestle table. There were two eyewitness accounts of the strange lights on Gallows Hill.

'Well, would you Adam and Eve it,' I said, trying to make light of it and handing the paper to Captain Holloway.

'Better take this outside, I think, Jack,' Captain Holloway said. 'Excuse us, Mr Feaver.'

We went and stood outside the tin tabernacle. The rooks were exchanging their gloomy sharp cries in the tall beeches of the Rectory garden, as usual.

'It's at times like these that I feel the need for my pipe,' Captain Holloway said, absently fumbling in his battle-dress pockets while reading the newspaper account. 'You've never gone in for the tobacco habit, have you, Jack?'

'Tried it – gave it up straight away. Not for me.'

'Helps me think straight; at least I tell myself that. Now, we are assuming that Viktor is somewhere in this area because he found out where Tom was from, and that he dragged his girlfriend, poor Miss Greville, into all this to give him some cover. It's all a bit thin, but we thought he might let that poor boy Tom loose on a remote air base just to see what he can do . . .'

'Fine – as far as it goes,' I said. 'Now we have a complication – the lights in the sky – and he will surely have seen this article or heard about it.'

'Exactly,' Captain Holloway said. 'It seems to me that Viktor will be tempted by that prospect far more than the chance to destroy a glider base or a bombing-run practice station. Here is his chance to get to the source, and as a good Nazi he will take it on, as sure as eggs are eggs.'

'So what do we do: stake out Gallows Hill and see what happens?'

'In the first instance, yes. If the lights really *are* back, we might just get lucky.'

'Just the two of us?'

'Good point, Jack. We could get some of our Essex

Regiment friends over at Burton Bradstock to lie in wait and surround the area, but my feeling is that: a) they wouldn't thank us in this lousy weather, and, b) the fewer people who witness what might happen, the better; if nothing happens, we would be seen as timewasters. What with all the invasion panic, we don't need to stoke up the rumour engine any further.'

'We'll manage, then,' I said, 'with just us and a camera.'

'We'll need more than a camera.'

'I have my rifle and Mr Feaver will have his stirrup pump.'

'Well, that's a comfort,' the captain said, and folded the paper. 'Give this back to him and say we'll return once it's dark.'

'Won't be long now,' I said.

CHAPTER TWENTY-FIVE

I had my army-issue rifle, of course – my Lee Enfield, the soldier's friend. I had fired a similar model a few times a year or so ago on a TA firing range. That was with 2.2 ammo, so effectively I was a novice at anything involving guns or fighting, but I had been accurate. Who knew what sort of force we would be up against later on Gallows Hill? I knew that Captain Holloway had his service revolver, which was a far less accurate weapon than my rifle, especially over any distance, so between us and Mr Feaver's tin hat and stirrup pump, what sort of a chance did we have? It was better not to think about it too much. We had Viktor's car registration, and I suggested that we send my new friend the local constable off noting cars around Langton Herring.

The evening bloomed with enough damp sea fret to hide a whole shipload of invading Nazis. I wondered what the real chances of the lights returning on a second evening were. I supposed that the odds were at least good enough to tempt Viktor to bring Tom out into the landscape – at least, if he was here somewhere.

The constable cycled up to the ARP hut at about seven in the evening to report, and he had a big smile on his face.

'Odd thing is,' he said between sips of Mr Feaver's eternally ready tea, 'I had a report from round there just yesterday. A woman came into the station – a regular visitor to us; sees a lot and hears a lot, if you know what I mean. She said a foreign voice, a German, had been heard thereabouts calling out from behind a hedge, and there was obviously a spy in the place. I said to her, *Are you sure it was German? Could have been a Czech or Polish voice, not German necessarily.* No, she was fairly sure it was German. This happens at least twice a day, I don't need to tell you, Mr Feaver. Folks are very jumpy, so I confess I ignored it. Then, when you asked me to look for a particular car, I remembered what she'd said, and so I went down there first. I checked the number plate, and blow me, there it was, large as life, in the driveway behind a closed five-bar gate. I noted it but did nothing.'

'Oddly enough,' Captain Holloway said, 'the nosy woman wasn't so far wrong, Constable. You have just made our job a lot clearer, if not any easier. We won't require any arrests – or, indeed, any intervention at all, at least not yet. We now have to spool out a little rope and let the suspect hang himself with it. There are others involved; we can't put them at risk so we don't want to spook him just yet. You did the right thing in leaving well alone. I assume you weren't seen?'

'Oh no, I was on my bicycle and the car was a way down the driveway from the farmhouse itself; didn't take me but a minute to spot it. Most of the locals thought the place was closed up and not used any more.'

'That all makes sense. I doubt it has been for a while.'

'Will you need me any more today?' the constable asked.

'I am afraid you are a luxury we can't afford, Constable. What we have to do we have to do alone and in secret. This is all strictly hush-hush, but by all means stay alert.'

'Right you are, Captain.' He put down his cup. 'Thank you, then, Mr Feaver, for the tea. I suppose this is all to do with those lights people been seeing?'

'Something like that,' I agreed.

'Well, you know where I am if everything gets out of hand, don't you,' he said. 'I can handle myself in a fight, you know,' he added, almost cheerfully.

'I'm afraid for security reasons we will just have to manage by ourselves for now. Thank you anyway – and, of course, not a word about it to anyone.'

The constable was soon away on his bike. I watched his dimmed rear light snake off back down to the main village street.

CHAPTER TWENTY-SIX

By seven the captain and I were setting off up the strange
white surface of Gallows Hill. Mr Feaver stayed back in
the ARP hut 'just in case', his buckets and stirrup pumps
at the ready. We had briefed him to expect an arrest
later and that was all. We took his dark lantern with us,
and his first aid kit. I had my rifle slung over my back
and Captain Holloway had taken charge of the camera.
About halfway up the hill that led to the main Honiton
road there was a passing place; a kind of lay-by with a
gate in the hedge and access to a field. On the higher
part of the field, a few yards from the road, stood an old
stone shepherd's bothy, from which we would easily hear
any motor cars coming up or down the hill – and any
other kind of traffic. We went inside and settled down
to wait.

'I've been thinking about where in the solar system these angel beings might come from, if at all?' the captain mused.

'I have too,' I said. 'Whatever craft they are travelling in seems to have been well hidden. Perhaps that's why they only appear at night, when there is a sea fog and overcast skies.'

'The only physical evidence we have is the lights. If we get Tom back – and it's a big *if*, I know,' Captain Holloway said, 'we must try and get him to remember what happened when they took him.'

'Most likely the experience has been hidden, either because it was too traumatic or because they wanted it that way.'

The captain went outside and looked up the hill towards the top road and the sky above. I followed him, and he turned to me.

'I've just remembered something. Tom took that little square of material he had with him. He put it back in his pocket. He's still got it.'

'We might discover what it was for, at least,' I said.

'Look,' Captain Holloway said, staring past me. 'Lights.'

They were over the crest of Gallows Hill: oval-shaped lights moving down towards the field. The captain got the camera out of his rucksack and started to take photographs. At the same time I heard a car climbing the hill. I heard the stop-and-start grinding of gear changes; the rumbling of the motor suggested it was having problems with the gradient.

'Car,' I said, and crossed over the wet grass to the gate. I watched it pull into a passing place on the other side of the road, just a hundred yards or so below us. The headlights were masked by the regulation slotted grille covers so that only just a little light escaped onto the the road itself.

The car sat there, just visible in the fogged dark. The engine was idling, coughing out smoke from the exhaust. I pushed myself up against the wet hedgerow as cover and used my army binoculars. The interior of the car was dark, but I could read the number plate clearly enough: NV 4103. It was Viktor's car all right.

'It's them,' I said.

The captain joined me among the wet leaves. I handed him the binoculars.

'The door's opening,' he said. There was a sudden rise in the light levels. The engine stopped running and I heard the car door slam shut. A shaft of light suddenly descended onto the roadway.

'Here they are,' the captain whispered, looking up.

The lights had appeared above us, and they were bright, but static overhead, just as they had been that first night on the hill. It was impossible to make out anything beyond the substance of the light itself, which was a bluish white, diffused and milky through the fog. The strange whining noise of the angels' engine was back too – and then there was the shuddering bass-drum thump as a shaft of light suddenly fell through the air and picked out the parked car. I could see three figures in the road close to the car. One was Viktor; the others were Tom Pile and Ruth Greville.

'Wait,' the captain said quietly.

The light was very strong, directly above them now. Viktor was wearing a raincoat with the collar turned up and a trilby hat. He looked like a plain-clothes policeman. Tom was still wearing my overcoat, and his head was tipped back as he looked up into the light. Ruth Greville had her hands protectively on his shoulders. I studied the dynamic between all three of them; their posture and attitude to each other. Something troubled me. Tom suddenly raised both his arms, pointing upwards, and I saw that in each hand he was holding something that glowed bright.

I heard the camera click and roll on, click and roll on as the captain tried to document what was happening.

'Do you see,' he said. 'Look at his hands: he now has two pieces of that strange material. Viktor must have brought the piece the Germans found all that time ago.

They really have been planning for this. I suppose it summons them or something.'

I looked at Tom's hands through the binoculars. The pieces of metal were pulsating, and I could see traceries of their colours leaching up towards the light, which suddenly shut off, plunging the hill into darkness again.

'Blast,' the captain said. 'What now?'

The shaft of light appeared again briefly, only higher up the hill towards the main Honiton road this time. I heard the car door slam and the engine kick in, and within a few seconds the car had driven slowly past us up the hill in pursuit of the lights.

We had left our staff car back down in the village. We had little choice but to follow as best we could on foot. The car was struggling so it was not hard to keep it in sight. The shaft of light seemed to be leading the way up to the main road and beyond. We kept close to the hedges by the side of the road.

'I doubt they can see us,' I said, leading the way up. There was no traffic at all on the top road, and I watched the car sail across the gap and up onto the crest of the hill on the other side, where it turned off into a field.

CHAPTER TWENTY-SEVEN

In the fog and cloud above the top road there was now a huge pale oval of light. The effect was of veiled moonlight, as if the moon itself had come down close to the Earth on a clouded night. The light was an intense blue-white, oddly cold-looking. Two or three shafts of it suddenly came down onto the field behind the main road at the highest point of Gallows Hill.

We could see the car in the middle of the field. It was parked at an odd angle, with all its doors wide open, as if the driver had been in a great hurry. Viktor was standing beside Tom, and Ruth Greville was partly hidden on his far side. From Tom's hands, two strong beams of red light answered the white light coming from above.

'Time we did something,' Captain Holloway said. He pulled out his service revolver and walked quickly forward through the gap in the hedgerow and into the field.

'Wait,' I said. 'I don't think . . .'

Too late. He pointed the gun straight up into the air and fired it once. Viktor turned, and at once ran towards the car. Ruth Greville stepped back a few paces. I had only a half-second or so. I had already tucked the Lee Enfield against my shoulder. The light was perfect and the slewed angle of the car meant that I had a good view of the target. It only needed the one bullet fired into the petrol tank to set it all off. The fireball leaped upwards and the car lifted a little from the ground as it exploded. Viktor threw himself down on the ground, and Tom and Ruth turned towards us. Captain Holloway crossed the field with his revolver held out towards Viktor.

'Stay where you are,' he called out.

Viktor kneeled up on the grass, his hands high in the air, a grin on his face. 'Thank God,' he called out.

Tom's hands were up anyway, each one pumping more light up into the sky. The noise of whatever it was above the fog and cloud was louder now. There was a downrush of air too; I could feel it on my face. When I looked up, I saw that the fog was blowing away and the lights were getting lower and brighter, moving down towards us.

'Get up,' Captain Holloway called out to Viktor, who was now lit by both the overhead lights and the burning car.

'Are you all right, Tom?' I called out.

He said nothing; he just continued to hold his arms up towards the sky and the lights.

'The boy is capable of anything now,' Ruth shouted, a big smile on her face. 'And I really do mean *anything*.'

I looked over at her; she was still tucked just behind Tom. I saw that she was holding a service revolver out at arm's length and it was aimed directly at Captain Holloway.

'God, Captain, watch out – she's got a gun!'

'If I you have any sense,' she shouted out over the noise of the machine in the sky, 'you will go back to London and leave all this to me.'

'What on earth are you doing, Ruth?' Captain Holloway shouted back at her.

'I've been on to her for ages, Captain,' Viktor called out. 'She only took up with me as cover. I found a whole case full of evidence she had stolen. I followed her onto the Underground, and then I tracked her and the boy here – there was no time to alert you—' There was a bang as Ruth fired the revolver, and Viktor sprawled forward onto the ground.

I had no clear shot at her. She was so close to Tom, I couldn't risk it.

'I can make so much better use of this boy and his talents,' Ruth yelled over the noise. 'I'm sure you know that his abilities are growing all the time. Of course, at the same time I will encourage his friends up there to join us down here.' She waved her pistol up towards the oval of light above us. 'To join us in other ways too. Never mind getting the Americans into your war – what about us getting *this lot* onto our side? Think of that – imagine an army of Toms and an army of *them*.' She raised her head and smiled. 'Even better, I think, than having God on your side.'

'I don't think so,' Captain Holloway called back. 'I'm afraid that your sorry game is up.'

'Oh no, Captain, I'm sorry to say that my game is only just beginning. Yours is the one that is up. You really have no idea.'

With her free hand she quickly reached into her coat and pulled something out of the inner pocket. Before either of us could respond, she aimed it vertically up and fired what looked like a bright signal flare towards the centre of the light. There was a hush, a half-second or so of nothing, and then the light flared into an intense blue-white. There was a deep low growl, and the angle of the light shifted as one edge of the oval dipped down towards the ground. There was a huge rumble, and a groaning sound, and I felt the air press down on me, as if a giant hand were forcing me to the ground.

'What the hell have you done?' the captain called out as he fell forward along with Ruth Greville. Only Tom was left standing. As I hit the ground, held down by the sheer weight of air pressure, I saw him still standing there, silhouetted against the intense light and the cascade of sparks falling from whatever it was above us.

There was an earthquake underneath me, and I felt myself being picked up and thrown down again. My rifle fell away across the ground, and then I saw it actually rise up into the air and hover there, suddenly freed from gravity. I saw part of a huge disc edged with intense white light slice into the ground. Huge chunks and clods of earth were thrown up into the air. The groaning metal noise continued, and a high-pitched scream was added to the rumble as more and more of the disc buried itself into the crest of Gallows Hill, as if it were burrowing down into the centre of the Earth.

The bright light suddenly went out, plunging the

hill into almost complete darkness. Chunks of earth, tree limbs, rocks and who knows what else tumbled down all around me. The burning black Austin, which had been lifted clear of the ground, crashed back to earth on its side. Tom Pile was still standing with his arms held out and his head bowed. Halfway across the field I saw bits of the wreckage of what had once been above us scattered across the ground.

Ruth Greville staggered to her feet and set off towards the wreckage, where some light still glowed.

Tom Pile pointed at her, and I saw her sprawl headlong, three feet in the air, hovering above the ground.

As I stumbled over the churned-up ground towards Tom, I saw the captain on his knees, rubbing the back of his head. I called out to him, 'Are you all right, Captain?'

'Fine – just had a bit of a whack from a rock or something, that's all. Go and see to Tom. I'll check on poor Viktor.'

Tom turned to me. 'She killed them,' he said quietly. 'She's killed the angels. I can't hear their music.' He had tears coursing down his face.

Large chunks of twisted metal lay scattered all around, their surfaces rippling with colours that echoed those I'd seen on the little fragment

Tom had originally had in his pocket. Even as I looked at them, they faded to a nondescript grey. There was movement under the ground – rumblings and quiverings through the Earth itself. I could feel the tremors reverberating underneath me like echoes; a shifting pattern that I could almost track in my mind as the disc rolled on down through the layers of the hill.

'Were the angels in there, Tom?'

'They were,' he said. He turned to Ruth Greville, still hovering on her front, paralysed, three feet above the ground.

'Perhaps we can rescue them,' I said.

'No,' Tom said. 'I think they're gone now.'

There was a final seismic shift under our feet, and I staggered and saw Ruth fall back down to the ground.

Captain Holloway came and stood next to me. 'Viktor has a wound on his shoulder – it knocked him out, but I think he'll be all right. My revolver's gone, though – lost somewhere in all this. We need to restrain our Nazi friend here.'

'My rifle's gone too,' I told him.

A voice called out of the darkness at the roadside, 'Is everything all right here?'

It was Mr Feaver and the police constable.

'There's been a plane crash,' the captain said. 'We'll

need some help from the garrison to clear all this. We also have a Nazi spy to place under arrest – but not a word of this must get out, mind.'

'Sounded like a bombing raid,' the warden said.

'Well, in a way it was,' Captain Holloway explained. 'The woman over there was signalling to the enemy. I think they were trying to attack the base at Warmwell. Could one of you get over to the garrison at Burton Bradstock and rouse my old friend Colonel Gauntlett and see if he can spare us some men and a large vehicle to clear this at first light? We also have a brave man down with a gunshot wound – he's in urgent need of medical attention. Oh, and before you go, handcuffs and key please.'

'Right you are,' the constable said, rummaging at his belt and handing them over before setting off at once.

Tom Pile was sitting on the ground next to the now slumped and oddly stilled figure of Ruth Greville.

'Arms behind your back please, Miss Greville,' the captain said.

She looked up at him with a blank expression and indicated that her arms were already locked.

'Let me handcuff her, Tom.'

Tom nodded, and suddenly Ruth's body jerked in spasm, as if it had been suddenly shocked awake. The captain wrenched her arms round behind her back and locked the cuffs in place.

'How did you manage to bring that thing down? What was that you fired?' Captain Holloway asked.

She looked back at him, her mouth clamped shut in a thin line, and shook her head.

'I see you want to play the silent game, eh. Well, it's your funeral, Miss Greville, or almost certainly will be. Sadly, I doubt if we will ever know how that happened. Looked like a standard flare. What a terrible waste. Just look at all this.'

Mr Feaver stood looking around at the lumps of scattered wreckage. 'Is this all there is of it, then?' he asked.

'This is all that's left after the explosion, yes,' the captain said. 'By the way, I think we should wait here and guard the wreckage until the army comes.'

'Oh,' said Mr Feaver. 'That won't be until nearly seven tomorrow. I ought to get back in case of more raids.'

'Yes, you are certainly free to go. Not a word about what has happened here to anyone. What we have is the remains of an experimental German aircraft, which will need to be kept secure. They will have heard it all over the county, of course. All you need tell them is that a bomber was brought down on its way to destroy Warmwell base.'

'Understood.'

Mr Feaver set off back down Gallows Hill to the village.

The captain pulled his pipe out of his battle-dress jacket, struck a match and, cupping the bowl, lit it. He walked over and kicked at one of the lumps of grey metal. 'I suppose we have to hope that the soldiers will accept these as bits of a downed Nazi plane. It all looks nondescript enough now.'

He crouched down next to the boy and asked, 'What happened, Tom?'

'I can't rightly say. I was in a terrible pickle after that Underground train ride and I ran off. Anyway, he saw me at the station, that man there. He was nice and he tried to help me – said I was in danger and I had get away. Then she caught up with us and she threatened him with a gun and said she understood all about the angels; said she was sent by them to help and all; said she knew all about me, and told me other things too.'

'I think she did know, Tom. She dug out the old newspapers and files about you, and Viktor found the evidence she'd collected and took it from her – silly, brave man.'

'She said the angels wanted to see me again, and we came here and you saw what happened.'

'Oh yes, we saw all right – what a terrible waste!'

It was then that the Earth rumbled again, deep under our feet, as if an underground mine had exploded. I found myself swaying, and saw one of the trees in the hedgerow simply topple over. Ruth Greville sprang to her feet as, from the other side of the field, a bright light burst upwards from the ground. There was more rumbling below, like an earthquake, and then something burst up out of the field. It was almost too bright to look at: a shining disc much smaller than the one that had ploughed down into the ground earlier. It leaped up and then hovered about twenty feet in the air, spinning and sparking out light. We all stood and looked up at it. It was in its way a thing of rare beauty. Here was an object from far beyond the moon or the rings of Saturn, hovering in the air above our heads. Tom walked forward and held his arms out to the spinning silvery disc. Two great beams of white light shot out from his hands, and as if in answer, a burst of coloured light like a spinning rainbow enveloped him. Then, after a momentary pause, the disc shot upwards and vanished behind the rolling fog bank. We could just see a trail of light as it streaked upwards, like a shooting star in reverse. And then there was darkness and silence.

'Looks like your angels said goodbye, Tom,' I said.

'I know,' he said with a grin. 'I heard their music again.'

And then we were left standing in the cold field, surrounded by extra-terrestrial wreckage, waiting for the sunrise.

CHAPTER TWENTY-EIGHT

A small force from my supposed regiment, the Ninth Essex, appeared at around seven a.m. There was a covered lorry, and an army ambulance. They were led by the captain's old friend, Colonel Gauntlett. The men were soon at work clearing the few scattered lumps of twisted and half-melted grey matter that remained, along with the burned-out Austin.

'I feel I ought to tell you, Colonel, that this is a strictly secret operation connected to a secret weapon. No word of the nature of this clear-up must reach anyone at all, no matter what. As far as anyone else is concerned, we brought down a bomber here, a fluke event. This is a top priority.'

'Fully understood, Captain,' the colonel said. 'The man Viktor has only a superficial wound, I am told.

The bullet passed through the muscle and tissue of his upper arm and came out again. Luckily your Mata Hari over there turned out to be a bad shot,' he said, indicating Ruth with his cane.

'Incidentally,' he added, 'you might remind your corporal here to salute an officer from time to time.'

By eight o'clock the soldiers had collected up most of the metal lumps and put them in a trailer attached to the back of the lorry. Apart from the gaping crater and churned earth, there was not much to show for the downed aircraft – though they had found my rifle and the captain's pistol and the very pistol Ruth Greville had used among the debris.

She stood watching it all, her arms cuffed behind her back. Her coat flapped in the wind, along with her normally perfectly brushed hair. As the soldiers were packing up, she suddenly shouted out, 'Heil Hitler!' Though of course, she couldn't salute the way she would have liked.

'You think that was a bomber,' she called out again, 'brought down here? Well, I can tell you it was not any sort of bomber. Where are the bodies of the crew? Were there any German markings on those bits of wreckage? No, of course not, because that craft was not of this world at all, but from another planet far from here, and soon the Reich will join forces with the beings from that place, and together we will conquer the world.'

'You tell 'em, Eva,' one of the soldiers shouted back at her. 'Look out, it's the Martians coming – oooh.' The other soldiers laughed.

'She's mad, of course,' Captain Holloway said. 'A Nazi spy and a fanatic. Put her in the back with the rest of the rubbish.'

Ruth was quickly manhandled into the lorry.

'Who's the boy?' the colonel asked, pointing at Tom. 'A local?'

'In one way, yes; now he's more of an evacuee,' Captain Holloway said.

Who knew where Tom was from now? It was impossible to let on that he was from this place, but forty or so years ago. It was also impossible to know the extent of his powers yet.

The captain turned to him. 'When we get back to London, Tom, I want you to talk about everything that has happened to you; everything.'

The craft, or the parts of it left behind, were of course already securely buried deep underground on top of Gallows Hill. Once the surface wreckage had been cleared, there was little to show for the extraordinary events of just a few days before. The grass surface was torn away in areas, and deeply scarred, but most of the disturbed earth had fallen back into the crater when the smaller craft took off. Once the grass had grown over the scar again, there would be almost no trace of the crash. The official version was that an experimental enemy bomber had been brought down and destroyed before it reached Warmwell aerodrome. The crash site was classified, and no news of the incident was ever published. Those locals who had seen the lights or heard the explosions that night had their own theories. After all, it was not the first time that unexplained events of this kind had occurred on Gallows Hill.

Tom Pile accompanied us to London for extensive questioning. He came to stay with my aunt Dolly, who welcomed him as the orphan that he was, and lavished her own brand of kindness on him, so that he soon blossomed. We still had no idea of the extent of his abilities or how the 'angels' had been able to modify and mutate his nature. By December he was feeling well enough to submit to new and more extensive interviews on what he remembered of his abduction.

Tom was seconded into Department 116 as an operative, along with Viktor Prejm, who happily made a full recovery. After all, the war wasn't won yet, and someone with Tom's abilities was a more than useful addition to Captain Holloway's roster. Of course, we knew that the Germans knew we had him, and they would surely try to get at him again. That was for another time; for the moment he was as safe as anyone could be in the middle of the Blitz.

Ruth Greville was the daughter of a Nazi sympathizer among the upper echelons of the aristocracy. There were many who played that game in the early days but saw sense when war came. He was interned, and she was eventually tried in secret for treason. Normally in wartime this carried the death penalty. However, with all her ramblings and testimony about beings from another world, she was certified insane and detained in a maximum security institution at Herrison in Dorset – the same place where old Gawen ended his days all those years before.

Tom Pile's verbal testimony

Excerpt from a wire recording made at Department 116
Thursday 14th December 1940

*'Tell us your story,' the voices said. 'We want to hear your
story – all of it.'*

*That was when I started speaking out loud to the night
stars all around me and to the music, the voices in my head.
They said, 'That's it. Go on . . . go on . . . tell us, tell us
all.'*

*I couldn't bring myself to shoot the stag. Something
stopped me. I don't know what it was. The animal stood
there, shining white in the darkness. It was alert too; it
knew something was up. Maybe it had the smell of us, of
old Gawen and me. He certainly smelled bad enough, did
Gawen, and even the stiff old poacher's sacks we had with
us stank of rancid meat and old blood. Surely a white hart
could sense that in the air; could sense us and our intention
to kill . . . Old Gawen took the gun from me.*

*'Go on,' he whispered to me with his rotten breath.
'Go on,' and he pushed the gun back at me, all fierce, and
said under his breath, 'Here's your chance, boy,' and he
spat that word fiercer than the rest. 'Go on, you damned
boy . . . prove yourself.'*

I looked down the barrel and the stag stood there, still.

'Go on,' he whispered at me. His chin was dug in hard on my shoulder. 'Time is a-wasting. Nice and gently now.'

I lowered the rifle and said, as quietly as I could, 'No.'

He snatched the rifle away from me again and spat out, 'Coward! Useless-arsed little whelp!' and he steadied the gun against the side of a tree.

The stag shifted, turned almost as if it wanted to present itself as an easy target. Its chest was now square on to us. Everything was quiet. The stag's breath misted out. I realized I couldn't let it happen, no matter how hungry we were for some decent meat. This just wasn't right – I knew it, and I had to stop it then and there. I broke the strange hush, I broke the silence, and I shouted out loud right at the stag.

'GO ON.'

Gawen fired the shot at the very moment I cried out, and the shot deafened me for a second. My ears sang and I heard a whistling noise.

The stag's front legs folded under it and it fell to the ground.

'You little bastard,' Gawen shouted harshly, right into my ear, and he struck me across the back in anger. 'What in Hell were you thinking of? You put me off my aim, and now that thing is mortal wounded and suffering. You'll have to go and finish it off, and right now.'

The stag was down but still alive. I could see it was

breathing 'cos its chest was rising and falling and its hot breath was still misting. Gawen came and stood in front of me and pushed an antler-handled knife hard into my hand.

'You'll go over there now, you little turd,' he said, spitting his words out at me in a fury. 'You'll deliver one quick blow to that thing's heart right now. Do it and I'll let you live. Do it and I'll let you cut it up and carry it back over your shoulder in sacks. Fail, and I will shoot you dead without a thought. What do I care for you! Not a whit, not a farthing.'

'I won't bloody do it,' I said.

'Then you'll get nothing but a bullet,' he said. ''Tis the last time anyone sees you, young Pile.'

I didn't care; I didn't believe he would do it. So I walked away from him, throwing his filthy sacks down on the ground.

'Give me the knife,' he shouted out, 'you useless—'

'No,' I screamed at the top of my voice, and then I threw the knife with its rough-edged antler handle. I threw it away as far as I could among the trees.

'You ungrateful little swine,' he screamed back at me in a fury. I shouldn't have thrown the knife away. Part of me knew that in one way he was right. I should have gone over and put the poor beautiful animal out of its pain and misery, out of its death agony; I should have killed it clean. But I ran off as fast as I could before Gawen could get a bead on me and shoot me, because I really thought that he would. So I ran towards the stag. I didn't care any more – not about being hungry or working for old Gawen or killing, or being killed even. It all drained away from me. It was as if there was a voice in my head, a gentle voice, though loud in my mind – a gentle, loud, whispering, shouting voice telling me to walk forward, to come on into the light.

Then there was the light.

The light was suddenly there – like the one my dad and me saw, only this was the brightest light ever. It was white or silver, and it filled the trees and the spaces between the trees. I was walking now. I couldn't run any more. I was walking into a wholly silver and white place which hurt my eyes, but I couldn't turn away. It was as wide as the sky and as high as the sky, which was not dark any more, and the white stag was somehow beside me, up on its feet, all mended. The light dazzled my eyes, but I could see that the stag was walking quietly beside me as if it were my own pet dog or something. I heard a shot from the gun that Gawen had taken from me – at least, I think that's what it must have been. It sounded like that gun, but it seemed loud and far away at the same time. Something hit me then, and bored into me. It didn't hurt, but I felt a hard tug at my upper arm. Then I felt a gentle sensation, but I couldn't tell what it was or what had made it. There were shapes moving: a darker – a very slightly darker white shadow against the brighter white. There were tall shapes, and they were like walking trees, and the shapes were talking to me. They were telling me to keep walking, and I did. The forest had gone away, and there was just this bright space which stretched all around me now, from side to side and from top to bottom. I could see nothing but the silver and white light. It was all around me, shining down in beams like you sometimes saw in those pictures we were given in Sunday school. Those special beams of light all around the halo on the head of Jesus. I knew then that these were the angels from Heaven, and thought that perhaps old Gawen really had killed me with my dad's rifle because he was that cross because I wouldn't let him kill the white stag.

I didn't feel dead, though.

What would being dead feel like anyway?

I could still feel the solid ground under my feet, even though it was white now, and brighter than the big snowfall of last January. That was when the snow came in the night, and the next morning, why, it was up as high as the tops of the hedges. That was when the white snow was as high as the hedge tops and you could walk on the hedges all the way up and down Gallows Hill if you dared to. If you fell, it was only into the soft cold blanket of snow in any case. Out in the woods near Powerstock it was even brighter than that snow had been under the most glaring noonday sun.

The voice in my head told me to be calm, but it didn't

say any words. The voice in my head wasn't really a voice; it was like a piece of music, but I knew what it meant without hearing any words. I knew that I was meant to keep walking until I was in the middle of the light; where it was at its very brightest, shining like a star, but a star that was somehow in the fallow field below the Rectory garden. If you were up in the tree in that field on a clear day, with no sea fret, you could see the sea itself in the distance – and, if you were lucky, the sun sparkling on the sea too. Now the centre of the white light looked like the sea sun sparks had landed in that fallow field. That is how bright it was.

I put my arm over my eyes and looked away from the light and at the stag instead. The poor animal was standing right next to me, and one of the angels was touching it or stroking it. Well, I thought it was an angel, but maybe it was just me talking to the beast and stroking its hot rough coat. In any case the light made it hard to see clearly what was happening, but the animal was calm enough, and it moved its head in turn towards me. I could look right into its big brown eyes. I could see how the whites were creamy and slightly bloodshot as its eyes rolled back a little in its head. It looked at me, and I understood then that it didn't understand me at all. It might look into my eyes, but it wasn't thinking about the whites of my eyes. It wasn't thinking at all, it was just . . . being.

I don't know how I understood or even thought about

that. The angels must have told me or helped me to think it.

I kept my arms across my forehead, shielding my eyes, trying to look away from the brightness. I felt a movement under my feet, as if I were being lifted high up into the air. In that moment the white light, the silver light, the brightness suddenly snapped off into complete blackness. I felt the stag buck under my hand. 'Whoa,' I said. 'Whoa. Gentle there,' as if it were the Reverend Stone's dear little trap pony instead of a lost and frightened wild thing. It backed away, and I felt the sharp antlers against my hand as it lowered its head.

I looked up and saw all the stars.

All of them.

I saw other things. I saw a blackboard with white letters, white words. The words were calling out to me. I knew then that there were others like me. Some might be out there, among the stars. Others were down on the ground. I wondered if I would ever meet them.

All the stars – so many stars, and all bright and shining clear. They were in a great arc shape over my head. The stars were clearer than I had ever seen them, even from Gallows Hill on a clear night, and they were all around me; not just above me, but below me too, and beside me and behind me. The angels had taken me floating in the sky on my way to Heaven with the white stag, which was healed now – there was no blood on its chest. The music in my head was gentle, like a lullaby that you might sing to a baby to get it to sleep. I felt sleepy too. My arms and legs were heavy. I wanted to lie down next to the stag, which was curled up next to me with its legs folded under it, asleep among the stars.

I thought that if I did the same thing as the stag, I would never wake up again; I would really be dead and asleep for ever under a mound of grass and cowslips in the churchyard at Litton Cheney, so close to our own little house. I might wake up in a wooden box like the one my mother was put in. Then I saw the grass on the tombs so clearly, all grown long, and I saw my father cutting it, heard the whisper of his scythe, all busy in the good days; and the voice music of the angels in my head told me now to go on, go on, talk . . . talk to us. Tell us your story – we want to hear your story, all of it . . .

Part 2

THE MIRACULOUS RETURN OF ANNICK GAREL

Author's Note:

Adolf Hitler's forces invaded France in the early summer of 1940. The French surrendered in June 1940, and most of France was occupied by German forces during the Second World War.

MEMORANDUM

FROM: Captain Holloway, Dept 116
TO: Colonel G. Clarke, War Ministry Liaison

STRICTLY CONFIDENTIAL

My dear Clarke (if I may – sorry, old school habits die hard, don't they?
How long ago was it we were there? My, how time flies!).

First, and most importantly, may I congratulate you on, and welcome you
to, your new position. One of the drawbacks of your job, I fear, will be
dealing with the likes of me and my raggle-taggle department. We really
are the 'awkward squad'. We don't fit in. So apologies in advance if what
follows seems far-fetched in places. We are neither strictly military nor
strictly scientific. We occupy a very odd space in the war effort; one which
I, and a select few including Winston Churchill himself, deem pretty
important. I am sure you will have been briefed on my remit, but this is to
bring you up to date.

I thought it would be useful to summarize where we are. First, a bit of
history.

Adolf Hitler's interest and belief in the supernatural are well
documented. He personally oversaw the setting up of the Office of the
Unexplained & the Supernatural in Berlin in the mid-1930s. His nefarious
colleagues have been pretty efficient at running things at their end, and
so far it has been very much to their advantage.

Our Department 116 was in fact set up before theirs. Its brief has been
to monitor and combat their efforts, where possible. Since war was
declared, this has become ever more vital. In every department we are now
in a race with the enemy; a race which could prove crucial to the outcome
of the war; a race which we must win at all costs.

In building my department I recruited a young man who now acts as my
right hand. This is Jack Carmody, my man on the ground; my case officer, if
you will. He is a young Londoner with exceptional gifts of perception,
language and much else. He is currently engaged in running tests on
subject A, the boy Tom Pile, of whom you may already have read in a series
of memos to your predecessor. Tom Pile was first encountered in mysterious
circumstances in the West Country (Dorset). He had spent 'lost' time with
beings he described as 'angels'. His experience found an exact parallel in
a case covered by the rival German office some years before.

They discovered a girl whom they codenamed Fräulein V. She was found in
similar circumstances to those surrounding Tom Pile. The Germans
characterized her as one of 'the returned'. They strongly believed that

there would be others. The girl also claimed to have been taken by 'angels', beings described by both herself and Tom Pile as being 'made of light'. Our belief is that the angels are in fact advanced extra-terrestrial beings. One of their craft crash-landed in Dorset shortly after Tom Pile was found. Most of the said craft took off again, but part of it is still underground at the site. We are currently investigating the remains, which appear to be made of an unknown metal alloy. This is being carried out under the cover story of an archaeological dig.

When discovered, both Fräulein V (according to our intercepts of German communications and files) and Tom Pile had on their person fragments of the same or similar metal alloy of unknown origin. The girl in Germany was tested and used by the authorities to the extent that she was (apparently) able to bring an aeroplane down out of the sky with just the power of her mind. I need hardly add that she, and other so-called 'returnees', are therefore potentially of use to the enemy as weapons. The testing evidently destroyed poor Fräulein V. Since then the Germans have been searching for another such subject. They certainly know of our Tom Pile, and attempts have been made to kidnap the boy.

Tom Pile has been shown to have similarly exceptional and potentially dangerous powers of control over his environment. The true extent of these are currently under investigation by Jack Carmody. Jack is closer in age to the boy, and a good bond of trust and friendship has developed between them. It seems that telekinesis – the power to move objects with the mind – is just one of Tom's abilities. This makes it even more vital that he, and any other figure in his position, be fully protected in the national interest.

I apologize – there is a lot here to take in. However, I thought it important to bring you up to speed. I will be piecing together the various elements of the ongoing story from a selected set of verbatim witness accounts, wire recordings and the like; and keeping records in a detailed journal. If there is anything I can help you with regarding this operation or any other matter, do not hesitate to contact me.

Your comrade in arms,

SECRET
WAR DEPARTMENT

Holloway

CHAPTER ONE

Douarnenez, Brittany, France
October 1941

It was not the usual kind of storm. There was no rain, for a start. Pierre Bouchard, skipper of the fishing boat *Le Sillon*, would have expected rain. The wet slate colour of the sky certainly promised it. There were low clouds too. They were darker grey, and stacked up well beyond the harbour wall. There were flashes of lightning inside the clouds, but there was no thunder and as yet no rain. The granite of the loading dock was relatively dry.

There was another dazzling but silent flash of light over the sea.

'*Sacrebleu!* Did you see that?' Bouchard said.

'Ball lightning,' said Pascal, his son, screwing up his eyes. He was tall, and looked older than his fourteen years. He had a head of unruly dark curls and eyes of a clear Breton-sea blue.

Skipper Bouchard nodded and spat on the ground. 'Either that or the Germans are up to something.'

'Should we be taking her out at all?' Pascal said, jumping down from the harbour onto the deck.

'It's always worth a try,' his father said, scanning round the harbour. Most of the fleet was still tied up, waiting out the weather. 'Chance to get a head start on the others. I hear they caught poor Madec. He was helping an Allied airman – fished him off a rescue buoy.' He shook his head. 'Fishing too far out, close to the limit.'

Bouchard himself had rescued more than one downed British airman and helped several more on the secret route back to Britain. 'If it's true, then Morvan said they might ban the fishing altogether. Even in-shore fishing.'

'They couldn't do that, could they?' Pascal said. He was over-eager and brave, only too anxious to do his bit; to help downed airmen, or anybody else who was fighting the Nazis.

His father shrugged. He never let on too much to Pascal about his Resistance work. Leaked information was dangerous. The Germans used any methods to crack Resistance cells. He couldn't expose Pascal to torture. He had heard stories.

'They're capable of anything,' he said. 'Mind you, if you ask me, it'll be cutting off their nose to spite their face. Where will they get their fish from? Spain, at twice the price? It won't last.'

He gestured to Pascal, who reached up beside the cabin window and pulled on the rope that operated the hooter. A single fierce blast echoed around the Place du Grand Quai.

'Let her go now, son. Take her out,' the skipper said. The rope was uncoiled from the bollard and pulled down onto the deck, and Bouchard jumped down after it.

'Here we go,' Pascal said while his father coiled the rope up around his elbow.

Another bolt of bright, silent lightning lit up the sky.

They chugged a kilometre or more out from the harbour, until they seemed to be almost in the eye of the storm. It still raged, strangely silent, overhead. Pascal had never seen a storm quite like it. Great flashes of ball lightning showed blue-white behind the clouds. The sea itself, though, remained almost calm. There was a swell, but that was to be expected in late October. The air felt charged with static electricity. The hairs on Pascal's arms stood up and he shivered inside his slicker.

He and his father set the nets and waited. There were no other boats to be seen as yet.

'I heard something about poor Malboeuf too,' Bouchard said.

'What about him?' Pascal asked.

'Arrested . . . German patrol caught him hiding two Poles in his house – Jews most likely. Times are hard – we must all be very careful.' As he spoke, he looked at Pascal intently, as if to emphasize the danger.

An hour later the heavens opened. The rain poured down, almost vertically out of the rolling dark clouds. The lightning flashes pulsed again. Shafts of light hit the surface of the sea, one after the other.

Pascal looked up and scanned the sky. 'Those look like searchlight beams, but shining downwards. I thought a plane was out looking for something, but there's no plane up there. No sound either,' he said, shielding his eyes again. 'Why is it all so quiet?'

'I wouldn't know, son,' Bouchard said. 'Come on – time to earn our soup.'

He had tacked in a half-circle. Now it was time to start hauling in the net. Cascades of thrashing silver sardines flowed out and onto the deck. Pascal swept them down into the hold with his hands.

Then the net yielded an even bigger haul. Among the flickers of silver he saw a darker shape – a slumped body. It lay face down, tangled among the netting and gleaming fish.

'Look at this,' Pascal said, waving over to his father. He struggled forward across the rolling, wet deck and did his best to untangle the body from the netting. 'It's a girl,' he called out.

He took a knife from his belt and cut the tangle of netting wrapped around the body. Once she was free, he turned the girl over onto her back.

She was wearing a long dark dress with a rust-coloured apron tied over it. She was as pale as the fish bellies all around her, her head haloed by a tangle of long blonde hair; her eyes gazed, apparently sightless, up into the rain.

'A proper mermaid,' Pascal murmured under his breath.

'Looks like it,' his father said. 'We've finally gone and fished one in. Poor drowned child,' he added, and felt her wrist. Then he lowered his head down to her breast. It was at that point that she suddenly coughed and sprayed a mouthful of seawater out into his face.

'It's a ruddy miracle,' Bouchard said, crossing himself. 'She's alive.'

'She is that,' Pascal agreed. 'I can feel her pulse, but she's very cold.'

'We must turn back.' The skipper took off his waterproof and laid it over the girl.

'Where did she come from? There's no sign of another boat out here,' Pascal wondered.

'Submarine?' Bouchard suggested.

'Maybe she just fell out of the sky,' Pascal said. 'She looks like an angel with that hair.'

CHAPTER TWO

As they made their way back, Pascal tried to talk to the girl. They had to be on their guard at all times, so he remained suspicious. After all, she might turn out to be some sort of spy or agent. It was quite possible that this was some sort of trap set by the Germans to catch them out; to break up the Resistance network which, Pascal knew, was run by his father. It seemed unlikely, but the way things were going with the occupation, you could never be sure of anything or anyone. Friends betrayed friends, neighbours betrayed neighbours.

The girl did not reply at first. She just stared ahead, unblinking. She appeared to be in a state of shock.

'Where are you from?' Pascal asked her more than once – without getting any response. He looked over at his father, who just shook his head.

But as they approached the harbour, she finally answered in a whisper, 'From there and from here.' She moved her hand out from underneath the skipper's oilskin and pointed up into the sky. 'From there too – and I saw you there. I know you.' Then she looked at the harbour area ahead, with the houses of Douarnenez rising up behind.

Once they had docked, they carried the soaking girl up the stone steps and sat her on a bollard by the harbour wall. She was still pale, and shivering, her arms wrapped tightly round herself. Her clothes appeared to steam in the weak sunlight.

'She's wet through,' Bouchard said. 'She'll need some dry clothes eventually; for now, this will have to do.' He wrapped a blanket from the cabin around her.

Pascal rubbed her cold, blue-white hands. She was clutching something in one of them: a fragment of metal. He took it out of her hands and tucked it into her pinafore pocket. Then they carried her over to the Café Atlantique.

A small group of locals soon gathered around them as they approached. 'What happened to her?' one of them called out. 'Is she safe?' There were mutterings, murmurs of suspicion. It was what Bouchard would have expected. Anything unusual was a cause for suspicion. People had very soon grown to mistrust even their nearest and dearest. Malboeuf had even been betrayed by his own sister. It was a sad state of affairs. As Bouchard – and some of his colleagues in the Resistance – had already saved more than one British airman and hidden him until his British contact had got him safely back, he had much to lose and much to fear.

'We saved this poor girl from drowning, that's all,' he said. 'She's very cold – she needs a hot drink.' He ordered a hot chocolate. 'Put a dash of something good in it,' he said to Mme Berthou.

'Sure that's not for you?' she said with a grin. 'Where'd she come from anyway, poor little thing?'

'Fished her out with the sardines. Astonishing – right in the middle of the sea,' Bouchard replied with a shrug.

By the time the girl was drinking the hot chocolate, some of the townspeople had come into the café.

'Was she just floating in the sea, way out there then?' M. Berthou, the owner of the café, was polishing glasses at the bar.

'We didn't notice her until we pulled in the net,' Bouchard said. 'There she was, all bundled up with the fish.'

'We thought she was some sort of mermaid. Well, we thought she was dead, to tell the truth,' Pascal said.

'Until she coughed up a litre of cold seawater right into my dad's face, that is.'

'She reminds me of someone . . . of something that happened years ago,' Bouchard said. 'It's the colour of that hair of hers.'

'What about her hair?' Berthou asked.

'The colouring – that very blonde colour; almost white. It reminds me of the Garel family. I went to school with one of them . . .'

'The Garels?'

'You know them. It was a while ago – maybe before you took over here at the Atlantique. Whole family – mother, father, two children – were lost. They all drowned in a storm. Over thirty years ago, it was. I was

just a lad myself, younger even than my boy Pascal here. Well, all but one. Just the uncle, Hervé – he survived. He still lives here in the town. You must know him . . . Hervé Garel – he often drinks here. It was his brother's family that was lost. He never had any children of his own. They all drowned that day.'

'Oh,' Berthou said, 'I know who you mean – he comes in here quite a lot; not every day, but regularly. Used to play boules in the square in summer. The coming of the Germans cheered him up no end. He likes order and the rule of law. It used to be just a coffee and a *pain au chocolat*; now he lays down the law with everybody he talks to. But what's he got to do with this girl?'

Pascal knelt down beside her. 'What's your name?' he said quietly, not wishing to break the fragile link he was sure he had established on the boat.

'I don't think I know my name,' she said. 'I can't remember much of anything except the sky and the sea.' She fixed him with her very blue eyes. 'Who are you?' she asked with a slight smile.

'I am Pascal Bouchard,' he said. 'I helped pull you out of the water. You can't remember how you got here, then?'

'No,' she said.

'What if I was to say the name "Garel" to you, my dear?' Bouchard interrupted.

The girl looked up. There was no reaction on her face. It remained a fixed and frightened-looking mask. She shrugged. Then she said, 'I was with the angels. The angels brought me here.'

He shook his head, then pulled Pascal to his feet. 'Perhaps she has escaped from an institution . . . Talk of angels by anybody but Father Duduyer is a sure sign that a person has something wrong up there,' he said, and tapped his head.

Then he looked up and smiled. 'Look, here comes Hervé Garel himself. Maybe he can shed some light upon this mystery. Go and fetch him over here, Pascal.'

The man coming into the café had a shock of very white hair, and the tanned and weathered face of a seafarer. He wore an old naval pea coat and a beret. Pascal brought him over to where Bouchard was standing. Beside him, the girl was sitting hunched over with her back turned, hands wrapped round her cup of hot chocolate.

'Ah, Monsieur Garel, good day to you,' Bouchard said. He stepped forward and took his hand. 'I'm sorry if I sound dramatic – it may be nothing at all – but I want you to meet this girl. We fished her out with our sardine catch this morning, and something about her struck me . . .'

It was then that the girl turned round and looked up at M. Garel. Bouchard's voice trailed off into silence.

Garel looked down at the girl for a moment, and the girl looked back at him. Suddenly he cried out, 'Oh my God, no, it can't be . . . our little Annick,' and then he fainted, and like a felled tree he crashed down among the surrounding tables, scattering glasses and cups.

CHAPTER THREE

Captain Holloway's office, Dept 116, London

I went down the stairs into the depths of the
department to see how Tom Pile was getting on. It
was late in the afternoon, and pretty soon it would be
time to for him to come home – that is, back to my
aunt Dolly's house.

I had been working for Captain Holloway for some
time now, and it had been the most exciting period of
my life. He had discovered me when I was a nipper.
This was partly due to the efforts of my Aunt Dolly.
She – and only she – had spotted things about me, her
late brother's only child, when I was very little. Some
of what I could do impressed her; some of it had
properly scared her, like the time I saw a real ghost.

I saw odd patterns in things; I noticed things. I could
predict thunder and much more. When I was in the

infants' school, I was very quick at sums and reading. I was soon moved up, and then on to special tutors. I was tried and tested over and over. That was when Captain Holloway heard about me. We went to see him down in the country – ostensibly so that I could study the moon through his telescope. Last year he recruited me for his new office, secretly investigating all sorts of strange and unexplained things. That was when we found young Tom Pile, down in Dorset. He lives with me at Aunt Dolly's house now.

Tom is very special indeed. A boy snatched up from his own time and dropped down into ours. A boy with powers, most of which we don't understand . . . Mind you, neither does he. So we are testing him and his abilities. Tom loves it, of course. Nearly every day he finds out new things about himself. The captain has given me the task of supervising the testing – which I had privately dubbed 'the Carmody Casebooks' – while he himself is down in Dorset with Staff Sergeant Shaw, a fierce lady scientist from the department, who is quite a match for him. They were working on the remains of something buried deep in a hill in Dorset.

I was letting Tom ramble on, but in a controlled way.

My aunt Dolly, bless her, had welcomed him to her house with open arms. The bureau cover story was that he had been orphaned in a bombing raid and was a ward of Captain Holloway's – which, in a way, he was. I now shared the big front bedroom with Tom. It used to be my study when I was growing up. Now there were two beds in it, one on either side wall.

Among her other qualities, Aunt Dolly was very good at managing our rations. For our tea that evening she had made a beef stew. There was no one to touch her at make do and mend. If she had skimped on any of the usual ingredients in her tasty stew – most things were now strictly rationed – we didn't notice.

'Too much parsnip for my taste, Jack,' she said, wrinkling her nose a little. She looked across the table and smiled at Tom. 'It's very good to see you getting a bit of meat back on your bones, Tom. You were that skinny when Jack first brought you here, and now look at you. You've filled out good and proper, in spite of all this ruddy rationing.'

'This stew is very nice, missus,' Tom said.

'There you go again, Tom. What have I said to you? You must get used to calling me Dolly – or Auntie, if you like – and there's an end to it. The secret to a good stew, I reckon, is the dumplings. You have to have proper dumplings in a stew, otherwise it's all a bit thin. How is the lovely Captain Holloway, by the by?' my aunt said, turning to me.

'Still down in the West Country,' I said. 'Can't say more than that.'

'Ooh, I might have guessed. It's always the same. Everything you do is so hush-hush, Jack. It does annoy me so. As if I'd go and say anything untoward to anyone about anything you and your department get up to.'

'You wouldn't mean to, of course,' I said, 'but something might slip out by accident and the wrong ears might be listening. Then where would we be? No, it's best to be like Dad, eh, and keep Mum.'

'Keep Mum?' Tom said, clearly puzzled.

'It's a phrase, Tom. You see it on the posters. It's a pun. "Keeping Mum" means keeping quiet, keeping your mouth shut – not a word to anyone, careless talk costs lives, and all that. But it also means looking after Mum – keeping her in the style to which she is accustomed. It's a double meaning, see.'

'Listen to him, Tom. Dear me, I always said he was vaccinated with a gramophone needle,' Aunt Dolly said, shaking her head.

For anyone who didn't already know about Tom Pile and his secrets, merely entering the underground room where he was being tested and seeing what was going on in there would have come as a monumental shock. I am sure Aunt Dolly would have fainted clean away.

That afternoon, for instance, Tom was sitting on a bentwood chair, his eyes closed. One of the lab technicians appointed by Captain Holloway was seated at a desk in the adjoining room, observing everything and making notes, while also recording what happened on 16mm cine film and a wire recorder through a large two-way mirror.

The room itself was filled with an odd assortment of domestic bits and pieces – pots and pans and so forth. I saw a brown enamel official War Ministry teapot, two saucepans, several shiny tin film cans and lids, some teacups and saucers, spoons, china bowls of precious white sugar cubes, a chair or two, and a government-issue paraffin stove. Nothing unusual about that lot, you might think, and normally you'd be right. No – what would upset the apple cart for the uninitiated, like Aunt Dolly and almost everybody else, was that all these things were up in the air.

They were circulating slowly around the room near the ceiling. They weren't dangling on fine strings like the stuff in the Claude Rains film *The Invisible Man*. No, these things were just floating around freely, all being controlled by Tom Pile; controlled by the force of his mind. I watched through the two-way glass for a minute. It was hypnotic. Tom sat in the middle of it all like the planet Saturn, and the stuff just revolved slowly above him like Saturn's rings, only made up of old kitchen stuff.

'He's able to control it better and better, the more he practises,' the technician whispered. 'I don't think the captain or any of us here is aware of a fraction of what this boy can really do or will do in the future.'

'I doubt whether Tom is really aware himself,' I said, a bit too loudly.

Tom must have heard my voice. He lost concentration, and all the stuff fell out of the air and landed with a crash on the floor.

I opened the door and went in.

'Sorry, Jack,' Tom said. 'I seem to have made a bit of a mess.'

'A few broken ministry teacups won't lose us the war, Tom,' I told him.

He stood up, stretched out his arms and then picked his way through the debris on the floor. 'Too much of this makes me feel very sleepy,' he said, covering a yawn with his hand.

'I can imagine,' I said. 'I reckon you could clean up on the music hall, you know. You'd be the best magician ever. Even the great Houdini couldn't compete with you, Tom. Shame you're not allowed to show everyone what you can do. I'd really like to see their faces.'

CHAPTER FOUR

Gallows Hill, Dorset

Captain Holloway stood on Gallows Hill, just above the village of Litton Cheney in West Dorset, and looked down at the sea. His grey hair, longish by military standards, was whipping across his high domed forehead. It didn't seem to trouble him as he sipped tea from the plastic Thermos cup in his hand.

Staff Sergeant Shaw, however, was forced to hold onto her headscarf with her free hand.

'As far as the local army barracks are concerned,' he shouted against the wind, 'we've brought down an experimental German weapon – all very hush-hush. As for the locals, I told them that the army had downed a bomber and it had opened up some interesting Roman remains.'

'I rather wish it had,' Miss Shaw said, turning away from the wind, back towards the entrance to the dig. 'The atmosphere down there is very odd . . . literally unearthly.'

She headed towards the earthworks, where an army sentry saluted her. 'At ease, Corporal,' she said. It gave her an odd kind of thrill every time she remembered to do something military. Her rank of staff sergeant was an honorary one. She had been seconded to Department 116 from Cambridge University, where she had published several papers on the possibilities of extra-terrestrial life, and was a founder member of the Interplanetary Society. She would have been dismissed by most as a crank, but not by Captain Holloway. She fitted into his department like a hand in a glove.

She and the captain walked down the slope that led to the hollow chamber. The remains of the craft left by the 'angels' Tom had talked about was partially uncovered: a curved grey hull with no distinguishing marks of any kind, not even a scratch.

'Gives me the willies every time we turn the corner and see it there,' she said, taking off her scarf and patting her hair.

'I know what you mean, Miss Shaw, but even so, I am still thrilled that we can even see and touch such an artefact.'

They went down the temporary wooden staircase and carried on with the work of easing away the clay from the underside of the hull.

'At some point, Miss Shaw,' said the captain, 'we shall get young Jack Carmody and Tom Pile down here to see what we have discovered. Perhaps we shall in turn find out what *they* have discovered.'

CHAPTER FIVE

Douarnenez

The procession left the little fishermen's church at eleven thirty in the morning, straight after mass.

The sun was bright and the sky unnaturally crisp and clear. The group were mostly dressed in the Breton style, the women's heads covered in elaborate white lace coifs. It looked like a traditional 'pardon' – only this was something more. In the centre of the procession, carried on high, was the plaster statue of a winged angel, rather than the usual one of St Anne or the Virgin. The model fishing boat that usually hung from brass chains over the altar was being held aloft too. At the front, dressed in white, walked the girl who had been rescued so mysteriously from the sea. One of her hands was held by M. Garel, a man who had lost his family to the sea, along with his faith in God – until, that is, the miraculous return of his niece; for he firmly believed that this was who the found girl was. The other hand was held by the local priest, Father Duduyer.

Pierre Bouchard and his son, Pascal, followed at the rear, just behind the small choir. The procession was heading for the beach. While they walked, the choir sang a hymn.

Bouchard had advised Hervé Garel not to go through with the service. 'It will only draw unwanted attention from the Germans, and surely no one wants that.'

The old man would not listen, though. 'Not all of us are so against the German presence here, Bouchard,' he said.

As far as M. Garel was concerned, in his renewed belief, a real miracle had taken place. Praise and thanks must be offered to the deity, to his angels, and even to the occupying authorities, in the proper way. He had shown an old photograph of his lost family to anyone who was interested, and especially to Father Duduyer. The similarities between the supposedly drowned Annick and the girl washed up in Bouchard's nets was indeed strong, almost undeniable. Father Duduyer was glad to help; glad to welcome back into the fold one of his flock in the shape of M. Garel. He had happily agreed to hold a service of thanksgiving on the beach, along with a sea blessing.

The procession finally reached the Plage des Sables Blancs. On the way, they had picked up a few more of the townspeople, including a reporter from the local *La Dépêche de Brest*. The wide expanse of sand seemed suddenly almost crowded. The black Sunday-best coats flapped in the strong wind like flags, and the women held onto their lace coifs. The short service began.

Further away along the beach, perched high up on the cliffs, was a group of late-nineteenth-century villas. They belonged to rich Parisians who came every August for their seaside holidays. The houses were large and spacious compared to the fishermen's cottages. They had balconies and pointed turrets, and offered wide views of the sea. They also had new tenants. The rich Parisians would no longer come for August. The German officers garrisoned in the town had commandeered the best houses as soon as they arrived. On that fine October Sunday, two of them had set out on their horses, freshly delivered to them by train from Berlin.

It was a perfect morning for riding on the beach, skirting the edge of the surf. It was low tide, and as they rounded a large outcrop of rock, they saw the gathering.

'Look at this, Hans,' said the local commander, Hauptmann Meier. 'A folkloric ritual right on our doorstep.' Meier was a ramrod-straight soldier from the romantic German tradition; one of the old-fashioned officer class. He even had a livid sabre scar on one cheek, of which he was very proud.

'I think they call this ceremony a "pardon",' his second in command, Leutnant Richter, replied. Richter was the opposite of Hauptmann Meier: the modern Nazi world incarnate. He had shrewd narrowed eyes behind large gold-rimmed glasses, and never looked as if he had shaved closely enough – for which he was often rebuked by Meier. 'Very primitive,' he said. 'I think their priest is blessing the sea or something. I'm sure our Reichsmarschall Goering would approve,' he added with a chuckle, slumped over in his saddle.

Meier felt that he had built up a good relationship with the local townspeople. Indeed, many of the older, more conservative ones had openly welcomed the stability brought by the Germans – so much so that he was himself a little surprised. There was resistance, but it mostly came from the young. Right now, he had no desire to blunder in and spoil the ceremony. He ordered Richter to slow down as they approached the congregation across the white sand. They watched for a few minutes from a respectful distance; Richter handed his superior a pair of field glasses.

The priest seemed to be blessing first the statue of a winged angel, then a girl of fifteen or so, dressed in white, standing at the water's edge. The sound of a hymn drifted across the sand on the gusting wind.

'Folklore and superstition masked as respectable Catholic religion,' Meier said. 'Perhaps she is a sacrificial virgin.'

They waited until the ceremony was finished, and then slowly rode over.

Meier turned to the leutnant and said, 'Best I stay back here. You dismount and go on ahead – sound out the priest.'

Richter dismounted and walked over to the congregation, who quickly parted in groups, scattering across the sand, clearly nervous. It always gave him a thrill to cause such confusion and fear among subjected peoples.

As he walked, he held his riding crop behind his back, nodding and smiling false reassurance. He had no real wish to upset anyone at that moment; he was just curious about the meaning of what they had witnessed.

The people closest to the priest parted like the Red Sea at Richter's approach. It was as if they couldn't wait to get away from him. No one wanted any trouble.

Father Duduyer stood at the water's edge, holding the girl's hand; a white-haired old man stood on her other side. He was smiling; he seemed not to care that his sabots had got soaked.

Richter tapped the peak of his cap with the riding crop in salute. 'Good morning, Father,' he said in his impeccable French, inclining his head and smiling at the girl and the old man.

'Good morning, Officer,' Father Duduyer said, and instinctively he pulled the girl a little closer to him.

'The hauptmann and I were just watching your ceremony. We found it most interesting. Was it a pardon, a sea blessing, or a baptism?'

Before the priest could answer, the old man, grinning from ear to ear, said quickly, 'We were giving thanks, Officer, sir, and for a real honest-to-goodness miracle.'

'A real miracle?' Richter asked. 'You did say "a *real* miracle"? Are you so sure of that?'

'A great blessing and a miracle, sir. My niece, who was lost, has been returned to us from Hades – from the underworld; from death itself. Given up from the sea by the angels,' the old man said. 'A miracle – a real, true, verifiable miracle – has taken place.'

Father Duduyer made as if to silence the old man. 'He is understandably a little overexcited, sir,' he said.

'The rest of his immediate family were drowned, lost at sea, and now it seems that God has indeed seen fit to return this one girl to us.'

'When were this family lost at sea, and why have I heard nothing of it? You are aware that martial law applies here?'

'Oh no, bless you, good sir, you wouldn't have heard about it,' the old man said. 'They were lost to us thirty-five years ago, when I was a young man – my poor brother and his family. They were all presumed drowned, but now, God be praised, one of them has been returned to us alive and well, as you can see.'

Richter nodded. 'If true, then that is indeed a miracle.' He touched the peak of his cap. 'Who found this girl?' he called out to the crowd.

The old man spoke up at once. 'Why, it was Pierre Bouchard, bless him. There he is – just over there.'

Bouchard steeled himself as Richter approached him.

'Excuse me, sir, but I understand that you found this little "miracle" here,' the German officer said.

'That is true, we did,' Bouchard said. 'You will most likely think that the old man is mad,' he added.

'I don't think I need a Frenchman to tell me what to think, monsieur,' Richter said.

'But, you see,' Bouchard went on desperately, 'we made no claims. We just happened to be the ones who pulled the girl out of the sea in our nets.'

'Before we go any further, monsieur, why don't you come and explain all this to Hauptmann Meier over here.' Richter raised his arm and indicated the two horses and the single rider over by the rocks.

Bouchard turned to his son, Pascal. 'I won't be a moment.' He saw that tired look on Pascal's face; the look of continual fear, of resignation. He watched the anxiety descend over his poor son's face like a cloud.

The congregation were dispersing, hurrying away now that the German officers were there with them on the beach. The priest and the old man stayed where they were by the shoreline, both close to the girl.

Bouchard followed Richter and then told the hauptmann what had happened.

Meier shook his head. 'You all believe this?' he asked, genuinely puzzled. 'That here is a girl who drowned some thirty-five years ago and has now been miraculously returned at the same age as when she was lost?'

'The old man believes it,' Bouchard said with a shrug. 'It is true that the girl looks very like his family. Whether she really is, I can't say. The likeness is there. God moves in mysterious ways, after all.'

'What does the girl have to say about this?'

'She can't remember anything – except she says it was the angels who saved her and who returned her.'

'You say you fished her out in your nets. Were there no other boats or ships near you?'

'No, none.'

'It occurs to me that there is a more likely explanation. This child is the survivor of a failed attempt to smuggle something or someone in or out of the occupied territory here – for whatever misguided reason. Nothing miraculous about that, wouldn't you agree, monsieur?'

'Well, no, if that really was the case,' Bouchard said, bitterly regretting his involvement in the whole saga and foreseeing nothing but more scrutiny, and so more trouble, ahead.

'You will please make sure, monsieur ... er ...' Hauptmann Meier paused and raised his eyebrow, his head on one side to indicate a friendly enquiry. The effect was the opposite.

'Bouchard – Pierre Bouchard, sir.'

'You will please make sure, Monsieur Bouchard, that the miracle girl, the old man and you present yourselves at my offices in the *mairie* tomorrow morning at ten sharp. Until tomorrow, good day to you.'

With that, the two officers rode away along the beach.

Bouchard trudged back across the sand to break the bad news.

Memo 6

Translated from German original intercept
FILED Dept 116, Captain Holloway's Office

MESSAGE READS

FROM: Kohler, Office of the Unexplained & the Supernatural, Berlin
TO: All head offices of Occupation, Northern Zone, France & Belgium

MOST SECRET

During the course of day-to-day interrogations, individuals may
present themselves with odd or unlikely stories of survival. These
may include claims of 'angel' help or sightings of strange lights,
and many other explanations as to their condition. Ninety per cent
of these will be lunatics and other refuse. However, it is just
possible that they may yet prove to be persons of great interest to
this secret department. Any such encounters, however unlikely,
should be reported through the most secret channels to this office.

CHAPTER SIX

London

I had noticed recently that Tom was sleeping, if not badly, then strangely. It wasn't just the usual occasional interrupted night that we all suffered – trips down to the shelter when there were air raids, and all that. No, it was more his general pattern of sleep. At first I thought he must have been dreaming vividly because of what had happened to him. After all, he had been plucked from one era in history and dropped into another and very different one, forty years later. What's more, he had found himself in the middle of a war. Tom had experienced things that perhaps only a handful of specially selected humans had been through. He had surely been changed by those experiences in ways I could hardly imagine. It was no wonder that he had broken sleep patterns and perhaps suffered from disturbing dreams.

That night I was woken suddenly, and sat up in panic; by now we had got so used to being roused by the sirens that the slightest thing disturbed us. This was different, though. I had my old 'thunder' feeling. When I was very young, I had held my hands over the ears of my aunt Dolly – who hated thunder – because I knew that a thunderclap was coming. That instinct – whatever it was – I called my 'thunder' feeling. It always meant that something very odd was up.

I could just make out the hands of the clock on my bedside table. Two a.m. As usual, the blackout curtains were drawn tight over the upper bay window and the room was in pitch darkness. I could hear Tom calling out something very quietly. I sat up and just listened at first. I didn't want to wake him.

He seemed to be talking in another language. Perhaps his 'angels' were communicating with him, I thought.

I kept a pad, pencil and a shaded battery lantern by the bed, and we had a special telephone link to the bureau set up in the room in case of emergencies. I fumbled for the pencil and torch, and finally managed to pick everything up without making a noise. I didn't want to risk waking Tom mid-dream. I did my best to write down what I heard, but it didn't make much sense. This is what I wrote:

> 2 a.m. Tom talking in sleep. Sounds like
> 'ohnge/onhger', then 'mair', then 'mary' twice,
> then 'moor', then 'blonk', then, finally,
> 'almond', repeated twice.

I tried to see a pattern in the words. I'm usually good at that, and at languages too. My French and even my German were really quite fluent. However, I was very slow on the uptake here. I could see nothing much but odd repeated sounds. At first it seemed like the sort of nonsense that might come floating up out of a weird dream; then it sounded like a conversation. There were pauses, as if someone was speaking to Tom, and he was replying in his sleep. It still sounded like nonsense, but now it was more urgent nonsense. I kept writing – but suddenly pressed too hard and the pencil lead broke off.

There was a blackboard and chalk in the room, left over from when I had used it as a study. I went over to it with the shaded lantern.

It occurred to me that if what Tom called his 'angels' were contacting him in some way, I should record it. I set the lantern down on a side table, pointing at the blackboard, then listened carefully and wrote down what I could hear in reasonably neat lines across the board. Some of the same words came up again – 'moor', 'almond', 'ohnge'.

As I wrote them down, I noticed that the shadow of my hand changed angle as I wrote. Suddenly the room felt a degree or two colder. The light source was moving up. I looked over my shoulder and saw that the lantern was rising very slowly, floating in the air a little way above the side table. The hairs stood up on the back of my neck. When I turned round, I could just make out Tom. He was sitting up in bed now, his eyes wide open. They looked bright in the dark room, as if somehow lit from within. He was staring at me, but at the same time it was clear that he couldn't really see me. Instead he was looking through me at the blackboard.

All at once I felt the chalk being pulled hard across the surface of the blackboard. I let it go, and it popped out of my hand and hovered there before moving across the board on its own, writing something in neat, flowing looped letters, quite independent of my hand. After it had finished, it dropped down onto the carpet.

Tom slumped back onto his pillow and appeared to be asleep again. The lantern bumped gently back down onto the side table with a tinny clatter and promptly switched itself off.

I stood there in the dark, allowing my eyes to adjust. Finally I made out what the stick of white chalk had written in the middle of the blackboard.

Aidez-moi. Help me . . .

CHAPTER SEVEN

Captain Holloway's office

'The captain is still in Dorset,' I said to the middle-aged man standing in front of my desk. If I hadn't known better – if I had been the proverbial 'man on the Clapham omnibus' – I would have sworn that he was some stray French peasant who had wandered in by mistake; one of those pre-war onion sellers who used to go door to door on a bicycle festooned with strings of onions; or, better yet, a tanned and weather-beaten fisherman. He wore an old, patched pinstriped suit jacket, dirty blue work overalls, a Basque-style beret, and a jaunty red and white spotted kerchief tied at his dirty neck.

Of course, it was all a carefully crafted illusion. I knew exactly who he was. It was the 'jolly old uncle' himself, Lieutenant Sperring, a colleague of Captain Holloway's.

He was part of the SOE (Special Operations Executive) – or the Baker Street Irregulars, as they were known around our offices. (Baker Street was where they had their HQ.) They were as hush-hush as we were, if not more so.

'He's down at our archaeological dig,' I added, 'on the Gallows Hill site. Can I help?'

'Oh, I see . . . That's what you are calling it, is it? Ho ho.' He winked and nodded, then sat down opposite me with a sigh and stretched out his legs.

'I don't know about any of that, young Carmody,' he said. 'I just wanted to leave the captain a little something that caught my attention. It seems to me it might be just up his street. It's confirmed by this piece in a French local newspaper. I was wasting a bit of time over in Brittany a few days ago. You know the drill – blending in with my Resistance helper friends; organizing the transport of an airman through the system. I was waiting for my ride back over the pond to Blighty when I heard this amazing story. I got it from one of the fishing families, the Bouchards. They are very pro-British. They've got a boy who's a bit younger than you – about fifteen, I'd say, Jack. His name's Pascal – like the sweets.

'Good people, the Bouchards, and very brave. Pierre runs a special safe house for us in Douarnenez. Anyway,

I know my old friend Holloway, and I know you and he go in for all that weird spook stuff. Don't deny it. From what I hear, your "dig" in Dorset is a very weird place indeed. You'll need to get this article properly translated. Read it for yourself – I hear your French is good enough. I've been up all night in a smelly fishing boat – otherwise I'd stay and tell you about it myself – but I'm off to my club for a good wash and brush-up. It's a strange story all right, though. Give the captain my best when you next see him.' Sperring chucked the rolled-up newspaper onto the desk. 'You'll see I've circled it in red. It's on the front page. I've an odd feeling I'll be seeing you again before too long.'

'Thanks, I'll read it,' I said.

Then he was gone.

A few minutes later I had managed to translate it, and I knew Sperring had been right about our interest.

I had another of my tingling sensations – a really strong sense of premonition. These feelings are rarely wrong. The story was more than just interesting; it was vital, and it was one that the captain should see at once. *Aidez-moi*, the chalk had written on the board . . . that meant 'help me' in French. Of course, all the odd words Tom had said in his sleep now fitted into place.

La Dépêche
de Brest & de l'Ouest

Edition de 5 heures

BREST
23, 27, a, 28
rue Jean-Jaurès
Tél 25.33-14.47
Bureau à Brest
Paris 33.13.3

MARDI
28
OCTOBRE
1941

DOUARNENEZ MYSTERY CATCH

Skipper Pierre Bouchard recently pulled up more than he had bargained for in his fishing nets. 'It was little after eleven in the morning,' he told our reporter. 'We'd been unable to fish earlier because of the weather. There was a strange storm at sea, if you remember. We hauled nets as soon as the weather cleared. Among the second catch my son, Pascal, saw a body. It was a girl of about fifteen. We pulled her free. She was cold, but astonishingly she was alive. There was no sign of any other vessel within range. I was naturally puzzled as to where she could have come from. We wrapped her up and took her to the harbour.' They landed the girl at the Grand Quai, and she was taken into the local Atlantic Café, where she soon regained consciousness. The girl's colouring and appearance reminded M. Bouchard of the family of a M. Garel, a resident of Douarnenez. Our records show that several members of the Garel family were drowned in a fishing accident some thirty-five years ago. M. Garel, the only surviving member, was fetched to the scene from his house on the rue du Pont. Upon seeing the rescued girl, he apparently collapsed in shock. When he had recovered, he fell to his knees and claimed there had been a miracle. He identified the girl as young Annick Garel, his lost niece. Indeed, she strongly resembled the girl in a family photograph. He said he was sure it was her. The girl, however, did not recognize him, and had no memory of how she came to be in the sea, except through the offices of the 'angels'. A service of thanksgiving for her return was later performed on the beach. The girl, her uncle and the crew were questioned by the authorities, and most were later released. The girl, however, was kept at the mairie in protective custody, awaiting further questioning and medical reports.

I had the relevant section of the newspaper photographed, along with my translation, and sent it off in a pouch down to Tom's old cottage in Litton Cheney, where the captain's billet was. I added a typed note about the dreams and the words Tom had uttered, along with my new thoughts. I had been very slow to notice what was so obvious in this case . . .

Word sounded like *ohnge*. In French this would be *ange*, which means 'angel'.

Sounded like *almond*. In French this would be *allemande*, which means 'German'.

Sounded like *meeor*. In French this would be *mur*, which means 'wall'.

Sounded like *blonk*. In French this would be *blanc*, which means 'white'.

Sounded like *mair*. In French this would be *mer*, which means 'sea'.

Sounded like *Mary*. In French this would be *mairie*, which means 'town hall' . . .

and so on.

Suddenly it all made sense. The mysterious girl who had been washed up in the fisherman's net was surely another of what the captain now referred to as 'the returned'. Just like Tom and that poor girl in Germany,

Fräulein V, who had not survived the Nazis' interrogation, this girl had been taken by the 'angels' at some point in the past, and then returned to our time. In her case it seemed that she had somehow been dropped into the sea. The captain was going to be very excited . . .

So far I hadn't said anything to Tom about his night talking, but now seemed the ideal time. After all, the girl must have been communicating with him in some way. Who knew what was possible between those who had been 'returned'? These were just three that we knew about. How many more might there be out there, and what else might they be able to do?

Tom was down in the underground room again, using his mind to shift a series of solid-looking weights across a table. He looked up and smiled when I came in. It was rare to see him smile broadly. I decided it was because he was bored with moving things about and welcomed a distraction.

'How about a cup of tea?' I suggested.

'Yes please,' he said.

A voice came through the loudspeaker from the observation room. 'Just make sure you get him back here when we need him. I've got a very excited Colonel Clarke coming from War Ministry Liaison – he wants a look at our Wunderkind here. He's a tricky customer; not a man who likes to be kept waiting.'

I sat Tom down in Captain Holloway's chair and laid my notes out in front of him, plus the copy of the French newspaper.

'This is a list of words I noted down while you were talking in your sleep last night, Tom,' I said.

'Was I?' he asked. 'Out loud?'

'Yes, out loud, Tom, and on more than one night too. I thought you must have been having some strange dreams. It sounded as if you were talking to someone too – the same words kept cropping up. I couldn't make much sense of them until I read this . . .' I pointed to the newspaper article. 'I realized that you were speaking in French. Does that make any sense?'

'Don't think I know any French . . . do I?' Tom said. 'But I *have* had the same dream a few times. I saw the light of the angels, and there was a girl . . . She spoke to me from somewhere, and she sounded – I don't know . . . sad or worried.'

'I think it's *this* girl, Tom. She's the one speaking to you.' I tapped the newspaper article. 'Here is the translation. Read it.'

Tom quickly read the article. 'They found her in the sea. In my dream I could hear the sea too.'

'She's asking for help, Tom. They've got her locked up – the Germans, that is. She is just like you – she was taken by the angels and then returned. It seems that she can reach out to you with her thoughts. It's like when Aunt Dolly listens in on the wireless . . . she has to tune into the station she wants on the dial. Because of who you are, you can somehow tune in and hear this girl over in France.'

'What will we do?' asked Tom.

'What we will do is talk to Captain Holloway. I've sent a copy of all this to Litton Cheney. I suspect we'll be summoned down there to talk to him face to face.'

CHAPTER EIGHT

Dorset

Sure enough, we were sent for at once. Captain Holloway met us at Dorchester station. His big forehead was tanned after all the time he'd spent outdoors. On our way to Litton Cheney we passed close to the 'dig' on Gallows Hill before turning down the steep road into the village.

'I'll let you both take a look at the site tomorrow,' he said. 'It's all very exciting and mysterious.'

Tom's quiet wariness returned once we were back in his old village.

'It must be difficult for you, Tom,' Captain Holloway said, locking the car, 'seeing all this again – the cottage, your old home, and so near to the place where your family is buried.'

'I keep thinking it will all change,' Tom said. 'That I'll be back here again as it was. That it'll all go back to how it used to be. Even though I know it won't ever be like that. Couldn't be, now, could it?' He looked back down over the hills towards the dark sea.

'No, you're with us in our time now, Tom, for better or worse. Come on in. I put one of Mrs Feaver's pies in the oven for supper.'

We sat in Tom's old kitchen. The captain had persuaded the army to do it up for him. The kitchen range had been fixed and the walls were freshly distempered in white. It felt quite cheerful in the lamplight. We ate rabbit pie and drank some cider. Later, by the fire in the parlour, we went over what had happened.

'It seems we are learning new things every day about what you are capable of, Tom. Now it appears that you can hear this girl in your head; that she is able to communicate with you, and over some distance. Did you remember the dreams when you woke?'

'Not really,' Tom said. 'I could just see the girl, I think. Something stayed with me – or at least, her voice did, even though I couldn't understand what she was saying.'

'Yes, awkward that. It's a shame that the beings – the angels, whatever they are – didn't build in an ability to translate. Luckily Jack here has good French and is pretty quick on the uptake.'

'My French is good, but I was really slow on the uptake in this case,' I said. 'I didn't realize what the words were until I saw that newspaper article.'

'Amazing luck for my old mucker Sperring to spot that. Mind you, he keeps his eyes open. He knows what makes me tick all right. I've alerted our listening station to pay special attention to radio traffic between that area of Brittany and Berlin. It can only be a matter of time before they realize what they've got locked away there. They will either transfer the poor girl to Germany, or send one of their own men up to interview and assess her in Douarnenez. We can't let either of these happen.'

'How do we stop it?' I said.

'Quite straightforward really.' The captain poured another glass of cider for himself. He let the cloudy drink settle and then grinned across at Tom and me. 'You two will have to go over there and rescue her. Then you can bring her safely back here. Imagine what we can achieve with the two of you, with both returnees.'

There followed what seemed like a long silence, broken only by the clock ticking on the mantel shelf.

'Us?' I said finally in disbelief. 'Us? You want *us* to go over to occupied France, into enemy territory?'

'Exactly that. You and young Tom here. People go over all the time in a very hush-hush way. Our friend Sperring will take you. He knows his way around and he speaks the local Breton lingo like a native. You'll take a British fishing boat, then a French boat, then a collapsible dinghy. Miles of shoreline there, and much of it still unprotected. He'll get you in and out again, if anyone can.'

I could feel my heart beating faster. I was both terrified and excited.

'Surely,' I said, 'we can't risk such a thing – not with Tom here. He can't be expected to know what to do faced with soldiers and guns and all that.'

'Will we have to fight, then?' Tom asked. He sounded puzzled, as if he were still digesting the information.

'I don't think so, Tom. You will be a very small and well-disguised party – civilians, fishermen. Just the three of you – and Sperring is a highly trained fighter, should it come to that. You, Tom, have ever-changing abilities, which I am sure you will put to good use if you have to. Imagine how easily you might demolish a lock or disarm a sentry! I have already arranged with my old friend Colonel Gauntlett, from the barracks in Burton Bradstock, for you to run through everything with Lieutenant Sperring tomorrow, at a secret safe house.'

'I can't believe it,' I said. 'You're going to send us off on a mission, merely on the basis of a few dreams and a French newspaper report?'

'Precisely,' the captain said. 'That kind of information is all we ever have to go on, Jack. Bed, now. Come on, we have an early start up at the dig. And watch out for those dreams, Tom.'

CHAPTER NINE

I couldn't sleep. My mind was racing with the thought of actually crossing the Channel and entering an occupied country . . . enemy territory. Tom had fallen asleep within a few minutes. Perhaps he felt more comfortable in his old home.

All through the night the church clock struck the hours. Eventually I got out of bed, pulled back the blackout curtain and looked out of the window. I saw old Mr Feaver, the ARP warden, out on patrol, holding up his shaded lantern, his scarf tied over his helmet. A sea fret had seeped in; it swirled around in the dim light. I saw him stop by Captain Holloway's staff car beside the old vegetable patch opposite. I drew back from the window and closed the curtain, worried it might give him a fatal shock if he saw me at the window, looking like a ghost.

It was then that Tom started talking. The familiar words came in the familiar order, just as I had written them down.

'*Aidez-moi* . . .' Help me . . .

I left the room and crossed over to where I assumed the captain was asleep – but he was sitting up at a table in his room. In front of him lay maps and charts; a fragment of the odd rainbow metal that Tom had brought back from wherever the angels had taken him glinted under a low lamp.

'Captain,' I said, 'come and listen.'

He turned to me and shook his head, as if I had just woken him. 'What is it, Jack?'

'It's Tom,' I said. 'He's talking in his sleep again.'

We stood in the doorway and listened as the French words left Tom's mouth, a little distorted by his Dorset accent.

'You see why I was confused,' I whispered.

'I do indeed, Jack,' the captain agreed.

'I saw her quite clearly in my dream,' Tom said at breakfast. 'It was as if she was gazing into a mirror, only I was the mirror. She had white-blonde hair . . . She looked very worried. I saw something else as well. There was a huge secret thing trying to get out from deep underground.'

'I'm guessing that this underground "secret thing" is the craft at the dig,' the captain said.

There was a knock at the door and Mr Feaver came in, his ARP helmet held out in front of him as if he was collecting pennies for a charity box.

'Well, good morning to you, Captain – and there you are too, young Corporal Jack. Blow me if it's not that boy we found as well! Goodness me!' He stepped back a little in surprise. 'Never expected to see him back here again. How is it up in London, then? All they bombs keeping you on your toes, I'll be bound.'

'Sometimes, Mr Feaver,' I said. 'Yes, they do. But London can take it. She'll pull through.'

'Oh, right you are. I have a message for you, Captain. Came in this morning from over at the barracks. There won't be anyone much to help guard the Gallows Hill dig today. They'll send a replacement sentry but they've got a bit of a flap on over at Burton Bradstock.'

'What sort of flap?' the captain asked.

'Special invasion training, or something like it, I would say.'

'Well, it suits me well enough, Mr Feaver. I've got these two to help me this morning. Cup of tea before you go?'

'Normally I would, but I've been on patrol all night and I'm just off home, so if you'll excuse me . . .' He put his tin hat back on his head.

After he had gone the captain said, 'Well, that helps in a way – no flapping ears at the dig. We can talk freely.'

'Tom's tests have been going very well,' I told him.

Tom concentrated on the empty tea mug on the table. Almost at once it rose up into the air and hovered there.

'Well, well,' the captain said. 'Look at that.'

'Better than a show at the Palladium,' I said.

'It certainly is.'

'He can move really heavy stuff too now – weights and bigger things. I've seen him.'

'What does it feel like, Tom, when it's happening?' the captain asked.

'Don't know really,' he said. 'I just picture it in my head, lifting, and it happens.'

'It's most important, Tom, that you keep this extraordinary gift between ourselves and those who are in the know about you – which is not very many outside our department. At the moment that includes our friend Sperring,' the captain said. 'Once you are in occupied France it will be even more important. If the

Germans were to get wind of what you can do, I dread to think what might happen. Of course, you may have to use that power of yours when push comes to shove, but don't go making French loaves float around the *boulangerie*!'

'He won't,' I said. 'I'll be looking out for him. He'll be fine.'

Communiqué

Intercepted and translated for
Captain Holloway's office, Dept 116

FROM: Office of the Mayor, Occupying Forces,
Douarnenez Headquarters

CONFIDENTIAL

We are holding a girl here. She is either a spy landed by means of a
British submarine, or a person likely to be of interest to your
department, as per your recently circulated MEMO number 6. She was
apparently dredged up by one of the local fishermen out of an empty
sea. Another local, a M. Garel, claimed her as his niece Annick, who
he believed drowned with the rest of the family some 35 years ago.
The drowning is on official record. The girl would thus have to be
well over 50 years of age, though she is no more than 15. She is
mostly unresponsive to our questions and claims/appears to have lost
most, if not all, of her memory. She has no proper account of how
she came to be in the sea. Her only explanation is that she was put
there by 'angels'. We can of course hold her here indefinitely. I
shall question her further and will report to your office again in
due course.

CHAPTER TEN

Gallows Hill, Dorset

The dig was securely fenced off. There were NO
TRESPASS and UNEXPLODED BOMB warnings, complete
with skull-and-crossbones signs. These were surrounded
by rows of double-stranded barbed wire topped with
razor wire. All were supported by tall metal fence posts.
There were some lights on gantries at intervals. It
looked like a deserted high-security prison camp.

'Best way to keep out the curious,' the captain said
as we stumbled over the churned-up earth. At the crest
of the hill there was a built-up entrance. It looked like
the opening of a mine working, all shored up with
dozens of sandbags, and then railway-sleeper-sized
wooden supports, all roofed over with corrugated iron.
Just inside the doorway hung some torches, along with
pickaxes and shovels and other paraphernalia.

'Take a torch each,' the captain said. 'We didn't really have to dig down that much – the craft obviously made its own tunnel, like some kind of burrowing mole,' he added as he ushered us in.

I sensed straight away that Tom was both nervous and excited – and fearful ... It was hard to read him sometimes. At first he stood awkwardly, half in and half out of the entrance, as if unsure whether to go on.

The captain was already heading down the shallow incline, his torch lighting the way ahead.

I felt something strange in the atmosphere of that place at once; something other than the damp chill. I sensed that it was caused by more than just the depth and the location. There was a strong intimation of something other; something wholly alien. I felt a sense of expectation too, which was not unlike my childhood experience at Mrs Burtenshaw's house, when I saw what was surely the ghost of a lady in a grey dress. That sighting got me and poor Aunt Dolly into a lot of trouble. Now, as on that other distant afternoon, everything around me felt suddenly unreal and heightened. It was as if time itself was slowing down, allowing me to experience every second just that little bit longer and more intensely. It was clear that Tom sensed something odd too. After all, we were now deep in the territory of his 'angels'. This was a place where they had left their mark – something solid and tangible.

'You coming in then, Tom?' I said, as cheerily and casually as I could manage.

He looked terrible – as white as a sheet – and he was shaking. 'If I must then,' he said.

'Come on, you two. No lagging behind,' the captain called out.

Side by side, we followed the beam of the captain's torch as well as our own. We were led down a gentle slope further into the hill. At first the sides and roof of the tunnel were shored up with timbers. It looked like one of those gold mines you see in Western films.

'The sappers from over at Burton Bradstock put in these supports,' the captain told us.

In my torch beam, his tall shadow rippled on the earthen walls as they curved round a bend. And as we turned the corner, a strange sight confronted us.

A huge chamber appeared to have been hollowed out inside the hill. Captain Holloway switched on an arc light on a skeleton gantry attached to a generator. A rickety wooden staircase led down to the floor of the cavern, which was at least seventy feet below us. Most of the space was taken up by the gigantic curved section of a hull. It could have been made of metal – or some kind of smooth stone – or even ceramic.

The captain led the way down the steps to the floor below. 'It buried itself here,' he said, tapping the side of the craft with the end of his pipe. 'The troops over at Burton Bradstock helped to dig it out, but only to a certain level. I exposed the rest myself, as far as I could, leaving the soldiers to guard the area. I couldn't risk letting them set eyes on this. As you can see, it is clearly not a German bomber of even the most experimental kind.'

I climbed down the shaky wooden steps to the earth floor of the chamber and looked up at the huge curved side. It was a dull battleship grey in colour. I could see no rivets – or any outward signs of construction at all: no metal seams or ridges. The surface was completely smooth and unbroken. Tom was still waiting at the top of the steps. I wondered if he was unwilling to come any closer. He was just staring at it – or perhaps, I thought, he was listening . . . It was hard to imagine that the object looming above us had come from some other and very faraway world. I reached out and touched it. It wasn't as cold as I had expected. There was a faint vibration, a kind of throb from somewhere deep inside it.

'I can feel something,' I said.

The captain took off his glove and put his own hand to the hull. 'That's new.' He put his ear against it and nodded. 'Perhaps Tom has made a difference to it just by being here,' he said. 'I think it recognizes him in some way.'

Tom was standing stock-still, his eyes closed. He raised his head, his eyes opening, looking at the top of the hull. I felt the vibration grow in intensity. Something was happening all right . . .

And then Tom raised his arms.

CHAPTER ELEVEN

It was as if a neat cut made by a very sharp knife was opening up (well, actually, it was down) the side of the hull. A segment like an orange slice folded out and down from the smooth surface, leaving a deep, dark fissure – and an entry point. A set of steps shaped a little like smooth teeth were revealed on the upper surface of the slice. I looked up, trying to see inside. I knew that, whatever had caused the entrance to open like that, it was not an invitation for me or the captain. Tom made his way down the wooden steps and approached it. Without hesitating, he climbed the steps into the hull, which lit up at once, piercingly bright. For a moment I forgot myself, and made to go in after Tom, but the captain held me back.

'No,' he said. 'I don't know what we should do next, Jack, but it's not that. It's a ruddy miracle, of course, and it's right here in front of us. We are but a few feet from what is possibly the greatest secret in human history. Part of me says we should follow him in. The other part says, stay here where we are safe, and wait.'

In any case, the question was resolved a few seconds later. The section silently lifted up, and the gap was quickly closed; the hull was as seamless as it had been before. There was nothing we could do now but wait. In spite of myself, I called out, 'Tom!' and banged on the side of the hull. My voice bounced off it and echoed around the cavern.

'No, Jack,' Captain Holloway said, shaking his head. 'I would have liked nothing more than to go in, but it opened for Tom and for Tom only. We would have been stopped anyway, I fear. We will just have to be patient.'

So we waited. The vibration from inside the hull stopped. The only sound was the dripping of water from the excavated walls around us. I will admit to feeling properly scared in that dark place. Not 'horror movie' scared, not 'scary story' scared, but a bone-deep, soul-deep fear of whatever was inside that craft with Tom. My apprehension meter, my personal fear radar, was off the scale.

Captain Holloway was nervously pacing across the chamber. He tested the hull, tapping it with the back of his hand every so often as if knocking on a door.

'Shouldn't bother really, I suppose ... They aren't going to let us in, old chap.'

'Not a chance,' I said. 'I suppose it was worth a try, though.'

Almost as soon as I spoke, the segment opened up again, and Tom walked down the steps. I tried my best to peer inside the craft. It looked enormous, bright and completely empty. I could see no features at all – a vast, dazzling emptiness, completely smooth at the sides. Then Tom was down, and the segment closed again, and it was too late.

Tom shook his head as if to wake himself. He smiled at me – unusual occurrence in itself.

'What happened, Tom?' I said.

'Where?' he asked.

'In there.'

'Was I in there?' he said. 'How long?'

'Not more than a couple of minutes,' the captain told him. 'What happened in there, Tom?'

'I don't know. I can't remember much after coming down the stairs there.' He pointed to the wooden staircase. 'After that there was a being of light sleeping deep underground. I have to help free it.'

'Well,' the captain said, 'we know one thing: this craft is still very active, but it will give up its secrets only to you, Tom. You are one of their chosen vessels. I suspect that the French girl is another. I can only imagine how frightened and disorientated she must be. We are her only hope now, Tom – and especially you.'

'I know I am. That's why I must go to her. I am one, and so is she,' Tom said, still smiling.

'You are very sure of that, Tom, aren't you?' the captain said. 'Every instinct says I should keep you safe with us, but I recognize the truth of what you say. We must prepare ourselves.'

We made our way back to the surface, where two different soldiers were waiting for us. One was a despatch rider, leaning against his motorcycle. He straightened and saluted the captain at once, handing over two bulky War Office envelopes.

The captain looked at them. 'You're not from Burton Bradstock then, Corporal?'

'No, sir. From London, sir. Direct delivery.'

'That bad, eh?' the captain said. 'Thank you for this, and I hope you have a safe return journey.'

After an exchange of salutes the despatch rider rode off on his motorcycle.

'I assume Colonel Gauntlett was at least able to spare you,' the captain said to the other soldier.

'Yes, sir,' he said. 'Sentry duty until eighteen hundred hours, sir.'

'Very good, Corporal. Remember, no one – and I must emphasize *no one* – goes into that place except me, my two companions here, and the staff sergeant. It is very dangerous and completely off limits to everybody else.'

After we had secured the entrance to the earthworks, we left the lone sentry guarding the wire perimeter and set off towards Burton Bradstock.

'Aren't you going to open them?' I said, referring to the envelopes.

'I think I'll wait until we are at the barracks and behind four walls. I suspect one of them is a bit of a zinger.'

A 'zinger' it was.

The captain let me read it.

WAR DEPARTMENT
WHITEHALL

Dear Holloway,

    I arrived at your offices this afternoon at 1500 sharp. I was told that not only were you yourself absent, but also missing was your protégé, the civilian named Pile - the one I was sent by the War Office to evaluate. I was told he was with you in Dorset. This really is not good enough. Your department is a civilian one, entirely funded by the War Office. In your memo to me upon my taking office, you told me that Pile has exceptional and potentially dangerous 'powers of control over his environment'; the true extent of his powers are currently under investigation, etc., etc. As you well know, there is a strong military interest in this foundling of yours. I was able to view cine film of his abilities at the premises. Those things can be faked. We at the War Office need to see proof of his abilities, and the remains of this craft, as soon as possible. If you do not return to London with Pile forthwith, I shall be forced to visit you.

Sincerely,

Clarke

Colonel Clarke

War Office Liaison

'Sounds angry,' I said.

'Hopping mad, I should think, Jack.' The captain turned to Tom and said, 'Trouble is, Tom, I think the War Office intend to take you over and use you as some sort of secret weapon. I am against that. We have barely scratched the surface of what you can do. It would be very ill-judged, and very dangerous, to use you in this way, however useful you would be to the cause. We know what happened to the girl in Germany, and no doubt there was more to that story than the Germans let on. We need to study and protect you. Which means that we have a big problem with our masters.'

The other envelope contained the translation of a message from the German commander of the garrison at Douarnenez to the Berlin Office of the Unexplained & the Supernatural.

Report 5

From the desk of Hauptmann Meier, Douarnenez, Brittany Department

I have now interviewed the subject – the girl who was washed up in the fishing nets. I have visited her three times, once with her supposed uncle, Garel, a French civilian with some German sympathies. She denied all knowledge or memory of him – so much so that the old man was in tears. He swears blind that she is none other than his missing niece. The fact that this girl is no more than 15 years old and his alleged niece has been missing, presumed drowned, these many years (35) seemed not to trouble him.

The girl was not exactly uncooperative, but she was withdrawn and her language was odd. Her French sounded archaic to my ears. There was obviously some old Breton argot mixed in with it. Even my secretary, whose French is flawless, had some difficulties understanding her. She has been well treated, considering her position. She is, in my opinion, quite possibly a spy, or even a mental defective. However, she referred to these 'angels' which your office is keen on identifying as per below.

Transcribed from Interview 2 with female subject:

> 'They came out of the heavens. Out of the clouds. They were brighter than the sun could ever be. They burned brightly in my eyes so that I could see nothing else all around me. I cannot remember their faces. I don't think they had faces. All I can say is that our boat was sinking in the big swell. We were overwhelmed by the water. I fell off the stern. I saw our boat upended by the waves, the mast come down. The sail wrapped itself around my poor father and dragged him under the water. Then hands of light lifted me up. My eyes burned, and I was taken up through the dark storm clouds. I was up in the blue of Heaven with the light all around me. I knew I was dead. I heard angel voices – gentle voices. They told me in their music not to be afraid. The voices were inside my head. They were closer to me than a whisper in my ear, but they were loud, and they were joyful too. They were like a peal of bells at Christmastide, or the choir at the Church of Our Lady, all singing in my head. They talked to me in the air. They asked me who I was, and I tried to tell them . . .'

That gives a good account of the tone of her discourse. Perhaps it is naïve religious nonsense, or perhaps it is clever playacting. I noted the intensity and sincerity of what she said and how she said it. The advice of my second in command, Leutnant Richter, is to ignore any supposed significance in this incident; to put everybody involved up against a wall in the town square and shoot them 'as a lesson to others'. I think that would be totally counterproductive: the evidence requires a more expert eye than we can offer. I suggest you send a representative to interview the girl. He will, of course, be made most welcome.

CHAPTER TWELVE

Dorset

'It's all falling into place,' the captain said after reading it. 'We now have more than a simple problem; we have a race against the clock. We must find the girl and bring her back here. It is vital that we do this before the Berlin Office of the Unexplained and the Supernatural get to her. That way I can also keep the War Office off Tom's back for the moment. You two will be taken over the water by Lieutenant Sperring. It'll be tough, but it means I can offer the War Office the promise of two birds in the bush rather than one Tom in the hand, if you follow.'

The captain left us in the charge of his friend Colonel Gauntlett at the Burton Bradstock barracks. The colonel was courteous enough, but obviously couldn't wait to pass on the responsibility to someone else.

We were told to change into battle dress and berets. I was surprised to see Tom in uniform. 'You look like a proper soldier,' I told him.

Ever since going into the abandoned alien craft, Tom had been behaving oddly. It was as if there was a dialogue going on inside his head which only he could hear. He nodded at me, but I wasn't sure if he had really taken in what I said.

We were driven away almost at once, and in silence, by one of the sergeants, and eventually found ourselves approaching an old house tucked away deep in a wood.

'Home sweet home,' the driver said finally as we drove in through the piled sandbags and loops of barbed wire at the gate. 'Good luck,' he added before he drove away again.

We walked up to the door, which opened in front of us; a familiar voice boomed out, 'Well, well, we meet again, Jack Carmody – and so soon, but in very different circumstances, eh?'

It was Lieutenant Sperring. He looked very different to the figure I'd seen in Captain Holloway's office. He was wearing khaki battle dress too. 'Good afternoon,' he said, grinning from ear to ear.

I saluted him, and Tom copied me a half-second later.

'We don't salute anyone here at HQ,' Sperring told us. 'This must be young Tom Pile . . .'

He reached forward and shook Tom's hand. 'You are a very mysterious fellow indeed, it seems. Both of you are under SOE orders from now on. Like the rest of us here, you are sworn to total secrecy – but then, you know all that. You are now, as it were, through the old looking glass – and I'm the white rabbit. You'll just have to trust me and follow me down a very dangerous rabbit hole. Our world is one of mirrors and deceit, where nothing and no one is necessarily what they seem to be. A telephone might be a bomb; a scruffy French fisherman might be an English ex-public schoolboy.' He pointed to himself. 'There are times when you wouldn't know by looking at me or even listening to me.

'So welcome, gentlemen. Soon, I know, we will travel together across the pond. I gather from Captain H. that time is of the essence. We have just three days to prepare you: count them – three days . . . one, two, three. No time to kick you both into shape, and I do mean *kick*. We don't operate under any sort of "Queensberry rules" here. This is not a fair and gentlemanly fight. We face a ruthless and efficient, not to say evil, occupying force. I know what they have been doing in Eastern Europe. Foul, horrible things.

They are ever alert. And some of the French have welcomed the German forces. You can't trust anyone, however plausible they are. This will be a very tough assignment for all of us. There may be no way back . . . You may well be killed. You can write last letters to your loved ones tonight. Only if you die will they be posted. Is that understood?'

'Yes,' I said, my mind racing at the thought of Aunt Dolly opening such a letter.

'When we finally meet up with that French fishing vessel mid-Channel, you must be ready – more ready than you can imagine or believe possible. I have to cram months of hard training into a few short and very critical days. Fail this, and all bets are off, I'm afraid. Let's hope you both survive it.'

The next three days were hell on earth. They passed quickly, though not quickly enough for me. I don't know about Tom . . . He was tougher than I expected and did better than me all round.

The first morning we were taken out early. A tough sergeant shouted at us and tried to kill us in so many ways we lost count – until it was time for a lecture. We had lots of those. It's funny how little bits stick in the mind.

'Observe and deduce,' the lecturer said, banging his lectern as he repeated it over and over. 'Observe and deduce. A face seen twice nearby, or a voice heard more than once, may indicate that you are being followed, so always be aware, take note, stay alert. In France, even the smell of real coffee might mean you are in the presence of a black marketeer who would sell his own grandmother for a can of petrol.'

After that long first day, I looked at myself in the shower-block mirror and saw that I was bruised all over. I looked like I had gone ten rounds with Joe Louis.

'There are two more days of this to go,' I called out to Tom as I stood under the stream of tepid water.

'I know,' he said. 'Must be done though, Jack.'

He was actually enjoying it, I realized.

I slept like a log in the mostly empty dormitory. I think Tom did too. I didn't hear anything until the sergeant got us out of bed at 5.30 a.m.

That day we ran up and down a field, our boots sticking in the thick mud. We crawled on our stomachs under lethally sharp barbed wire and through foul ditch water. Our bodies ached as we sat through yet more lectures. Next we were sent through the woods and were stopped by two German soldiers. They interrogated us in French. Tom had no choice but to play dumb – he couldn't speak a word. I managed all right, but I wasn't a patch on Lieutenant Sperring, who sounded like a real Frenchman.

Finally we were taken up to a clothes store in the attic.

'This stuff is made for us by refugee tailors and seamstresses,' Sperring said, holding up a jacket. 'They cut and sew the clothes as they would have done at home so that none of this stuff looks or feels in any way British. Then someone ages it all – breaks it down so that it doesn't look new; smokes filthy French Caporal cigarettes all over it so it smells right too. Where we are going, only collaborators can afford new.'

We chose our outfits – nondescript grey clothes: threadbare, patched shirts without collars, dirty grey flannel trousers. We were told to sleep in them for the next two nights.

'We have to mix with the local population. I have plenty of experience of this. You two have none,' Sperring told us.

At the end of three days, it seemed that no one was pleased with our progress.

The lieutenant shook his head. 'The sergeants aren't very happy with the results of your basic survival training. We may have to rethink . . . change the plan. Otherwise you'll just end up getting us all shot – or worse.'

Captain Holloway was sent for. We lined up in front of Sperring like two naughty schoolboys: he sat behind his desk looking like a disappointed headmaster, nursing an unlit pipe.

'It won't do, Captain,' he said. 'My men have done their best, but we have insurmountable difficulties here. This one' – he indicated Tom with the stem of his pipe – 'knows no French at all; this one' – he pointed at me – 'knows a passable amount. This one' – Tom again – 'handles himself well in combat – wiry, tough, unafraid of pain – good agent material in maybe five years. This one' – me – 'is not as tough but bright as a pin and sharp as a tack, as you know. Blend them together and we have an excellent agent. But as individuals, no – suicidal. Can't be done.'

Captain Holloway nodded and said, 'I never said this was going to be an easy mission. We have a most difficult situation here, Sperring. Over in the SOE you know all about secrecy. Well, we do too. This mission is top priority – vitally important to the future of this country . . . and, it would not be an exaggeration to say, of the world as well. It just happens that because of certain . . . secret qualities that my two operatives possess, they are the only ones I can send to effect the necessary rescue. They have been sent for and they have to go.' He paused and spread his hands wide. 'It's as simple as that. I can't explain the reasons. You will have to trust me, Sperring.'

'I do trust you. But can I trust *them*? That's my worry . . .'

Tom broke the silence. 'You *can* trust us,' he said firmly, staring fixedly at Sperring.

There was a pause.

'We'll do our best,' Sperring told the captain, 'but I want it put on the record that I lead this mission against my better judgement.'

'Duly noted,' Captain Holloway said. 'You won't regret it.'

'Oh, I think I shall,' the lieutenant replied.

CHAPTER THIRTEEN

English Channel

I am a London boy, as I think I have mentioned before –
in fact, I think I may have said it too many times. So
crossing the English Channel at night in a small boat
was not something I looked forward to.

From the moment I first stepped onto the deck and
felt that unsteady rolling movement under my feet, I
hated it. In fact, I felt seasick almost from the word go.

I wonder if it was all part of my abilities to read
pattern. I could somehow calculate the rolls of the
swell. My brain raced ahead, anticipating, and I
couldn't keep up, and so the nausea began. Tom, on
the other hand, seemed totally used to it. He took to
the unsteady, stinking little boat 'like a duck to water'!

'I used to go fishing with my dad and uncle off West
Bay near Bridport,' he said as he stood at the prow,

looking across the choppy dark water with something like excitement. The wind had whipped up the waves and the boat was lurching about – and we were still in the shelter of the harbour.

'You all right there, Jack?' Sperring asked when we reached the open sea. 'Only you look a bit green about the gills, old man. I'd advise you to go below decks, but I think that would only make it worse, what with the smell of old fish and the diesel fumes! Best stay up here and brave it in the fresh air.'

So I did.

I'll never know if I would have felt any better down in the hold . . . Looking back on the trip, I reckon it was as bad an experience as I've ever had to endure.

It seemed to take for ever. I was very conscious of the water below us. Such deep, treacherous stuff. The only saving grace was that it was dark and I could barely see the constantly shifting horizon, although that did grow clearer as the grey dawn finally appeared after the longest, most miserable night of my life.

In the cold light of morning I felt only a little better. At least the swell had calmed mid Channel. Sperring grinned at me as he poured some tea from a flask.

One of the sailors was scanning the sea with a pair of binoculars. 'I see her,' he said, turning to the lieutenant. 'She's a mile off.'

'She' was a large rescue and salvage buoy; shipwrecked sailors or downed air crew waited for rescue there. It looked a bit like the conning tower of a submarine with a tall radio mast sticking up out of the water. We were to be left there and picked up by a French fishing boat; then we'd take a rubber dinghy ashore somewhere on the coast of Brittany.

Tom jumped off the rolling boat and onto the similarly rolling buoy as if he'd done it all his life. I admit that I had to be helped across the gap like a child. I could feel the wiry strength of Tom's arm as he pulled me to relative safety behind the buoy's guard rail. A deck hatch led below to a little room with bunk beds, emergency rations and a first-aid kit. I sat on one of the beds and felt the buoy bobbing in the water.

Lieutenant Sperring soon joined me. 'Tom seems happy enough out there in the wind, but you don't care much for the sea life, do you, Jack?'

'I hate it, to be honest,' I said.

'Maybe we can hitch a ride home on a nice aeroplane,' he said, 'when it's all over.'

'Some hope,' I said, closing my eyes, trying to let myself drift with the motion.

Sperring and Tom stayed up in the conning tower, keeping an eye out for the French fishing vessel.

After what seemed a long time but was probably only an hour or so, I heard shouts. I climbed up and saw a single-masted vessel with two men on deck approaching. It sat low in the water, its sail furled; I could hear its engine. As it nuzzled close to our buoy, Sperring hopped across onto the deck. From the cabin at the stern, the skipper waved to him, and one of the deckhands – clearly an old friend – clasped him in a bear hug. 'Ah, *mon ami*, eet eez good to see you,' he called out as he clapped the lieutenant on the back.

Sperring turned and beckoned to us. I elected to go first, hoping to redeem myself. Luckily the buoy was a good three feet higher than the fishing boat. I timed my jump carefully: when the boat was at its closest, I swung myself down, holding onto the mooring rope. Tom untied the rope after me and threw it back across to Sperring, and then jumped down onto the deck as if simply stepping off a London bus.

I must have found my sea legs, because the rest of the journey was much better. Perhaps the sea was calmer, or perhaps the French boat had better stabilizers.

Tom enjoyed himself. He helped the fishermen haul in their catch, and by the time sunset came his clothes were silvered with fish scales; he certainly looked the part.

Once it was completely dark Sperring went into action. He pumped up the rubber dinghy. 'We'll slash this into ribbons once we land,' he said. Then he spread a scarf map out on the deck and shone his torch on it.

'Won't we need the dinghy to get out again?' I said.

'We'll be leaving by another route altogether,' he said. 'Don't worry about it now, Jack. We'll hit land, I hope, on one of the beaches somewhere between Audierne and Plozévet.' He pointed at the map with his pipe. 'I know this area pretty well. Fewer patrols and so on. We head north to Douarnenez, and there we'll be met by my contacts, and we can finally work out our plan of action. I've got this camera with me – you'd better take charge of it, Jack.' He handed me a package the size and shape of a small book.

*

Half an hour later we were huddled together in the dinghy, paddling through the darkness towards the dangerous coast of Nazi-occupied France. I had some idea of what awaited us once we were ashore. Hanging over everything else was the certainty that if we were caught, we would be shot – immediately, if we were lucky; most likely we would first be tortured by the Gestapo. I had heard things; I'd even seen some photographs. Some agents were issued with suicide pills – fast-acting poisons – but I had no idea if Sperring was carrying anything like that. I wondered if I would ever have the courage to take such a pill if the situation demanded it.

CHAPTER FOURTEEN

La Mairie, Douarnenez

The girl sat opposite Hauptmann Meier. He found it hard to read her, but he had to admit that, despite himself, he was intrigued. Was she being stubborn, or was she simply bewildered and frightened?

She looked deceptively angelic, with her white-blonde hair – more Scandinavian than Breton. At first he'd been certain that she was nothing to do with any angels; the girl was surely a spy, or was being used in some cynical ploy, on her way in or out of the Occupied Zone, and up to no good, when she ended up on the fishing boat. However, doubts had slowly, gradually eaten into him – especially after the memo and the repeated messages from Berlin showing interest. The putative old uncle, M. Garel, a would-be collaborator, turned up at the *mairie* almost every day asking if he might see the girl. Since her first rejection of him, Hauptmann Meier had been minded not to let him in – though the old man seemed convincing, with his letters and his family photographs and old newspaper clippings. Meier had kept them all to show the visitor from Berlin.

'Tell me again,' he asked the girl in his clear but accented French, 'how you managed to get into the middle of the sea.'

'I've already told you,' she said. 'I was delivered by the angels, praise Jésu.' She crossed herself.

'I don't think so,' Meier said, leaning forward. 'I think you have been sent here as a spy.' He tapped the table with his finger. 'You are at the very least a Resistance agent, a terrorist of some description. I have done my best with you. I have been fair. I have only asked the questions I must ask. In the end you have failed to answer them.

'In you I see either folly or courage – I can no longer tell which. In the next day or so a very important man is travelling all the way from Berlin to interview you. If it were not for his interest in you and your strange fable, I would most likely have had you put up against the wall in the courtyard out there and shot as an enemy of the Reich. I have done that before, you know . . .' He hesitated, uncomfortable under her steady gaze.

'As it is, once my guest has finished interviewing you and expresses no interest in your story, then we shall be forced to question you all over again – using rather different and specialized methods. Either way, we will get to the truth.'

The girl's expression did not change. There was not even a flicker at the quiet threat of impending torture or execution.

The corporal was summoned and the girl was taken back to her secure room in the cellars of the *mairie*. Meier was convinced that there was something very odd . . . something frightening about the girl. He could not identify exactly what it was, but there were times as he was talking to her when his mind seemed to go blank. It was as if she was somehow inside his head, and he found himself conjuring up the image of a black square that blocked out everything else – like a door that had suddenly been closed. At first he had put it down to overwork or schnapps, but he knew it was more than that. Deep down, he knew that it had something to do with the strange girl – though he would never have admitted it, even to himself. Maybe Berlin was right to be interested in her. For his part, he was increasingly frightened of what she represented and what she might be capable of.

CHAPTER FIFTEEN

Coast of Brittany

It felt good to be standing on solid ground again. Even the soft sand felt firm underfoot, and I was very grateful. After Sperring had destroyed the rubber dinghy and hidden the fragments, we trekked up the beach in single file, heads down. Spread out across the sand were X-shaped concrete stanchions and rolls of barbed wire. We negotiated our way through them well enough. It was still dark, but the crescent moon shone weakly through the clouds. The sand gave way to pebbles, and then a line of bigger rocks stretched away into the distance on either side.

We scrambled over them and finally found ourselves on the coast road. I could see a line of whitewashed houses on the far side. The windows were shuttered and dark and there was no street lighting.

Sperring whispered, 'This way – quietly.'

We walked through the sleeping village and regrouped among some trees near the church.

'Now we must head inland to reach Douarnenez,' Sperring said. 'The coast road is patrolled regularly, and it goes all the way round the peninsula – known as a *presque l'isle* in French. Much quicker to go cross-country. Anyway, we are due to meet our contact somewhere near here. We are fishermen – don't forget that.'

Almost as soon as we'd left the road, we heard the roar of a motorcycle passing through the village behind us.

'There you are,' Sperring said. 'German patrol, most likely. I can't imagine many locals are allowed out on motorcycles at this time, what with the curfew and no proper fuel. Most cars now run on wood burners.'

Once again Tom Pile proved to be at home. He surged ahead, sure-footed, through the countryside. At one point he turned to me and said, 'Not so different from Dorset really.'

Later we stopped in a stand of trees, and Sperring dished out our ration packs. 'K rations,' he said. 'We're lucky – American stuff; you can't always get these.'

We ate Spam and dry biscuits and cheese, and there was orange juice too. We took care to bury any trace of ourselves afterwards.

'It'll be market day in Douarnenez,' Sperring said. 'Best time for getting around – plenty of people about, easier to pass unnoticed. Remember your training; remember the interrogation in the woods. If at any point you are asked for your papers, look bored, sullen, give a Gallic shrug, hand them over. It happens to you ten times a day, a boring event. Betray no interest. Most of the German soldiers are just as bored. Try not to say anything at all.'

So we walked on through the night. The skies had cleared and the waxing crescent moon hung in the trees above us. We passed farmhouses and outbuildings; all were dark and quiet.

'There's a blackout – it's just as strict as the one back in London,' Sperring whispered.

Below us, disappearing into the distance, we could see a straight road. 'That's the D765,' he told us. 'We need to keep close to it.'

After a couple of hours we reached the crest of a hill. Sperring and I sat down and rested, while Tom stood looking up into the sky. After a minute or two I went to join him.

'What is it, Tom?' I asked.

'She's been calling to me,' he said quietly, 'even when I'm awake. She seems louder, closer. I can see her face too.'

'Do you think she knows we're coming?'

'Oh, she knows.'

An aeroplane, a Junkers transport, passed high overhead in the clear sky. One red navigation light blinked on the tail.

'Most likely on its way over to Brest,' Sperring said. 'That's where the U-boat pens are now.'

Tom looked up at the plane. 'I could pull that down out of the sky,' he said matter of factly.

Together we watched it head off towards the coast.

'Save that thought, Tom,' I said. 'We might need it later on.'

MEMO

FAO Captain Holloway

Intercept
Translated from the German

FROM: H. Kohler, Office of the Unexplained & the Supernatural, Berlin
TO: Meier, Northern Occupied Zone, France

MOST SECRET

Our representative, Herr Mustchin, is travelling on a night flight
from Berlin to Brest. He will arrive tomorrow morning and will need
to be driven first to a top-secret site near the town of Monteneuf,
and then to Douarnenez to interview the girl. You will arrange
transport to meet him promptly on landing at 4 a.m. Ours is a
civilian department, so he will not be in uniform. However, he is to
be offered every assistance; he has the highest possible clearance.
I should remind you that the Führer himself takes a great personal
interest in all matters relating to our investigations.

SECRET
WAR DEPARTMENT

CHAPTER SIXTEEN

Brittany

The French countryside seemed completely empty that night as we trudged on across it. The air was cold, but it smelled sweetly enough of grass and leaf mould and all the other country things. A contrast to old London, which always smelled of burning coal, soot, town gas, steam and hot iron.

'I've arranged to meet at a safe house – we should reach it in an hour or so, just before daylight,' Sperring said, and then he pulled me forward so that we were walking a few paces in front of Tom.

'What did young Pile mean back then?'

'Mean?' I said. 'When?'

'Don't play silly beggars, Jack. He said he could "pull that plane down out of the sky". I've heard rumours about him and his abilities. Can you explain?'

'Sorry – I can't.'

'Can't or *won't*?'

'I suppose for now it has to be *won't*,' I said.

'I see. I don't want him going off at a tangent. I suspect he's just a bit dangerous – am I right?'

I said nothing as I trudged over the tussocky grass.

'Your silence, as they say, speaks volumes, Jack,' he said. 'I don't blame you. I know how it is. Fall back now, there's a good chap.'

Not everyone in all the various secret departments knew about Tom Pile. It was clear that Lieutenant Sperring was only partially aware of what we were about. He was a man of action, not science. His brief was to get us in, and then get us out again safely, along with the girl.

I thought it slightly odd that he should suddenly question me like that, but then, Tom was an oddity. A special case. There was bound to be rumour and curiosity. Sperring was no doubt wondering about me too. After all, what was so special about any of us, and why was he risking his life – and – ours to get the girl to England?

By now we had been walking long enough for my eyes to be accustomed to the darkness. But my extra perception had also kicked in, and I could make out the rounded hills in various shades of grey, as if they were laid out on a map.

We passed a barn, and a lone dog sensed us and barked. I could hear its claws scrabbling, and another bigger beast stamping and snorting. The dog was pulling on its chain, trying to get at us over the fence; it set off another dog, and their barks echoed across the night landscape.

It was then that I saw someone watching us in the lee of a stand of trees – a dark figure outlined in white, as if with chalk. Friend or foe? I wondered. Clearly Sperring hadn't seen anything yet.

I suppose we must have stood out against the clear sky as we made our way down a gentle slope towards the figure, who seemed to be waiting.

Suddenly whoever it was seemed to light a cigarette. A little flick of orange light stood out in the surrounding grey – and then Sperring stopped with his arm raised. We stopped too.

After that things happened very quickly. The figure came running towards us out of the trees. I knew that Sperring had a pistol hidden somewhere in his shabby clothes. I heard him click back the hammer in readiness.

A woman's voice called out, 'Elgar?'

'Yes,' Sperring said in French. 'It's Elgar – and you?'

'Berlioz,' the voice said. 'And the others with you . . .' The woman was close now. 'How many?'

'Two,' Sperring replied.

She switched on a covered torch, and I saw that she was young and wore a headscarf and a bulky overcoat, with a shotgun slung across her back. She shone the torch briefly at us and then switched it off again.

'Come,' she said, and pointed further down the hill.

'Come on,' Sperring said, turning to us. 'She's one of ours. We must follow her.'

We headed downhill, away from the trees, and soon hit a narrow dirt road. At the bottom of the slope we reached a junction with the D road we had been shadowing. A truck with a tarpaulin cover over its flatbed was tucked away by the hedgerow.

'Change of plan, Elgar,' she said. 'Sorry – couldn't be helped. You must go on to Douarnenez tonight. The safe house here is sadly no longer safe.'

'What happened?' Sperring asked.

'The two were taken to Brest for questioning. They found nothing at the house and all may still be well. No doubt a neighbour denounced them, hoping to get more rations from the Germans. It happens. They will most likely return safely, but from now on they will be closely watched – you'd better warn London. We can't rely on them any more.

'I will drive you to Douarnenez now. You will have to hide under our cargo. We have a curfew permit.'

'What is your cargo?'

The woman smiled and lifted the edge of the tarp.

The lieutenant sniffed. 'Ah, of course – it could only be fish,' and then he laughed. 'At least,' he added, 'it can only add to our cover.'

We lay down on blankets, then more blankets were piled on top of us, and then flat planks, and then the crates of fish were laid over those. Tom was lying beside me, and I remembered how much he hated confined spaces. I reached across and held his arm.

'It's all right, Tom. We won't be under here for long.'

And we weren't . . .

The truck ran on charcoal, just as Sperring had said. Any diesel was reserved for the Germans. The fumes drifted around the back of the truck.

By the time we reached the outskirts of Douarnenez it was just light. The truck stopped in a side street not far from the fish market, and we got out. Smuts like those from a train-carriage window had settled all over us. We certainly looked and smelled like the kind of fishermen who might operate a smokehouse curing herring.

We stood together on the street corner. It was cold, and we were damp and stiff from lying under the crates. We blew on our hands and stamped around, trying to get our circulation going.

I could hear the ropes and cleats rattling against the masts of the fishing boats in the nearby harbour. I hoped we were not going to be put onto another boat. Across the street a woman was opening up a café-bar. It was the Café Atlantique – the very one mentioned in the newspaper report.

It was then that I saw my first German soldier. I suspect he was just coming off a night shift – he had a rifle over his shoulder. He stopped and said something to the woman who was lowering the café awning.

'That's Madame Berthou,' Sperring said. 'She runs the bar with her husband. We can trust them, when and if the time comes.'

The German soldier waited while Mme Berthou went into the café. Sperring's contact – Berlioz – had already slunk quietly back into the cab of the truck. The soldier looked across the street, directly at us. He was young, not much older than me, and I felt a sudden surge of pity for him. I know I should have wanted to shoot him or cut his throat with a bayonet or blow him to pieces with a hand grenade. The Germans had bombed London, and much worse, strafing refugees from the air and the like. But somehow I couldn't hate him. He looked cold and awkward, standing there in his ill-fitting uniform, a vacant expression on his face. Here was a young private, sent to guard this backwater, denied the glory of Paris. I had a queasy feeling about him, and the smell of roses suddenly came to me. This was always a warning sign – for ever associated with my sighting of the ghost when I was young. It was as if the young soldier was already a ghost. I saw his face darken, his already thin cheeks grow sunken, his uniform char. A halo of flames seemed to shoot up all around him. In that split second, that flash of premonition, I was seeing his future death – I was sure of it. Over the years I had tried to ignore these visions. They always came without warning, and now I struggled to conceal my shock.

Mme Berthou emerged from the café carrying a china bowl. The soldier leaned his rifle against one of the tables and took the bowl, smiled, then drank his coffee.

'The French use breakfast bowls instead of cups . . . That will be real coffee,' said Sperring. 'A real *café au lait* – no ersatz acorn stuff for him. Not like the stuff the poor French have to put up with. I could just do with some of that.'

The young soldier finished his coffee and picked up his rifle again. He saluted Mme Berthou and then continued along the street. Groups of fishermen were arriving now, greeting one another as they milled about outside the café. Life was carrying on, as it usually did, in spite of defeat and oppression and the many hardships of the occupation.

'We'll go over in a minute. Our contact has given me a name. We will be in his hands until tomorrow.' Sperring banged lightly on the side of the truck. The woman nodded, then started up the engine, pulling away from the kerb in a cloud of black fumes; she was soon lost to view.

We were on our own again.

'Jack, your French is up to it – just go into the café, take a seat and order something for you and Tom,' Sperring told me. 'You'll have to use the ration cards and stamps. You play tired, Tom. Keep yawning and say nothing to anyone. I'll follow on in a minute or so. I can pass as French, after all. I'm pretty well known in there, so just ignore me until I signal otherwise.'

By the time Tom and I crossed over the road, the café was busy with the early shift of stallholders and fishermen. We went through to the part where tables were laid. An elderly waiter in a long white apron came to take our order.

'Coffee for two please,' I mumbled in my best French.

'Bread with that?'

I nodded. Tom yawned and kept his eyes fixed on the tablecloth, as if half asleep. Two china bowls of sour coffee substitute and half a dry, grey loaf soon arrived. The café was full now. All around us there was noisy conversation and a fug of cigarette smoke. I hoped we didn't stand out too much, although we were clearly strangers. My hope was, and it was a slim one, that most working folk would be anti-German, anti-Nazi. My accent was not perfect – the waiter might have been on the telephone already, alerting the authorities. It was gamble we had to take. I had deliberately chosen a table tucked away in a corner. Most people were standing at the bar on the other side, drinking wine as well as their ersatz coffee. The café smelled very different from the Lyons Corner Houses in London, with their aromas of toasted teacakes, Woodbine cigarettes and damp wool. The cigarettes here smelled very much stronger, and the clothes smelled of the sea, not London rain and fog.

Sperring came in, ordered a cognac and started talking in French to one of the men at the bar. Next to the man stood a youth of about my own age. He had very dark curly hair – Aunt Dolly would have said he was a 'gypsy'.

Tom ate his half of the loaf and drank his bowl of bitter coffee down in one draught, with a muted sigh of satisfaction. When we had both finished our breakfast, I dug out some coins to pay, remembering to leave a few centimes as a tip.

Sperring looked across and beckoned us over. 'This,' he said in perfect French, 'is Pierre Bouchard, skipper of *Le Sillon*, and his son, Pascal.'

We shook hands. Pascal had a firm handshake; he looked straight into my eyes and gave a brief nod. I found myself liking him.

'Pierre suggests,' Sperring said casually, 'that we go and look over his boat this morning – now, in fact.'

Outside, four young German soldiers were sitting at a corner table in the weak sunshine. One of them was writing; the other three were talking and laughing, taking no notice of us. It gave me a turn, seeing them sitting there in their uniforms, looking just like something out of the Gaumont newsreels. I was relieved that they were ignoring us. We had obviously passed as native. Just as we were about to cross over to the harbourside, one of them called out in German-accented French, 'Hey, you – here a moment.'

I turned round and saw that the soldier was addressing me.

My stomach lurched. I felt sure I was going to be sick. I took a deep breath, and then I turned, looking as bored as I could manage. The soldier beckoned me over to their table. He was older than me, an officer, his uniform smart and crisply pressed. As I stood there, he picked something up off the table – a leather pouch that looked like the holster for a pistol. I half caught sight of Tom and Sperring reflected in the café window. They had followed Bouchard and Pascal across the road without looking back. I knew the drill that Captain Holloway had drummed into us: if anything went wrong, Tom was the priority; if I was caught, too bad.

The German officer unclipped the pouch and pulled out a camera. 'Here,' he said. 'Take a picture of us please, kind sir.'

I took the camera and raised it to my eye, looking through the viewfinder. The soldiers bunched up together and smiled. I clicked the shutter and wound on the film. My hand was shaking. I had to hope they wouldn't notice.

'One more please . . .' At least they were polite. I took another, and wound on the film, and then another from slightly further back. The café awning made a sharply defined shadow across the tables and the cups. The silverware glittered. The soldiers smiled broadly; they looked like they were on holiday. I froze the moment for them with one more click. I imagined them sending the photographs back to their sweethearts in Germany – *Having a lovely time. Wish you were here* – surely knowing that all around them were people who wished they weren't there at all.

I handed the camera back, and the officer smiled politely and nodded. 'Thank you.'

I crossed the road to find the others waiting anxiously with their backs turned, looking out across the harbour.

'Bad luck,' Sperring said. 'Did they say anything?'

'Just thank you.'

M. Bouchard spat into the harbour. 'Come,' he said.

CHAPTER SEVENTEEN

Monteneuf/Mairie, Douarnenez

Herr Mustchin wore a civilian overcoat, a hat and gloves – though he still had the air of a military man in full dress uniform. The coat was Loden – a very dark forest green; the hat, an almost black grey homburg, was worn low so as to shade his eyes; his moustache was a salt-and-pepper row of toothbrush bristles in emulation of the Führer. Leutnant Richter spotted him at once, making his way down the steps from the Junkers transport plane with the half-dozen other passengers.

'Oh, that'll be him,' he said quietly to himself.

The man stood beside the arrivals board, a black suitcase by his side and a black briefcase held close to his chest, as if fearful of being robbed.

'Herr Mustchin,' Richter said with a relaxed smile. 'Welcome to the Reich's Northern Occupied Zone.' He extended his hand.

'Heil Hitler,' Mustchin replied, shooting his arm out. Then he shook Richter's hand, but through his leather glove. He smelled of a sharp kind of lemon disinfectant.

'The car is this way,' Richter said. 'Good flight?'

'It's satisfying to cross over a country and know that it is under solid German rule.'

They walked across the tarmac strip to a waiting Mercedes staff car.

'First,' Mustchin said, 'I must be driven to these coordinates . . .' He had pulled out a detailed map of the area to show the driver. 'The town of Monteneuf. I will be there for less than one hour, then I will meet this girl.'

They drove in silence through flat wooded countryside. Monteneuf was a ghost town. Everything was closed up, empty. A manned and sandbagged barrier stretched across the entrance to the high street. Mustchin stepped out of the car and approached the guard. They spoke for a minute. The barrier remained closed.

Herr Mustchin returned. 'You will wait here,' he told Richter. 'You may step out of the car, but you must remain within sight of the sentry. I will be one hour.'

'What is happening here? Why is it all closed off, and where are the people?' the Leutnant asked.

'Your department is not privy to everything. This is a highly secret operation about which you need to know nothing.'

Richter got out and leaned against the bonnet of the Mercedes. He nodded at the sentry, then walked over and offered him a cigarette.

'Not while I'm on duty, thank you, sir.'

'What goes on around here anyway?'

'I have no idea. Something in the forest. Slave labourers digging – building something in there, as far as I know.'

The forest surrounded the town. The trees were dark and dense. Richter could see no sign of activity at all.

He walked up and down, peering into some shop windows. Every building displayed a sign – CLOSED AND EVACUATED BY ORDER, AREA COMMAND. *What, he wondered, is so special about this place that even we are kept in the dark?*

Herr Mustchin returned on the hour. They set off back towards Douarnenez.

'Instead of putting you in a hotel or barracks,' Richter said, 'I have found a little villa for you with charming views, right on the seafront.'

'That is a most kind gesture, but not really necessary. Views and charm do not interest me. I am concerned only to interview this girl as soon as possible. When may we start?'

'I thought you might want to relax for a day, Herr Mustchin – take in the sea air perhaps?'

'As I just said, my only concern here is to interview the girl and discover her likely origin. Where is she at present? Is she secure?'

'She is under detention at the *mairie*. She is being well-enough treated, as far as I know. Hauptmann Meier has tried to engage with her, draw her out . . .

Between you and me, I think she is a fraud and a spy.'
He took one hand off the wheel and mimed firing a
pistol. '*Blam*,' he said.

'I shall be the judge of that,' Mustchin said. He stared
straight ahead for the rest of the journey, pointedly
ignoring the dramatic views of the sea and the coastline.

It was a little after ten when they arrived at the
mairie. Hauptmann Meier was not in his office.

'Perhaps you would wait here in this antechamber,
Herr Mustchin. May I take your coat? One of my men
will bring you some coffee.'

'First and before anything else I want to see the girl.'
The visitor seemed restless. He fiddled with the handle
and locks of his briefcase.

'Very well.' Richter picked up the internal
telephone. 'Could you arrange to bring the Garel girl
up to the interview room please?' He paused, listening.
'Yes, of course . . . Now . . . Yes, at once, and then
arrange for some coffee and rolls too.' He put down the
phone.

'You know, Herr Mustchin, I was on the beach here,
the Sunday after the girl was found. There was a
ceremony, a kind of "pardon", at the water's edge.
Women in traditional coifs, plaster saints, the lot. The
fishermen said they pulled this girl up in their nets.
Apparently she fell out of the sky, dropped there by

"angels". If you want my opinion, she is feigning madness in order to avoid being shot as a spy. As I said before, I am all for shooting her – *bang* – and the fishermen too – *bang, bang* – as examples.'

Herr Mustchin turned his gaze on Richter. 'That would be a most terrible mistake,' he said. 'If my investigation works out as I think it will, this girl may well prove to be most vital to our war effort. Consider this: shooting her as a spy might have lost us the whole war, and Hauptmann Meier and your good self would also have been shot, or hung from piano wire for treason – a slow, lingering and painful death.'

The adjutant was soon bustling in with coffee and bread rolls.

'Real coffee,' Richter said with a fixed smile, rubbing his hands, shifting the subject away from possible hangings. 'Not the ersatz stuff the peasants are forced to drink.'

'The girl?' Mustchin said.

'In the interview room, sir,' the adjutant told him, clicking his heels together.

'Good, good,' Richter said, turning to Herr Mustchin. 'Please, sir, bring your coffee with you. It's this way.'

The girl sat at the table in a side office. The blind was drawn and the desk lamp was on. Her head was propped on her hands, her elbows resting on the desk. She was wearing a simple grey orphanage smock over a white blouse, and her pale hair was carefully brushed and tied back with a black ribbon. She made no move to stand up or change her position when the two men came in.

The older man in the suit sat down opposite her, took a folder out of his briefcase and laid it on the table. The officer called Richter sat on the far side of the room, stretching out his legs, sipping his coffee and lighting a cigarette. The adjutant looked through the window in the door for a moment, and then was gone.

'Good morning,' the older man said with a smile; he spoke perfectly accented French. 'I am Herr Mustchin. Have I the honour to address Mam'selle Annick Garel?'

'I'm told so,' the girl replied. She was puzzled by his tone; it was so very different from that of the soldiers who had been interviewing her so far. 'I can't really remember.'

'You were found, though, in a fishing net, and pulled out of the sea just beyond the harbour here – is that correct?'

'I was taken up in a storm, and then, some time later, I was dropped.'

'That particular storm, if the reports I have are correct, would have been over thirty years ago – is that right?' Mustchin showed her a page cut from a newspaper. 'Here it is – the article is all here. It reports the tragic loss of a fishing family, the Garels – your family apparently. Their boat capsized and all were drowned in a storm just off the coast here. It happened in 1906. Does any of that story sound familiar to you?'

'Some of it does, yes. The old man who says he is my uncle said the same thing. I can only remember being thrown into the water as the boat capsized, and seeing my father tangled up in the sail and going under. Then I was taken up.'

'Taken up, you say . . . How, and by whom?'

'By the angels. By the bright ones. The ones so bright you can't look at them.'

Herr Mustchin shuffled through the folder on the desk and then read aloud, '*Bright like looking into the sun at noon . . . And it was the sun that spoke to me in my head.* Was it something like that for you?' He looked over at her.

'Yes, it was like that. I didn't say that to anyone, did I?'

'No, you didn't. That was said by another girl some years ago – a German girl. I believe she saw the same angels as you. Did the angels you saw teach you anything, or show you anything?'

The girl sat up straight and looked directly at Herr Mustchin. 'I don't think they did – except the silver bubble I found myself in . . . I think I would have remembered anything else.'

'This silver bubble . . . were you in that when you came back to the sea?'

'I must have been.'

'Have you felt any different since you were with them? Can you do things you couldn't do before? It could be anything at all, however small . . .'

The girl was wary now. She didn't like the soldiers. They threatened and bullied her. They didn't believe her. She was frightened of them and what they might do. That was why the angels had shown her how to send 'help' signals out into the night sky. They knew that another would see them, and understand, and come and rescue her.

Herr Mustchin nodded and pointed to a family photograph which he had taken from his folder. 'Monsieur Garel claims that the girl pictured here is you. I have to say, there is a very strong resemblance. He also claims that this man is him.' He gestured to a figure in the photograph. 'He claims to be your father's brother. According to the reports, he has been trying to see you. You don't know him at all, though – is that correct?'

'An old man came to see me and he was crying. He said he was my uncle but I didn't remember him.'

Richter looked over from the other side of the room, a smile on his face as he drew on his cigarette.

Herr Mustchin continued. 'If that picture really is of Garel and he is your uncle, and if you are the girl in that same picture, that would make you at least forty-nine years old, and yet you don't look it, do you?'

'It can't be me, can it?' the girl said, tentative now, perhaps believing that this could be true, that anything might be possible with the help of the angels.

Richter suddenly sat up straight and laughed. 'Of course not, girl. Admit it – you are a spy for the communists, a petty smuggler, a thief on the run; something everyday, something boring. You've never seen an angel.' He pointed his cocked finger at her. '*Bang!*'

Herr Mustchin turned and fixed him with a disapproving and penetrating gaze. 'I was under the impression that *I* was conducting this interview, Leutnant. I wonder if you would mind leaving us. The adjutant can surely stand guard outside. You are creating a negative force, and you are fouling the air with your cigarette. You are aware that the Führer forbids smoking among his officers?'

Richter stood up and saluted, then left them to it.

'Good,' Mustchin said, switching on a wire recorder on the desk in front of him and then looking at the girl again. 'Now, in your own words, tell me everything you can remember of what happened to you that day.'

'That morning I went out with my parents and brothers. All I can remember is the mast falling and the sail pulling my father under the water, and then the feeling of being lifted up very fast, and voices in my head singing and sounding like bells. Then, some time later, I fell back into the water, and they say I was all tangled up in the net. Then, in the café, the man came and said he was my uncle. Later they took us down to the beach, and the priest blessed the sea and me and thanked the angels. The old man was there, and he said again that he knew who I was, but I still didn't know him.'

The man was following what she said – following it eagerly. He wasn't scoffing at her ideas or speaking harshly like the others had done. It seemed that he might believe her about the angels – though this didn't make her any less scared. In fact, she feared him more. She was sure that if he believed her, then he didn't want to help her; he wanted to contact the angels and hurt them, and her, in some way. She'd been fearful ever since the angels had let her go.

She had reached out for help and found the other one; he was very near now.

The girl opened something in her head. The angels had shown her how to do it by holding onto the little piece of rainbow metal. It was like pulling back a curtain and revealing a bright window. She allowed what she was seeing in front of her to go back out through the reflecting glass . . . It travelled high into the sky, where it could be viewed by the boy she saw all the time – through the window in his own head. He had also been touched by the angels. She opened the window now and showed him the man who was asking her questions. She kept her head still and concentrated on him. She didn't blink.

She hardly noticed what Mustchin asked her next, so hard was she concentrating on sending out the image. The little piece of metal had been in her old pinafore. The head soldier had taken it and put it in the folder that was on the desk in front of her. She had to get it back before this man saw it. The boy was very close to her now, in both space and time. Like her, he had been chosen, had been lifted up by the angels. He would come for her soon, and she would be ready.

She could do things now. Inside her was a growing awareness of a dormant power. It was tamped down like a tightly coiled spring. She had tried it out in very small ways in her room at night. No one else knew what she could do. She could most likely do much more, especially with the help of the boy who was coming to save her. She couldn't tell anyone else about this power – especially not this man. She just knew that, like all the others, he would turn out to be vicious underneath. She saw right through him. She was on her guard now, convinced that they all meant her harm.

Leutnant Richter opened the door and came in again. He deliberately lit another cigarette, as if daring Herr Mustchin to comment, and then clicked his heels.

Mustchin stood up, obviously annoyed. The girl loosened something in her mind, slowing time itself . . . or something like it. Perhaps she herself speeded up. It was something she'd discovered she could do. She looked at Herr Mustchin's open folder; at the papers spread out across the table next to the recording device. The typed sheets were very thin; the breeze from under the blind was making them ripple. She shifted her gaze over to the smart, cruel soldier, Richter. His head was back and he seemed to be enjoying his newly lit cigarette. Then she looked at the pile of papers again and, using the power in her head, lifted them as if the breeze had grown stronger. They rustled, and she suddenly sent them high into the air so that they scattered, then slowly drifted down to the floor. At the same time she made the lit cigarette fall out of Richter's mouth in a shower of bright red sparks, which caught the sheets of paper; flames blossomed out across the floor. All this seemed to her to take place in slow motion. Then, at her speed, she reached out and took back the little disc of rainbow metal, tucking it into her pocket . . . and reset time so that it ran at its normal speed.

Herr Mustchin shouted and stamped on the papers. 'Shut that window,' he screamed at Richter, who shot forward at once and slammed it shut.

The papers were picked up. There was no serious damage, just some singed edges. Herr Mustchin set the papers back on the desk and put a heavy glass ashtray on top of them.

'Now perhaps you will understand why I was anxious to prevent smoking in here.'

He looked at the girl. She sat in the same position, unmoved, her hands flat on the table. She had done nothing – although he also knew at once that she had done everything. *Confirmed*, he thought. *You are indeed one of the returned, and have just this moment become not only very dangerous but also very valuable. That was no simple unplanned accident.* He knew what their previous captive, Fräulein V, had been capable of. He had been there at the aerodrome on that fateful afternoon when she pulled the aeroplane out of the sky. After that, despite the horror of the outcome, his department's funding had suddenly been tripled.

Annick Garel closed the curtain in her head. She clutched the little disc in her pocket and summoned up the schoolroom blackboard. In the dark space in her mind she wrote again in white chalk the words she always wrote: *Aidez-moi* . . . Help me.

'After this interview,' Herr Mustchin told Richter, 'we will need to remove this girl to a secure unit.'

He shuffled the papers back into the folder. Tucked in amongst them were photographs he had just brought back from Monteneuf. The clearance was going well. What they had partially uncovered could be seen as a 'silver bubble', he supposed, albeit an ancient one.

CHAPTER EIGHTEEN

Douarnenez

At the harbour we split up. Sperring went off one way to meet further contacts. We stayed with Pascal, while M. Bouchard went out on his boat as normal.

This was a relief – I was sure we were about to go out on a fishing boat again. No. We were all to meet up later at the local cinema, the Rex. The streets were already busy with the market. I hoped against reason that we wouldn't be noticed. Anyone who looked at us was a potential traitor. Arousing even the slightest suspicion could prove fatal. It was hard to get used to; and drained any energy I might have had. I began to notice people's faces and expressions.

Pascal led us along the crowded cobbled streets. There were fruit and vegetable stalls on either side, and a red painted butcher's shop with a horse's head outside – a *chevaline*, a horse butcher.

Just like the market near Aunt Dolly's house there were shady-looking types hanging around, offering things from inside their overcoats. Here, though, German soldiers were patrolling the streets. We kept away from them as much as we could.

'Things have been very difficult since the Germans came,' Pascal said as we walked. I had taken to him at once. He struck me as a fearless type, not afraid to put himself in danger in order to help us. I'm not sure I would have been as brave if our positions had been reversed. He was hiding us in a hostile town, risking himself for a boy about whom he knew nothing; he had no idea that Tom was in any way special.

'There are shortages of everything,' he went on. 'Though we are lucky here – we have fish, and our relatives in the countryside bring us fresh vegetables and fruit. Here in the Northern Occupied Zone, city-dwellers are already going hungry. No one complains. No one says anything. They keep their heads down. If you protest or complain officially, anything like that, you're sent off to work in Germany.'

I translated this for Tom as we walked, keeping my voice low, looking around as I did so. I remembered the SOE lectures: 'Stay vigilant.' One of the shady-looking characters was close behind us; he was bundled up in a dark overcoat, looking down at his feet as he walked. He didn't seem interested in us, but 'stay vigilant' were the watchwords.

We finally reached Pascal's home – the safe house.

His mother opened the door to us and quickly ushered us inside. 'You can't be too careful,' she said. 'Some people delight in spying on others.'

'Someone was walking close behind us just now,' I said.

Pascal nodded. 'Oh, him', he said. 'I saw him too. It takes some getting used to, all the mistrust; all the suspicion. I know who he is. I don't think he means us any harm, but you were right to mention it. People will report anything out of the ordinary to the authorities – even the slightest thing. Neighbour turns on neighbour. They think they'll get more rations or better treatment. It's terrible.'

We were taken through into a back parlour and warmed ourselves by the fire in the big granite fireplace, well away from any windows.

Pascal left immediately to unload fish under the noses of the Germans. 'We'll be fine,' I told him in my best French when I shook his hand.

'Stay low and keep away from the window. I will be back at six to take you over to the cinema,' he said, and stay low we did.

I looked at Tom and saw that he'd gone into a kind of trance. His eyes had glazed over and he was muttering something under his breath, just as he had back in London.

However, he soon snapped out of it and turned to me. 'She contacted me,' he said suddenly in the quiet room.

I leaned forward. 'What did she say?'

'I think she wanted to show me something. I saw a man talking to her, but he was speaking French so I couldn't understand. After that I saw the blackboard with *Help me* written on it.'

'What was the man like? Was he a soldier?'

'He had a moustache and he was wearing a suit and tie. It looked as if he was reading from some papers, and then he was staring straight at her, and so at me too. The image was as clear as if he had been sitting here with us. Then there was the blackboard and the chalked words, *Aidez-moi*.'

Later, at noon by the mantel clock, Mme Bouchard brought us some bowls of soup.

'*Potage grandmère*,' she said. 'Made with vegetables sent in from my cousin's garden. We must make the best of them while we still have them.' She looked at me. 'Do you understand French, monsieur?'

I nodded, and then tried the soup. It was thick and smooth, and a pale yellow colour. I was used to the thin, powdery stuff that they served at the Lyons Corner Houses – called *crème de legumes*, in an attempt to sound sophisticated – but it didn't taste like Mme Bouchard's.

She was serious and concerned. 'I hope you never have to suffer invasion and occupation in England,' she said. 'We live this nightmare twenty-four hours of every single day. Pascal says you have come to rescue the girl who was caught in our nets.'

'We're going to do our best,' I said.

'Well, you cannot do any more, can you? Why is she so important, this girl? There are so many rumours about her. Pierre told me that she looked very thin and pale. There was a thanksgiving ceremony on the beach – some said she had come back from the dead. Monsieur Garel says it is his missing niece and it is a miracle – he says this to anyone who will listen.' She crossed herself. 'That caught the attention of the Germans, and so they locked the poor girl up.'

She waited while I translated what she had said for Tom.

'Just why is that girl so important?' she asked me again.

'She is very important,' I said. 'I can't say any more than that.'

She nodded, crossed herself again, and then cleared away the soup bowls. I noticed how red and raw her hands looked, and how tired she seemed.

I couldn't explain to anyone that the girl they had fished out of the sea had earlier been communicating with Tom by mysterious telepathic means. They would think we were mad. It was too soon for any of that.

'Looks like they are questioning her, then,' I said after Mme Bouchard had gone, 'if that is what she showed you, Tom.'

'The man looked fierce and intense . . .' he told me. 'Though he was controlling his anger. I think he was scared of her.'

'The sooner we can get her out of there, the better,' I said.

Mme Bouchard suggested we might like to take a bath. We both had a welcome, if lukewarm, soak, then sat and waited by the dwindling fire as the afternoon slowly passed.

CHAPTER NINETEEN

Just before six Pascal came back. We left the house with him.

'There is a curfew,' he said. 'No one is allowed out after nine unless they have a good reason and a special pass. That's why the cinema is showing the film early – it means we'll be out just after eight. We don't get any Hollywood films any more – no English language films at all. It's mostly German propaganda pictures, but tonight there's a French film with Suzy Delair. There'll be a big crowd of young people, so you'll both fit in all right.'

The cinema – a big building with low lighting in the foyer – was on the junction of two streets. As expected, there was a crowd of young people wrapped up in overcoats and scarves – we had been warned there would be no heating in the cinema. I saw Sperring

chatting to a man; he was standing under a poster for the French film: *Le Dernier des Six* – The Last of Six. It looked like a detective flick. We went over and shook hands with them.

'This is an old friend, Labarre. We can trust him – he knows the layout of the *mairie* well.'

We went into the auditorium and I sat in the back row next to Tom. M. Labarre sat between me and Sperring; Pascal was furthest from me. There was a buzz, a happy sense of anticipation among the audience. They were excited to see a new film, no matter how cold it was there. The lights went down, and some of the young bloods whooped and whistled before being shushed by the older patrons.

The curtains were drawn back and we heard the newsreel fanfare. *France – Actualité – Pathé – Gaumont* flashed up on the screen. First, of course, came the news of the war. We saw German soldiers marching, then a big eagle with a swastika in its talons. As soon as Hitler appeared, there was a loud chorus of coughing and spluttering, along with a few muttered boos. The noise carried on throughout the newsreel – until the lights suddenly came up again, and we saw half a dozen German soldiers standing in the aisles. Silence fell. An officer pointed to various young people in each row, and they were dragged out, one after the other.

'These are clear signs of rebellion!' The officer's eyes flicked to and fro, and then caught mine; he pointed directly at me. 'Outside!' he shouted in French.

One of the soldiers grabbed me and pulled me to my feet. The older members of the audience looked firmly at the washed-out images of the war on the screen; no one wanted to acknowledge what was happening all around them – though some of the young ones were standing up as if ready to leave. I looked at Tom and then at Sperring, who shook his head very slightly.

I was bundled outside with a random selection of young people – perhaps a dozen in all. We were surely to be made an example of in some way. We'd most likely be birched or whipped, I thought, and very nearly pissed in my trousers. It had all happened so fast, I'd had no time to think of a strategy for dealing with the situation. Here, there was no pattern for me to discern, no strange feeling to analyse. I had simply tumbled head first into big trouble. I just hoped that the others had a plan. I should have prepared myself, I thought. After all, this sort of thing was always a possibility.

We were lined up against the outer wall of the cinema, and I noticed that the young man next to me was crying. As the German officer walked along, inspecting each of us closely, I noticed a grey army truck parked on the pavement nearby, its tailgate down. My heart pounding, I half expected to see a machine-gun ready to mow us down. At the department we had heard rumours and seen photographic evidence of the atrocities inflicted on civilians in the Eastern Occupied Zone.

There was no machine-gun. When we were ordered to get into the truck, I saw that it was empty, apart from benches on either side. I was last on, and two soldiers piled in next to me, carelessly pushing me and another boy aside. The officer sat up with the driver. When the engine started, I was conscious of the smell of diesel fumes, sweat and leather boots. I just gazed down at the rough flooring, trying to appear fed up and bored; not terrified, despite my pounding heart. I was worried about Tom, left behind, unable to speak French. I was sure I'd end up being shot.

When we set off, I looked back and saw a crowd of people milling around the cinema. They had obviously given up on the film and were spilling out into the road, heading home.

The truck's engine echoed loudly off the walls in the quiet streets. Way behind us, I thought I saw Tom and Lieutenant Sperring running after the truck, and quickly turned away. I didn't want to draw attention to them. When I looked back again, I saw that Tom had stopped ahead of the rest of the group; he raised his arms up above his head, as if in a gesture of surrender.

I braced myself, holding onto the bench with both hands – and then the truck suddenly lurched right across the road, as if negotiating a sharp bend – except that there was no bend. The soldiers fell over – one face down on the truck bed, the other backwards. With a screech of tyres, the truck turned sharply the other way, lurching out of control. I saw sparks flying up off the road where the metal wheel rims had scraped against the granite kerb. The soldier who had fallen forward didn't move. As the tailgate shuddered down, the other one fell out onto the road.

I heard shouting from the cab. Most of the other prisoners had got to their feet; now they started to panic. The truck's dim headlamps suddenly burned with a blue-white light – a light I recognized only too well. All this took place within the space of a few seconds at most, though it felt longer. The truck suddenly accelerated, and then, equally suddenly, screeched to a halt, sending everybody flying. It reversed across the road and slowly tipped onto one side; the remaining prisoners leaned over to try and counterbalance it. I took my chance and leaped out of the back before it went over. I hit the road and went into a forward roll like a parachutist. At least I had picked up something at our training sessions with Sperring. I turned in time to see the truck crash into a streetlamp, which juddered and slowly toppled over. The other lads either climbed or jumped out of the truck, then scattered and ran off in all directions. Suddenly I heard gunshots. The officer had emerged from the cab, and was firing his gun up into the air. The bright headlamps faded to nothing. Pitch darkness.

To anyone watching, what had happened to the truck would have just seemed like a malfunction. An accident. I knew better, of course. As I ran back towards the cinema, I passed the fallen soldier, who was now lying in the road – unconscious, by the look of it. I heard more gunshots behind me. The officer was still firing into the air – at least, I hoped it was him. The crowd outside the Rex were fleeing in panic. No one wanted to hang around when there were guns going off all over the place.

A freak accident had apparently saved a dozen young hotheads from a beating, or perhaps worse . . . Well, I knew that it was no accident.

It was Tom Pile.

When the Germans came to examine the truck afterwards, what would they find? Just a burned-out electrical system? Surely there would be no physical evidence of sabotage. No excuse to take hostages . . .

I stopped for a moment. My knee hurt from when I had hit the road. I limped forward for a couple of paces, and then felt a hand clamp down hard on my shoulder. I turned.

It was a French policeman.

'Stop . . . Pass . . . Come on – papers.' He had obviously singled me out as I ran back to the scene of the 'crime'. It was my own fault. I should have headed off into one of the side streets. I had wanted to protect Tom. A major error. My pass was a fake, of course, but it was the best the SOE could come up with and was nicely weathered. Besides, it was pretty dark now.

'Next time you and your little communist friends feel one of your coughing fits coming on,' he said, 'suppress it, will you? Use a handkerchief or take yourself off to the doctor for some cough syrup. The Germans will not tolerate insults, as you should know. Now go on – get lost, before I arrest you.' There was sudden and more urgent shouting from the truck. 'I said, *get lost*, go on!' The policeman kicked out at me so that I stumbled forward. Then he turned and ran off back down the street towards the crashed truck and the shouting officer.

I had been saved by Tom. Now I just had to find him again.

CHAPTER TWENTY

Mairie, Douarnenez

Annick Garel lay quietly in the darkness of her secure room at the *mairie*. Or, rather, floated there. The darkness did not oppress or scare her as it might once have done. No locks or chains could hold her. Darkness was her medium now. She soared, sending herself out into the darkness like a hunting bird, an owl or a hawk. Out through the ceiling, through the roof of the *mairie*, and up into the night sky. She flew over the sea and the town and the surrounding countryside. She watched everything, and all the while her body remained on the truckle bed in her cell. Whenever the guard checked, there she was, exactly where she was meant to be. All the while the voices of the angels who'd saved her from the sea spoke and sang to her. They did not use words, but the sounds they made were easily understood.

They wanted to understand her. Whether she lay quiet on the bed or soared high in the night sky, they asked for her story; the joyous voices uplifted her and empowered her.

'Tell us,' they said. 'Tell us everything.'

Time was in flux. As they spoke to her and she answered them, there seemed to be no past and no present. All time was present. She could ramble on for what seemed like hours or days – or was it merely seconds? At times she floated higher than the clouds, up among the stars. Then it seemed as if she was curled inside a warm silver bubble with the stars spread out all around her.

'Tell us,' the bells said.

The blackboard was there with her in the big schoolroom that was also a silver ball. She could write on it with the white chalk and could use it to block others from seeing into her star-filled head. She had only to imagine the blackboard filling her mind to close the door into her soul.

'In the summer we went to the beach, and I felt the sand between my toes as I walked amongst the seaweed and the tiny white shells. The cold surf washed in and out, white with blue bubbles at the edge. My mother picked through the shells. She held out the prettiest ones to me. There were white ones shaped like a fan.

There were stripy curled ones. When it was calm, we went out in the fishing boat. After a long day at sea, my eyes always felt hot and tired. My father was busy on the deck hauling in nets; tipping the torrent of silver fish into the baskets. I looked over the edge of the baskets and saw all the shining eyes. Even then I knew that they weren't looking back at me; they had dead button eyes and their mouths were open, their bodies silver like the angels'.

'When my mother brushed my hair, she said it was the hair of the angels; my white-gold hair, so like her own. Then the storm came. I saw my father fall into the water. I saw the mast break, and then fall, slowly, taking with it the sail, like a shroud, and then he was wrapped in it and pulled under the waves. Then the hands came – only they weren't hands but light, and the voices were like bells. They held me. They lifted me out of the sinking boat. I saw it so clearly as I rose into the air. Below me, I saw the boat break up and sink, taking everyone I loved away, away, down into the dark grey foaming sea. I did not cry out. I was too busy talking to the angels and writing in white chalk on the black dome of the sky beyond the clouds, beyond the blue, *Help me*. There in the star-filled darkness I saw a boy with dark hair whirling in his own silver ball. I stepped out of my ball across the blackness, across the bridge of light and time. The boy was looking out at the surrounding stars, and his eyes were bright and searching. He reached out his hand and I took it.

'I felt the charge, the connection between us through my whole body. I could see him in his bed, far across the water. *Help me*, I said. *Help me*. I wrote in white on black. *Walls, the white walls, the mayor's office, the sea, the Germans and the angels are here . . . Come and help me*.

All this was happening at once as I lay on the narrow bed in Douarnenez. There were times when I was in the cold water looking up at the boiling dark clouds. The beams of light burst from the sky and touched the water; they engulfed me and lifted me up into the sky. At other times I was falling, tumbling end over end in the air like a bird diving down to catch a fish in the water – a guillemot – but flying so slowly, at the end of the long beam of light, down into the water, where I was tangled in the net.

'And there, waiting for me, was a different boy – the boy with sea-blue eyes. The boy called Pascal. He held my hand and spoke to me when I was cold, in my dream of now.'

CHAPTER TWENTY-ONE

Douarnenez

The report of the incident at the cinema and the accident with the truck was on Hauptmann Meier's desk the next morning. After lunch he took Leutnant Richter down to the big Renault garage that had been requisitioned for German army vehicles. Against the back wall, upside down so that they could see the blackened chassis, was the truck, still attached to the French breakdown lorry's tow chain.

'What happened?' Meier called out. 'Was it sabotage? A device of some kind?'

A German mechanic in grey overalls was standing by the truck. He had a lamp and was running it all over the underneath. 'Not that I can see,' he said. 'Nothing has been attached. It just went haywire – driver error, electrical fault – I really don't know. Certainly the electrics have all shorted out, but I can find nothing that would have caused that crash.'

'You're sure?'

'I am very sure, hauptmann. I am used to servicing these vehicles. I know them like the back of my own hand. No sign of any interference at all: nothing added, nothing taken away.'

'Just as well,' Richter said. 'Retaliation is always unpopular among the peasants. It only encourages the scum to rebel. At worst some young people got lucky. None of our soldiers were badly hurt, and the peasants got a fright.'

'True – and we'll have fewer of the communist "coughing fits" in the cinema from now on.'

They left the garage and went down to the sea, where the tide was out. It was cold, but sunny, and the curving beach was inviting, so they walked back towards their villas past coils of barbed wire and tank traps laid along the shoreline. Here they met Herr Mustchin. He was walking straight towards them, tightly buttoned up in his forest-green overcoat.

'Here comes our "spook" doctor, our seeker of the irrational,' Meier muttered under his breath.

'Good afternoon, Herr Mustchin,' he said out loud, touching the peak of his cap. 'Your villa is to your liking and the servant is looking after you well enough, I hope?'

'Yes, all that is satisfactory. I wish to interview the man Garel. Could this be arranged please?' he asked brusquely.

'I am sure it can be arranged very easily – he is a man possessed. A man only too eager to help us. Will tomorrow morning be soon enough for you? I will confess that Leutnant Richter and I are intending to go riding on the sands before dark today.'

'Tomorrow morning will be satisfactory. I am about to send a confidential report to Berlin. I need to cross some t's and dot some i's.'

'You heard about the accident last night?' Richter said.

'No, what happened?' Mustchin asked, his interest piqued at once. 'After all, anything unusual might be connected.'

'One of our trucks taking some young communist hooligans to HQ for a beating suddenly went out of control and crashed into a streetlamp. They all ran away, the truck was badly damaged, but none of our soldiers were hurt.'

'Was this an act of sabotage – a bomb, sugar in the tank?' Mustchin asked.

'No, apparently not this time. A failure of the system, out of the blue. The driver wasn't even drunk. It's a mystery.'

'What of the girl? Was she observed at this time? Where was she exactly?'

'She was in her cell at the *mairie*. Where do you think she was? She was nowhere near the scene of the accident – she was safely locked up.'

'Oh yes, of course,' Mustchin said. 'I understand.'

He watched Meier and Richter stroll on along the beach in their crisp uniforms and their shining boots. They were so confident of their superiority, so blissfully unaware of that other, larger world which was now so close to their own. It appeared that Berlin's English source had warned of this very possibility – that the English had found a 'returnee'. There might well be two of them now.

Herr Mustchin turned round and went back to the little villa on the front. The documents he had brought with him on the 'found object at Monteneuf' were no longer safe. He went up to his bedroom and pulled his suitcase out of the wardrobe. No one would ever have guessed what was inside.

He opened it and took out the precious folder, along with the file of photographs, transferring them to his briefcase. They must remain with him wherever he went now. They must not leave his sight. If necessary, he would chain the case to his wrist like a nervous bank messenger fearful of a hold-up.

There they were: the photographs; part of the mysterious craft. It had been found only six months before, buried deep among the remarkable and mostly hidden ancient menhirs, the standing stones, at Monteneuf. The menhirs were scattered amongst a dense forest. Fräulein V had indicated the area – the 'place of lights', she had called it – in one of her interviews in 1936. She had pointed it out to them on a map of France.

The locals of Monteneuf knew little or nothing about the hidden standing stones. Herr Mustchin and an assistant had visited the area, posing as tourists, long before the outbreak of war, before any thoughts of the possibility of an invasion. They took secret measurements and photographs. By 1940, when the Germans invaded, his department had already organized an extensive and secret archaeological dig at the forest site with the full approval of Reichsmarshall Goering.

After he had finished interviewing Garel and the girl, he would return to Monteneuf and supervise the operation. Here was a chance to test his theory on sacrifice and the Ancients. He would take the girl along too. Who knew what might happen once she was on the spot where his team had found the craft? Depending on the outcome, he could then either arrange for her to go to Berlin for rigorous tests on their new secret weapon . . . or for the quick disposal of her body. With luck he might even flush out the returnee held by the British and deal with both.

MEMO

TO: Herr Kohler, Office of the Unexplained & the Supernatural, Berlin

FROM: First Field Expedition, Northern Occupied Zone, Monteneuf,

Codename V

Success. Have located the buried remains of the 'object', as originally located on the map by Fräulein V. She was not far out in her supposition.
 Suggest team continue examination of site in secret. Will report further. Photographs attached.

CHAPTER TWENTY-TWO

'That crash wasn't just luck, was it, Jack?' Lieutenant Sperring said as we made our way back to the safe house. 'Tom made that accident happen somehow, didn't he? I was watching him.'

'I can't discuss it,' I said. 'Our mission is to rescue the girl and get her back home. That's it.'

'Do the Germans know anything about any of this odd stuff?'

'One of the reasons why we are here is to stop them finding out,' I said. 'They have their own bureau of "odd stuff", as you put it, in Berlin. They have done for a while now.' I stopped, sure that I had already said too much.

Tom was walking behind us with Pascal, who had found him standing very still – 'like a statue' – in a side street behind the cinema. The two of them seemed to be getting on even without the use of language. They both had the same roots, after all, one from the soil, one from the sea. They shared everything except a language.

Up in the attic of the Bouchards' house, hidden among the parts of a treadle sewing machine, was a radio transmitter and receiver. Sperring sent a follow-up coded message to Captain Holloway's office to confirm his contact with the local Resistance. There was a short burst of a reply: 'Understood'.

We were to sleep here. The roof timbers looked like the upturned hull of an old ship, and the whole place was full of old stuff. There was a dressmaker's dummy as well as all the sewing gear.

'My grandmother was a seamstress,' Pascal explained. 'It seemed like a good place to hide the radio. My grandfather used to own *Le Sillon*, our boat. It will be mine one day, all being well.'

He said goodnight, and left us to it. I settled down on a pile of blankets. Above my head was a round window set in the roof. I looked up into the night sky: the distant stars, the curve of the Milky Way. I thought about what Tom had experienced – somewhere out there; somewhere beyond our understanding. He was asleep, already muttering bits of garbled French under his breath.

'Whatever's that?' Sperring said.

'Tom has these dreams,' I explained.

'Does that include speaking in tongues – well, bad-sounding French anyway?'

'Seems it does,' I said, and buried myself under the blankets.

The next morning we made a frugal breakfast. M. Bouchard had already gone out fishing; Pascal had stayed with us.

'We will need to visit the *mairie* this morning,' Sperring said. 'We must pay close attention to the guards and to all the possible entrances and exits. I have a contact on the inside. I telephoned him yesterday. He will meet us in the gardens opposite at nine a.m. and bring us a plan of the interior, I hope. We'd better get moving.' It was already eight o'clock.

I turned and saw that Tom was once again staring off into the distance. He appeared distracted, as if he was watching and concentrating on something that the rest of us couldn't see.

'They are moving her,' he murmured suddenly.

'Explain please,' Sperring said.

'Later today,' Tom said. 'They are taking her somewhere else.'

Sperring looked at me and then gestured over to Tom, who was now sitting bolt upright with his eyes closed. 'How does our own Nostradamus here know all this stuff, Jack? I just don't buy it. I know you and old Holloway run some kind of spook station, but this is going too far. We are in occupied territory here, and I am supposed to trust to the notions of this boy as if I was a giggling schoolgirl and he a gypsy fortune-teller on the Palace Pier at Brighton?'

'He is able to communicate with the girl,' I said, realizing I was digging myself a very deep hole.

'I am supposed to entrust our safety, our lives, to some sort of telepathy, if that is what it is?'

'Seems so,' I said. 'It's worked so far. Although up until now Tom hasn't been able to understand French. Maybe it has gone beyond language – I don't know; none of us do.'

Sperring shook his head. 'Can't be done,' he said. 'I knew this mission was a mistake – I said so from the start.'

Tom opened his eyes. 'I need a pencil and paper,' he said in a flat voice.

They were found, and Tom wrote, as if his hand was being guided by something – or someone – else: a single word.

MONTENEUF

'What does that mean?' I asked.

'It's a place name, a small town – hardly even that,' Sperring said. 'A few miles from here.'

'She heard them say it,' Tom said, as if he had woken up again. 'She wrote it on the blackboard,' he added, 'along with what she always writes – *Aidez-moi* . . . Help me.'

'Are you seriously telling me that Tom sees what she thinks or writes down?' Sperring said.

'I'm not telling you anything,' I said firmly.

'We still have to go and meet my contact near the *mairie*. Either we get her out of there today or, if they really are moving her, we have to follow them to this other place, Monteneuf, and that won't be easy. We'll need transport.'

Tom, Pascal, Sperring and myself set off for the *mairie*. I carried a fisherman's basket, trying to play the part. The gardens in front of the *mairie* were laid out in a formal pattern. The bare trees and hedges had been severely pruned, and there were benches placed at regular intervals. A few children ran about, jumping over the divisions in the parterre. Old men in overcoats sat slumped, smoking or playing chess near a boarded-up café. I could see the *mairie* on the other side of the road. Two flags – a tricolour and a swastika – flew together over the entrance, and grey army vehicles were lined up in front of the building. A soldier stood sentry by the main door.

Pascal saw his contact immediately – it was a young man with a beret sitting on a bench. He led me over while Sperring and Tom went to sit on another bench.

Pascal introduced me, and the man nodded to me and then handed over a small envelope, which Pascal quickly put away in his inside pocket. I looked around the gardens. The old men seemed to be taking no notice of us, but remembering all the talk about neighbours betraying neighbours, I thought that any one of them might be up to no good.

'Might be a change of plan,' Pascal said. 'It seems that our particular parcel might be moved today to a spot further inland.'

'How much further?' the contact asked.

'Not far – seventy kilometres or so. Monteneuf.'

'Really? Monteneuf, you say? Now, that is a very strange coincidence. That whole area was cleared within a few weeks of the Germans arriving and then locked up tight as a drum. The whole village was evacuated.'

'Well, that's where our parcel might be bound for,' Pascal said.

'You have one advantage,' the young man told him. 'That area is one big forest. You can approach through the trees – that way you might just get in unseen. It will be very risky, though.'

'Thanks,' Pascal said. 'Hear that, Jack? It makes me wonder what they're up to. Are they building a prison camp or something?'

'If they are,' the contact said, 'then it's one without any actual prisoners, as far as we can tell – unless they are just waiting to transfer some poor souls from elsewhere.'

I turned and noticed that Tom was sitting very still, staring intently at the *mairie* as if he could see inside. He had gone off into one of his trances. I went over to him and Sperring.

'We should leave,' the lieutenant said. 'Now.' He got up and walked away from the bench.

Tom said, 'They are taking her away this afternoon.'

'How do you know?' I asked. 'Surely they were speaking in French.'

'Yes,' he said. 'But now I understand everything.'

'You surprise me more and more, Tom,' I said, replying in his new-found French.

'They want to show her something – well, the man with the moustache does. The others don't really know what he is talking about,' Tom told me.

'Come on,' I said.

We followed Sperring out through the gates. Pascal joined us and we walked back in the direction of the Bouchards' house.

'I have the map of the inside of the mairie,' Pascal said. 'Not that it matters, if they are moving her.'

'They're moving her this afternoon,' I said.

'How do you know?'

'Tom knows,' I explained. 'Before you ask how, he just *does*. He heard them talking about it. He apparently understands more French than I thought. He's been having lessons.'

'Nothing I can say to any of this, is there?' Sperring said, stopping suddenly and shaking his head in frustration. 'You ghost ops lot really are spooky, aren't you! Well, we haven't time to get your girl from inside the *mairie*. We'll just have to follow them as best we can.'

'Our contact tells me there are strange things going on over at Monteneuf,' Pascal said.

'That all fits somehow.' Sperring sighed. 'Chasing ghosts and notions. We'll need to organize transport.'

'We can borrow a van,' Pascal said. 'It's almost new – a Citroën TUB; it belongs to my uncle. We have a permit too. I can drive you there. Fuel might be a problem, but we should be able to manage it. No need to check with my father – we don't have time. We'll just go and take it.'

'Won't you get into trouble?' I asked.

'You need the van now – I'll have to risk it,' he said. 'I feel sorry for that poor girl, locked up in there. What are they planning to do to her? I wouldn't put anything past them.' He spat on the kerb.

'Where is this van?' Sperring said.

'It's tucked away in a garage – maybe five minutes away.'

Observe and deduce – the training words sprang into my mind as we walked on. One of the men who'd been sitting in the gardens was walking some way behind us. I had seen him before: he had been behind us in the market too. Here he was again. He was plump and bundled up in the same dark overcoat and the same distinctive grey Fedora-style hat. His face was pink – flushed with cold perhaps, or was it that he lived a little too well compared to his neighbours, taking extra rations from the Germans in return for information received? He looked down at the ground as he walked, not at us. I didn't like it one bit. *Observe and deduce.*

CHAPTER TWENTY-THREE

Douarnenez/Monteneuf

'Don't look round now, but I think we're being followed,' I told the others. 'Someone has been behind us ever since we left the gardens.'

'Is it just the one?' Sperring said.

'Yes – a man.'

'Keep an eye on him, but don't be too obvious. It might be nothing at all.'

We followed Pascal up through the steep streets, away from the harbour and the market. We passed some small modern whitewashed factories and warehouses. Everything was unnaturally quiet; hardly anyone was about. Our follower was still there, keeping pace with us. We came to a builder's yard with the name BOUCHARD painted in big blue letters on a wooden fascia board across the entrance. Inside I could see lengths of timber and sacks of cement, but there was no sign of any building work, or even any workers. It was like a ghost town.

'Lots of men have been taken away to build fortifications for the Germans along the coast, especially at Brest,' Pascal told us. 'No one is building any new houses here at the moment.'

We went into the yard proper. The man behind us carried on past the entrance without even glancing in. We tucked ourselves away behind one of the stacks of timber and waited. He did not return.

'He could be reporting us to the local police even now. I'm afraid too many of them here toe the Nazi line. He could even be alerting someone at German HQ,' Pascal said. 'Or it could be nothing. It really doesn't matter. Either way, we've no time to waste.'

The Citroën van was hidden under a tarpaulin in a locked garage at the rear of the yard. It was almost new and in good order.

'My uncle hid it in here when the Germans first arrived. They were requisitioning vehicles,' Pascal said.

'The supply chain is better now, I'm guessing,' Sperring said. 'Not quite so much need to steal from the locals as there was.' He ran his hand over the bodywork. 'She'll do very well. Of course, we don't know if they really *are* moving the girl, or their exact destination – or anything else for that matter. It's all in his head.' He indicated Tom.

'I'm sorry, but we have to rely on Tom,' I said. 'It's the nature of this mission. We can't do it any other way.'

Tom was gazing off into the distance again, his expression vague and distracted. He seemed to spend as much time communing with the girl and other entities as he did talking to us. His reality had gradually shifted ever since he'd visited the remains of the craft in Dorset.

'We should go now,' he said in French, grabbing Pascal by the elbow. 'They will pass us on the road and then we can follow them.'

'Now we have to trust another sudden prediction out of nowhere?' Sperring said.

'It's everything – it's all we have to go on,' I insisted.

Pascal went into the office and rooted around in a desk drawer. He emerged with the spare keys for the van.

We set off cautiously, Sperring at the wheel. We had official permits, and according to Pascal the tank was full of precious fuel.

'I'll explain it all to my uncle later, somehow,' he said, and grinned.

'We'll pay him back for the fuel,' Sperring said. 'I promise you that, and it's a promise from the British government.'

Pascal sat up front, next to Sperring. Tom and I sat in the back, watching the road spool away behind us. We were stopped by the police at a checkpoint by the turning towards Brest. After the van had drawn to a halt, Tom went into action. He concentrated his energy – or whatever it was – on the policemen: they didn't even bother to look in the back of the van. They just checked the passes and waved us on.

After an hour or so Tom said, 'They are behind us. I can see the car. She is showing it to me. It has a small flag flying from the bonnet.'

I stuck my head into the cab and said to Sperring, 'Tom says they are somewhere on the road behind us.'

'Really,' he said. 'If that is the case, then I'll eat my hat.'

I stayed there, scanning the cars as they passed us. There weren't many.

It was another fifteen minutes before a German army staff car finally passed by. A small swastika flew on the bonnet.

'That must be them,' I said. 'Get out the frying pan, Lieutenant – it's time to cook a hat.'

It was impossible to see into the car itself, but I saw a frightened-looking, pale face framed by blonde hair look quickly back out of the rear window.

'That's her,' Pascal said.

Tom called out, 'She knows I'm here – I've told her we are coming to help.'

'I'm impressed,' Sperring said. 'I don't know how you do it, Tom. You should perform in the music halls.'

'We don't want to stay too close,' Pascal said. 'We should drop back a little. If the place is locked up as tight as our contact said it was, then we'll have to approach on foot. We'll need to hide the van too – somewhere we can find it easily later.'

'Let's just hope that there *is* a later,' Sperring muttered.

We were crossing a flattish plain; in the distance the forest stretched away on both sides of the straight road.

A road sign loomed up. Sperring stopped and climbed out. The place name on the sign had been painted out with what looked like tar or pitch, but he managed to scratch away part of a letter M and an O. This was Monteneuf all right.

'We'll drive in among the trees and find a hiding place for the van,' Sperring said.

We carried on for several more kilometres until we were deep in the forest, where the trees were dense.

'The ancient French kings used this place to hunt for wild boar,' Pascal told us.

One or two tracks snaked off from the main road, where the trees had been cut back. We drove cautiously a little way along one of them, and then Sperring reversed under a canopy of low branches. We camouflaged the front of the van with broken boughs and leaves until it was almost completely hidden.

'How will we find it again?' I wondered.

'I'll know where it is,' Tom said. 'Don't worry, we'll find it.'

In the distance, through the trees, we could hear drilling and hammering – the sound of construction work.

'I suppose we should head in that direction,' I said.

'I think we should split up,' Sperring suggested. 'We are too big a target like this. We stand a better chance in two groups. Pascal – you come with me, and you go with Tom, Jack. Keep within sight as far as possible.'

So Tom and I walked roughly in the direction of the sound, and it wasn't long before we came upon something very strange indeed.

Captain Holloway's Office

INTERCEPTED MEMO
Translated from the original German

FROM: Mustchin, Northern Occupied Zone, France
TO: H. Kohler, Office of the Unexplained & the Supernatural, Berlin

MOST SECRET

I am in the process of moving the girl to the site of the 'found object'. I have cameras and other equipment set up to record any outcomes. I will report in due course.

CHAPTER TWENTY-FOUR

Gallows Hill/Burton Bradstock, Dorset

At the time the above memo from Herr Mustchin was being decoded in London, I was deep below ground on Gallows Hill. Since Tom had entered the ruined hull, mysterious things had been happening.

It was gradual at first. The ARP warden, Mr Feaver, had come to see me; he was concerned.

'Some of the locals have reported seeing lights in the sky, Captain,' he said. 'They think it's enemy aircraft activity. Two or three have seen them over Gallows Hill, where your dig is.'

It seemed that Tom's contact with the craft's hull had set something off – a kind of alarm system maybe, or a beacon.

I tried to reassure him. 'My colleague and I will be up there today and we will still be there tonight, so we'll keep an eye open. If we see anything, I'll alert the anti-aircraft batteries over at Burton Bradstock and Dorchester.'

Staff Sergeant Shaw and I had continued excavating around the hull of the craft, finding little fragments of grey metal – much like the stuff the soldiers had carted away to the base at Burton Bradstock, where they were kept in a locked and guarded hangar. It had all seemed pretty inert – that is, until one of the sentries told Colonel Gauntlett – who in turn told Mr Feaver – that he'd heard odd noises coming from the place.

I had the only keys, so the day after the warden made this latest report, I drove to the base with Miss Shaw.

'I don't mind admitting I'm alarmed at what we might find – either in the hangar or under Gallows Hill,' she said.

'I am more curious than scared,' I replied. 'I like to believe that these beings, these "angels", are benign. Of course, we have no proof, no evidence of any such thing, but somehow I *feel* they wish us well.'

After coming to greet us, Colonel Gauntlett soon left us outside the hangar. He seemed only too keen to get away. 'I'll leave you chaps to it, then,' he said after a hasty salute.

I unlocked the doors and switched on the overhead arc lights. I had insisted that the smaller pieces of wreckage be laid out on rows of trestle tables all the way along the hangar. The pieces were more or less graded by size, with the larger bits of wreckage furthest from the door; some had to be laid on the floor. At once I saw that there had been changes. Normally, twisted and damaged pieces of metal from a crash site would have deteriorated even more after being left exposed. Instead, the pieces seemed brighter, newer; in some cases they were positively dazzling. One or two larger chunks looked as if they might not even be solid, but made of mercury or some kind of liquid metal. They were now silvery, reflecting the fierce light from the overhead arcs. It was a good job the blackout blinds were drawn.

'Look at that,' I said. 'It almost seems as if the pieces have joined together again.'

It was true. On the floor, bits of metal were stretched out like a sort of shining silver taffy, linking to pieces on the tables, which similarly stretched down to meet them. It was a very strange and chilling sight. They looked like tendrils of plants in a greenhouse seeking the light. In this case, they were seeking not the light, but one another.

'I think I was right to be scared,' Sergeant Shaw said. 'I've never seen anything like this before. What is this stuff anyway? Is it metal . . . liquid . . . what?'

'I don't know. It's some unearthly element, for sure.'
I set off across the hangar, studying each of the trestles
in turn. It appeared that each piece was in the process,
not only of renewing itself, but of trying to find other
pieces to which it had once been joined.

'Left to itself for long enough,' I said, 'I believe the
craft would have put itself back together in a version of
what it once was.'

'Then what would have happened?' Sergeant Shaw
asked, looking around at all the wreckage.

'I don't know, but it would be a very powerful thing.
I'm not sure I know how to contain it,' I said. 'The
soldier reported strange noises.'

'Some of these pieces look like conventional
aeroplane engine parts, or perhaps even weapons; but
then they also look organic, like plants. Where would
you start? Where does one thing end and the other
begin?' She picked up a melted-looking chunk of silver
metal.

It was then that we heard it . . .

It was somewhere between a ringing bell and a voice –
very hard to describe. It rang like metal, but the voice
part 'Oohed' and 'Aahed' like a choir singing a
wonderfully harmonic chord. It appeared to be
happening both inside my head and all around outside it
too. The sound echoed up into the rafters of the hangar.

'What the—?' Miss Shaw dropped the twisted lump of metal she was holding; it fell back onto the table and immediately dissolved into a shining puddle of silver. 'Sounds like a banshee,' she said, frowning and blocking her ears. 'Or a witch's sabbath.'

'If that's what the soldier heard, no wonder he complained,' I said.

The sound stopped as suddenly as it had begun.

'I imagine that was some kind of distress or alarm call to the rest of the wreckage. I suspect that this stuff has been communicating with what is left of it under Gallows Hill,' I mused.

'Look at that.' Sergeant Shaw pointed at a shining cube of silvery metal. It had apparently just surfaced from the twisted wreckage on the far table. Although it was silvery, it also shone with all the colours of the rainbow – just like the fragment that Tom had with him.

CHAPTER TWENTY-FIVE

Monteneuf Forest

We stopped in our tracks amongst the dense undergrowth. The light was fading; what was left of the sun was low on the horizon, but within the tangle of trees in front of us we saw a huge ancient standing stone. The kind they call a menhir.

It loomed over us, at least twelve feet high. I could see another one some way off. It was just as tall and just as mysterious. It had clearly affected Tom: the atmosphere all around was suddenly charged with a kind of fierce electricity. He stood there looking up at the weathered stone surface. Through the trees I could just make out Sperring and Pascal moving forward, unaware of what we had found. I couldn't attract their attention – I didn't want to risk making any noise; I just had to let them go on their way.

'Are you all right, Tom?' I asked.

He didn't reply. He just gazed up at the ancient stone. His lips moved, and he muttered something very quietly under his breath, almost as if he was having a conversation with the slab of stone itself.

'It's like Stonehenge, Tom,' I said, trying to elicit a reply. 'I imagine these stones have been here for thousands of years too,' I carried on, to fill the odd silence. 'It looks like the forest grew all around the stones and kept them hidden. You wouldn't think it possible, would you?'

Tom said nothing.

Suddenly I remembered that I had the camera. How excited Captain Holloway would be to see all this. I took it out of my pocket and then out of its case. Tom walked forward a few feet and pressed himself against the surface of the tall stone. I heard something then – a low, deep rumble; a vibrating sensation that felt as if it was coming from the ground under our feet. At once little flickers of blue-white light played very quickly around and over Tom's body. I took a photograph, wound the film on and took another. I hoped it would come out in the dim light. Then Tom let go of the rock and staggered backwards, his hair standing on end. He shook himself like a dog that had come out of the

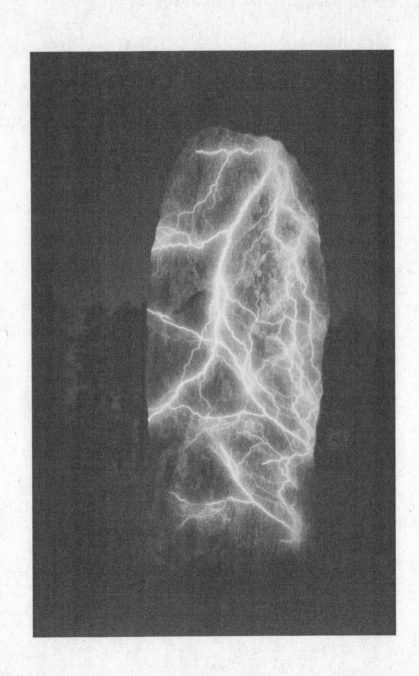

sea, then ran forward into the darkness under the trees. For a moment I was too shocked to move. Tom had vanished. I stuffed the camera back in my pocket, realizing that I had no choice but to run after him. I found it hard to keep up. I passed several more of the tall standing stones. Dozens loomed up among the trees. I could hear Tom's boots crashing through the undergrowth ahead of me. I had to stop him running into any German sentries or French policemen. After all, we had no good reason to be in the forest, let alone in a forbidden zone, in the near dark. It would be hard to talk our way out of it if we were caught. And it seemed increasingly likely that we *would* be caught and then shot.

Gasping for breath, I stumbled on after Tom, eventually coming to a small clearing. Tom was standing amongst the menhirs, which were set in a half-moon shape . . . The pattern struck me suddenly, and I realized that, among other things, they might serve as some sort of astronomical calendar.

'Tom,' I said, gulping between breaths. 'Wait, please. What is it?'

He turned to face me, his eyes unnaturally bright in the gloom by the stones. He approached me, his expression intense but fixed somewhere beyond me.

'It's the angels,' he said. 'They are here – somewhere very near. I can feel them – they've been talking to me. Can you hear them too, Jack?'

'No,' I said. 'I can't hear anything but my own breathing.'

'They have been here before,' Tom told me. 'They have been here many times before.'

'There is a strange energy here, Tom,' I said. 'I can feel it. Just now, for instance, when you touched one of the standing stones, there were flickers of light all around you – like a kind of St Elmo's fire.'

'There is so much here, Jack,' he went on, 'and it's just waiting. There is a real force; something is buried deep under here: some power – but what sort of power I don't know what exactly.'

'What should we do?'

'I don't know, Jack. The angels haven't told me much yet – they've given me no clues about that or anything else. I think they're just pleased that I'm here – they were welcoming me . . . But there is more to be found.'

'We should keep going then, and we don't want to completely lose sight of Sperring and Pascal.'

The fact was, of course, that we *had* lost sight of them. I had a very bad feeling in the pit of my stomach. My thunder feeling, my roses smell – they were firing off like rockets, and I could see flames framing a human shape. I was sure Pascal and Sperring had been caught. Now we would have to rescue them as well as the girl. I started to panic.

'We should go on, yes,' Tom said. 'Yes – we must.'

We half ran through the dense undergrowth. The standing stones were everywhere – sometimes grouped in patterns, sometimes standing alone like mysterious sentries. I suddenly realized that they may well have been just that: sentries guarding a sacred place – sacred to the ancients and to the 'angels'. So this place was dangerous as well: not just to us, but to the Nazis. I wondered again exactly how much they knew. It was clear that they had brought the girl to this place for a purpose. It was no coincidence. They thought they knew what they were doing; *we* thought we knew what we were doing too. But did any of us actually know anything?

We stumbled on in the gloom, and then, when it was almost completely dark, a harsh voice in front of us called out, '*Hände hoch!*'

CHAPTER TWENTY-SIX

Two German soldiers were standing under the trees – I could make out the glint of a rifle barrel, which was pointing straight at us. Neither side moved. In that split second I realized that Pascal and Sperring might be miles away by now. We were effectively on our own.

I spoke to them in French. They were Germans, so I hoped that they wouldn't notice my English inflection.

'We mean no harm, sir. We were just out looking for food, sir. I am sorry, sir.'

One of the soldiers stepped out from under the trees. He was young – not much older than us. He looked nervous, but he had his rifle pointed straight my chest.

'You should not be here at all – it is a forbidden zone. Where have you come from?'

'My uncle had a farm back there near Monteneuf. We were hungry.'

'All the farms and villages were cleared months ago.'

'Yes, our uncle is no longer there. We stayed behind – we've been hiding in the barns.'

The other soldier spoke out of the darkness. He sounded older. 'Take them to the camp. We can't question them here, in any case. We'd better be quick – it will soon be time.'

The younger one gestured with his rifle that we should walk ahead of him. 'Keep your hands where I can see them,' he said.

Tom and I walked side by side, our hands held high above our heads. We said nothing for a moment or two; then I decided to lay it on thick.

'Might we get fed please, sir, at the camp?' I said plaintively.

'I doubt it,' the younger soldier said. 'You'll most likely be shot. No one is allowed in here for any reason. You aren't the first.'

'I don't see why, though,' I said. 'It's just a forest, with trees and stones and wild boar.'

'There are no wild boar, so you can forget it. The whole place was cleared – you should know that. You were spying, and spies always get shot.'

'Please don't shoot us, sir,' Tom suddenly piped up, in his newly acquired perfect French.

'Not up to me,' the soldier said. 'Now keep quiet and walk.'

It was not long before we reached a mesh and barbed-wire fence – a double layer right across the path that led through the trees. On the other side I saw another group of standing stones – proper twelve-foot-high menhirs. Each was lit by an individual lamp suspended from a tall metal platform. I could see them extending into the distance, with wires linking the stones.

If this was the camp the soldier had mentioned, then it was very extensive. We were marched along the fence until we reached a gate, where a sentry nodded at the two soldiers and let us in. Now I could hear the noise of machinery some way further into the forest. We were led to a clearing occupied by half a dozen wooden huts and several vehicles – including a couple of Mercedes staff cars like the one that had passed us on the road. The others were trucks and armoured personnel carriers. We were taken into one of the huts, and I saw a poorly lit desk, typewriters and filing cabinets. It looked like a rough admin office. An officer came through from the back of the hut. He shook his head at the sight of us, and drew on the cigarette he was smoking.

'Not more of them, surely,' he said in German. 'I thought the area had been cleared.'

'They say they were looking for food – out poaching in the woods,' the young soldier said.

'Are you idiots?' the officer said in heavily accented French. 'Poaching is as bad as looting, punishable by hard labour or even death, and yet you peasants still persist in it – pathetic half-men.'

'We are sorry, sir,' Tom said, suddenly stepping forward. 'We were starving. We had no idea what was here.'

At that moment I got a strange sensation. My old instincts kicked in again. I looked over at Tom as he spoke. His bright eyes were fixed on the soldier. I sensed that 'slowing of time' effect; at least, that is what it felt like.

The officer very carefully stubbed out his cigarette and shook his head. 'Take them over to the holding pen. There's too much going on tonight. We'll deal with them in the morning.' He paused and looked at Tom. 'Better give them something to eat.'

The two soldiers exchanged glances at this; one raised his eyebrows. I sensed that the offer of food was not the usual treatment meted out to poachers.

'Are you sure, sir?' the older one said.

'Of course I'm sure. Now go and do as I say.'

We were taken to another hut at the far end of the row. A sentry stood guard outside.

'Two more,' the soldier said, nodding his head at us. 'The sergeant back there says we've got to feed them.'

'What about the one who's already in there?'

'Better to be safe than sorry. Go and get some soup from the mess tent. We'll deal with these two.'

This hut was dingy, with a row of slatted wooden bunks on either side. There was a table in the middle, and a dim orange light bulb was suspended above it. Away from the table, the interior vanished into deep shadow. I could just make out a human form sitting on a bunk.

Tom and I stood there awkwardly. The person on the bunk called out in French, 'I'm hungry.' It was a girl; she sounded young.

'If you shut up,' the young soldier replied, also in French, 'you might just be lucky enough to eat tonight. Enjoy it while you can. There won't be any more where you are going.'

The sentry was soon back with a big metal saucepan, which he dumped on the table, along with a half-loaf of bread. 'There you are. Sort yourselves out, and stay away from the windows.'

The soldiers left, and the door was locked.

The shadowy figure emerged into the dim light – a girl with long dark hair and wearing a shabby dress. She made straight for the bread, tore off the heel and dipped it into the soup. 'Mm,' she said. 'Cabbage soup – not bad.'

She divided up the bread and tossed us each a piece.

'How did they catch you?' she asked. 'I'm Françoise Ulrici,' she added, holding out her skinny arm.

'Jacques,' I said, shaking her hand. 'We just ran into two soldiers. We were out looking for something to eat.'

'Join the club,' the girl said. 'Where are you from anyway? Not round here – not with that accent.'

'No,' I said. 'Not originally. We are from Holland – we've been living in Douarnenez. We ran into a bit of trouble with the Boche – coughing in a cinema when old Goebbels was on the screen,' I added, thinking quickly. 'We've been hiding out near here ever since.'

'I was being hidden too,' she said. 'They caught the people sheltering me and brought me here to the forest.'

For a while we just ate the soup, dipping in the bread and sucking it up as best we could.

Françoise perched on the edge of the table. 'There's something very odd going on round here,' she said quietly.

'Really?' I said. 'What kind of thing?' I looked back at Tom, but he looked distracted.

'I think they're making some sort of secret weapon.'

'How do you make that out?'

'I've known this area all my life. Not many people know about the Ancients, but I do. My father is a historian.'

'The Ancients?' I queried.

'You saw the tall stones among the trees?'

'Yes, we did.'

'Put there by the Ancients, my father said, and for a reason. It was a sacred place to them. The Germans moved all sorts of stuff in here – special lights and generators – truckloads of it. The whole place is wired up. They've had people digging for weeks as well – deep in the forest, away from everything. They use slave labour: Polish people for the most part – not so many French, unless they are Jews like us. My parents were working away in there. I was well hidden, but this afternoon the Germans found me. They've dug a huge hole to hide something. I expect all the Poles will end up buried there in the end. I haven't seen any of the workers – not a trace for a few days now. Just German soldiers.'

'Perhaps they are trying to find something,' Tom said, 'not bury it.'

I was still amazed by Tom's sudden knowledge of French and German and his new-found authority. In that altered brain of his, things were developing quickly and in very mysterious ways.

'I hadn't thought of that,' the girl said. 'Might just be the buried treasure of the Ancients down there – old Breton gold. Those Nazis are greedy, as well as superstitious.'

'We can't stay in here all night,' Tom said.

'We can't do anything else.' Françoise shook her head. 'We're locked down tight.'

'Oh, but we can.' Tom went over to the window. 'There's only the one sentry.'

'Yes, but the whole place is crawling with soldiers. We wouldn't get far, even if we managed to get out of this hut.'

'We *have* to get out,' he insisted.

CHAPTER TWENTY-SEVEN

Annick Garel sat in a comfortable leather armchair, her hands clasped around a mug of herbal tea. Opposite her sat Herr Mustchin.

'That tea is a favourite blend of the Führer's,' he said. 'I never travel without it, in his honour.'

It was dark now. Outside, the trees were already impenetrable – though Annick could see lights far off through the dense scribble of branches.

'When you've finished your tea,' Mustchin went on, 'I have a little test for you. Nothing difficult. Later I'm going to take you outside. You are to be the centre of an important ceremony. I will show you something that we have found. I think you will find it most interesting. First there is this . . .'

He opened an envelope and shook some cards face down onto the table, picking one from the top of the pile. He held it in his palm, away from Annick, and looked at a silhouette printed on it – a black circle.

'Now I would like you to concentrate. I am looking at an image on this card. I wonder if you can tell me what it is I am looking at . . . ?'

Annick saw the black circle clearly in her mind – or at least in one part of it. The other part, the larger part, the deeply submerged part, was concentrating on the boy, Tom Pile. She knew that he was almost with her now. She knew that he knew she was there. She had sent out her strongest signals yet. Others were with him – that much she knew; the boy who had pulled her from the sea, Pascal – she sensed him nearby too. She felt warm inside at the thought of him.

She sent the circle image out to Tom, then looked over at Herr Mustchin. 'Black circle,' she said.

'This one?' He was looking at a triangle.

She sensed the presence of the angels who had saved her. They were here, everywhere, hidden in plain sight. Their energy, their voices, were all around, among the dark trees, and somehow contained within the strange tall slabs of stone. The bells rang with the slow swinging harmonies she recognized from her time in the sky – the bridge of time between one sea and the other. Had it been a long time, or had it been no time at all? There was no way of telling.

'Black triangle,' she said.

'And this?' Mustchin had picked a card bearing the image of a cat.

'A cat,' she said.

Herr Mustchin looked very pleased with himself. Annick sensed both his impatience to reveal whatever it was he was planning to show her and his mischievous delight in holding it back. It would surely not be long now. She also knew that, in some way, she was, and always had been, in mortal danger; the others too. She turned her head away as Mustchin picked up a fourth card – a house – and looked out of the window again. She could already sense odd swirls and flashes; bright blue lines like a tracery of veins were visible on the standing stones close by. It seemed that only she could see these things. Mustchin did not react to the sudden bursts of light or the gentle, metallic angel bells echoing through the forest like a strange chorus of birds; the sound of a whole new kind of nature. Herr Mustchin simply didn't hear it.

Annick turned back to him, feeling divided now. Part of her was in the here and now, sitting in the wooden hut in the forest, apparently playing guessing games with the man with the moustache. The other part was among the trees, seeking Tom Pile, sniffing him out like a bloodhound. That part of her followed the traces out there . . . She found him soon enough. There were two soldiers outside another hut at the end of the row. Through the window she could see a dim light and shadowy figures. This was the closest she had ever been to him. Barely a kilometre of forest separated them.

They would soon be together. She sensed Pascal was close too; she felt a strong bond with him. He was as important to her as Tom was.

'This one might be more difficult,' Herr Mustchin said. His card showed a simple line rendering of Adolf Hitler.

'A man with a moustache like yours,' Annick said.

'I think we have finished for now.' Mustchin stood up and put on his overcoat. 'We must go now. I need no further proof. The time is right.'

He opened a cupboard and took down from a shelf two crowns made of plaited leaves. He gave one to Annick. 'Put this on please,' he said.

From a lower shelf he took a white cloak covered in shiny gold stencils – a stag, a swastika and stylized wings – then put the second plaited crown on his own head. For the first time in ages Annick Garel was tempted to laugh. However, she suppressed the urge and allowed the gold and white fringed cloak to be draped over her shoulders.

'Come,' Mustchin said, and she sensed his growing nervousness; he was both excited and frightened – she could smell it on him. There was fear under the oak-leaf crown; a sour stink in the drops of sweat on his forehead; fear in the rank damp patches under his arms.

He opened the door. Outside stood a dozen soldiers. Two held up flaming torches; between them, another soldier carried a Roman-style military banner showing an eagle clutching a swastika in its talons.

Leutnant Richter was there too. He stood at ease behind the line of soldiers, observing everything. He stared at Annick and Mustchin in their ritualistic outfits. He too was tempted to burst out laughing at the sight of Herr Mustchin in his crown of leaves. *It's all becoming too ridiculous*, he thought. *Mumbo jumbo and nonsense.*

At a signal from Herr Mustchin, a soldier at the end of the line blew a fanfare on a hunting horn. Mustchin set off, marching in time to the beat as a single drummer struck up. Annick joined him, heading into the trees towards a brightly lit area. Richter followed slowly, some way behind, shaking his head.

CHAPTER TWENTY-EIGHT

Monteneuf Forest

A sudden blast of a horn echoed amongst the trees.

'That's it – it's starting,' Tom said. 'We must go right now.'

'How do you expect to do that?' Françoise said.

'I have ways.'

'Wait.' I grabbed Tom's arm. Only I knew what he might be capable of in that confined room. 'Is this a good idea?' I asked.

'We have no choice. It must be now.' He turned to Françoise. 'You stay here. This is something we have to do. It need not concern you. It is our risk.'

She sat back on the edge of the bunk and shrugged. 'Do your worst, but you won't get very far, whatever you do.'

'Ready?' Tom said to me.

'If you survive,' Françoise said, 'bring me back something more to eat. I'm still starving.'

'When we run – and we will run – you should run too. Run far and run fast. Don't look back,' Tom said. 'Things are going to be happening.'

There was another blast on the horn.

'What things?'

'Big things.'

Tom went over to the locked door, his arms down by his side. He lowered his head, fixing his gaze on the lock. A moment later the metal part started to glow – dark red, then orange, then yellow. Finally it turned almost white before falling out in a shower of bright sparks and rolling across the bare floor, darkening as it came to rest by a bunk bed.

'Sacrebleu,' Françoise said. She stood up and backed away into the darker part of the hut. I didn't blame her.

The door swung open and stood gaping wide.

The guard came and stood outside, clearly puzzled. Tom just stayed where he was: the light bulb suspended from the flex over the table suddenly brightened, burning with an intense, cold, blue-white light. It was as if the tungsten flash from a press camera had simply stayed on. The hut interior was painfully bright, and the soldier in the doorway looked dumbfounded, frozen in the harsh glare. Françoise ran forward, wide-eyed.

The bulb suddenly brightened even further, so that the light was dazzling, and then it promptly exploded. Red-hot fragments of glass showered down onto the table and around the dark hut.

'*Halt!*' the soldier shouted. Still blinded by the intense light, he now found himself in a completely dark interior. His rifle clattered onto the floor, and he cursed. Then another sentry blundered in through the dark doorway, crashing into him. There was the sound of further cursing and more metal crashing onto the wooden floor.

'Now!' Tom shouted.

I followed him, along with Françoise, and somehow we made our way through the confusion of bodies in the doorway. Once we were outside in the half-light, Tom looked back at the hut and raised his arms. The door slammed shut as if a hurricane had blown it to. There was a sustained burst of intense white light in the hut, and then darkness again. Françoise didn't stop, didn't look back; she just ran off into the trees.

'Come on,' Tom said, now firmly in charge.

I hurried after him as we followed the sound of the horn and the drum, which we could still hear through the trees. As we ran, I wondered about the two sentries in our hut. If they were alive, they would surely soon be after us.

It was not long before we came across another clearing with a hut much like the one we had been held in. Inside, the lights were on; a single sentry was on guard.

Tom stopped and stared at the hut. 'Pascal and Sperring are in there. We must get them out,' he said.

'How?' I said. I was still nervous and listening out for sounds of pursuit.

'Stay here,' he told me.

I ducked down and watched from behind a tree. Tom went and stood directly in front of the hut, eyes fixed ahead. I hoped he couldn't be seen.

There was a sudden burst of bright light from the lock on the door, where Tom had focused his energy. As flames burst out around the door frame, the sentry turned and shouted out.

There was a brief pause, and then the door was pushed down flat from inside. The sentry didn't stand a chance. A crowd of men burst out – ragged figures lit by the rising flames. Panicking, they trampled over the door, crushing the guard underneath.

The light from the burning hut was dazzling now. As Tom ran forward, I emerged from behind the tree and joined him. The escaping prisoners barged their way past me. They looked half starved; their clothes hung off them in rags.

Someone in the middle of the fleeing crowd called out, 'Tom, over here!'

It was Pascal. He was pulling Sperring away from the flames as the ragged figures ran off in confusion into the dark trees.

We ran towards them.

'Thank God,' Pascal said. 'All the lights suddenly blew. We saw the flames around the door and everyone panicked. The door fell down . . . I don't understand what happened.'

'It was all my doing,' Tom said.

'No need to explain all that now, Tom,' I said quickly. 'What happened to Sperring?'

'Guards hit him on the head when we were caught,' Pascal told us. 'He's still a bit dazed.'

'I'm all right. Really I am,' Sperring said, brushing himself down. He looked over at Tom and shook his head. 'You really did that, didn't you, Tom?' He gestured towards the flames consuming the hut.

In the distance we heard the drum still banging its rhythm.

'We must go now,' Tom said. 'Soon it will be too late.'

CHAPTER TWENTY-NINE

It was not long before we reached another kind of perimeter fence. This one was taller but single, and there
were lights set along the top at regular intervals, trained
inwards onto a wide clearing, which was surrounded
by an almost perfect circle of ancient standing stones.
In the middle, a huge hole had been excavated. Within
the stones stood a row of soldiers. Flaming torches were
arranged in a semi-circle, and in front of them was a
girl with white-blonde hair. She was standing next to
the bare trunk of a single tree close to the hole.

'Is that her?' I said quietly. 'Is that Annick Garel?'

'Yes,' Pascal said.

She was oddly dressed, her shoulders draped in a
cloak covered with gold symbols. She looked like
something out of one of the *Flash Gordon* serial
films. On her head sat a crown of twisted leaves, just
like the one worn by the man standing next to her.

'I've seen him before,' Tom said – so quietly that I suddenly realized I'd heard him in my head. 'She showed him to me when he was asking her questions.'

I looked closely at him in the light from the fence. 'You spoke to me – but only inside my head,' I whispered.

'Of course I did,' he said. It happened again – I could see that he'd spoken without moving his lips.

'When did this start?' I said.

'I'm not sure. I didn't really need to use it till now.'

'What should we do now, Tom?' I whispered.

'We wait,' he said in my head.

The man standing beside Annick read aloud from a scroll – though I couldn't hear the actual words. He spoke in a kind of sing-song voice, like a priest. Whatever it was he was saying, it sounded rehearsed. The soldiers all stood to attention, though Annick Garel seemed uninterested in what was happening around her. She looked almost hypnotized, her attention focused on the hole in the ground in front of her. The man droned on, but she continued to stare into the chasm. I looked over at Tom, who was no longer speaking to me but staring intently through the barbed-wire fence, concentrating on Annick. He touched the wire on either side of his face. I was worried that he might be seen in the spill of light from the fence, but everybody was intent on the ritual. Except for one person . . .

Annick. She suddenly raised her head and stared straight at the spot where we were hidden – and all at once my thunder feeling returned.

There was a sudden hush, and I realized that the man in the leaf crown had stopped reading from his scroll. He rolled it up and dropped it on the ground.

I took the camera out of my pocket and pushed the lens through the leaves and wire so that I had a clear view of what was happening. I took one or two pictures of the gathering, and then focused on Annick. As my attention moved to the soldiers behind her, I started to smell roses, and my head felt swimmy. The thunder feeling was strong now.

More fanfares, and then the steady drumming began again. Scanning the soldiers' faces, I picked one out – surely the one I'd seen earlier, outside the café in Douarnenez . . . with the halo of flames around him. He was wearing the same ill-fitting jacket and had the same sunken cheeks, the same vacant, staring eyes. I peered through the viewfinder at him and, for no particular reason, took some snaps.

I turned to face Tom. 'Something is going to happen – I can feel it,' I said.

'I know it is,' he agreed.

'What is it?' I whispered.

'Wait,' he said quietly, straight into my head.

CHAPTER THIRTY

Gallows Hill, Dorset

We drove straight back from the barracks to the dig. We were both shaken by what we had seen; by the strange, almost organic nature of the wreckage from the alien craft; by the way it had sought to mend itself, re-joining with its matching parts and making itself whole again.

We passed the warnings – the skull-and-crossbone flags; trespass notices; the rolls of barbed wire. From the store we each took a powerful torch and made our way down into the dark underground chamber.

The hull of the craft had changed colour since we were last down here. Instead of battleship grey, it now looked silver. As we went down the wooden staircase and approached it, I saw a shadowy, distorted reflection of our faces, and remembered laughing at the crazy images during visits to the hall of mirrors at a seaside pier.

Only now I wasn't laughing. Something was happening to the hull. Close to, the surface had become dimpled; almost fleshlike in texture, and the colour of dull mercury. I was sure that the 'something', whatever it was, had been triggered in turn by some outside event or force. Things were on the move.

'It looks so different . . .' Sergeant Shaw stopped some feet away from the sheer curved wall. She appeared reluctant to get any closer.

'Something has stirred it up,' I said. 'Something has awakened whatever it is in there – whether it's just the bits of wreckage over at the hangar in Burton Bradstock calling to it in some way, or something else, something bigger, I really don't know, Miss Shaw.'

I reached out and touched the hull. 'God – I swear it rippled under my touch,' I said, and drew my hand back. 'This is all beyond anything we could even hope to understand.'

The surface had felt warm, and for a moment I was sure that the whole thing was somehow alive. It was a terrifying sensation. I stepped back – as if standing a few feet further away would somehow save me from the elemental, unearthly force contained in that silvery hull.

'What should we do?' Sergeant Shaw asked.

'I suppose that, however unstable it is, we should try to observe it from a distance.'

'I have the camera,' she pointed out.

'Yes, I know. Take some pictures from up there.' I nodded towards the stairs.

We went up to the top; we were no safer there, but at least we could make for the exit in case of some kind of disaster.

Sergeant Shaw started taking pictures. We used a specially formulated film, designed to operate in low light levels. I had equipped Jack Carmody with a similar camera and film.

'Take another if we see any kind of change.'

I hoped that, wherever he was, Jack might be using his camera to similar advantage. Sergeant Shaw took another picture as the light increased, as if from inside the hull. She wound on the film . . . and then, suddenly, we heard a tremendous *thump* on the earth above our heads, quickly followed by another from above ground. Loosened soil rained down on us, and one of the wooden pit props shifted.

'We are being bombed, by the sound of it,' I said. 'Come on.'

We ran up the slope, out onto Gallows Hill. A streak of light was hurtling towards us from the south-west, arcing up from the ground a few miles away, not dropping from the sky. Whatever it was, it landed with a tremendous crash a few yards behind us and then vanished underground.

I raised my field glasses – just in time to see another tracery of light launch itself and arc into the sky overhead. I followed it as it sped towards us.

'What the hell . . . ?' Sergeant Shaw said. 'This is not possible.'

'It seems it *is* possible – it's the wreckage from over at the barracks making its way back here piece by piece, by the look of it.' Even as I spoke, more bright streaks crossed the sky.

'How are we going to explain it?' Sergeant Shaw said as she photographed the streaks of light heading towards us.

'Tracer fire that went wrong . . . a false air-raid alarm . . . a trigger-happy ack-ack soldier . . . I don't know – we'll think of something.'

My words were drowned out by further thumps and crashes as the pieces of metal fell all around us. They seemed to burrow their way underground as soon as they landed, seeking out the rest of the craft, I assumed. I was tempted to go down and watch the strange process at work, but it was just too dangerous. After all, we had no real idea of 'their' intentions (odd that we had to

imagine the 'angels' as a 'they' – an entity that we might understand – when in truth, whatever they were, these beings were beyond our understanding). They had apparently treated Tom with kindness and returned him – but what had they wanted from him in the first place? Why had they blessed (or cursed) him and the other returnees we knew of with their apparently growing powers and abilities?

The shower of metal parts continued. It looked like a glorified firework night display. The whole thing must have lasted for more than half an hour. It was fortunate that there were no houses near our Gallows Hill dig. As it was, I was already expecting dozens of alarmed reports to come in. The soldiers over at Burton Bradstock were covered by the Official Secrets Act, but goodness knows what they were making of it. I would need to call my old friend Colonel Gauntlett first thing and explain a thing or two. But first, once the display was over, I had to go back down into the underground chamber to see the craft.

Sergeant Shaw agreed, and we both headed for the entrance. Some of the supports had been damaged, but the approach tunnel was still intact. However, by the time we reached the chamber where, only minutes before, she had been taking photographs, everything had changed.

The craft was now glowing, pulsating with light in controlled bursts. At first there was no noise; it seemed that the pieces had finally stopped burrowing down to the hull. They must all have been absorbed into the body of the craft – I could see no sign of any spare pieces. The regular pulse of light from the craft suggested a kind of countdown or timing mechanism. I was sure it was getting faster, and began to time it on my watch. I wondered what was controlling the machinery, if that is what it was. Perhaps the machinery itself was the 'being'?

Had Tom going inside somehow woken it all up? There was no way of finding out the answer. We just stood and watched while the pulses of light came faster and faster. I'm not sure when I first noticed that the craft was moving. It began slowly, imperceptibly. It was building to something.

Suddenly it seemed to shake off the banks of earth around it. There was a rattle of stones and clods of earth as they fell back onto the floor. Then the hull rose up to the roof of the chamber. The lights stopped flashing; now they shone continuously, and another strong beam of light descended from the base of the craft as it hovered there before us.

'I hope you're getting all this,' I said to Sergeant Shaw.

'I'm doing my best,' she replied.

'It's surely going to break out of here,' I said. 'There'll be an almighty cave-in. We should get out of here while we still can.'

We turned and ran up to the entrance and out onto the workings at the top of Gallows Hill. Scattered beams of light shone up through the various holes in the open field. It would not be long now, I thought.

'We should get some distance away,' I shouted to Miss Shaw.

We both stumbled along as best we could until we reached the edge of the field, where we waited for a few seconds to catch our breath. Then the rumbling started. It rose to a pitch, and a great vertical shaft of light came up through the ground: the silver hull was rising out of the underground chamber. I heard the carefully constructed entrance to the tunnel collapse under the weight of displaced earth. All too soon that chamber would be filled in and inaccessible.

'Good God – look at it!' Sergeant Shaw exclaimed.

We watched the round craft as it slowly rose above Gallows Hill, sending beams of light in all directions. I was both excited and saddened by what I was seeing.

'Please tell me that you have some film left in that camera,' I said.

'Oh yes,' she said, and she photographed the craft as it gradually climbed up to cloud level.

Feeling like a fool, I waved as if there was some relative on board. The fact was, I wanted the craft to come back. I wanted *them* to come back. I had not discovered the first thing about them – whatever, or whoever, they were. Now it seemed that whatever evidence they had left behind would be buried under tons of earth. We had lost them completely; perhaps for ever. Why had they chosen to go now? I doubted whether we would find an answer. The file would just have to remain open. At least we would have some new photographs to add to it.

Finally the craft was lost in amongst the clouds. A tremendous silence and almost complete darkness followed its departure.

Sergeant Shaw lowered the camera. 'What did we just witness?' she asked.

'One of the most astonishing moments in history,' I said. 'A final contact with an unearthly civilization which is now perhaps lost to us for ever.'

'What exactly was in there? How, I wonder, were they operating the craft? What propelled it?'

'I have no idea,' I answered. 'I have speculated about their nature but have really got nowhere with it. Their mystery remains.'

'They might just come back,' Sergeant Shaw said.

'They might,' I agreed, though I doubted it.

CHAPTER THIRTY-ONE

Monteneuf Forest

The man in the leafy crown suddenly turned and barked out an order, and the line of soldiers behind him went into action. I took photographs as two of them pulled Annick back against the tree and tied her hands behind her. Then all the arc lamps were switched off. Now the only light came from the guttering torches, and also – strangely – from the gigantic hole in the ground.

In my head, Tom said suddenly and clearly, 'I'll save her.'

I made to stop him, but he had already vanished, and I hadn't even noticed. I backed away from the fence.

Behind me, Pascal took me by the shoulder. 'Let Tom go. We must wait here – look . . .'

I turned and saw that Sperring had collapsed and lay curled up on the ground.

All at once a great shout rang out; it sounded as if it had come from the other side of the path where we were hidden. I turned and looked through the fence again. I realized that the light emanating from the hole was stronger now, and took more photographs. There was a rumbling noise too. I couldn't work out where the shout had come from or what it meant. It was then that I noticed that there was a gap under the fence here. I got down onto my hands and knees and then wriggled forward under the wire. I felt the sharp barbs catch and tear my clothes, but I ignored them and continued to crawl into the forbidden zone. Once I was through, I took more photographs, still crouching low. Surely everyone would be too busy watching the hole to notice me, I thought. I crawled forward through the trees to get a better view.

It was a very strange sight. Something bright was slowly rising out of the hole. Annick, tied to the tree trunk, looked as if she was to be a sacrifice – but to what?

The drum and the horn had stopped, and the soldiers inside the standing stones had raised their rifles, training them on Annick, as if they were about to carry out an execution.

I looked around in panic: Tom had run off somewhere, and Sperring was lying on the ground in a faint. What should I do? I wondered. Suddenly Pascal ran forward in front of me – he had followed me under the fence. I stood there, mesmerized by what might be coming up out of the ground.

There was another shout, and then an explosion; several shots rang out. I ran towards the sound, following Pascal. As I did so, the forest all around me grew brighter and brighter.

Suddenly I saw a rifle floating past me in mid-air; then another, turning end over end as it flew by my head. More of them floated above head height. Emerging from the trees, I stopped dead in my tracks.

The German soldiers stood frozen in position. They were no longer holding their weapons – which were hanging in the air a few feet above their heads. The man with the crown of leaves was on his knees, apparently in supplication, while Tom and Pascal were standing next to Annick – all framed in a great halo of light. Tom and Annick's hands were clasped and raised above their heads; they were holding up the little pieces of shining rainbow metal. It seemed as if they were keeping everything around them in a kind of stasis. And then I saw, above the edge of the hole . . . a huge, vague shape that seemed to be made of light, which towered above everything. There was something both beautiful and terrifying about it; something beyond my experience or understanding.

I ran further into the light. Tom saw me but did not move. It was as if he and Annick were waiting for something. The being of light remained at the edge of the hole, its outline wavering and shimmering.

Beyond the circle of stones I saw a lone German officer, the light reflecting off his wire-rimmed glasses. He was frantically jumping in the air, trying to grab his Luger pistol, which was hovering high above his head.

I turned back to see a beam of light slowly coming down from the sky with a loud rushing noise. I looked up and saw a craft like the one at Gallows Hill. The beam finally hit the ground with a huge thump – a sound I also recognized from before. I was lifted off the ground, along with some large rocks and logs, and the rifles floated even higher . . . and then I saw that all the soldiers were in the air too, crying out in terror, surrounded by the bright light. The young soldier from outside the Atlantic café was haloed by flares, just as I had envisioned him. I couldn't tell if these were flames or just intense light – though I felt no heat.

I spotted the German officer again: he was still firmly on the ground. He must have been just far enough away to escape the gravitational influence. I saw him turn and realize what had happened to his troops, and run off into the trees in panic. At least one of the Germans had escaped.

I suddenly remembered Sperring; I hoped he was all right. Pascal stood with his arms around Annick. I floated, fixed in mid-air; I thought of those old formal portrait photographs where the subject's head is clamped into position by a kind of neck brace.

Then the alien being that seemed to be made of light slowly twisted in the beam. I thought I could make out what might have been limbs and eyes, and there was a cavernous space that might have been a mouth. It wasn't human, though. It rose slowly up within the beam of light, as if pulled up on invisible wires towards the hovering craft.

It passed close by; I felt the light brush against and around me and heard a kind of joyous noise like ringing bells, with a voice somewhere in amongst them. The standing stones were lit with traceries of blue light, which rippled and flickered across them. I could see them spreading out like beacons all across the forest.

As the being rose towards the craft, the beam of light was slowly rising too. Below me, the ground was dark; above me, the light was brighter than ever. Finally the beam receded further, and I fell back down – slowly, slowly onto the mossy ground.

I lay still for a moment. I didn't even try to move. I felt sure I was still locked tight by the brace effect. Then, suddenly, the sensation was gone. I was able to stretch out my arms and legs. I jumped up and looked around. The ground was covered in odd debris: bits of twisted and broken rifle; fragments of charred uniform; and bullet cases. There was no sign of any of the soldiers.

I crawled back under the fence to check on Sperring. He was sitting up and rubbing his eyes.

'What the hell happened here, Jack?' he said. His face was ashen.

'Something we can't even . . .' I said, and then I trailed off into a confused silence. I looked around for Tom, Pascal and Annick, suddenly fearful. The hole was now dark; the man with the leaf crown was lying on his front beside it, staring down into its depths.

I was stunned; I couldn't grasp what had just happened myself. 'I can't see the others,' I said.

Sperring looked up into the sky; he raised his arm and pointed. 'What is that – an aeroplane? What was it doing? I don't understand . . .'

I followed his gaze. The craft was almost lost in the night sky, though it remained a glowing circle for a moment or two. We watched it grow smaller, until it seemed no bigger than any of the distant stars.

'A dangerous and experimental aircraft of some kind,' I said.

'Is that your department's official line?' Sperring said; he was panting, as if he had been running. He was clearly suffering from the blow on the head, and now he looked shaken to the core: he had just witnessed something way beyond our understanding. I'd had some idea of what to expect – though of course I couldn't have warned anyone else.

It had been a rescue mission, I thought. The angels had finally come to collect one of their own. The Germans had uncovered either a craft or some evidence of the being. It had all been left there, waiting under the ground amongst the mysteries and ley lines of the menhirs. Now it was gone. I had felt the angel being as it passed by; I had heard fragments of voices – the strange music of the spheres.

I was puzzled about the whereabouts of the soldiers. I could see the ruins of their rifles, but where had they gone?

'I can't explain what we have seen here,' I told Sperring, then turned as I heard a shout.

It was Pascal. 'Jack!' he called out.

I hurried back through the fence towards him, past the slumped figure of the man in his leaf crown, and saw that Annick was standing on a high branch of a tree, half hidden by foliage. Nearby, in another tree, was Tom.

Pascal was looking up at them. 'I think you should both come down – before it's too late,' he shouted.

'I won't even ask how you got up there, given everything I've seen tonight,' I said.

'Surely someone will have seen that aircraft, those lights, and heard the gunfire,' Pascal added. 'German reinforcements will be here very soon.'

Tom and Annick climbed down from the trees.

'He is right,' Sperring said, who had followed me under the fence and was holding out his hand to Annick. 'I am Lieutenant Sperring from England and we have come to rescue you.'

She ignored him. She went straight over to Pascal and embraced him. They stayed there, locked together, for a moment or two.

'I know who you are,' she said, turning to take Tom's hand again. 'I have been asking you to come, and now you are here.'

'This is Jack Carmody,' Sperring carried on regardless. 'Between us we must get you back to England. It won't be easy. We must set off now, before anyone comes.'

MEMO

MOST SECRET

Captain Holloway's Office
Translated interception

TO: H. Kohler, Bureau of the Unexplained, etc., Berlin

FROM: Leutnant Richter, Northern Occupied Zone, Monteneuf, France

I was sent with your man, Herr Mustchin, and the Garel girl to the secret
site at Monteneuf. I am not sure how much you are aware of or have already
been told about what happened there. After some ritual business,
something terrifying emerged from the deep hole at your works. At the
same time a strange aircraft appeared in the sky. The troops were not only
attacked by some kind of new weapon; they vanished without trace. Most
were sucked up into the air, as if by a hurricane or tornado. I barely
escaped with my life. I have no idea what happened to your Herr Mustchin.
If this is some kind of secret weapon we are testing, then it worked only
too well, and sadly, against our own side. If this is something developed
by or run by the Bolsheviks or the Allies, then we are doomed. Will report
again fully and then in person asap.

CHAPTER THIRTY-TWO

Monteneuf Forest

We headed west, back through the forest. It was deathly quiet, empty of everything but silent trees and stones. No birdsong, no little creatures running about... nothing.

'What happened to those soldiers?' I wondered.

'The angels took them away,' Tom said.

'You mean they killed them?'

'No,' he replied. 'They just took them away.'

Sperring was walking a few yards behind us, keeping an eye out for the enemy. We had not gone far when a figure suddenly stepped out from behind a standing stone. '*Halt.*' It was the man wearing the crown of leaves, and he was aiming a rifle at us – though even in the dim light I could see that he was trembling with fear.

'It would be best,' he said in shaky French, 'if I were to kill those two now. I will make it quick. They will know no pain. I cannot let them live after what I have seen.'

Pascal immediately stepped in front of Annick.

'That won't help,' the German said. 'I'll just have to kill you too.'

I felt Tom tense beside me.

'I would put that down if I were you,' I said.

However, now the German aimed the rifle at Pascal – and it was suddenly wrenched out of his hands. It floated away, drifting up high amongst the branches above him.

He took a step backwards. 'No,' he muttered, shaking his head. 'No.'

I heard the click as Sperring cocked his gun.

'Leave him,' I said. 'He can't do anything to us now.'

Annick stepped forward and approached the German. He backed away, his eyes wide with terror, but she simply reached up and took the plaited crown of leaves off her head and handed it to him.

He took it carefully in both hands, holding it as if it was an unexploded bomb. 'No,' he repeated. 'No, please . . .'

Annick took the white cloak from her shoulders and dropped it on the ground at his feet, staring at him as she did so. He backed away as both she and Tom continued to stare, then suddenly clutched at his chest as if in pain. He fell forward onto the white cloak, and lay still.

Sperring went over and lifted the man's arm; as he let go of it again, it fell to the ground, limp. Then he turned the body over: the eyes stared up at the sky, sightless; the cheeks were sunken. Suddenly the man looked hollowed out, as if he was a thousand years old.

'Heart attack,' Sperring diagnosed.

We left the man where he had fallen. I turned back once; I could just see his white face, but he was soon swallowed up by the darkness.

Before long we heard motorcycles and heavy trucks ahead of us. I guessed we were walking parallel to the main road at the edge of the forest. The Germans were already responding to the lights and the fire.

'How will we find the van in the dark?' Sperring wondered.

'We'll find it,' Tom replied.

He did find it too – took us straight to it in the darkness. Tom and Annick rode in the back with me. Pascal and Sperring sat up front.

Sperring drove back to Douarnenez very slowly – agonizingly slowly. We didn't want to draw attention to ourselves. 'Our best bet is to head back to the safe house and send a message requesting rescue – and fast. There will be a full-scale alert after all that has happened tonight,' he said. Every so often military vehicles roared past us in the opposite direction.

'How are we off for fuel?' I said.

He tapped the gauge. 'Touch and go,' he replied. 'But I've been thinking: I know of another safe house – it's closer than yours, Pascal. I doubt we'll make it all the way back to Douarnenez. They've got radio equipment there – I know because I supplied it.'

'It's very late though,' I pointed out.

'I know, but we'll have to risk it; otherwise we'll have to walk back to Blighty.'

CHAPTER THIRTY-THREE

Brittany

Tom and Annick held hands as we rattled along. It looked like they were clinging to each other more for protection than anything else. Annick's hair caught whatever light there was and shone. They looked across at me in the dim light, but I could tell they weren't really seeing me at all. They were off somewhere else inside their heads. I smiled at them every so often, but their fixed expressions didn't change.

Sperring pulled the van over onto the verge and studied his silk-scarf map by torchlight. After that he drove on slowly for another mile or two, then turned off the main road and bumped down a long unmade track until we came to a stop at a barn. The engine clicked as it cooled, and for a moment it was the only sound I could hear. We all sat in the van – each of us, I suppose, trying to make sense of what we had seen and what had happened just an hour or so earlier.

In the farmhouse beyond the barn a light went on, and it wasn't long before a young woman in a scarf and an old overcoat emerged carrying a shotgun and a shaded lantern. She stopped a few yards from the van, and as Sperring wound down the window, I recognized her.

'I'm Elgar,' he said.

'I'm Berlioz,' the woman replied.

We slept up in the hayloft. The animals stamped and snorted below us during the night. I slept badly. I had understandably vivid dreams – the creature of light had Tom's face and was tearing people's heads from their bodies – and woke early.

Tom and Annick had gone. I quickly climbed down from the loft without disturbing Pascal or Sperring, and went out into the yard. They were both there, standing side by side, hands clasped together as if they were praying; looking up into the grey sky, searching for something.

I saw our rescuer, 'Berlioz', at the farmhouse window. She beckoned me over. She was brewing up coffee on the stove in the big dark kitchen.

'She must be something then, this girl of yours?' she asked.

'She is important, yes,' I said.

'You have come all the way from England – you have risked everything. I wonder why . . . She holds a secret, yes?'

'In a way,' I admitted cautiously.

'It will be dangerous guiding your aircraft in tonight. It is important to us that she is important. We take the risks.' She tapped her heart.

'She is very, very important,' I told her.

She nodded. 'Those two must be cold out there. Bring them in here for some breakfast. The other boy has been brave too, I think.'

'Yes, he certainly has,' I said. 'Properly brave. He's put himself at risk and will receive no real reward.'

'The reward is to get one over on the Boche. Did he manage that?'

'Oh, many times over,' I said.

Over breakfast she promised that she would take Pascal back to Douarnenez. 'In time,' she said, 'we will get the van back to your uncle's yard too, once we can scrounge enough petrol.'

'What about your uncle? Will he mind?' Sperring asked Pascal.

'Not when I explain,' he replied. 'I shan't say anything to old Garel. He is pro-German, for a start – he would most likely report me soon as look at me. I pulled his niece out of the sea – that is enough. No, the Germans will have to explain to him what has happened to Annick.' He smiled over at her. 'I'm sure they will have a story worked out.'

Tom spoke directly into my head: 'They will come after us in some way. They will want her back after what has happened. They will want me as well.'

I shook my head very slightly. I couldn't reply – I didn't want to alert the others to any more of Tom and Annick's abilities. Sperring and Pascal had already seen enough to frighten them. I didn't want to add to their problems.

Berlioz's charcoal-fuelled truck was brought round and Pascal got ready to leave. He had clearly formed a strong attachment to Annick and was reluctant to leave her.

'Au revoir, Annick,' he said. He pulled her towards him and kissed her very politely on both cold cheeks.

She responded by holding onto him, laying her white-blonde head on his shoulder. Even though she couldn't share the same experiences with him as she did with Tom, she definitely felt something for Pascal too: a different kind of closeness; a more normal, everyday attraction. She liked him. He liked her.

'*Au revoir*,' she said, finally letting go of him. 'Thank you.'

Pascal climbed up into the cab and was driven away in a cloud of dirty exhaust.

We spent most of the day up in the hayloft. It was just slightly warmer than outside. I cheered myself up with the thought that at least we would not be returning by boat.

Tom kept his internal conversations with me to a minimum. Annick just slept, while Sperring spent the time nervously checking his pistol, his ammunition, his maps and his camera – no doubt distracting himself with mundane tasks from thinking too much about what had happened in Monteneuf.

He was a different man now, I thought; quieter; no longer so breezy and affable; no longer naturally in charge. I think he was shaken by what he had seen. Before we left home he hadn't been aware of Tom's powers. As far as he was concerned, he had just been lumbered with a pair of ingénues by a rival – and only hazily understood – department of the War Office. We were being sent to pick up a vulnerable girl from occupied France. Only his knowledge and skills would get us through safely, he thought. Then he had seen what Tom could do; what he could do in conjunction with someone else: a fragile-looking girl. And then – without any warning – he had witnessed the alien and transforming power of the angels. I suspected that he felt betrayed by those around him, especially me. I had failed to warn him about Tom.

Once or twice during that long cold day he seemed about to ask me a question. In the end he said nothing to me until after Berlioz had been back for a while.

He was helping her to load the truck in the near dark.

'I have been in touch with my colleagues,' Berlioz told us. 'They will organize lights on the landing field. We will have to act quickly once your plane lands. No fond farewells, eh, Elgar?'

'Sadly no, not from me,' Sperring said; then he turned and pulled me away from the truck. 'In case I never get the chance again, Jack . . . What in hell's name was really going on over in the forest last night?'

'I can't say too much,' I told him. 'The Germans found something ancient over at Monteneuf. We found something connected to it at our dig in Dorset. I can't explain it all. No one can. The Germans want Tom and Annick for their "total war" machine. Imagine if they could somehow harness the power you saw . . . We had to stop that.'

'God,' Sperring murmured as we stood together in the autumn twilight. 'Who would ever believe any of it?'

'No one – that's why I didn't tell you anything about Tom or the girl. You would have thought I was completely barmy.'

'True, Jack, I would have – but then, I do anyway.' He punched me playfully on the arm. It was the first I had seen of the old Sperring all day.

We set off as soon as it was dark. This time we were hidden under a covering of vegetables instead of fish. Tom and Annick held onto each other in the confined space. Sperring rode in the cab with Berlioz. We rattled along the side roads and then bumped our way over some fields, finally coming to a halt.

The truck was parked at the edge of a wide field. When we got out, we saw a group of armed figures emerging from the shadows and gathering around Sperring. The night was cloudy – *nuageux*, the French would say. As my eyes grew accustomed to the dark, I saw that there were piles of wood and twigs running down both sides of the field.

Sperring came over to us, checking his watch. He was holding a stick with a rag tied to it. I could smell oil on it. 'We'll wait until we hear the Lysander coming before we light the fires,' he said. 'Can't leave them burning for too long.'

We all stood in silence and listened hard.

'It's coming,' Tom said.

'I don't hear anything.' Sperring frowned.

'Light the fires now.'

Sperring looked at me and I nodded assent.

'You sure, Jack? Only I don't hear it. We only get one pass at this.'

'If Tom can hear it, it's here. Light them,' I told him.

Sperring lit his torch and the others did the same. They spread out along the field, lighting the bonfires on either side. The flare path was set up: the whole area was suddenly bright – we were totally exposed. I stood listening with the others, expecting to hear the shouts of German soldiers, followed by gunfire.

Then we heard the familiar drone of an approaching aircraft. It was low in the sky, and circled the field a couple of times, descending a few feet with each circuit. Then it landed, bumping across the ground and coming to halt on the far side, its propeller still turning.

'It can take off again in a very tight space,' Sperring said. 'I'm staying here, by the way, Tom. There won't be room in the cabin otherwise. I'll make my way back by boat. Go on – off you go. Hurry.'

The pilot opened the cabin door. He was wearing a leather flying helmet and goggles. He threw out some metal canisters, which the shadowy Resistance fighters collected up.

'Good luck,' Sperring shouted after us as we ran over to the plane.

I turned and waved. I had to help Tom push the nervous and confused Annick ahead of us into the cockpit. We climbed in after her.

'Hello there,' the pilot said. 'Get settled – belts on and hold fast. We're off!' He turned the plane in a tight circle and headed back down the field, picking up speed.

'First time in the air for me,' I shouted to Tom.

'For you,' he said quietly in my head.

Then I felt the sudden lurch in my stomach as we left the ground. We were soon climbing steeply. I looked down in time to see the bonfires being extinguished as quickly as they had been lit.

It was noisy in the plane. We couldn't really speak to each other. The pilot turned every now and then and gave us a reassuring smile or a thumbs-up sign. I looked out of the side window: the dark earth was rushing by beneath us. All being well, in a couple of hours we would be back in good old England.

CHAPTER THIRTY-FOUR

Gallows Hill, Dorset

I was woken by a telephone call. It came from Mr Feaver, the ARP warden in Litton Cheney. He sounded breathless; he was clearly panicking.

'Captain Holloway, sir – they're back . . . I've seen them.'

'Who is back?' I answered him blearily. I had fallen asleep staring at the little piece of rainbow-coloured 'stuff'. It always sent me into a kind of peaceful trance.

'The lights up on Gallows Hill – well, just the one light so far, but it's a proper bright one – making noises too.'

'I'll be with you as soon as I can,' I said. 'Stay where you are.'

I got into my staff car and picked up Mr Feaver from his tin shed. We were soon on the lower slopes of

Gallows Hill. There was no mistaking it: a bright beam of light like an arc lamp was visible up near the remains of our dig. Once we had crested the hill, I saw the familiar outline of the once-buried craft shining through the low cloud layer.

'What on earth is that?' the warden asked.

'Good question, Mr Feaver,' I replied. Of course he was witnessing the strange alien phenomenon up close for the first time. My dilemma was how much to tell him.

'All we know is that this is some sort of experimental craft, possibly made by the Nazis. No markings, as you see, and these powerful lights make it hard to see any detail.' It was hovering just above the cloud layer, directly over the ruins of our earth workings.

'What happened here?' Mr Feaver said, noticing the freshly churned earth and damaged fencing.

'A raid the other evening. A Junkers came in from the coast and dropped a stick of bombs – superficial damage really. It was kept quiet for operational reasons.'

'So that was what Mr Fry was on about the other evening – said he saw tracer fire overhead in the middle of the night.'

'Something like that,' I said. I was unaware that anyone had noticed the 'fireworks' display.

Mr Feaver suddenly pointed upwards. 'Have you a weapon with you, Captain?'

'The only thing I have is my service revolver, Mr Feaver. No match for that aircraft up there.' I followed the direction of his quivering finger. Dark shapes were slowly falling down through the beam of light towards the ground. When I looked through my field glasses, I saw several German soldiers, seemingly unarmed, slowly tumbling head over heels down through the bright beam. I pulled the revolver out of my coat pocket and cocked it. Better to be safe than sorry.

'It's parachutists – German parachutists – and they're heading for us right now,' Mr Feaver exclaimed.

'I see them,' I said. 'About ten of them at most. What do they think they're doing?'

'Invading us, of course, Captain. What else?' Mr Feaver said in a hushed voice. 'This will be the advance party. They send in the elite troops first to soften us up, then follow up with the big landing party. I'd better ring the church bells. This is it . . . Finally, the invasion.'

'Wait just a minute, Mr Feaver,' I said.

I didn't have the heart to tell him that the invading soldiers had no parachutes. They were just gently free-falling, suspended in the beam of light. One after the other, they landed on Gallows Hill.

I walked over to them, my pistol drawn, doing a quick count. There were eight of them altogether. They stood close together, shivering and fearful, looking back into the sky, up into the beam of light. They looked thoroughly defeated, their uniforms scorched and ragged. These were certainly no elite troops. This was no invasion.

'Hands up nice and high,' I said in German.

They seemed only too happy to oblige me. One of them pointed up at the craft behind the clouds and shook his head. He looked terrified.

The ARP warden came to join me.

'Don't look much like an invading army, do they, Mr Feaver?' I said.

'They look like prisoners already,' he said.

'That's exactly what they are.'

The light beam was suddenly extinguished, and we were plunged into darkness. I looked up, but could see nothing now – just clouds and one or two faint stars.

I made the soldiers sit on the ground with their hands on their heads and sent Mr Feaver off to telephone the garrison at Burton Bradstock.

At first light the army truck arrived, and the grateful, shivering prisoners were loaded up.

'Parachutists,' I said to my old friend Colonel Gauntlett.

'So I see,' he said. 'With no parachutes? Much like your aircraft wreckage, which suddenly decided to fly away, all on its own . . .'

'Can't say any more, I'm afraid,' I told him. 'I wonder if you could arrange for these prisoners to be fed, and get their names, ranks and serial numbers for me . . . I'll come and debrief them soon. After that we can arrange for their transfer.'

'There are some very rum things going on around you, Holloway,' the colonel said, shaking his head. 'All I can say is I'm very glad to be your friend, old man. I shouldn't want to be your enemy. Good day to you.'

The truck drove off, the soldiers sitting slumped in the back. One of them waved to me as they left – I had the impression that they were grateful; I had somehow understood what they'd been through. I hoped that they would let me interview them and record the truth about what had happened to them.

I trusted that Jack would soon be safely back – along with Tom Pile and, all being well, the angels' other 'passenger', the mysterious French girl.

CHAPTER THIRTY-FIVE

Powerstock, Dorset

Just as dawn had broken we finally landed safely in another field: an RAF glider airstrip just above the main A35, and not far from Powerstock, the place where Tom had been 'lifted' by the angels.

Captain Holloway was there to meet us. His first words to me were: 'What's happened to old Uncle Sperring? Is he all right?'

'He stayed on,' I said. 'He thought the Lysander would be too crowded. To be honest, I think he was in a state of shock – he wanted to get away from us and be on his own.'

'Yes, of course he would have been spooked,' the captain said. 'I can't say I blame him. I was pretty shocked when I saw a load of German soldiers floating down out of the sky without parachutes, I can tell you.'

He went on to explain what had happened the night before.

I told him about the alien craft appearing in the forest at Monteneuf, and the vanishing soldiers.

The captain arranged for Tom and Annick to be taken back to London as soon as possible. He was keen to interview them and hear, in their own words, exactly what had happened.

'I will have to face up to the War Office too, Jack,' he said. 'I am against setting those two up as some sort of freakish secret weapon. That seems to be Colonel Clarke's notion, and I suppose I'll have to offer him what I promised before I sent you off to France. It'll be two birds in the bush, after all.'

Captain Holloway's Office, London

When I got back to London, I was summoned to see the captain in his office.

He was studying a piece of paper. 'Look at this, Jack,' he said, passing it to me.

'You see, Jack, they are rattled now, and doubly dangerous. Mind you, so are our returnees. We need a place of greater safety for them. I am afraid even your delightful and formidable Aunt Dolly could not hold off a division of crack German commandos.'

'They'll never manage to get over here,' I said confidently – though I knew full well that if we had slipped so easily into occupied France, then a team of commandos would find it equally easy to land here.

'We shouldn't make the mistake of underestimating them. There are sleeper cells and Nazi sympathizers all over the country. They could be called on to help and we would have very little idea.'

'That is true,' I said.

'By the way, Jack, I have had both sets of films developed. Over here – look.'

The captain had had the prints enlarged, and they were pinned to a board on the back wall of his office – a set of big black-and-white images, both of the craft and of the forest at Monteneuf.

'I suppose that' – the captain pointed to a picture of the German in the leaf crown – 'is the Nazi equivalent of me. From their special bureau, no doubt.'

'Dead now,' I said. 'He was finished off by the horror of what he'd seen, and by Tom and Annick staring him down.'

There were some pictures of the hole with the first beams of light coming from it. Then there were Sergeant Shaw's pictures of the craft leaving Gallows Hill.

'Look at these and compare,' the captain said. 'The craft that appeared over you in France is clearly the self-same one that was buried at Gallows Hill. Something woke it up; something sent it over to rescue whatever it was the Germans thought they had exposed or summoned with their ritual.'

'I saw what it was,' I said. 'Something impossible to describe or photograph; something huge, and alive, and made of light – or so it seemed. It brushed past me as it rose up out of the hole, and I heard bell-like sounds – like church bells, only not mournful or annoying. *Joyous* would be the word I'd use, and yet the thing itself was terrifying. Just ask those German soldiers. They'll tell you; they'll sing like canaries.'

MEMO

Intercepted and translated from the original German for DEPT 116

MOST SECRET

Captain Holloway's Office Only

FROM: H. Kohler, Office of the Unexplained & the Supernatural, Berlin

TO: Central Headquarters
COPY TO: The Wolf's Lair

We have debriefed Leutnant Richter. He confirms all the events mentioned
in his first communication, and more. The late Herr Mustchin was correct in
all his assumptions regarding the site at Monteneuf. Richter's version of
events was further confirmed by several recaptured labourers and the
surviving soldiers. An enormous craft of unknown origin was in some way
summoned – whether by Mustchin's ritual or by the returnee girl, subject A.
In any case, she is now missing, believed to have been taken to Britain in
a plane organized by a local Resistance cell. Our priority must be to
mount a mission to secure her return, and that of the returnee boy
already in British hands. If the proposed invasion of Great Britain is in
any way postponed, then I strongly suggest that a commando raid is
mounted at the earliest to achieve that end.

CHAPTER THIRTY-SIX

London

Aunt Dolly was very flustered at the thought of having a French girl living in her house.

'Whatever will I give her to eat? She will be wanting garlic, snails and frogs' legs for her tea – where am I supposed to get them, with everything on the ration?'

'She'll love your cooking as much as I do, Auntie,' Tom said.

'Hear that, Jack? Tom just called me Auntie at last – and about time too! Well done, lad. I won't ask where you've been all this time, or how this French girl turned up in your lives, because I know just what sort of an answer I'll get: none,' she went on.

'Captain Holloway himself is bringing her over to meet you,' I said.

'What's she like?'

'I don't know her that well. She is very blonde – a bit like Jean Harlow used to look,' I said.

'Ooh hello, are you sweet on her? Is she your girlfriend then, Jack?'

'No, Auntie,' I said, and I'm sure I blushed. 'She is not my girlfriend. She is keen on a French boy she knows called Pascal.'

'It's true,' Tom said, nodding.

The captain arrived in his staff car at six o'clock that evening.

'Don't know what the neighbours will make of the army turning up here like this, Jack, I'm sure,' Aunt Dolly said.

I had managed to persuade her that whatever she normally cooked for our tea would be more than all right. 'You don't have to go off making all sorts of fancy stuff,' I assured her.

The captain led Annick in, and she looked around in surprise. She was still getting used to everything that had happened.

'I hope this is not too much of an imposition, Miss Carmody,' Captain Holloway said.

'Not at all, Captain. You'll be setting me up as a hotel for waifs and strays next,' she said. 'By the way, call me Dolly, please, and in any case we must all pull together and do our bit for King and country.'

She welcomed Annick with some attempted French. '*Bonjour*, my dear. You sit yourself down here.' She indicated a chair at the dining-room table.

But before she could sit down, Tom went over and embraced her. They stood locked together for a moment, staring straight into each other's eyes.

'I thought you said her boyfriend was someone else altogether, not our Tom,' Aunt Dolly said.

'He is,' I said. 'She is just grateful to Tom for his help.'

'Help for what?'

'Can't really say.'

'Well, we are very grateful for *your* help, Dolly,' the captain said. 'It will only be for a little longer. I need to arrange new accommodation nearer to our work. My staff sergeant, Miss Shaw, will look after her there.'

Aunt Dolly stared at me and then turned to the captain. I could see the thought crossing her mind – and then it came out.

'What work would that be, then?' she asked, her arms folded across her chest.

'I wish I could tell you, I really do,' the captain replied with a smile. 'Let's just say it is very important, and that young Jack is very much doing his bit. We would be lost without him and his abilities.'

Realizing that she would get no further with all the 'hush-hush' stuff, Aunt Dolly went off to the kitchen. While she was out of the room, Annick sent her plate up into the air and over to Tom's place, where it landed with a gentle bump on the best tablecloth. Tom made his plate soar across to Annick, with the same result. They both got the giggles.

'Now now,' the captain said. 'Enough of that.'

Annick now focused on the carving knife; it rose up just as Aunt Dolly came back into the dining room carrying a hot pie. The knife hovered three feet in the air.

Aunt Dolly put the tray down in the middle of the table. 'There,' she said. 'This ought to be a good old-fashioned steak and ale pie. Well, it's trying its best to be that – it's all a bit of a muddle under the pastry crust, but it means well . . .'

Captain Holloway looked daggers across the table at Annick. She sat staring down at her plate, still grinning.

'Now, what about the two little waifs and strays sitting there like butter wouldn't melt, trying not to laugh? I don't see the joke, or am I missing something?'

There was an awkward silence. The knife still floated above the table. The last thing Aunt Dolly might have expected to see above her best tablecloth.

'Now,' she said. 'Where's that knife . . . ?' And she plucked it out of the air and started to cut into the pie.

'Perhaps I'm not as daft as you all think I am,' she said, lowering a slice onto Captain Holloway's plate and smiling round at us all.

We said nothing.

A week later a postcard was delivered to the office in the general mail. It had been posted in England and showed a colour photograph of a French fishing boat.

SOUVENIR OF DOUARNENEZ

it said in bright letters over the photograph. On the reverse was written

WIRE RECORDING MADE AT DEPT 116/DECEMBER/1941

Captain Holloway's Office & War Room only
Copy to Col. Clarke

MOST SECRET
Subject A = Tom Pile
Subject B = Annick Garel
Referred to in Transcript as: A & B

A. I first heard the girl's voice in my head in my dreams. She asked for
help by writing things down on a school blackboard. I could see them
clearly - her words written on the board. She wrote 'Help me' on that
blackboard. At first it was in her own language so I couldn't understand
it. I tried to answer her, but I was never sure if she had heard me. Then,
later, I was able to see her face because she made a mirror in her head and
then looked into it. When I first saw her, her eyes stared at me in the
glass.

B. After I was pulled out of the water, I was in the sky among the stars,
and I saw the boy, the other one, just for a moment. Then afterwards, after
a long time, I was put back into the water. Pascal saved me and took me to
the town. I was led down to the sea and blessed, then locked away in a
white room. The angels had left me, but I still heard them. They sang to
me. They showed me that there was another - the boy I had seen among the
stars. He would help me. I asked him to help, and he came. He came all the
way across the sea. I saw him, and I knew him at once when his face
appeared through the leaves. Together we took away their guns and held
them back when the lost angel came up out of the ground. Together we made
a bridge, hand to hand, arm to arm. The angel climbed across our bridge
and then up into the light.

A. I saw the boy, Pascal, and the man, Sperring. They were locked away with
the slaves who had dug the hole. I burned through the lock. I burned the
hut so that they could escape. I sent the rifles up into the air and
silenced the drum and the horn. I thought of the white hart - the
beautiful creature I couldn't kill for Old Gawen. I saw its noble head and
held it in my heart - the creature that had shared space and time with me;
the creature healed by the angels. We owed our lives to the angels. I
watched from the high tree as the lost angel soared up through the beam
of light.

B. When I opened my eyes - after the sea and the sky - I looked into the face of the boy, Pascal. He cut me free and saw that I was alive. He talked to me and brought me back to life. He cared about me. Now he is lost to me. The old man was there, weeping because I was returned. He was my uncle and he was cruel to me in my other life. He beat me. He was not a good man. I will never see him again. I will see Pascal, though. I will send out my signals, but he won't be able to hear them or see me in my mirror. I can do things with twice as much power now, because of Tom. He speaks my language; he thinks with my words. He thinks inside my head and I think inside his. We are as one.

We share the pictures.

We share the stars.

I understand everything and I understand nothing. My old world is lost to me. Sometimes I can see it as clearly as the white wall that I stared at in the room at the mairie. It was there that I found I could make things happen: I scattered the papers and made them burn. I was strong, and now, with Tom Pile, I am stronger still. Tom can pull things up from the ground; I can pull things out of the sky. Together we will do many things. My brother in light, Tom.

A. My sister in light, Annick.

AFTERWORD

Thanks to Annie Eaton and Natalie Doherty for their encouragement and patient editing. To my son, Laurence Beck, for his document designs and for the many photographic manipulations.

There was a real Tom Pile and there was a real Michael Holloway but they never met. Tom Pile worked as a part-time gardener for my late parents-in-law in the real Litton Cheney in Dorset in the 1950s. Michael Holloway and his wife, Iris, showed great kindness and encouragement to me when I was a callow art student in the mid 1960s. My fictional Captain Holloway has, I hope, absorbed some of the sterling qualities of the real Michael Holloway along the way.

Both books had a long gestation. They began the way many stories start – in this case almost forty years ago – with a set of vague and muddled ideas. On my first visit to the real village of Litton Cheney I saw the marvel of the stars on a clear, cold winter night with no streetlight pollution. To see such a sight is to properly experience the numinous and the transcendental. It set me thinking about mysterious lights in the sky, and an Edwardian village child's possible reaction to them. And about the Nazi regime's possible interest in all kinds of strange and occult matters. Over the years I just took them all a little further down the path of adventure until they seemed ready to be written.